I0749904

# THE BOGOTÁ FILE

A JACOB HUNTER THRILLER

DAVID ARCHER

DAMIEN WILD

RIGHTHOUSE

Copyright © 2026 by Right House

All rights reserved.

The characters and events portrayed in this ebook are fictitious. Any similarity to real persons, living or dead, is coincidental and not intended by the author.

No part of this book may be reproduced in any form or by any electronic or mechanical means, including information storage and retrieval systems, without written permission from the author, except for the use of brief quotations in a book review.

ISBN-13: 978-1-63696-468-3

ISBN-10: 1-63696-468-0

Printed in the United States of America

www.righthouse.com

www.instagram.com/righthousebooks

www.facebook.com/righthousebooks

twitter.com/righthousebooks

**JACOB HUNTER THRILLER**

The Kyiv File (Book 1)
The Bogotá File (Book 2)
The Havana File (Book 3)
The Amsterdam File (Book 4)
The Saint Petersburg File (Book 5)

# ONE

## ONE DAY BEFORE DEPLOYMENT TO COLOMBIA

Jacob Hunter had been enjoying the brief stopover in his home town of Glen Bridge, Ohio. For the most part, the trip down memory lane gladdened his cynical and scarred warrior's heart. The cool, late October weather, strolling along familiar streets. Jerry's bakery on Main Street, still pumping out that delicious sourdough bread, brownies, and muffins folks drove twenty miles for. The library he'd spent countless hours in, reading history and classic adventure stories by Mark Twain. The old playground where he and his only true friend Magnus Ohlson played one-on-one hoops, with 6'6" Gus usually taking the honors.

It wasn't all pleasantries, though. Jacob was on a private mission of vengeance. However, before he could exact said vengeance, he first wanted to make sure his hunches had some foundation beneath them. He wasn't the type to dish out violence for the sake of it. There had to be a reason—a very good reason. And when he found it, there was no holding back.

First, he had to speak to a number of people, tell them what his hunches were, get their views on the matter. To see if he was on the right track. These folks were old schoolmates and a couple of teachers whom he hadn't spoken to in many years. They'd long since abandoned little-old Glen Bridge, spreading out in all directions. Those with career ambitions, at least, had fled. There wasn't a helluva lot to keep a person in town once they'd graduated high school. Many of the people he most wanted to talk to lived at opposite ends of the country; a couple in Canada, Europe and the UK, one as far away as New Zealand. Jacob was sure these people knew things, important things, that they held the key to a riddle he'd been trying to solve for close on twenty years. And to get the information he wanted, he was convinced only in-person conversations would work. Phone calls, emails, messages— people had and would continue to dodge answering them. Get 'em face to face, though, and the chance of receiving honest answers rose exponentially. Especially with Jacob's powers of persuasion.

So he'd brought them together in the old home town, like Detective Colombo rounding up the witnesses and suspects and grilling them all in one spot. Jacob had created a closed Facebook group, ostensibly dedicated to a fancy Glen Bridge High School reunion—one that was never going to happen. The woman he'd rescued from his last mission in Moscow, IT guru Irene Frobisher, formerly known as Irina Frolova and to him always Irina, had put together a bunch of promo material for the fake reunion that few could resist. A good many old classmates were going to be mighty pissed when they turned up to the non-party tomorrow night.

He'd reached the pointy end of the week-long investigation. As a result of some fruitful and at times animated conversations, he'd narrowed his focus down to one man.

And now, here was that vile man, trussed up tightly and cooking from his insides like a Thanksgiving turkey. To reel the rube in, Jacob had treated him to a free lunch, a couple of beers, some bullshit palsy-walsy chat, and voilà: the dude was putty in his hands. To get him to follow Jacob to the trap was a cinch: the promise to ogle photos of a couple of women who used to attend Glen Bridge High but were now involved in amateur porn on the

Internet. It had the sicko salivating at the prospect. *I've got a computer set up at the place I'm staying*, Jacob had said. *Because it's so hot, almost illegal, I can only show you that stuff using a special encryption.* Those magic words did the trick. Jacob could barely keep up with the guy as he marched down Main Street.

"Hey, isn't this your old place?" the asshole had asked when they reached the address. "I recognize them big trees with the tire swing. Still there after all these years."

Jacob nodded. "Yeah. My parents are friends of the couple who bought it from them." A lie but swallowed eagerly. "Guess they liked the house pretty much the way it was. Tire swing and all."

"We gonna stand here gasbagging all day, or are you gonna show me videos of those dirty women?" The perverted man had been practically hyperventilating.

Fast forward thirty minutes and the man, now getting acquainted with Jacob's interviewing methods, could barely breathe.

Jacob slackened his two-handed grip around the man's throat, thick as a small pumpkin and nearly as hard. The fella managed to inhale a couple of massive gulps of air before Jacob reapplied the pressure. Jacob's fingers ached with the effort; it was like squeezing solid rubber, not flesh and ligaments. He gritted his teeth and pressed harder. Another thirty seconds of choking and it would be lights out for the guy, permanently. Jacob couldn't afford to kill him, though: he needed a confession to make it all worth the effort. The app on Jacob's iPhone was recording everything. Irina would later edit the sound file with AI to make the man's voice sound less strained, like he was voluntarily laying it all on the line, then she'd delete Jacob's voice completely. Jacob would anonymously send the doctored file over to the homicide cops in Columbus. After that, hopefully, justice would be served.

Simpering Steven Finkel, one of the few graduates of 2005 to stay put in Glen Ridge, was the best suspect Jacob had found in many years of searching. Physical evidence was scant to the point of being non-existent, and the leads Jacob had been chasing over the years had gone cold. A confession it would have to be. As a bulwark to his theory, the classmates Jacob spoke to believed that yes, Finkel could very well be the killer.

Jacob let go of the suspect's neck and took a step back, regarding the brute through narrowed eyes. He remained silent, wanting Finkel to be the first to speak.

The man's shaking hands shot to his fat neck as he gasped for air, his mouth opening and closing like a whale's blowhole. He blinked away pearly tears. "I'm...not the guy...you want," he managed to huff. "I never done nuthin' to her." The denial was followed by vigorous shaking of his closely shaved head.

An extended finger poked right in the middle of the man's throat, hard and fast, causing him to gurgle as his spider-veined eyeballs bugged out. "You *are* the guy, Steve. People have ratted you out." Jacob's voice was soft and reassuring now. "You are the psychopath who killed someone I loved very much."

"No!"

"Yes, Steven, yes."

Finkel open his spittle-covered mouth as if to scream for help. Jacob fired him a laser stare that shut down that thought in a flash. "Don't you dare yell out," he added for good measure. Jacob paced back and forth, tapping the blade of a long knife against the palm of one hand, then against his thigh. "Now either you open up and tell me the truth and I call the cops—that way you get to live—or you continue to stonewall me and I slit your throat here and now." He tilted his head slightly to one side and showed one open hand and one upraised knife. "Your choice, Steven."

Jacob put the knife down on the ground in an act of conciliation. "Last chance, fat man."

Finkel swallowed hard a couple of times, no sign of an Adam's apple in his blubberous neck. "I'm very thirsty. Can I have a drink of water, Jake?"

"Do *not* call me Jake, understand?" Jacob thundered. "We're not in the schoolyard."

"Sorry," came the timid reply. "I didn't mean..."

"Can it, asshole." He was already sick of the man's sniveling. At high school, Steven Finkel had had the reputation of a mean bully, but also a coward. Seems he hadn't changed much. Adding to Jacob's irritation, a piece of gristle from the T-bone steak he'd demolished thirty minutes ago was wedged between his teeth and annoying the shit out of him. Not nearly as much as the sweating tub of lard tied to the chair in front of him, though.

Jacob paused a second to scan the surroundings in his parents' dimly lit basement. True, it was someone else's property now. There was so much familiarity about it. His mom and dad had sold the house five years ago and moved to Florida to enjoy the sunshine in their twilight years. The new owners at 198 Hotham Drive, Jeff and Alice Millard, were, as far as Jacob was able to determine, at work in their legal practice in downtown Columbus, hence no cars. Their two teenage kids were at school, five blocks away at Glen Bridge High. No one should be returning home any time soon.

One thing the Millards hadn't attended to, even after five years of ownership, was fixing the defective side door to the garage. There was a knack to jiggling around in the lock with a paperclip or piece of bent wire. Get it in the right spot, and the door opened obediently like Aladdin's cave. The worst burglar in the world could break into this garage. The Millards' lack of care was understandable, though. This was a safe neighborhood in a safe town, Jacob remembered. Break-ins were few, crimes against the person very rare.

But not unknown. Like everywhere, innocent people sometimes got themselves killed.

Jacob placed his boot in the middle of Finkel's crotch, barely able to wriggle his foot into position on account of the captive man's broad, spreading thighs. With a bit of effort, though, he got there. He gave a firm double-pump push with his foot. Finkel yelped, sweat streaming from his face like a leaky faucet. "Ow! Don't kick me in the nuts!"

"You'd be lucky to find any nuts in that pool of lard. Now why did you kill her? Tell me!"

Jacob's high-school sweetheart, Sally-Anne Vincent, had been murdered nineteen years ago. The cops had worked hard to find the perpetrator but came up empty. Now it was a cold case, all but forgotten. Jacob would never give up trying, though. Steve Finkel, unemployed deadbeat and someone Jacob had suspected from the beginning, was firmly in the crosshairs.

"I didn't do it. I swear. You gotta believe me!"

"Don't lie to me." Jacob jammed his foot even harder into the man's balls, drawing a high-pitched squeal. "I've spoken to ten independent people, *ten*, Steven, who swear blind you were totally obsessed with Sally-Anne in high school. I noticed it at the time, too. But I dismissed it as me being overprotective of her and you just being a pathetic loser. But those ten people believe you really were crazy enough to have killed her. And I tend to agree."

"I wouldn't hurt a fly..."

"I would," said Jacob, administering a lightning-fast open-handed slap. It gave off an echoey crack but was delivered with only a fraction of the force Jacob could have unleashed.

"Ow! Why did you do that?"

"Because...you're a fucking murderer, Steven."

Finkel shook his head hard, tears and gunk from his lips fanning left and right. "You don't seriously think I hurt Sally-Anne...do you?"

Jacob sighed heavily. "I think you might have, yeah. But then again, it takes a degree of courage to kill someone, and you've never been a brave fella, have you?"

Finkel's mouth turned upside down into a spittle-covered frown moments before Jacob delivered a slap to the other side of his jowls, this one with plenty of power.

A scream. "Please stop..." Finkel jerked back in his chair, mumbling incoherent words. Tears poured down his marshmallow cheeks like there was no off switch. "I honestly don't know anything."

Jacob pressed his forefinger and thumb to his chin as he coolly regarded Finkel. The slumped shoulders, vacant stare, and wracking sobs were too real. A coward like Finkel would have had 'tells' if he was lying. There were no tells, dammit.

Finkel looked up, ropey snot dangling from both nostrils like a slimy Goth piercing. "I wish I could help you, I really do. I liked Sally-Anne, but not in that way. I know you loved her. She..."

But Jacob wasn't listening anymore. He took a pair of scissors he found on a workbench and cut the snap-ties around Finkel's wrists. "Get up, dickhead. We're done here."

Much as he wanted Finkel to be the killer, Jacob's gut told him he was wasting his time. A jolt of shame coursed through Jacob's mind as he realized he'd derived a small amount of pleasure from roughing the man up. Not his style, but Finkel was so loathsome the enjoyment obtained was almost justified.

"You know what?" Jacob grinned and folded his arms across his chest. "I believe you, pal."

"Then why did you–?"

"To be absolutely sure. Look on the bright side, Steven. Now that you're vindicated in my mind, you get to live. That's a pretty good deal, huh?"

The cops' theory back in the day, that it was some opportunist, probably an out-of-towner, a drifter, who had murdered Sally-Anne and left her lying in a snowy ditch late December 2005, was most likely correct. Finkel was innocent.

Standing on wobbly legs, Finkel smudged the tears away with the back of his pudgy wrists. He gave Jacob a feeble smile, one that said *please don't hurt me anymore*. But his tiny brain couldn't help but spit out the first stupid thing that came into it. "You know, you're going to regret doing this to me."

"No, I'm not." Jacob shook his head. "I wasn't even here. You weren't here, either."

"Yes I was. And I'm not as dumb as you think I am. I'll be able to prove we were here."

Jacob raised his fist as if to strike, and Finkel's hands went up defensively at the same time as his head ducked to the side.

"You mean your cell's GPS will leave a trace of your movements?"

Finkel dared to look back at Jacob through his fingers. "Yes." He reached into his pocket, fumbled around, and then surprise pulled his eyes into big round circles.

"Looking for this?" Jacob dangled the phone in an outstretched hand. Before Finkel could answer, the banged-up Samsung dropped to the concrete floor. Jacob's size 11 right boot stamped on it repeatedly, shards of glass and plastic crunching. He smiled benevolently at Finkel. "Time for a phone upgrade, pal."

# TWO

Paul Brohman tugged up his zipper and moved away from the raised urinal. Tonight's celebration was a day early, but the icing on the cake would come tomorrow. One step closer to exposing the conspiracy. Some semi-incriminating background files were already in his possession. Stored on his laptop, a USB and, for good measure, uploaded to the Cloud, from where they could be retrieved and submitted to Deputy Director McDonald in Langley.

But those files were full of circumstantial evidence and meant nothing until he got the final piece in the puzzle. The piece that would lead to arrests and jail sentences. For whom? That remained to be seen. Brohman had his firm suspicions, but as of now, that's all they were— suspicions. But dear God, he hoped he was right about this.

Tomorrow, at 7:30 a.m. sharp, Miguel would meet him outside the National Shrine of Our Lady of Carmen, the candy-striped church that towered over the historic La Candelaria District. Inside the church, Miguel would pass on the secret recording. It only cost $500, but to Miguel, it was a king's ransom. And it was money well spent— enough to expose the dirty turncoat and stop an unthinkable crime.

First, though, Brohman badly needed a woman to slate his strong carnal urges. A sex addict who saw no need to be treated or cured for his affliction, he washed and dried his hands meticulously and headed back into the belly of the night club.

He wobbled back from the bathroom, tipping finger waves of apology as he bumped into people on the way to the bar. He couldn't see, or even sense, that he was off balance; only those around him could see it. If he collided with others, it was because *they* were drunk. He forgave them, of course. Paul Brohman was famous among friends and colleagues for being a happy drunk, never violent when he'd had too many beers, tequilas, vodkas, or whatever the locals were imbibing.

Now, at 11:45 p.m. on a Wednesday night, the smooth-talking American from Dallas, Texas, had reached that special state of inebriation, the state where you think everything's under control, you are the smartest guy in the room, the best singer and dancer, and women find you *irre-fucking-sistible*.

And to be fair, Brohman was a very good-looking hombre. Smooth, wrinkle-free skin due to good genes. Brilliant white teeth never affected by nicotine. A rock-hard body, low BMI. Working out for two hours every day without fail for the last ten years meant he not only looked sharp in a suit or Speedos, he had the stamina to party all night if needed. He shunned the popular party drugs, especially now that he was forging a new path in Colombia. The risks of falling into a dangerous trap here were immense. No cocaine or funny little pills for him. Good old alcohol was his poison of choice, and he would stick to it. He trusted it, knew its effects, and could deal with the consequences of even the worst hangover. Of which he had suffered many.

Yet even when tanked to the gills, his tall, well-muscled figure, thick, stylishly cut blond hair and classic chiseled features, teamed with the body of a welter-weight boxer, were the assets that got him laid when he was out on the prowl. The financial mogul generally had plenty of luck with the ladies. On the other hand, his distinctly Nordic look sometimes had negative consequences among the male population of Bogotá. Especially in the night clubs he liked to frequent.

"Oye, mira por donde vas, gringo!" A man dressed like John Travolta in Grease eyeballed Brohman with an accompanying sneer.

The only word Brohman understood was the last one. The intent was clear, too. *You are a guest in our town, so don't be a jerk.* If it came to a fist-fight, thanks to five years in the Marine Raiders as a younger man, he had the skills to defend himself. Even when he'd had too many drinks. Brawling was always a last resort, and he never initiated trouble. True to his happy drunk persona, Brohman gave the man a shrug and a beatific smile of innocence. It worked perfectly, as the young man made a conciliatory hands-down gesture and allowed Brohman to go on his way.

Straight back to the bar. One more beer, then home.

He nodded at a couple of men at the far end of the bar. They waved at him, gave polite smiles, then resumed their conversation. An Englishman and an Australian, like him they were businessmen working for Fortune 500 companies with branches in Colombia. Unlike him, these dudes were married and most likely heading home soon if they wanted to avoid the rolling pin.

Pepe's nightclub, in the pumping Zona Rosa to the north of the Colombian capital, was a popular spot for some R&R with both ex-pats and locals. Brohman's style when he visited was to network early with the foreign crowd until he'd had enough of their boring conversations, then ditch them and switch to predator mode. Quite often, Brohman would pick up a cute señorita and take her back to his apartment.

Tonight, though, he wasn't feeling it. There was no new meat at the market as far as he could tell. Just women he'd bedded already, wise enough to know he wouldn't go back for a second bite. Like a vampire, he craved fresh blood, young and virginal if possible, but after a lean trot, he'd happily bed a new woman aged between 25 and 40. No one would guess Brohman himself was the wrong side of 50.

Ten feet from the bar, he spotted a gap opening that he figured on sidling into and occupying. Out of nowhere, he felt a sharp poke in the right side. He turned to offer his customary apology, but the words froze in his mouth. The woman flicking her hair from side to side was the most breathtakingly beautiful he had ever laid eyes on. A dress not much bigger than a handkerchief revealed medium-to-large breasts, but the legs, his favorite part of a woman, were so perfect he almost drooled. She was slightly out of his preferred age range, but this was an opportunity only a fool would pass up. He detected a touch of African heritage, perhaps, maybe some native Mayan blood infused with that of the Spanish colonizers. Whatever the lineage, she fit squarely into the category of drop-dead gorgeous. She stopped flicking her hair, flashed him a wicked grin, then barked a collage of rapid-fire Spanish he had no hope of understanding.

"No hablo español," he said loud enough to be heard above the funky music. "Hablas inglés?"

"Si, I do," she replied with a coquettish pout. "But not very well. I watch you from the other side of the bar. You are a very handsome man. Americano?"

He nodded as he felt the smile on his face broadening. Her come-on was so strong, he considered for a moment whether she was a hooker. Dammit, she was so beautiful he might even consider compromising his principle and pay her for sex if he had to. Without broaching the question, the only thing he could think of to say to this radiant goddess was the lame cliché, "Would you like to have a drink with me?"

"Si, señor. Con mucho gusto!"

As Latino music, heavy on trumpet and drums, throbbed in the background, he extended a hand to help her mount her seat; she'd be lucky to be five foot tall, although the stilettos added several inches.

His gut told him she wasn't a prostitute. A gold-digger? Quite possibly. The version he wanted to believe was that she was a horny modern woman looking for a one-night stand with an experienced stud. And why not? This was far from the first time a hot female had approached him in a bar with devilry shining in her eyes. In Rio de Janeiro, where he'd spent two years in the early 2000s making a stack of money investing in coffee futures, it was even easier than here. It was almost like he needed a repellent to keep women away. A handsome blond man was considered so exotic, getting laid was almost unavoidable. Less of a certainty here in Colombia, but his strike rate was still impressive.

Five minutes later and $50 lighter, he'd learned the woman's name was Carolina. Without prompting, she even volunteered a last name, Ortega, which, in his eyes, made her even sweeter. Only an innocent from the countryside would do that. Carolina was 23 years old—*bingo*—and, of all things, crazy about baseball. She had been raised in a small village outside of Medellín, where her family had been farming bananas and rice for four generations. They made a basic living selling their produce locally. She found country life utterly boring, so last year she'd moved to the capital.

"To chase your fortune?" said Brohman, ogling her cleavage over the top of his glass. "To become a pop star, maybe? An actress? You've certainly got the looks and sparkling personality to be a roaring success."

She giggled like a schoolgirl before sipping her drink. In the glass was a Colombian specialty, a Pacific mule: a blend of vodka, strawberry liqueur and peach schnapps, ginger ale and lime. It purportedly kicked like the animal it was named after, so Carolina said she would only have a couple.

As the volume of the rhythmic cumbia melodies pouring out of the speakers increased, he leaned in closer. "Do you like this kind of music?"

"Si, mucho." She placed her hands on his thighs, squeezing gently. "Our Colombian music is very romantic, no?"

"It sure is," he agreed. The heady scent of her perfume, a subtle blend of frangipani and jasmine, wafted across to him. Combined with her own natural musky odor, the aroma was activating responses in his basal ganglia, the part of the brain in charge of primal instincts. Those instincts were telling him, *Get this woman out of the bar and into your bed before she changes her mind and disappears.*

"Would you like to take a walk with me?" he said, struggling to place his empty beer glass in the middle of the coaster. "It's a nice evening for it."

"Si," she said with an eager nod. "And then we go back to your place?" She paused for a moment. "To fuck."

*Oh, my,* Brohman thought. This was going to be one of those nights legends are made of.

Before he could respond to her brazen offer, she hopped down from the barstool, grabbed his hand, and led the way to the exit. He thrilled at her intensity, her sense of purpose. In his professional life, he valued people who knew what they wanted and let nothing stand in their way. With her attitude, Carolina would kill it in commerce. He never mixed business and pleasure, though, so he wouldn't be offering her a job.

His mind raced as they walked; they would soon be as one, bodies entwined on his king-size bed, going at it like rabbits until the early hours. Her small fingers felt oddly cold as they interlaced with his larger ones. No problem, she'd be very warm soon enough.

They slalomed past a group of people near the bar, stomachs gyrating and arms twirling to the cumbia music. Brohman's eyes remained riveted to her perfect legs, which led all the way to the holy grail. His heart thundered with the anticipation of his conquest.

Before exiting the club, Carolina extracted a token from her purse, exchanged a couple of words with the attendant, and fetched a gabardine coat from the cloakroom. Bogotá might be near the equator, but due to its elevation of 8,660 feet above sea level, it enjoyed a temperate climate. Brohman was fine with the cooler evenings; his suit jacket never came off when he was out on the streets. There was a loaded ultra-compact Beretta 950 Jetfire snuggled in a holster under his left armpit. He might like to avoid fights, but he was smart enough to be extra careful in this city. Although Pepe's bouncers used metal-detector wands to stop weapons entering the venue, Brohman got a pass because he paid all the managers to turn a blind eye.

Out onto the bustling Calle 82, aka 82nd Street, the night's bracing air was like a refreshing glass of water. Despite the flashing neon lights of the bars and clubs, the honking of the traffic, the shouting street vendors, and people scurrying about like ants, a feeling of immense calm descended upon him. He and Carolina were in their own little bubble, and nothing else mattered. They ambled their way along the sidewalk, hand in hand like long-time lovers. They'd walked about fifty yards or so when she tugged on his arm. "Hey. I've got an idea. Let's go down this alleyway, guapo, and have some fun." Her voice was husky, almost breathless. "I can't wait to feel you inside me."

"I'm not sure about that, my dear." Calling him 'handsome' certainly appealed to Brohman's ego, but his conservative side rose to the surface; he hated that side because it squashed spontaneity. "It will be much more comfortable back at my apartment. It's a quick trip by cab."

"Look at the traffic, mi amor. It will take over two hours to get to your place." She pulled him with surprising strength toward the dark entrance to a narrow laneway. "Don't be, what do the gringos say? A pussy? Come on, Pablo, show me what you got in your trousers."

She was right. You only live once, and at this surreal moment in time, he was convinced Carolina had more pluck in her than any person he'd ever known. For once in his selfish, misogynistic life, he might even be...in love?

No. Strike that. He was sobering up now, gusts of chilly night air accelerating the process. Two failed marriages to women with smart lawyers, who continued to strip him of a large percentage of his vast fortune, was lesson enough. Never again.

Carolina was a heavenly vision, but he wouldn't allow himself to be hypnotized into complete submission by her beauty. Still, the effects of the Cialis tablet he'd dropped earlier this afternoon were beginning to make themselves known in his loins: her idea of coupling down the laneway now seemed an inspired idea.

The alley ran between a closed souvenir shop, its steel shutters awash with multi-colored graffiti, and what used to be a taco joint but was now boarded up. Before he knew it, Brohman was tiptoeing carefully around a couple of homeless guys sitting on either side of the alley like bookends, their bearded faces barely visible under filthy blankets. In front of them were woolen hats containing a handful of lousy coins. Brohman couldn't help himself. He turned back, peeled off a couple of Ben Franklins, and dropped one in each hat. The men grunted; whether it was in thanks or not was impossible to tell.

Carolina strutted down the lane like a model on a catwalk, her generous hips and butt swaying like a metronome. She suddenly stopped about twenty yards in. Lights from the windows of buildings along its sides cast a gentle light, spotlighting an area free of trash. She leaned against the brick wall, one leg tucked up against it at a 45-degree angle. Her hand disappeared under the front of her dress. She finger-rolled a black G-string down her legs, under her shoes, then flung it away disdainfully. "Come and have a taste of the good stuff, guapo." A fleshy tongue ran around her plump lips, unenhanced by cosmetic intervention.

He was upon her now, unbuckling his leather belt, ready to drop his trousers, hoist her up in the air, and impale her against the wall. Her glistening eyes stared back at him, unblinking, challenging him. He wrapped his arms around her waist, closed his eyes, and leaned in for a kiss.

"Atáquenlo, muchachos!" she screamed around the side of his neck.

*What the fuck?!*

He heard the approaching pounding footsteps an instant before a savage blow connected with the side of his head. But it was time enough to take a slight evasive action that stopped him being KO'd. Whoever—and whatever—hit him achieved just a glancing blow.

The reprieve was temporary.

He turned to see two big men lined up against him. They were dressed head to toe in dark clothing, one brandishing a baseball bat, the other a huge knife. He cringed as he took in those scruffy beards: they were the 'homeless' assholes he'd just donated $200 to!

This was a fucking set-up. A honey trap. He couldn't believe he had been stupid enough to fall for it.

But they wouldn't get him with the simple weapons they had. He reached into his jacket to grab the...

"Looking for something, guapo?"

He spun toward the sweet voice. Carolina stood, feet set shoulder-width apart, aiming his own pistol squarely at his head.

"You fucking bitch!"

With his back turned to the men, one of them delivered a vicious stab kick to the side of the patella, and Brohman dropped like a stone. "That's no way to talk to a lady, pendejo!"

The pain stung as if someone had poured boiling water down the back of his leg. The men descended on him in a second, like wolves pouncing on a wounded fawn. He struggled gamely for as long as he could—a matter of ten seconds. A powerful hold that threatened to snap his wrist put an end to all resistance. He knew it was time to submit: these gorillas were too strong and too well-trained to be bested by a middle-aged ex-Marine Raider with seven—or was it eight?—large beers under his belt. Snap ties went around his wrists, and the men frog-marched him down the alley away from the busy street.

Incoherent words full of derision and laughter exchanged between Carolina Ortega—definitely not her real name—and the goons added to his humiliation.

As they neared the other end of the alleyway, which exited onto a smaller, less busy street, a rough hessian bag went over his head. He heard car doors open and another two male voices.

There was a shove in the small of the back and arms around his shoulders, guiding him into the passenger seat. There was already someone sitting next to him. Someone with a big and menacing presence.

The car took off like a rocket, the music on the stereo blasting out the same cumbia music that had been playing in Pepe's. "Where are you taking me?"

Instead of an answer, the presence beside him unleashed a massive closed fist under Brohman's rib cage, sucking the air out of his lungs.

Through the clearing fog of alcohol, the clues were now so obvious he couldn't believe he'd missed them. One: the bitch understood every word he had said in English, despite claiming to not speak it very well. And two: how the hell did she know it would take two hours for a cab to get to his apartment? She knew where he lived, dammit. She had known *everything* about him. His captors, too, must know *everything* about him. Including his side role with the CIA. A role he should have taken more seriously, thinking with his head more than with his dick.

If the hombres who snatched him were anything to do with the new cartel, his future looked bleak.

There was only one positive to be drawn from this horrific experience.

He was still alive.

# THREE

"You don't need me to manipulate the man's voice now?" said Irina.

Jacob swapped the phone to his other ear as he scanned the board to find his flight back to JFK. "No. You don't need to do anything. The whole trip was a waste of time." Not entirely true; joy had been obtained from tormenting Finkel. "The man's an asshat, but not a murderer. Still, it was worth a try. The search goes on."

"I'm so sorry to hear that you didn't get the result you wanted."

"Thank you." Irina seemed only too willing to assist Jacob track down the murderer, yet he felt there was an underlying resentment. They'd been dating for a couple of months now, and he already knew he loved her. He'd told her as much. The first time he said it, oddly not after love-making but at the end of a grueling two-hour gym workout, she'd broken down into tears. *I love you, too, Yakov*, she'd said, using the Russian version of his name like she always did. *Since the moment I met you.* Yet he couldn't shake the suspicion Irina thought he was still in love with Sally-Anne, a woman dead for twenty years. He swore he was only interested in seeking justice, that he was being true to a promise he'd made to himself when it happened that he would leave no stone unturned to find her killer. Irina said she believed him, but did she really?

"And why are you speaking English?" said Jacob.

"Because I need to practice more." Her tone was businesslike. "Speaking Russian with you all the time doesn't help to advance my development, you know."

"Come on," he said, gripping the handle of his carry-on luggage. "Your English is excellent. Perfect, in fact. Wait a second." He scrolled to the Facebook app on his phone. Twenty people had accepted the invitation to the dinner tonight at the Golden Duck Chinese restaurant in downtown Glen Bridge. Comments were running hot, people eager for the event. Shit, they didn't deserve to be duped like this. "Hey, do you think you could make an announcement in that Facebook group that you...I mean I...apologize for the last-minute cancellation, but the reunion is off? Say something about an unexpected grave illness."

"Khorosho, zaichik. Okay, darling." She reverted to Russian, but it was only a fleeting lapse. "And I delete the group?"

"Wait until"—he glanced at his wristwatch, a new Breitling he'd indulged in after the massive payout from the Department of State following his successful mission in Moscow last year—"an hour before the event. They're all in town, I guess, most of them anyway. Geez, I feel bad about this."

"Don't. Maybe they can contact each other and come up with another party? One where they'll curse you to hell but laugh at it like it's an epic prank."

He hadn't realized how busy John Glenn International Airport had become lately; people scampered in all directions, racing for flights, looking for lost kids, taking a last-minute leak. Another check of the information board: his own Southwest Airlines flight was departing from Gate 6 in ten minutes. Time to move a bit faster.

"How are things at home?" Jacob meant how were things with Irina's son, Valentine, previously Vladimir, whom Jacob had help extricate from Russia with his mother. He was dealing with bullying at his high school: Russians weren't exactly flavor of the month, plus he was staying loyal to his outmoded Goth/emo subculture, which also attracted derision. Yes, he had an English name now, but there was no hiding the accent and lack of linguistic fluency. The kid was bright, a math and science prodigy thanks to good genes from Mom, but honing communication skills was going to take some time.

"He will be fine, Yakov. Don't worry about him."

"I can't help it." Jacob cradled the phone against his ear as he handed the pre-printed boarding pass to the smiling attendant. "His problems are your problems, which means they are my problems. Maybe you could have another think about home-schooling the boy? Maybe a tutor?"

A sigh. "Maybe, zaichik. I'm not keen, but if you can convince me..."

"Okay, gotta go. I'm boarding."

As he took back the pass from the attendant at the gate, a text message alert buzzed in his hand. His boss, Grant Fletcher. He switched to flight mode and pocketed the phone. Whatever Fletcher wanted would have to wait a couple of hours. The failed mission to nail Finkel had left Jacob drained like he'd been on a three-day boot camp. A couple of relaxing drinks on the two-hour flight home, browse a couple of mind-numbing travel magazines, a power nap. Then he'd deal with whatever shit storm Fletcher had in store.

---

AT 30,000 FEET, curiosity got the better of him. Fletcher had been quiet for several months, and he hardly ever sent a message simply to enquire about his employees' health. Something serious must be up.

He flicked out of flight mode and read the encrypted text, broken into two sections because it was so long-winded.

*Jacob. If you have plans for the next couple of weeks, cancel them. I don't care if it's chemotherapy, a heart-lung transplant or your own mother's funeral. Tomorrow evening you fly to Bogotá, Colombia. The deputy director of the CIA's Directorate of Operations, Joel McDonald, called me, desperate for assistance. They've got a big job lined up for us, and by us, I mean you.*

*Damn you, Fletcher.* The same corny "I mean you" line every time. As the lights dimmed ahead of imminent landing at JFK, he turned up the screen's brightness to better read the SMS.

*Dozens of CIA operatives in the key centers of Bogotá and Medellín are becoming compromised. In fact, not to put too fine a point on it, they've had to pull out some of their best agents. There's a mole among their number, and the leak needs to be plugged before the cover of all agents is blown. A couple of so-far uncompromised agents will be assisting you when you hit the ground in Bogotá. I recommend you take a seat for this next bit.*

*Got that base covered,* thought Jacob. He couldn't stand now if he wanted to with the fasten seat belt sign flashing and the undercarriage dropping noisily.

*The new-age cartel that's reformed in Colombia and extending into Mexico is proving to be more powerful than its predecessors.*

Jacob placed the phone in his lap and took a deep breath. Central fucking America. No way. Last time he was there, in Nicaragua, he'd undergone indescribable torture. Saved at the last minute by a stranger with a gun. There was no get-out clause in his contract with top-secret agency Skia, taken from the Greek word for *shadow*. There had to be some way to formulate an excuse for avoiding this mission. *Damn it, Hunter. Pull yourself together. You don't even know what the assignment is yet. Could be a walk in the park.*

He read further: *It's predicted that the guy in charge of the cartel, Adolfo 'Hitler' Sanchez, will soon make Pablo Escobar look like a Sunday-school teacher by comparison. He's been flexing his muscles from behind an impenetrable screen—the Colombian and Mexican governments and law enforcement authorities are failing to curb his excesses. The CIA believes he is involved in the identities of their key agents being blown. And more bad shit besides. The mission handed to us may require that you infiltrate this organization to find out crucial information. Your skills make you the only possible Skia agent capable of getting the job done.*

So no walk in the park, then. For once, Jacob was glad Fletch was providing a ton of background in his message. He could technically access the Boeing 737-800's Wi-Fi, but for some reason, he wasn't anxious to dig too deeply into this Sanchez guy. As he sipped flat Sprite from a plastic cup, he gave himself a mental head slap: Colombia is in South, not Central America. However, there was no comfort in that knowledge.

*As you know, a presidential election is scheduled for this year. The polls have the incumbent, Daniel Claxton, and his rival, Hannah McIvor, neck and neck. At this point in time, however, President Claxton is our boss, and he has aligned himself with this case.*

*What case, Fletcher?* Jacob wondered. *You haven't even mentioned the specifics of any fucking case yet!* Why did he always take so long to get to the point?

*An influential American businessman, Paul Brohman, has disappeared— presumed kidnapped— and the president wants us to get him back ASAP.*

There it is, at last...

*I'll give you a full bio of the guy when you get back to Manhattan. Yes, you can google him, but there's a lot of information about him that you will never find online. Here's the main thing you need to know. The abducted man was a key contributor to the president's campaign fund. We're talking a large percentage of the overall budget. With Brohman's disappearance, his personal accounts—containing a shit-load of money—are inaccessible. It's going to have a huge impact on Claxton's campaign if these funds aren't available.*

Jacob's head shook from side to side involuntarily as he took in the information. Still light on detail, this mission was starting to look like one of those prefixed with the word *suicide.*

*And here's the second main thing you need to know, the part that even the president isn't aware of. Brohman was also a CIA operative of sorts, working on flushing out Sanchez, infiltrating his network, including links with the mole and/or moles who are exposing the CIA's top assets. He'd befriended a guy in Bogotá who runs a chain of gas stations, used to work with Sanchez in Mexico before he turned dirty. Well, dirtier. The CIA thinks this Mexican, who shares Brohman's penchant for Colombian women, could be a useful lead.*

So absorbed was he in reading the SMS, Jacob barely noticed the bump as the airplane touched down on the tarmac in a perfect landing.

*Brohman, a former Marine Raider, is a staunch supporter of the president and a patriot prepared to do his duty in the interests of his country. However, he has a huge weakness for young women. The top rumor running around the ex-pat community right now is that he did a Leroy Brown— made advances on a woman with a jealous husband who has killed Brohman. We have no reason to believe this is true— the local police are telling us they're doing their best to find Brohman, but I have very little faith in them. As you know, corruption is rife in the Colombian government, military and police.*

*I hope I've given you enough to whet your appetite, Jacob. Check in with me the minute you get back to NYC and you will be fully briefed on your mission.*

The rest of Fletcher's text dealt with petty bitching about the worsening standards of public order in New York City and lamentations about the fate of the Jets football team, which Jacob skimmed over.

Reaching for his carry-on bag from the overhead locker, Jacob sighed. The irony hit home: He would probably have a better chance of tracking down Brohman than he would of ever finding the asshole who murdered Sally-Anne Vincent. Whether or not he'd get out of Colombia alive, that was another matter altogether.

Outside the terminal, he peeled off $100 and slipped it to the taxi dispatcher, who let Jacob cut the line and take the first available cab.

"Nice flight, sir?" asked the polite Indian driver.

"Excellent."

"Where to, sir?"

"Tribeca. And step on it." The sooner this was over and done with, the better.

A call to Irina. She'd be expecting him for dinner at her apartment in Harlem. "I'm back."

"I'm delighted to hear it." She spoke English from the get-go. She'd made up her mind this was how it was going to be, and he realized he'd have to get used to it. "I hope you're hungry. I spent all day making traditional Russian golubtsy."

He smiled. It was one of his favorite dishes, and she knew how to make it perfectly. "Do they reheat well?"

A silent pause. "Hmmm. Fletcher called you already, I see. Before you even speak to me? The man has some, what do you say...balls."

"He's sneakier than that. He sent me a text. He knew I wouldn't be able to resist reading the damned thing. He calls me, I just block it. The man is smarter than he looks."

"They do, by the way."

"What?" She'd lost him.

"They reheat well. So you can still come over and have a nibble before you go back to your place."

He laughed. "Oh, right." Jacob craved her physical touch even after only a short time away. He was addicted to her. "I'll be having a lot more than just a nibble."

She burst out laughing. "Me too!"

The taxi pulled up to the curb outside Fletcher's refitted luxury warehouse apartment.

The time for flirty banter was over.

# FOUR

THE MASSIVE AQUARIUM WAS A MAGNET FOR THE EYES. It was the first thing you saw when you exited the private elevator into Fletcher's open-plan apartment. Thirty feet long and filled with more that 3,000 gallons of water and a kaleidoscope of fish, it dominated the space. Brilliant neon colors glowed inside it, from artificial lighting and the bodies of the fish themselves. Fletcher had upgraded from a modest 55-gallon model, splashing out with abandon after the State Department had awarded Skia a massive sum of money as a thank you for Jacob's successful mission to Moscow last winter. Jacob did very well out of it financially, too. His money, however, was invested sensibly in the stock market. Most of it, anyway.

"Like the new acquisition?" said Fletcher, undoing the squeaky cork of a bottle of Hennessey XO and pointing the neck at the middle of the gargantuan tank.

"Sorry?" said Jacob. He tugged his trouser legs at the knee, then sat himself down in a luxurious black leather armchair. He shut his eyes to savor its sensual embrace. A moment passed, then he snapped them open again and said, "It's all a mass of scales and fins. You know I can't tell one of those creatures from another."

Fletcher touched a finger to the side of his nose. "Understood.

You're not an enthusiast like me. By the way, do you actually have any hobbies?" Before Jacob could answer, he said, "I've acquired two new Albino Asian Arowanas. Can you see them?"

He pointed; Jacob sought them out and failed. Still, he gave a nod. "Oh, yeah."

"It took me a month to track them down," said Fletcher, almost breathless with excitement. "I bought them off a dealer based in Indonesia. Then they were shipped stateside in a special container on a cargo boat that docked on the Hudson. Delivered to my door in a truck I had to order for the job, can you believe it?" He scratched a spot behind his ear before dropping ice cubes into Waterford crystal cognac glasses and pouring drinks for himself and Jacob.

"Very pleased for you, boss." He accepted the tulip-shaped glass and inhaled the fragrant scent. The vapors seemed to warm the inside of his chest. "I hope they bring you much joy."

"They freakin' better. Each one cost me fifty grand, you know! And that's not even counting the freakin' freight costs and import tax."

Jacob nearly spat out a mouthful of cognac. "You're kidding me, right? A hundred thou on a pair of fish?" He shook his head. "And you complain about your ex-wife taking you for a ride? I don't get it, Fletch."

"They're among the rarest aquarium fish in the world, Jacob! I got 'em each for 20 grand less than you'd normally pay. Pretty good deal, huh?"

"If you say so." Jacob hoped that if he kept his answers short and didn't engage with the conversation, the topic would exhaust itself and Fletcher would eventually get to the point.

"They might only be five inches long at the moment, but in three months, they'll be double the size. I wish I could do that." He laughed at his own lame joke.

Jacob responded with a grunt as he crossed one leg over the other and stared at the ceiling.

"Sorry, champ. I do prattle on about my damned fish, don't

I?" He slugged the rest of his cognac and poured himself another. Jacob declined the offer of a top-up. "But I can easily afford it now." He lowered his voice conspiratorially. "I paid Nancy a fat lump sum after the Kyiv business, and she agreed to leave me alone. For fucking ever! And it's in a legally binding agreement." He made a dusting-off-the-hands gesture. "Finito!"

"Does that mean I never have to hear about her again?" said Jacob hopefully.

"I can't swear upon it, but most likely, that's it as far as she's concerned. The bitch is out of my life now, and good riddance. Last I heard she'd moved to California with her masseuse."

"Even better news than the deal on the fish." Jacob saluted with his empty glass. "Now I'm desperate to get back to Irina and sample her golubtsy, so if you could get on with the briefing..."

"Sample her *what?*" Fletcher's eyebrows arched and elevated at the same time.

"Cabbage rolls stuffed with ground beef, pork, rice, and some other ingredients. Delicious."

"Thank God for that. I thought it was code for her..."

"Enough, Fletch!"

A look of contrition softened the laugh lines around the boss's mouth. "I didn't mean anything by it."

"I know you didn't." Jacob puffed out his cheeks. "Still, can we please get to the point of why I'm here?" The professional relationship of virtual equality meant the men could speak their minds about anything without fear of discipline or recriminations against either party. It was an unwritten rule, but one the men abided by and appreciated. Less room for bullshit.

A box of contraband Cuban cigars appeared, but only Fletcher indulged. "I've given you some of the background information so you could get a feel of what's going on. As far as we know, that is. Our intel is sketchy. What we do know for sure is this: Paul Brohman has vanished, and we need to find him." He sent out a couple of smoke rings, sipped cognac and smacked his lips. "The rest of it shouldn't take too long. I'll do my best not to detain you much longer."

"Appreciated."

"However, I'll expect you here tomorrow morning at 8:00 a.m. sharp for a full session with the deputy director of the CIA Directorate of Operations. He's flying in from Langley especially to speak to you."

"Jesus, Fletch. Couldn't it *all* have waited until tomorrow morning, then?"

"No." He tossed a manila folder onto the glass coffee table separating the two men. "The so-called brains at the CIA have created a legend for you. I wanted your opinion on it before I... uh...throw you to the wolves, so to speak." He laughed uneasily. "If it sucks, we can change it. Better to do it now before you 100 percent commit to the role, don't you agree?"

"Sure," said Jacob flatly, snatching up the folder. He licked a finger, flicked to the first printed page, and read aloud. "Name: Carlos Iglesias." He glanced up at Fletcher. "Literally Charles Churches in English. I like it." He continued to read the file. "Born in Pamplona, Spain. Only child. I spent my early years in Bogotá, where my parents worked as school teachers before the family emigrated to the United States when I was eight. I went to high school in Missouri, then graduated from Wharton Business School, University of Pennsylvania. I worked for New York's largest insurance broker for ten years before branching out on my own as a broad-brush financial adviser. Current role: international freelance business consultant specializing in drawing up trade contracts between the US and foreign companies. A fake company with a real street address and two local employees, Gunderson Holdings SA, will be my base in downtown Bogotá." Another wide-eyed look at Fletcher. "Dammit, why another finance guy role? It's not my thing, man. I'm tempted to change it. Why can't I be...I don't know...a music producer or a Hollywood agent?"

Fletcher waggled a finger. "I had a feeling you might object, but don't dismiss it immediately. Think how brilliantly you pulled it off in Russia. Skia's greatest result in its short 30-year history."

"God only knows how! I was totally lost in the arcane jargon, the legalese, the 'financialese,' to coin a word. Shitting my pants every minute of every day."

Fletcher stood and walked to the window overlooking a quiet cobblestone street. He pressed his hands against the sill and spoke with his back to Jacob. "Yes, you had some close calls, but you succeeded." He turned, pointing a finger. "You *always* succeed. And this time will be much easier. You'll have freedom of travel, no official employer to answer to. This cover will be a cinch to maintain by comparison with the Russian Ministry of Finance. Now read on, please."

The boss had valid points about the 'ease' of the role this time. However, the price of exposure was the same in Colombia, Russia, or anywhere else, for that matter. Death. If you were lucky, it'd be quick—unlucky, a spot of torture to deal with first. He took a deep breath and continued.

"Marital status: single. No children. Language skills: Native Spanish speaker with an accent slightly influenced by growing up in the USA. Basic Portuguese from a stint in Brazil five years ago."

"You confident your Spanish is up to scratch?"

Jacob side-eyed his boss. "Are you joking? And what if I said it wasn't? Would it relieve me of the mission?"

An awkward expression twisted Fletcher's lips. "No."

"Well, lucky for you, my Spanish is as perfect as it can be. I'm a little out of practice, but a day or so in Colombia and it will all come back. And you know I can imitate any accent." He cleared his throat. "My Portuguese is totally rusty, but since the bio says 'basic,' so that'll do. Anyway, I'm a linguistic savant, in case you'd forgotten."

"It's 90 precent of the reason we recruited you, son. You're one of a kind, and that's also why you're the highest paid spook in the history of the United States." Fletcher clapped Jacob on the shoulder. "Okay, champ. Get back to your woman." He glanced at his gem-encrusted gold Rolex. "It's getting late. I hope Irina's dumplings are still warm enough for you." He winked as he ushered Jacob up a couple of steps and summoned the elevator.

"Fuck you, Fletcher. If you weren't my boss, I'd break your nose for that snide comment."

"No, you wouldn't," said Fletcher. The doors closed with a ding.

*Yes I damn well would*, thought Jacob.

---

"IT'S PRETTY LATE. You sure you're in the mood to eat, zaichik?" Irina ladled two portions of stuffed cabbage onto his plate, then filled a glass with water from a jug.

He tilted his head and grinned. "After all the trouble you've gone to, how could I refuse?" Sentiments aside, his stomach, aided and abetted by his nostrils, had already made the decision for him. He sliced one golubets in half and almost swallowed the piece whole. Satisfied noises of contentment brought a smile to Irina's face.

She wiped her hands on an apron and took a seat opposite Jacob. "Can I have the bad news first?"

He swallowed hard, then said, "What the hell are you talking about? What bad news?"

She pursed her lips for a moment and gave a slight shake of the head. "You've just spent an hour at your boss's office. Something's up, I know it. In these situations, there's usually a bit of good news and a bit of bad news. I want the bad news first so it's over and done with."

His heart squeezed for a second as he scanned the modest Harlem apartment. Nothing like the luxury of his Tribeca condo. Pride wouldn't allow Irina to take advantage of the rewards bestowed upon Jacob. She'd vowed only to buy things for herself and her son with money she had earned fair and square. America had done them a massive favor by accepting her, giving her a home and a fresh start after escaping a regime she despised. Jacob wanted to shower her in money and gifts, but she would have none of it. And he loved her even more for her principled stand.

"I fly to Colombia tomorrow, and I don't know when I'll be back."

A small fly appeared from nowhere and settled on a piece of bread. Irina obliterated it with a flick of a dish towel like a cowboy cracking a whip. The bread sailed across the small kitchen, hit the wall buttered-side first, and stuck there. As if nothing had happened, she said, "That doesn't sound like bad news. It's not as dangerous as it used to be there, is it?"

"No, it's much safer than it was. But from what Fletcher tells me, there's a dude down there trying to resurrect the bad old days who's set himself up as the new Pablo Escobar. Crime is escalating, and it's all drug-driven again."

She interlaced the fingers of both hands and placed them on the top of the kitchen table like she was about to invoke a prayer. In her head, maybe she was. No words, just a slow nod.

"Not curious what my assignment is?" he goaded with a smile.

Big, glistening blue eyes stared back at him, unblinking. "No. You once told me every mission is potentially your last one, so no. I don't want to know anything about it."

He frowned. "It's a moot point, anyway. You're well aware that I'm not allowed to go into the specific details of my work with anyone. Not even you."

She opened her mouth to object, but he held up a finger. "I know what you're going to say. In Russia you knew plenty. But Russia was an exception because you were helping me achieve what had to be done." He twirled his fork on the empty plate, like he was winding on invisible spaghetti. "This time, it's different. Unless you're part of the mission, I have to keep you in the dark. Even if I wanted to tell you more, I couldn't. It won't be until tomorrow that I learn the full picture myself."

She cleared the plates away and placed a slice of medovik honey cake in front of him with a clatter.

"I know you're upset," Jacob said in his best calming voice, "but..."

She dabbed at her eyes with the corner of her apron. "If something happens to you...I can't imagine how I will cope. You are everything to me." She held back a sob.

He walked around the table and put an arm around her. "Shhh. I could get killed by some crazy whack-job on the New York subway. Crossing the street is an act of faith." He squeezed her shoulder and whispered, "In fact, watching the news, sometimes I think we're better off out in the countryside. Perhaps we could move to a quiet farm in the Midwest, where I was raised. It'll be good for your son. For you. For us."

She sniffed, shaking her head. "No. Not yet. I have to wait until Vova finishes high school. Two more years."

"You don't have to wait. You can enroll him somewhere else."

"If I do it now, it will disrupt his education."

"He's young and smart. He'll pick up where he left off in a new school. There are plenty of good ones in rural areas. I went to school in a small town. It's not an educational barrier here, like it might be in Russia. There are good schools all over the country. To be honest, the kid's going to be better off in so many ways by moving out of the city."

"But my job is here, in the financial district." Soon after arriving in America, Irina had scored a job at a respected global bank on Wall Street. Her IT skills allowed her to get a ground-floor position with scope for rapid promotion if she could prove herself. Without the security clearances organized by Skia, she would never have landed the role. But the application, the interview, the practical tests— it was all her own doing, and she was damned proud of her efforts. Nearly as proud as Jacob.

"You can get another job. You're smart." He turned to face her, brushing a strand of hair from her forehead. "You don't even have to work, baby. I make more than enough to support you and

Vova. Your parents and brother, too, if and when they decide to leave Norway."

She wriggled out of his embrace. "No! I am not a fucking charity. I love you, but do not take pity on me."

He gritted his teeth when she swore in English, something she only did when she was really pissed off.

"I'm not...geez..." He didn't know how to play this. Perhaps it was a hormonal thing, something else going on in her personal life: the kid, her parents, her brother. She was fully aware of his job and, in particular, his obligations to his employer. No get-out clause. "Listen, maybe I should go home and..."

Irina's small strong hands grabbed him by the waist and pulled him close. She rested her head against his broad chest. "Don't go home." She thrust her groin against him. "Not yet, anyway."

*Thank God*, Jacob thought. He couldn't have imagined leaving on his potentially last mission, as Irina had so rightly phrased it, on bad terms.

The way her hand squeezed him between the legs with a slow, erotic kneading motion told him they'd be parting on very good terms indeed.

# FIVE

Joel McDonald looked every inch the loyal government bureaucrat. Steel gray suit to match the serious, steel gray eyes. Conservative navy blue tie perfectly knotted at his throat. Sparkling silver cufflinks, chunky watch with a black leather strap. He gave off the subtle aroma of a popular aftershave that was marketed widely as a manly scent guaranteed to attract females, but to Jacob, it reeked of cloying, sweet femininity. McDonald's voice wasn't the most masculine he'd ever heard either, its whiny tone reminding him of his mother's off-key soprano.

"I cannot impress upon you enough just how urgent this unfortunate situation is," squeaked the CIA deputy director. "Nor how important it is that you succeed in carrying out the president's orders with the minimum of fuss." Fletcher's secretary, a 28-year-old curvaceous woman with barely an original thought in her head, Susan Stonehouse, poured the guest a tar-black coffee. McDonald accepted the offering with a thin smile and a curt nod. He promptly ignored the busty woman and her fluttering eyelashes and drilled his gaze into Jacob. "Now"—he tapped a pen on the edge of the glass table—"I know absolutely nothing about you, Mr. Hunter. Apart from the fact that you come highly recommended by President Claxton."

"The president has never met me, or seen my face, as far as I'm aware. Same goes for Grant." He gestured toward his boss. "We've spoken on the phone, but he's not allowed to see our faces. You've got one up on him, sir." Jacob took a chocolate chip cookie from a plate and dunked it in his latte. "You must have security clearance higher than God to be sent here personally."

"Indeed," said the VIP guest without the slightest trace of emotion or even feigned interest. A well-trained functionary, barely human. The perfect man for the job. "None of that concerns me. What does concern me is that President Claxton wants Paul Brohman found and brought back to the United States alive. If he loses an arm or a leg in the process of extricating him, that's okay. Nuts cut off by bandidos, also fine. As long as he can sign a piece of paper to make a healthy withdrawal from his bulging bank accounts, that's all that matters."

"Yes, sir," said Fletcher, who had given small head gestures of approval at almost every word McDonald uttered. Now and again, a finger pressed to his lips in focused concentration. Jacob knew it was a ploy, not an act of respect or deference. In his own mind, Fletcher thought he was better than everyone else. And in reality, as chief of Skia, he was more important to the government than the CIA man, a fact McDonald would not necessarily be aware of. Since its inception thirty years ago, Jacob knew that each successive president had sworn to keep all information about their dealings with the 'non-existent' organization secret. Divulging that knowledge was rumored to come with severe consequences. What they were and who enforced any penalties for breaching the oath, he could only guess. Probably someone like McDonald but in a black hood. So far so good: every president had kept his mouth shut.

"Why is his financial backing so important?" said Jacob. "Surely one man's contribution, or his company's, isn't going to make or break Claxton's re-election campaign."

McDonald rubbed a spot behind his ear, leaned in over the table, and unnecessarily lowered his voice. "Of course, you're right. There's more to it than that. Yes, he's dropping many millions into Claxton's coffers. He's the biggest individual donor, and Brohman's donations will certainly help Claxton compete with the odious challenger, who's leading the polls by a slight margin. But Brohman was also on a quest. Ultimately, and with the benefit of 20-20 hindsight, he was the wrong man to deploy, but we have to live with our decisions."

Jacob eyeballed Fletcher. The unspoken message: *they're not living with the decision—we're going to clean up their fucking mess.*

"We've learned there's a traitor in Bogotá, maybe more than one, whose actions could bring down our government. Brohman was about to dish the dirt on who they are. Sadly, from what we've seen on video footage from inside the nightclub and cameras on the street, before he got the final piece of the puzzle, he fell for a honey trap of epic proportions. The kidnappers have made no contact with authorities, made no demands. We don't know if he's been murdered, but we have to hope he's alive. The fact there's been no ransom note could mean they've either killed him or they're keeping him alive as some kind of leverage for later.

"The man is renowned for chasing skirt to the detriment of his assignments, but he's never let something like this happen before. He's also a staunch patriot and a close confidante of Claxton's to boot. I guess that's why we decided to risk it."

Jacob leaned back in his chair. "I've only been to Colombia twice. And it was a long time ago. A time when the Norte del Valle cartel was flourishing. I hated every moment of it. I've never been to the capital, so I'm not familiar with the territory. I'm going to need solid assets on the ground to help me out here. I mean, I don't even know where to start looking for your guy."

McDonald slurped coffee noisily, then reached into a briefcase. He handed identical folders to both men. "It's all in there, but I'll read the summary for you. Last page, gentlemen. Stop me if you have questions." A pair of glasses appeared from inside a jacket pocket and were on McDonald's face in one fluid motion.

"Wait, wait, wait," said Fletcher. He buzzed the secretary, who was in Fletcher's 'real' office, a separate room that Jacob had never set foot in, and asked her to make more coffee. The so-called office contained, according to the boss, boring administrative materials, archives and the like. Jacob suspected it was also a space where Fletcher got close and personal with Stonehouse when the fancy took him. The coffee she made was lousy, as were the home-baked cookies. Her organizational skills when it came to booking flights and accommodation were abysmal. The only logical conclusion one could come to was that Fletcher was banging her.

Jacob sipped tap water as he read along and McDonald recited from the page.

Thirty-five minutes later, the CIA man and Fletcher considered Jacob fully appraised of his mission and ready to fly out at 16:25 that afternoon. Backstops were lined up by the backroom team; a safe place to stay had been set up in the well-heeled Bogotá suburb of Rosales; two strong-arm local employees of 'Gunderson Holdings SA,' Gilberto Vicario and Ricardo Diaz, who were also on the CIA payroll but unaware of the full details of Jacob's mission, would meet him at the airport and escort him to his accommodation.

"Weapons?" said Jacob near the end of the briefing.

"At your apartment you will find an untraceable handgun, ammunition, and keys to a safe containing more magazines."

"Can I take my own pistol?"

McDonald nodded. "You'll have a special security clearance at the airport in Jersey, and no one will even look at you at the private airstrip in Bogotá, so if you feel desperately attached to your own weapon, by all means, pack it."

"Thanks. As it happens, my Glock 19 is like a favorite pet."

McDonald plowed on in his whiny, girly voice. "Fair enough. In Bogotá you will have access to more discrete weaponry, such as knives, knuckle dusters, a whole arsenal of goodies. Finally, for paying any bribes, there'll be a large cache of greenbacks and the local currency, whatever that is."

"Pesos," said Jacob. "I checked the exchange rate last night: one US dollar gets nearly 4,000 pesos."

"Fascinating," said McDonald blandly. Jacob's faith in the puppet master, not especially strong before, took a dive. If the dude didn't even know what money was used in Colombia, heaven help him. "A driver will pick you up from this address at precisely 3:00 p.m. to take you to Teterboro airport. Be ready; the airport's busy and Kanye West is arriving sometime this afternoon with a sizeable entourage. You don't want to be getting under each other's feet."

Jacob smiled. He could imagine the nerdy McDonald wearing oversized headphones, secretly listening to Kanye. Jacob had never used the mainly private facility, located a short drive away, across the Hudson River into New Jersey. It was famous for being used by top celebrities flying charter jets who wanted to avoid the limelight.

"Don't expect the luxury treatment at Teterboro," said McDonald with a tad too much pleasure. "You'll be onboard and flying into Bogotá very soon after you arrive." He stood to leave. "Last thing you need to know is your codename. Montoya."

"After the Colombian F1 driver?" Jacob smoothed a wrinkle that had formed in his jeans. "Nice touch."

McDonald gestured toward Fletcher. "His idea, not mine. I've never heard of the guy."

The men wound down the briefing with some small talk and shook hands. McDonald exited with a confident stride, his briefcase tucked close by his side. With the CIA chief gone, Fletcher offered his top agent more cognac, 'one for the road,' but Jacob politely refused. "I'm heading home to pack a few essentials."

Jacob had been to hell and back on his last mission to Moscow. Killed more people than he'd anticipated. One was too many. This assignment, to a region where the criminals had a reputation for cruelty and brutality on steroids, had his guts working overtime. A bottle of Pepto-Bismol would definitely be going into the travel kit.

He descended the elevator deep in thought. He almost missed his own street as he sucked in pints of cool afternoon air. Something deep in his gut told him this one was going to be worse than Moscow by an order of magnitude. And, as always, if he was exposed and captured, the budget and number of personnel that would be dispatched to save his ass would be exactly zero.

# SIX

Sweat pooled in Brohman's armpits and crotch. Everywhere sweat could escape from his body, it had. A gallon of water would go halfway to rehydrating him properly. He blinked droplets from his tired eyes. Why was he so damned tired?

Through the wet bleariness that stung like shampoo under the eyelids, a hazy image of a face appeared. He blinked more to squeeze out the sweat. The image became clearer, but that wasn't a good thing. The man staring into his eyes was the embodiment of mindless, senseless, pure evil.

The man howled like a hyena. The high-pitched sound was somewhere between hysterical laughter and an air raid siren. He took a step back, pulled out a plastic pouch, and carefully rolled a cigarette. A mottled reptilian tongue flickered before it licked the gum and sealed the smoke. A giant flame danced around on the end of a gleaming Zippo lighter. The acrid, sweet stench of tobacco mixed with pot filled the air. He spat out a loose leaf and dragged a stool across the room; the sound it made on the tiled floor set Brohman's teeth on edge. The man spun the chair around and sat on it backwards. A jet of foul reefer smoke homed in on Brohman's face unerringly like a tracer bullet.

"You look like you been in a freakin' hot sauna, man." The

last word sounded like mang, the way Tony Montana spoke in the movie *Scarface*. "You shoulda just kep' yo head down, yo nose outta everybody's business. But no, you had to go and fuck everything up."

Brohman wanted to protest his innocence to this arrogant punk. To lie his head off. *No. You got the wrong guy. It wasn't me.* The tape around his mouth stopped him from doing anything but make pathetic humming sounds. He made one now, hoping it sounded like *Take the damn tape of my mouth, you son of a bitch.*

Paul Brohman couldn't speak, but he could see with a clarity and awareness borne of abject fear. His days in the Marine Raiders, when he was young and brave, seemed so long ago now. An almost forgotten chapter. Life in the corporate world had made him soft. He dropped his head and noticed he was sitting on a chair. A bit of grainy tan color on either side of his quivering thighs told him it was a wooden chair. He couldn't see the rope around his wrists at the back of the chair or the rope around his ankles that bound him to the chair's legs. He didn't need to see them to know they were there. He was stuck fast. The rope around his chest, coiled three times, was visible if he tucked in his chin. Also visible was his wrinkled and slightly shriveled genitalia.

He was cold, so that explained the minor shrinkage. But not the profuse sweating. Had they injected something into him? He remembered a similar reaction to a dye injected into his arm prior to an MRI scan a couple of years ago. He thought then that he was going to die. A similar feeling gripped him now.

A spot in the back of his head ached and throbbed without pause. It seemed to be spreading; he so wanted to rub it, make it feel better. Or ask someone to take pity and rub it for him.

None of that would happen.

He'd been found out, and his grim fate awaited.

The vital recording would not be handed over tomorrow morning. Or was it already today? Perhaps yesterday? He'd been knocked unconscious, waking up just five or so minutes ago. He had no concept of how much time had elapsed since that fucking bitch had lured him into the alleyway and those goons tossed him into the waiting vehicle.

The man who'd just spoken approached from the far side of the room, joint dangling from the corner of his mouth. He waddled with one of those ridiculous gaits that rappers favor: a lumbering crouch with pointed fingers of both hands criss-crossing as they go. The performance reminded him of Groucho Marx's funny duck walk, yet he saw no humor in it.

"There's good news for you," said the young man, crouching down low and placing tattooed, thick forearms on Brohman's thighs. He glanced at the prisoner's crotch and gave a short laugh. Brohman felt his face flush with shame. The kid, who couldn't have been more than 19 years old, took a step back. Despite his youth, his English, a Hollywood mobster-gangster dialect, was well practiced. "And that good news, man, is that we ain't gonna kill you..."—he winked, but all Brohman could focus on was the angry pink scar that ran down the length of the kid's cheek—"... yet." Brohman couldn't be a hundred percent sure, but it appeared that one of the boy's eyes was made of glass. What he wouldn't give to poke the other one out for him. "I'll be back soon. I got something for ya. Don't go away, okay?" He let out a shriek, departed through a door, and slammed it behind him.

Brohman's nostrils flared as he tried to ingest every ounce of nourishing oxygen that he could. He must be hungry, judging by the gurgles coming from his stomach, but food was the last thing on his mind.

Miguel.

He was most probably dead.

They would have killed him and intercepted the recording of the American who was supposed to be spearheading the big crime, the so-called *Operación grande*. The audio material was going to reveal not only who was behind it, but when, where, and how it was going to happen. Rumors were running wild in the spook community that something huge was afoot: assassination of the Colombian president; assassination of the US president;

worldwide release of a deadly and highly infectious pathogen developed by mad scientists in the Amazon jungle.

Fucking Miguel Herrera was a coward. Too scared to simply tell Brohman over the phone. Influenced by too many stupid spy movies. This wasn't Russia or Washington. Phones were tapped occasionally here, but it was a rare thing.

And then he realized the truth. He must have been hit over the head so hard he'd lost the ability to think rationally. Through pulsating aches in his skull, he began to remember. A huge government scandal involving the president, illegal wire-tapping, stolen money, something to do with a nanny accused of working for the Gulf Clan cartel.

The criminal network in Colombia was complex, hard for most people—even those players involved in it directly—to wrap their heads around. Brohman thought he had a good handle on it. He'd studied the history of narco-crime in Colombia, going back to the two-billion-dollar-per-annum earning Cali Cartel of the 1990s, headed up by Escobar and Rodriguez. The Norte del Valle cartel that ran until 2012, then the BACRIM, the so-called bandas criminales emergentes, in English known as the emerging criminal organizations.

But the web was so intricate and diaphanous, he often got lost trying to stay on top of it. This leader would rise, then get killed. That gang would gain ascendency, then get crushed by a rival. A roller coaster characterized by anarchic unpredictability.

Then, if that weren't enough, there were the paramilitary groups anxious to destabilize everything and get their cut of the loot. New incarnations of FARC and the M-19 militia, the latter now parading as a legitimate political party. As things stood, to fulfil his mission, Brohman had only needed to grasp the big picture as it looked today. The Gulf Clan, aka the Gaitanistas, was on top; Cartel Moderno headed by Adolfo 'Hitler' Sanchez with its Mexican connections was rising and looking set to become number one; minor cartels were trying hard, but they would never be the equal of the other two; and finally, Colombia's first leftist government was floundering but was also jam full of criminals.

*Dammit, Brohman. How naïve can you be!* Miguel might have been a coward, but he was right. There was plenty of scope for covert surveillance inside Colombia. Everyone with a stake in the game was capable of conducting it, alongside carrying out brutal physical measures. Witness his own current, pathetic predicament.

That last phone call must have been traced—or maybe Miguel's actions had been caught on a hidden camera. How else would they—whoever *they* were—have known about the handover? Miguel swore on his mother's grave that he'd been totally discrete and carefully covered his tracks every step of the way. *Nobody knows what I'm doing*, he'd said. In other words, no one could have ratted him out. But maybe Miguel was wrong. Maybe he hadn't been as careful as he thought, confided in the wrong person.

He heard bustling noises on the other side of the door. Loud laughter. The door burst open. The first thing he saw was a pair of bare feet sticking up in the air. Bent, twisted toes blue and black and ugly. A body lay on a trolley. Made of shiny steel, it looked like a hospital gurney. Reminded him of those corny cop shows he loved to watch, where the coroner wheels in the stiff and the detectives check out the body of a victim.

The rest of the trolley followed the feet into the room. The body, piled on it like an afterthought, unlike in the sanitized TV shows, was a bloody mess. Like a slaughtered animal thoughtlessly dumped on a butcher's block. It was sliced down the sides of the torso, intestines hanging out like strings of sausages. The head was angled so Brohman got a good look at the face, reduced to a pulpy red mass. Even with the features destroyed beyond all recognition, Brohman had no doubt about the identity of the corpse.

The wild mop of curly hair, an afro better suited to the 1970s.

It was his source, Miguel.

Sticking out of his mouth, like an apple shoved in a pig's maw prior to roasting, was a cell phone. The instrument of his own capture. Judging by the stench that overpowered any lingering cannabis odor and made Brohman's eyes water, poor Miguel had either been dead for some time or left out in the open air, which had hastened decomposition. The urge to puke was strong, but the tape firmly stuck to his mouth made vomiting a non-option. No way would he give them the pleasure of choking to death in this stinking room. He would get out of here somehow and bring all these sick motherfuckers down.

It was only then that Brohman noticed the other two men in the room. The young man from before who had steered the gurney, and an older man, although perhaps ten years younger than Brohman. The two of them conferred in hushed tones, hands as active in communication as their words, which did not reach Brohman's ears. The kid gave a nod and pushed the gurney to within inches of Brohman, who closed his eyes and wrinkled his nose in a futile attempt to block out the stench of rotting flesh.

A stinging slap across the face. "Open your fucking eyes, Señor Brohman."

*No. I won't obey.*

A jolt of electrified pain surged through his body, agony he'd never experienced before. His eyes burst open to see the kid beaming with satanic joy and brandishing a taser. The pain disappeared in a flash, but it was something he didn't want to experience again. What if the kid held it against his skin for more than a few seconds?

"You will do as we say, dirty Americano dog, or you will end up as ground beef like your dumbass amigo, Miguel. Entendiendes? *Understand?*"

He could barely raise the strength to nod.

The hand to the face this time executed a soft pinch followed by a gentle double tap with a cupped hand, like an Italian mafia don praising his prodigal son turned back to the fold. "Good," said the kid. "This way we will all get along fine."

The older man standing by the window snapped out an order in Spanish. The kid instantly turned meek. "Si, si, jefe. *Yes, yes, boss.*" He pushed the remains of Miguel out of the room, but the odor of decay lingered.

"I see you are not used to the smell of death?" said the newcomer. The man had a neatly trimmed mustache and a mane of slicked-back hair that gleamed under a generous helping of product. "Young Javi and I don't give it a second thought anymore. We have been surrounded by death for many years." He produced a bottle of red wine from a drinks cabinet, poured two glasses, and set them down on a table. "Our enemies kill us, we kill them. Natural justice." He picked up one glass, swirling it in the bright light coming through the window. "Miguel was an enemy."

He tugged at the cuffs of an expensive-looking business shirt poking out of an equally expensive-looking jacket. They teamed well with his designer jeans, Brohman reflected, even if the cowboy boots were kind of gauche. He then wondered why, in such a dire situation, fashion was figuring in his thoughts.

The man placed one hand close to Brohman's ear and gently tugged away the band of tape with the other. There was a slight sting as skin and hairs stuck to glue, but compared to the taser, it barely registered. Brohman gasped, his chest rising and falling like a bellows as he sucked in a gallon of air. The chance to breathe through his mouth instead of his nose and thereby not suffer from the stink of death was a momentary godsend.

"In that wardrobe, you will find a dressing gown to cover up." The man waved a hand in the general direction of Brohman's shriveled manhood. "Javi was excessive in taking away your dignity. Not something I would have done to another man, but never mind. You will now take a shower and change into clean clothes. After that, you and I will then enjoy a glass of wine and have a cozy chat. And finally, we will have some dinner. You like Mexican food?"

Brohman smiled weakly. This 'nice treatment' bore all the

hallmarks of a captor setting him up to be the classic Stockholm syndrome victim. "Thank you," he mumbled.

"For what?" The man tilted his head and smiled, all lips and no teeth.

"For..." Dammit, what was he thanking him for? His genteel manners? Dinner and drinks? "I don't know."

"Ha ha! You are thanking me because you are still alive and I'm giving you a reprieve from Javi's ill-treatment. Logical for a man in your position. You have probably heard that Adolfo Sanchez is a cruel man. The reality is far different. If I'm gonna kill you, I do it quick." He paused. "My employees sometimes get ideas about being creative, using torture, for example. I don't condone it, unless I need very important information. Foot soldiers like Javi are so loyal to me"—he chuckled throatily—"that I cannot find it in my heart to discipline them for exuberance."

Sanchez walked behind the chair. Brohman felt a tugging sensation and heard the sounds of a knife cutting through his rope bonds. Well, at least he now knew who the kidnapper was. The one he'd suspected all along was one party to Operación grande. If only he knew who the other party was. Sanchez's English, although accented, was so fluent he must have studied long and hard to reach this level. From what Brohman knew about the man, his formal education was limited to ghetto primary school. "Sanchez, did you say? I've never heard of you."

His hands sprang free, then his feet.

"Please," said Sanchez. "There's no point lying to me. I know all about you, who you work for, both officially and in your clandestine role. It's all out in the open, thanks to Miguel. He, if you'll excuse the expression"—Sanchez grinned again, showing a set of top teeth boasting two gold premolars either side of his mouth—"spilled his guts."

Brohman sighed and took a deep breath. His hands had moved to cover his modesty. Sanchez's eyes drifted to the very spot where Brohman's hands were fidgeting like he had palsy, covering his previously exposed crotch. "If you figure on keeping that equipment, then I'd advise you to tell me no more lies. None. Or I'll be forced to turn a blind eye while Javi separates you from your cock and balls. And from what I hear, you like using them with the ladies."

Brohman swallowed hard. Sanchez was messing with his head big time.

"But enough of that. Stand!"

Brohman stood on wobbly legs.

"Oh dear," said Sanchez. "You need help." The drug lord went to the closet, pulled out a black silk dressing gown with a dragon motif on the right breast, and tossed it to Brohman.

Fifteen minutes later, the reluctant guest was showered and changed and sipping excellent Merlot on a deck overlooking a well-tended garden.

"Now I'm going to ask you a series of questions, and I expect honest answers to all of them," said Sanchez. He handed the glass he'd poured earlier. "The wine has had time to breathe. And so have you. Here's to you taking many more breaths. Salud!"

Brohman clinked his glass with a wide-open stare and a forced grin, like a certifiable idiot. All he could think about was his impending demise.

# SEVEN

THE FLIGHT IN THE LUXURIOUS GULFSTREAM G650 WAS ultra-smooth most of the journey, with only one small episode of turbulence that upended his coffee and stained his chinos. No biggie; he changed into the spare pair he'd brought and soldiered on. The entire six-hour trip had seemed to take fifteen minutes, but that impression may have been due to Jacob's immersion in the historical material he was reading. So much to take in. From Simon Bolivar way back when, right up to last year's elections. One thing the country couldn't shake off, like a bad cold that won't go away, was the ongoing drug running and violence associated with it, and new criminal organizations, like Cartel Moderno, taking the place of the old cartels.

He breathed a little easier when he got to the end of the comprehensive article. Once described as the most violent country on Earth, recent reforms by determined Colombian leaders had seen a massive reduction in many forms of crime. In particular, murder had plummeted to levels even the most cautious tourist would find acceptable. As positive as that sounded, those statistics were little comfort for a man about to go toe to toe with the most brutal of the brutal, Adolfo 'Hitler" Sanchez.

The private jet had traversed the approximately 2,500 miles

from Jersey to Bogotá in a tick under what it would take a Boeing 777 to cover the distance. No advantage in speed but vastly superior in three main aspects: comfort, safety, and avoiding detection. Gulfstreams in the CIA's fleet led the way in advanced aviation communications systems, in particular secure voice and data transmission. In short, what happened on the plane stayed on the plane.

There was no other aviation activity in Guaymaral Airport tonight. The pilot, a bespectacled woman called Cynthia from Bristol, UK, who bore more than a passing resemblance to the actress Julia Roberts, told Jacob a couple of air traffic controllers were the only staff left at the airport. Oh, and a couple of flight maintenance mechanics to help refuel and make sure she was good to fly back to New York without issue.

"I would have expected a bigger airport for a capital city," he remarked disingenuously. He knew they were taking a circuitous route to get to his new temporary home, using a minor hub. What time they lost in flying would be made up for in speedy ground transportation to his downtown pad.

"I don't generally question my flight plan, but for some reason, you've been spared the headache of negotiating the main airport, El Dorado." She smiled broadly. "Which is kind of fortunate, because that place is super busy." She scribbled something in a logbook. "And I've been spared, too. I much prefer landing in these out-of-the-way places." Her broad mouth formed a warm smile. "I'm not much of a people person. Me and the sky, that's my happy place."

Jacob shook her hand and thanked her for her skillful flying. She waved away the praise. "It's all computers. I just sit here at the pointy end of the plane in case something goes wrong."

He stepped down the short flight of boarding stairs at precisely 11:38 p.m. All around was dark and quiet, save for the chirping of insects. Moist, cold air stung his cheeks; he re-gripped the handle of his heavy sports bag as it began to slip off his shoulder. No customs clearance or security of any kind meant he was able to not only bring his Glock 19 but also a back-up Sig Sauer P320 and plenty of ammo. A pair of thick-soled jungle boots added to the already considerable weight in the bag. Sure, he could go on a shopping spree and buy new ones in Bogotá, but old, well-worn-in footwear is a much safer bet. You never knew where you were going to end up on a mission like this one, full of unknowns.

A casually dressed man waited at the entrance to the terminal, fidgeting and wriggling his hips like he needed the bathroom. Normally, this nervous body language would be a bad sign, but Jacob gave him the benefit of the doubt, putting it down to the chilly temperature. As he neared, the man squared his shoulders and set his jaw. Hand extended, he asked, "Cuál es su nombre en clave?"

"Mi nombre en clave es Montoya," said Jacob, giving the code name that was so politely requested by the stranger. He exaggerated his American accent but still spoke quickly and confidently.

"Bien. My name is Gilberto. I'll drive you to your accommodation. Please come with me."

The two men's footsteps echoed through the deserted terminal, if you could call the oversized shed a terminal. An eerie feeling gripped Jacob deep in his guts. He was on the alert for surprises, someone leaping out of the shadows. He told himself to calm down; it was just the nerve-jangling acoustics you get in empty spaces combined with hard surfaces.

But one never knew, so it paid to keep your hand close to your weapon. A deserted terminal on the edge of a dangerous city was the perfect place to encounter an ambush. "Espera un momentito. *Wait a second*," he said, staying Gilberto with a light touch on the elbow. He retrieved his Glock 19 from the bag, loaded a magazine, and tucked the weapon under his belt. Gilberto watched with an approving eye.

Through a side door and out onto the deserted street, the sense of foreboding lifted somewhat. A starless night with a gentle breeze seemed completely ordinary. They strolled a couple of yards toward a parked black Land Cruiser with tinted windows, mounted spotlights, and an intimidating bull bar. Gilberto graciously held open the front passenger door, and Jacob grabbed the handgrip and hoisted himself inside. There was already another person sitting in the back seat. To ask questions or not? He decided to play it cool, staring out the front windscreen. Gilberto sat behind the wheel, kissed a crucifix hanging from the rearview mirror, and crossed himself. He pressed the start button, and the engine kicked in with a throaty rumble.

Exiting the airport's small parking lot, the driver clarified the situation. "The man sitting in the back seat is Ricardo, your bodyguard," said Gilberto in Spanish slowed down so a dumbass gringo like Jacob could understand. He dropped down a gear as the powerful high beams picked out a dead cat lying in the middle of the road, the unfortunate creature's innards a patch of jam on the asphalt. Gilberto then turned to face Jacob and for some reason switched from Spanish to English. "He is strong, very reliable, and obedient. He give you no trouble, Montoya."

"I don't need a bodyguard," said Jacob, sticking to Spanish. This condition of a bodyguard hadn't been agreed to at any point. The last thing he needed was another person hanging around when he was supposed to be infiltrating the Cartel Moderno. Curious enough now to want a better look at Ricardo, he turned his head to see a grin mostly lost inside a bushy beard. The man extended a hairy hand; half of the index finger was missing. "Encantado. Pleased to meet you," said Jacob, eyeballing the damaged digit before pumping the man's hand. "I'm afraid I won't be needing you for this—"

The Land Cruiser skidded to a halt, fishtailing to the right.

"Puta madre! *Holy crap!*" Gilberto's voice rose an octave.

Jacob let go of Ricardo's hand, instinctively spinning and ducking his head. On the way down, he had a moment to glimpse the outlines of what he guessed to be two men. After skidding, the car wasn't facing them square on; the headlights had no chance of illuminating them fully.

*What's going on?*

He curled into a ball, wedging his left ear up against the glovebox. Some shit was going down early. Way too fucking early. He reached for the Glock. Gilberto and Ricardo would be tooled up, but who knew what they were confronting? Jacob's heart beat out of his chest. This mission would be over before it began. How many were out there? These gangs usually traveled in packs. Any second now, bullets would tear through the windshield, perforating Gilberto. He'd be next, then Ricardo. He recited a quick prayer. *God, look after Irina.* Not Irene, never Irene. She would always be Irina to him. *God look after...*

A cough, then Gilberto mumbled a couple of words of annoyance. From behind, a husky chuckle.

Jacob breathed a sigh of relief. It wasn't a hold-up.

He quickly uncurled his body and sat up straight in the seat. He placed his Glock on his lap as a precaution and turned to face Gilberto but ended up looking at the panther tattooed on his neck. "What the hell's going on here? I nearly had a heart attack." The words hung in the air unanswered. The driver wasn't paying attention; instead he was busy chatting with a pair of unsmiling, granite-faced officers. Jacob had read up on the structure of the *forces* in Colombia, both police and military. Judging by their uniforms, they were from the local branch of the National Police based in Bogotá, the Región de Policía No. 1.

"License, please," said one of the officers, waggling fingers impatiently. "Pronto!"

Gilberto handed his over with a smile. "What seems to be the problem? I'm sure I wasn't speeding. You can't on these shitty roads, even if you want to."

"One moment, señor."

"Hey!" he exclaimed as the officer strolled back to his patrol car, parked at the side of the road under a dim yellow street light covered in spider webs. "Where's he going with my damned ID?" he barked at the second cop.

"Please, relax, señor. There's been some car jackings out on this road during the last week. People flying into the regional airport have been robbed, two even stabbed to death. This is just a random stop. Nothing to be concerned about. Can I ask why you are traveling on this road at such a late hour?"

"We were picking up my colleague from a charter flight." He jerked a thumb toward Jacob, who tipped the cop a salute garnished with a grin. "It was delayed by several hours due to bad weather in Cali." He lit a noxious cigarette and expelled a plume of smoke close to the cop, who sneered as he waved his hand in an effort to disperse the nicotine cloud.

While Gilberto was engaged with the cop, Jacob turned to the bodyguard and whispered. "How are you supposed to protect me from the back seat when trouble starts?"

Ricardo gave a lopsided smile. He reached between his legs and half pulled up, so the cop couldn't see it, a compact weapon, dull-black and menacing, that looked like it could wreak a lot of havoc. "With this bad boy. My best friend."

"What is it?"

"A micro Uzi. It can fire 1,250 rpm." He gestured at his tinted window and whispered, "I could drop those two stupid cabrónes in three seconds." He pursed lips through the lush facial hair. "You don't need to be afraid of anything when I'm around, gringo."

The first officer returned and handed back Gilberto's license with a flourish. "Everything seems to be in order. I'd just like to check the ID of your passengers."

"Why?"

"Because my mother lives in Cali. I just called her. Perfect sunny weather there all day and the same forecast for the rest of the week. Why are you lying to the police, señor? Very suspicious, if you ask me. Perhaps you are the carjackers we've been trying to catch."

"Give me a break," said Gilberto with a sarcastic laugh. He tapped ash out of the window then spat to the right of the cop, missing him by inches.

The second officer was already at Jacob's window, making a roll-down-the-window gesture. Jacob's jaw clenched as he pressed the button with one hand and tucked the Glock under his left thigh with the other. He fished out his passport. "Would you like to see my ID? No driver's license, I'm afraid. I'm too nervous to drive the streets of Bogotá." He laughed, trying to make light of the situation.

"Gracias," said the man in a robotic tone. He hummed tunelessly as he examined the inside of the document; his eyes flicked back and forth between Jacob and the photograph in the passport. It was from a recent photo, high quality, and there could be no doubt in anyone's mind that the bearer and the photo were one and the same person. The man folded up the passport and handed it back. "Before we let you go, I'd like to ask you a couple of questions, Señor Iglesias, if you don't mind." The man's tongue circled dried and chapped lips. *Dude could do with some lip balm*, Jacob thought. Or a drink. He took an unopened bottle of water from the console and took a deep draft himself, made a satisfied 'aah' sound, and wiped his mouth with the cuff of his shirt. The officer sneered, unimpressed.

Dammit, this was taking too long. Another couple of minutes and it would be clear whether these two upholders of the law were seeking a bribe. Jacob had enough cash in his wallet to satisfy even the most bent of cops.

"Sure, ask whatever you want. Fire away." He took a couple of deep breaths. He was Carlos Iglesias now; he summoned his photographic memory to visualize all the details of his legend as they were written in the file.

Thanks to one tiny glitch, he needn't have bothered.

"Why is there no entry visa stamped in your passport?"

"I beg your pardon?" Jacob felt his blood pressure hit levels he hadn't experienced in months. Someone in the tech department had fucked up big time on this assignment. Colombia didn't require visas for short visits, but there had to be a stamp in the travel document. Everyone got one on arrival.

The cop tilted his hat back on his head, placing a hand on his hip. "You have entered this country illegally. There are severe penalties for breaking Colombian immigration laws."

"I assure you," said Jacob, "the official at the airport back there just waved me through. Go and ask him why he made a mistake. He's the one that needs prosecuting, not me."

By now, the other cop had joined his companion at Jacob's window.

"What's the problem, Julio?"

The cop scratched his chin thoughtfully and gestured toward Jacob, who tried to maintain his calm and look as innocent as possible. "I don't know. Something fishy could be going on here. Wait a second while I go and run a check on the license plates."

Before Jacob could contemplate his next move, Ricardo made the decision for him. The bodyguard shouldered open the rear passenger door, commando-rolled a couple of feet out of the danger zone, then squeezed off a series of rounds from the spitting Uzi. The cop dropped like a bag of cement. As he fell, Jacob saw the man was riddled with bullets, jets of dark red blood spurting out of a number of holes.

Jacob raised his butt cheek and fumbled for the Glock and took aim at the second cop, but all in vain. He was gone. Jacob gripped the weapon so hard he thought he was going to make an indentation in the handle. A shove and the door was open. He crouched and held his breath in the semi gloom.

"Get back in the car, Montoya, quickly," said Gilberto, who stood over the body of the second cop. "We have to get out of here. These weren't police."

"Are you sure?"

"Seguro. *Sure.*" He nodded. "Look at their shoes."

Instead of boots, the men wore brand new Nike sneakers.

"Who are they, then?" said Jacob.

"No idea. You and Ricardo, help me drag them off the road."

A couple minutes later, the bodies were concealed in bushes at the side of the road, their 'police' vehicle rolled into a ditch.

As the car tore along Calle 235, Gilberto's knuckles white on the wheel, Jacob said, "They were from Cartel Moderno, weren't they?"

"You're smarter than you look, gringo," chuckled Ricardo from the back seat. "There's a good chance they were. But then again, maybe it was some random bandidos looking for an easy score. Whoever it was, they made a big mistake!" He tapped the driver on the shoulder. "Hey, Gilberto. Turn up the stereo, huh?"

The driver obliged, a rhythmic melody pouring from the speakers.

"You know, muchachos," said Ricardo, bobbing his head to the tune, "there's nothing I like better after plugging some bad guys than to listen to happy music."

"You object?" Gilberto was already reaching for the button on the dashboard as he glanced at Jacob. "I can turn it down if you prefer."

"Not at all. Just get me to my apartment before we run into any more of those pricks."

The strains of Latin American pop music filled the car as it sped toward the center of the city.

# EIGHT

THE APARTMENT WAS ON CARRERA SÉPTIMA, PERCHED on the thirteenth floor of a red brick building in the well-heeled suburb of Rosales. From the front, it overlooked the broad main thoroughfare. To the rear, streetlights below illuminated lush parks and gardens, occasional mansions surrounded by electrified razor wire and security cameras. The vast, sprawling city of twinkling lights was lit up like a Christmas tree. He could pick out a few brave souls wandering the streets, but for the most part, it was quiet.

Before checking in with Fletcher, Gilberto and Ricardo had some explaining to do. Jacob ambled to the double-door stainless steel refrigerator and pushed a glass against a lever. Ice dropped into his glass, then a gush of water. The agents at first refused his offer of a drink, then relented when he insisted. Once they'd got nice and comfortable in matching leather recliners, it was time to get some answers. If they were satisfactory, Jacob would let them go home, wherever that was.

He looked from one man to the other, taking his time before he asked bluntly, "Who do you both work for?"

They exchanged a look of confusion.

"Ah, for the CIA?" said Ricardo uncertainly, massaging his jaw.

"Correcto," chimed in Gilberto, tweaking a curtain and peering into the street below. His answer carried the certainty of knowledge. "We thought you knew."

"They are paying you, I assume. Or this phony company I'm here working for, Gunderson Holdings SA, is. Not important." He pointed at each of them in turn, like a coach reprimanding players that should be performing better. "Until my job here is completed, you two work for me, no matter where your paycheck comes from. You take no orders from anyone but me. Claro? *Understood?*"

The men nodded slowly.

"If you deviate from this simple directive, I will have both of you replaced." It was an empty threat; who would he replace them with? He sipped water, and the others copied him, their eyes never leaving Jacob's face. He noticed the American twang to his Spanish had begun to slip; his natural inclination to speak the language perfectly was hard to curb. A mental head-slap to be more careful. Being too fluent might lead the men to think he was shady.

"Tell me everything you know about Paul Brohman." He turned to Gilberto. "You first."

"I only know what's been circulating the city as rumor." He looked at his nails for a moment. "And some intel we've gathered ourselves."

"Tell me the rumors first, then the intel." Jacob made a get-on-with-it motion with his left hand as he sipped more water from the glass in his right. He'd never felt so dehydrated: during the long flight, he'd had a couple of dry crackers and three strong coffees, so absorbed was he in reading about the history of Colombia. Now he couldn't get enough water into his system.

"Okay." Gilberto wriggled in his seat. "Everyone knows he's a businessman who's backing US president Claxton."

"That's not a rumor."

Gilberto cleared his throat. "Sorry, I'll get to that." An uncomfortable giggle. "Sometimes it takes me a while to get to the point. What everyone doesn't know is that he's also a CIA agent. I suppose you know that, too?"

Jacob nodded. "It's half of the reason I have to find him and save his ass. Assuming I'm not too late already."

"Bien. *Okay*. The rumor is that Brohman was killed by the wife of some jealous husband. Body was disposed of and the police will never find it. We, I mean me and Ricardo, have been keeping an eye on him for a while. The theory that he pissed off the wrong dude and got offed for it is, of course, a possibility, but unlikely."

"Why do you say that?"

"The women he slept with were all single, as far as we can tell. At least the ones he picked up in Pepe's nightclub."

"That was his favorite hunting ground," added Ricardo, arms crossed. After Jacob had laid down the law about their commitments, Ricardo had seemed cool as a cucumber compared to Gilberto. Which meant he was either unflappable or he wasn't concerned about the consequences should he fail to live up to Jacob's expectations. After the way he'd taken care of the 'cops,' the latter seemed plausible. The guy was fearless, and Jacob would have to be vigilant with him.

"Was it his only hunting ground?"

"No," he admitted. "We know he was using dating apps, too."

"Why do you think that?"

Gilberto cleared his throat. "This is why the jealous husband theory I mentioned before, the one fueling the rumor, is unlikely." He blinked hard a couple of times. "Here's where our intel gathering comes into play. We created a fake profile on Tinder that we knew would appeal to someone like Brohman. A pretty girl with lusty appetites."

Jacob waved a hand in the air. "Wait a minute. On whose orders did you create this dating profile?"

"Jim Stynes asked us to set it up. He even used his own

Colombian secretary in the trap." Gilberto shook his head in disgust.

"And Brohman met up with this woman?"

"Si," said Ricardo. "And now her brother is also missing."

*What the—?* Jacob's brain was running at a million miles an hour. It was 1:09 a.m., and he was dog tired and starving. But the list of questions he wanted answered by these men was long and growing. This new information needed clarification and thorough processing. Starting off tomorrow as businessman Carlos Iglesias would be a helluva lot easier if he knew the answers to these questions before he put his head on the pillow. He reached for his wallet. "Do they do late-night Uber eats in this city?"

"Similar services exist here," said Gilberto. "But nothing good is open after 11:00 p.m., so no point calling them."

An examination of the contents of the pantry and refrigerator revealed enough raw ingredients to feed a small army. Ricardo volunteered to put something together. "Cooking is my passion." Killer and cook, Jacob pondered. Quite the combination.

Half an hour later, the three men were chowing down on the most delicious chicken enchiladas Jacob had eaten in his life. He might put Ricardo's name forward for some kind of medal.

Jacob wiped his lips with a cloth napkin and said, "Tell me about this Jim Stynes." He already knew that Stynes worked as the main liaison between the Agency and Colombia's National Intelligence Directorate. An important role, at the coal face of the fight against the drug traffickers and paramilitary but with a lot of scope for being turned. A meeting with Stynes at the office of CIA Clandestine Operations was on the top of Jacob's to-do list for tomorrow.

"First of all," said Ricardo, "he is an asshole. Second of all, he is our"—he made air quotes—"handler."

Lips pursed tight, Gilberto nodded vigorously. "True. I do not like him either. But he is efficient, and his counterpart at the NID, a woman called Laura Torres, thinks his shit don't stink.

Stynes will be in the seat he currently occupies for another ten years."

Jacob chewed the last of his enchilada as he pondered this. HUMINT, or human intelligence, was often worth more than raw data and surveillance videos. The men's inside take was gold. "Do either of you believe Stynes could have had a hand in Brohman's disappearance?"

Both men frowned and showed open palms, which was only to be expected. Neither a yes nor a no. "Fair enough. What do you know about the date with...what's her name?"

"Carmen Hererra."

"Was she a willing participant?"

"I don't think so," said Ricardo. "She is only about 25 years old, I think. A naïve girl from the countryside." He paused, sipping water. "But Stynes is very persuasive. I wouldn't be surprised if he threatened to fire her—or worse—for not following his orders."

"Who else knew about this?"

"Just us two," said Ricardo, "because Stynes sent us out to tail them on their date."

"Date, singular?"

"Si," said Gilberto. "Even though she is a beautiful woman, Brohman is only interested in the conquest, not forming a long-term relationship. No doubt in my mind she slept with him—she didn't leave his apartment until after 9:00 a.m. the next morning. We sat in the car all night freezing while we watched a dark window! Did I tell you Stynes is an asshole?"

Jacob nodded. "What I don't understand is this. Brohman and Stynes are on the same team. What was the point of this entire exercise? My reading of the background material tells me nothing about Carmen working for the CIA."

Ricardo tapped his finger on the armrest of his chair. "Stynes would not divulge why. We have discussed this and can only come up with two options. First, he suspected Brohman of being rotten and that he was working with Adolfo Sanchez or some other criminals. Stynes wanted Carmen to get evidence out of him about that, trick him into giving up some kind of secret information."

"The second option?"

Gilberto said, "He was using Carmen as a conduit to somehow set Brohman up."

"How?"

"Well, Señor Iglesias," he said with a smirk, "there would be no point in taking compromising photos of him having sex with her since he's not married and can't be blackmailed that way. My guess is she would have been tasked with hiding a recording device somewhere in the apartment. To catch Brohman out betraying his country or committing some kind of drug-related crime."

"But you don't know about a listening device for sure?"

"No," said Ricardo. "Stynes gives people specific jobs and doesn't necessarily let others involved in the same assignment know what others are up to."

"I'm inclined to think you may be right about Carmen's objectives." Jacob decided to share his own possible scenario. "Has anything come to light about Brohman after the date with Carmen?"

"Nada," said Gilberto. "Apart from poor Carmen looking miserable, ashamed almost. If the sting brought information to Stynes, he hasn't shared it with us."

"What if Stynes is the one working with Sanchez?" said Jacob. "What if he thought Brohman was going to expose *him* and decided to get in first? Get some kompromat?"

The two men nodded.

"He could be the rat, Señor Iglesias," said Ricardo, cracking gnarled knuckles. "I don't trust Stynes in the slightest."

First job in the morning was to check in with Stynes and give him the letter of introduction. Would his opinion of the man diverge from that of Gilberto and Ricardo? Time to find out about the mysterious Mexican.

"What can either of you tell me about a guy Brohman knows who owns a chain of gas stations in Bogotá?"

Ricardo pouted. "You mean Felipe Zapata?"

"Do I?" said Jacob cryptically. Let them join the dots without prompts.

Gilberto nodded. "You must mean him. As part of our brief to surveil Brohman, we couldn't help but notice Zapata. But I gotta point something out. When you say 'chain' of gas stations, that's an exaggeration. Turns out he owns five gas stations in central Bogotá. He operates under the Brazilian Petrobras label, so it's kind of like a franchise set-up."

"You said you couldn't help noticing Zapata. How's that?"

"It's interesting, actually. One night Zapata shows up at Pepe's, takes a seat at the bar right next to Brohman. They get chatting, and over the next month or so, it looked like they became best buddies. They would often have a couple of beers at Pepe's, chatting away and laughing. Usually, Felipe would go home before 8:00 p.m., and Brohman would continue to party on, looking for a chica to take home."

Fletcher had mentioned that a Mexican in Brohman's circle used to work with Sanchez. Was this the same person Gilberto was talking about?

"What else do you know about Zapata?"

"He likes to tinker with car engines during the day. But at night, he's like a caterpillar who turned into a butterfly: dresses like a gangster, lots of gold jewelry, fancy suits. Has a personal driver. He's easily 60 years old, maybe close to 70. Looks like a pervert hanging around in that nightclub."

"You know anything about his background in Mexico?"

A shake of the head, then a look of realization. "Wait a minute. Zapata is a Mexican? We never got up close enough to hear his accent. Are you suggesting there might be some connection between him and...Adolfo Sanchez?"

Jacob nodded. "My intel suggests Sanchez used to work for Zapata back in Mexico City before Sanchez spread his wings and turned into a drug baron. It's got to be more than a coincidence that both of them end up in Colombia. In my experience, the overwhelming majority of Mexicans who leave their country head for the United States, not here." The last sentence ended with a prolonged yawn. His eyes began to droop, and his body cried out for sleep. "Listen, guys. I've enjoyed the company, and what you've told me has been really useful. But go home now. Rest up. I'll be fine on my own."

"You don't want me to stay?" said Ricardo. I'm your bodyguard, after all." He smiled.

"Not necessary." Jacob crossed his arms high on his chest.

"Even after what happened with those fake cops tonight?"

"I'll be okay."

"You sure? I have an overnight bag in the car."

The man was insistent. And he could probably rustle up a hearty breakfast in the morning. Jacob checked his watch again. Nearly 2:00 a.m.. He had an 8:00 a.m. appointment at CIA Clandestine Operations tomorrow. "How far away is your home?"

"An hour's drive away."

"Go get your bag."

"And me?" Gilberto wore that morose look of the ugly girl not invited to the dance. "I live even farther away. And then I have to come back here and take you two to the office."

"You got an overnight bag too?"

"Ah...no."

"You look about the same size as me. Perhaps a couple inches shorter. I guess you can borrow some of my clothes in the morning." He'd already checked the main bedroom. He'd been supplied with enough changes of clothing for two weeks.

"Gracias, Señor Iglesias!"

He lay his head on the soft, cool pillow, head spinning with information and white noise. From the living room came soft snoring. From the second bedroom—loud snoring. He closed his eyes, drifting into a yogic meditating technique that blocked off all external stimuli. Soon, he fell into a black, dreamless sleep, the kind you experience under general anesthetic.

A firm hand shook his shoulder. "Get up, quick!"

Jacob jolted awake. Hadn't he only just fallen asleep? No, it was morning. Light streamed in through the sheer blinds at the end of his bed. "Are we under attack?" He fumbled for the bedside drawer; in an instant, he found the loaded Glock and pointed it squarely at Ricardo's face.

The man burst out laughing. "No, Señor Iglesias. You overslept. Stynes has been on the phone, wondering where the hell you are!"

Gilberto's stubbly face appeared beside Ricardo's. "Hurry up, Señor Iglesias. The traffic is already crazy. The longer we wait, the later you're gonna be. Stynes won't be happy if you keep him waiting."

"Fuck Stynes," Jacob mumbled, rolling out of bed.

# NINE

An office is an office is an office. Pretty much the same wherever you go. Except when it's a clandestine CIA office. The 'station' was located at the embassy, and in an authoritarian country like Russia, that's all you got. One station, safe from outside interference—at least on paper. The security of even the Moscow embassy had been seriously breached a couple of times, most notoriously in the 1980s.

But in a 'free and democratic' nation like Colombia, there was more room for creativity. And so, in addition to the embassy station, the CIA had set up a number of offices around Colombia, the biggest of them in downtown Bogotá. The sign out the front was for the fictional law firm Servicios Legales Bogotá SA.

Jim Stynes rose from behind his desk, extending a large hand toward Jacob. "Welcome to our hotbed of intrigue, Señor Iglesias," he said. His skull was the epitome of male-pattern baldness. With his bushy silver mustache and Texan drawl, Stynes reminded Jacob of TV's famous Dr. Phil. "Deputy Director McDonald informed me that you've been sent here to help us find a missing US national. Coffee?"

"Yes, please," said Jacob. "Black with one sugar."

Stynes buzzed in an order over his desk phone, thanked the

woman on the other end, and beckoned for Jacob to take a seat opposite.

Jacob sipped the coffee, which was excellent and a welcome pick-me-up after a night of so little sleep.

"You were lucky with your timing last night," said Stynes. "There was some real drama on the same road Gilberto would have taken to bring you to your accommodation. Which is up to your expectations, I hope?"

"Perfect." Jacob gulped the remains of the coffee and clanked the cup down into the saucer. "Whoever furnished it has impeccable taste."

"Wonderful." Stynes beamed. "Anyway, the police found a couple of dead men out near the airport. Shot up real bad with a high-caliber weapon. It's all over the news this morning."

"Really?" said Jacob with an arched eyebrow.

"Uh-huh. The bodies were dressed in local police uniforms, but they weren't cops at all."

"Have they ID'd the victims?"

A shake of his shiny dome. "Not yet. This story will have a short lifetime in the press. Probably gang members trying a shakedown but picking the wrong target. Life can be a bit like that out here."

"So I understand. I lived here until I was eight years old, but I barely remember any of it. My parents decided to leave when one of their friends was assassinated in a case of mistaken identity. They figured if that could happen to an innocent school teacher, it was time to get the hell out of here."

Stynes nodded along understandingly as Jacob lied his head off. "It's been a lot better in this country since the '80s and '90s, even the early 2000s. But every now and then, something happens that makes us stop and pause, take a reality check, as the saying goes these days."

Jacob's turn to nod. His strategy: let the man talk until he ran out of steam. Then hit him up with the big surprise.

"The business with Paul Brohman is the classic example. More coffee?"

"I won't say no," Jacob said. While the young woman fussed around with the coffee pot, Jacob examined the room. Much smaller than he would have expected but exquisitely decorated with reproductions of paintings by the famous Colombian artist Botera, as well as expensive and, he guessed, very new furniture and office equipment. Shiny as a pin.

"Thank you, Carmen."

Jacob's ears pricked up. "Espera un momento!"

Carmen stopped, offering a weak smile that was obviously forced. "Si, señor?"

Jacob decided to grill her on the spot, firmly but politely. Stynes would have a good grasp of Spanish—he wouldn't be sitting in that seat if he didn't—so there was no point trying to be sneaky. "Do you know Paul Brohman?"

"Of course she does," interjected Stynes. "Please allow my employee to go about her duties. I will answer all your questions relating to–"

Jacob snapped his head toward Stynes, shooting him a withering stare. "Please don't interrupt while I'm speaking." Without waiting for a response from Stynes, he readdressed Carmen. He toyed with the idea of standing, but she was barely five feet tall, and his towering frame would certainly intimidate her. He continued in Spanish, "Did Mr. Stynes here ask you to do something you weren't entirely comfortable with?" The anger and discomfort rising in Stynes were almost palpable in the room.

She shook her head, too fast to be a truthful gesture. Then she looked anxiously toward the door, as if her salvation from this impromptu interrogation lay behind it, her arms swinging awkwardly by her side.

"Let me ask you another question. Is your brother missing?"

"He...ah..."

In the blink of an eye, Stynes was on his feet and ushering Carmen, already sobbing, out the door. In seconds, the CIA man was standing in the threshold, face scarlet. "Now I don't know who the hell you think you are, but I run this ship, do you understand me?" He strode to his office chair, sitting in it so fast it rocked on its casters. "I've been told to afford you all courtesy and assistance while you are here, but there are limits, sir."

"No," said Jacob, shaking his head. "There are only the limits that I choose to set."

He reached into his jacket pocket and held it open to extract the letter from Joel McDonald. "What the fuck is that?" said Stynes, a degree of wariness in his voice.

"A letter from your superior. Take your time reading it, and then I'd like you to ask Carmen Herrera"—he noted the look of alarmed curiosity on Styne's oily face when he used the woman's last name—"to come back in here so I can get the information I want."

Stynes' shaking hand took a pearl-handled letter opener. He sawed open the envelope, tossed it aside, and began to read the handwritten note. Even though the envelope had been glued up, Jacob could recite the contents. McDonald had temporarily granted Jacob seniority over the entire office until he left and it reverted to Stynes. Provided, of course, that the current boss of the operation didn't end up being found guilty of anything serious. Stynes' brow furrowed deeply as he read; Jacob understood why Gilberto and Ricardo had such a low opinion of the man. There was something about him that was hard to pin down, but whatever it was gave a seriously bad impression.

Folding the letter back up again, Stynes cleared his throat, then took a sip of water from a neon-purple sports bottle that sat beside his laptop. "I'm supposed to believe this is genuine, am I? Never in my life have I..."

Jacob nodded at the beige telephone on Styne's desk. "Give him a call if you like. The letter is a hundred percent genuine." He laughed gently. "I didn't seek this, Jim. McDonald himself said the only way to expedite this crucial mission is for me to have full control over your office. And I expect your complete and unfettered cooperation." He stood to his full height of 6'2" and ambled to the window that overlooked a convenience store and a veterinarian's clinic. With his back to Stynes, he added, "Which includes an introduction to"—he checked a small spiral notepad, although he knew the name by heart—"the head of Colombia's National Intelligence Directorate, Laura Torres, as well as access to all your files, paper and digital."

"Fucking unbelievable," muttered Stynes. "If you don't mind, I'm going to call the head of station at the embassy first, then Deputy Director Joel McDonald. You are not an employee of the agency, yet you seek to take charge? This is most unorthodox and, quite frankly, Mr. Iglesias, I have to do my due diligence. Will you at least allow me to do that?"

"Of course," said Jacob in his most magnanimous voice. "I'll give you half an hour to make the checks. After that, I'm in charge. Entiendes?"

"If I find out you're bullshitting me..."

Jacob laughed. "We'll see. Once the penny drops, I'll be making some requests. The first of which is to view the CCTV footage from Pepe's nightclub and the surrounding streets and a copy of the local police report into the abduction. I am right in assuming the crime has been reported to the Bogotá cops?"

"Of course. Brohman's personal assistant called it in when the boss didn't turn up for a regular business meeting the next morning and failed to answer his cell phone."

"Your people have also gone over his apartment?"

"Naturally. Do you think we are clueless incompetents out in the sticks?"

"Not at all. I want to see all your internal reports relating to what you've managed to uncover. Since your boss sent me here, I've a feeling that's not much. Now"—he pointed at the phone like it was a time-bomb—"make the calls, please, Jim. I haven't got all day. And nor has President Claxton."

---

"WELL, now that we've established I was telling the truth and the letter I gave you is genuine, I want to review all the material you've got relating to the Brohman abduction. Stuff you've gathered, any information shared by the police, all of it. When I'm done with that, I'd like to continue my conversation with Carmen Hererra."

Jacob was secretly glad Stynes hadn't rolled over meekly. It was his duty to check out the bona fides of a man he'd never met before who was making all kinds of claims. Besides, as far as Stynes knew, Jacob was merely a businessman with way too much swagger and some kind of high clearance going all the way to the White House. All that aside, he still didn't like or trust the man on an instinctive level.

Stynes was beaten. He languidly lifted the receiver, made a call, and in a droning voice asked someone to send Juan to the office. A man in his early 30s wearing a dark suit 'and sporting a glittering pair of diamond earrings appeared wheeling a steel cart. On the top shelf sat a pot of coffee, under that, cardboard boxes and a pile of manila folders. With an affable smile, he ushered Jacob into a small room. He switched on a computer, in a heartbeat created a temporary guest profile on the internal system, and left Jacob to get on with it.

One hour and fifteen minutes was plenty of time for a speed reader with an IQ the size of Jacob's to analyze each and every piece of paper in the files, as well as each second of CCTV relevant footage from the nightclub and surrounding streets from the night of Brohman's abduction. The image of the woman who'd lured Brohman away was clear as crystal. There was no record of her in any government database, meaning she wasn't a Colombian citizen. Facial recognition software also failed to identify her. Her image had been sent to Interpol—again, no hits.

The images from the street cameras showed Brohman and the woman entering an alleyway. A few minutes later, footage from a camera at the other end of the alley picked up two other men shoving Brohman into a van before they and the woman got in and sped off. The vehicle bore fake license plates, made even more unrecognizable by the gray tape that was clearly distinguishable on the video.

According to Bogotá police reports, a number of people from the nightclub had been questioned, as well as business and social contacts and Brohman's PA. None were suspected of any wrongdoing, nor were they able to assist. The CIA internal report, based largely on HUMINT provided by Gilberto and Ricardo, suggested efforts should concentrate on Felipe Zapata, revisiting the nightclub and grilling patrons, and also a digital forensics deep dive into Brohman's life.

Sound recordings made at the CIA listening post from data sent by the device Carmen Hererra had planted in Brohman's apartment were largely unintelligible. There was a suggestion that Hererra had failed to activate the bug as instructed or had dropped it or damaged it in some other way. She'd insisted that she was careful and the device itself must have been faulty.

Head swimming in the detail, none of it pointing Jacob in an obvious direction, he returned to Stynes' office and told him he was ready to speak further with Carmen.

"Of course. I'll just go and get her."

Jacob held up a hand. "No need, Jim. I'm going to treat her to an ice cream at the café down the street. I think she'll be more frank with me away from the office, don't you?"

The CIA officer didn't respond to the rhetorical question, escorting Jacob to the reception desk position at the top of a single flight of stairs. The entire office occupied one floor, no elevator. Jacob imagined that whoever had muscled the giant photocopier and all the other large pieces of equipment up the narrow stairwell would have let loose with some choice cusswords.

Carmen tucked a wayward strand of hair behind her ear as she looked up from her computer monitor at the approaching men, apprehension narrowing her almond eyes. Stynes said in English, "Take a break, Carmen." He rapped his bony knuckles on the countertop. "Our guest, Señor Iglesias, wants to follow up on the questions he started to ask you before."

She took a deep breath. "What kind of questions?"

"Important ones," said Jacob in Spanish. "I'm here to help you find your brother."

She burst into tears, burying her face in a large lace handkerchief. Wracking sobs soon followed. She blew her nose, then briefly stared daggers at Stynes. "Bien. No one else seems to care about him."

"Please," said Stynes, clearly embarrassed by her effrontery but unable to chastise her now that Jacob was top dog, "go with him." His face reddened. "Tell him what he needs to know. Remember, we all want what's best."

"For you, maybe!"

Jacob clocked Styne's face, angry veins throbbing in his temple. "Jim, listen good. If this woman is fired for speaking out about...anything at all...your feet won't touch the ground on the way out." Without waiting for an answer, he slipped a hand around Carmen's waist and carefully led her down the stairs, out into the brilliant sunshine, and across the street to the modest café.

# TEN

An acne-faced waiter wearing braces on his teeth who couldn't have been more than sixteen years old placed two ice cream sundaes on the table. Carmen picked up a long-handled spoon, dug around in the treat, then let go.

"Not hungry?" said Jacob, picking up a mound of vanilla ice cream covered in chocolate sauce.

"No," she replied flatly. "I seem to have lost my appetite over the last few days. Can't imagine why..."

She was in the mood for sarcasm, so the best way forward was to be direct. "Is Jim Stynes a good man?" Jacob asked, dipping a spoon into his ice cream.

Her eyebrows nearly shot to the back of her head. "What a strange thing to ask!"

"Well, is he or not?"

"No! He is a horrible bastard. Only thinks of himself."

"Surely he can't be all bad. Is he conscientious about his work, at least?"

She frowned and stared off into space. Jacob followed her gaze and saw the imposing Eastern Hills that formed the boundary of the city peeking between two buildings. "You said you wanted to help find my brother. Who told you he was missing?"

"The two men sent to pick me up at the airport last night." He sipped coffee from a tiny cup and grimaced. Disappointingly bitter. "My main job, apart from my usual business affairs, is to find another businessman called Paul Brohman. It's very important I find this man. In fact, the disappearances of both men are probably connected, and you had a hand in one of them. Which means you are indirectly responsible, even if only partly, for whatever happened to Miguel."

"How dare you!" Carmen swept the untouched sundae from the table, sending it crashing to the floor. A beefy man, who was getting cozy with a woman at a neighboring table, stood with bunched fists, demanding to know if everything was okay. Perhaps he suspected Jacob of instigating a domestic dispute in public. "It's fine." Jacob stood to show the customer he was bigger and broader than him. "She found a bug in her food and freaked out. You know what women can be like with creepy crawlies."

The explanation seemed to satisfy the man, who laughed heartily. Before he resumed his seat, he added, "Make sure you get a free replacement on that ice cream."

"Will do." Both men sat back down as if nothing had happened. Jacob reached across the small wrought-iron table, searching Carmen's eyes pleadingly. "I'm sorry to be so blunt, and I didn't mean to offend you. I'm sure you acted out of good faith when you agreed to be the bait for Stynes. You would have had no idea there could be repercussions for Miguel."

"How do you..." She choked back a tear. "How do you even know he's in trouble?"

"How long has it been since anyone heard from him? Three days, correct? One of my men called his employer, and the manager of the supermarket says he's getting worried."

She gave a couple of sniffles. "Maybe he just...I don't know... decided to be alone for a while. He sometimes travels to the beach at Cartagena up north, goes surfing for a couple of weeks without telling anyone his whereabouts."

Jacob shook his head. "Bullshit, Carmen. His boss said Miguel was practically begging for more shifts." She was clutching at straws with this surfing nonsense. "Stynes' men, Gilberto and Ricardo, who are now working exclusively for me, have been tailing Brohman over several months. Recently, they noticed him interacting with your brother on a number of occasions. Did you ever mention to Miguel what Stynes was forcing you to do? That you were going to sleep with him, that you were on a mission to get compromising material on Brohman?"

"I did sleep with him, it's true...Jim would have fired me if I refused. But it was just one time!" She paused as two noisy motorcycles ripped past them. Jacob's fingers instinctively reached for the Glock under his jacket. Satisfied it was nothing, he gestured for Carmen to continue. "When he was taking a shower, I put a bug in his apartment." She nodded slowly, then her hands shot to her face. "And yes, going back to your other question, I did discuss what was going to happen with Miguel. We share almost everything. Hostia! *Holy crap!* What have I done?"

"How did Miguel react when you told him what you were going to do?"

"What do you think? He hit the roof! Swore he would kill Stynes."

"Not Brohman?"

Her face froze. "No. Because I didn't say who the target was. I just said it was an enemy of the people whose identity I didn't know. I said I was sacrificing myself...my dignity at least...for the greater good."

"Miguel bought that?"

"Ha! Of course he didn't."

*Let's see if she's true to her oath of service*, Jacob thought. "Does Miguel know you work for the CIA?"

She shook her head. "No. It's the one thing I can never admit to him. He thinks I'm an employee of a law firm and Stynes is a specialist manager who was recruited from America."

He squeezed her hand gently, she made no move to pull away. "It's okay. None of this is your fault. You have been manipulated."

She nodded. "I should have said no!"

"Have you tried calling your brother?"

"Si. Many times. Straight to message bank."

"Is that typical?"

"No. He always picks up after a couple of rings. If he misses a call, I don't have to wait long for him to call me back."

"Have you called the cops to report him missing?"

A head shake. "Stynes said to wait. But I cannot wait much longer!"

"What do you think Miguel and Brohman might have been talking about?"

"What do you think?" She tugged her hand away from Jacob's grip. "Miguel would have told Brohman to leave me the fuck alone. That if he..."

"If he tried anything on with you, he would be sorry? Something like that?"

Her nostrils flared. She was a beautiful woman, even when angry. The perfect bait to dangle in front of a predator like Brohman. "Yes," she growled in the back of her throat. "Something like that."

Jacob wriggled in his seat. This was going to be uncomfortable for Carmen to contemplate. "When you speak of 'the greater good,' do you think Miguel could have a world view like that?"

Confusion knitted her finely plucked eyebrows. "What do you mean?"

"What I mean is, perhaps he hated Stynes so much that allowing you to...go through with his plan...was something that Miguel could leverage to bring Stynes down."

She cradled her head in her shaking hands. "No, no, no. He would never do that."

"How do you explain the fact that, according to the guys surveilling Brohman, he and your brother appeared to be very friendly with each other?"

"Coincidence. Or Miguel was...ah, I don't know. I told you, I never mentioned anything about Brohman." She shuddered at the mere mention of his name. Jacob could only imagine what the bastard had put her through.

"I don't believe in coincidences. In a city of 10 million souls, what are the odds Miguel and Brohman knew each other?" Jacob pulled out a couple of bills to pay the check. "Either there's a mole inside that building"—he jerked a thumb towards the office across the street—"or you're not telling me the truth!"

He pulled out his phone and dialed Gilberto's number, exchanged a few words, and hung up. He narrowed his eyes as he looked back at Carmen. "You and I are going to take a little drive across town."

---

THE RIDE FROM THE CAFÉ, where Carmen's presence had taken Gilberto and Ricardo by surprise, was mostly silent. At least inside the car. Outside there was honking, crazy traffic. After they'd been driving for less than 30 seconds, Ricardo had reached across to amp up the volume of the quietly playing music, Latin rap that Jacob generally found highly entertaining but not today. "Turn that shit off," he snapped. "I've got a headache, and that's not doing me any favors." He tapped the console. "Remember, from now until I go back to the United States, you answer to me and me alone. No arguments or backchat."

Gilberto's face split into a grin. "Fine by me. Better than doing Styne's bidding all the time."

"Me too," readily agreed Ricardo. "We're both thinking of getting out of this gig, trying our hand at private security. If we can finish on a high helping you, we'll both be happy."

"Amen to that," said Gilberto, flicking the indicator to go around a broken-down van.

Soon they found themselves wedged in a dense snarl of midmorning traffic as they crawled their way toward the particular Petrobras gas station where they knew Felipe Zapata spent a lot of his time. No guarantee he would be there, but it was worth a shot. Three calls to the listed number of the business went to voicemail every time.

Ricardo opened a packet of Haribo soft candies, took one, and handed the packet over his shoulder to Jacob. He readily accepted, tossed three gummies into his mouth, and felt the sugar rush he'd missed after abandoning 90 percent of the sundae. The bodyguard's offer of candy to her was met with a decisive head shake. She seemed to be content sourcing nourishment from the fingernails she constantly chewed as she stared out the window.

"How far away is this damned gas station?" said Jacob, scrabbling around for another gummy but finding he'd absentmindedly consumed them all.

"Four blocks. Might be faster if you walk, Señor Iglesias."

"Seriously?"

"Yeah."

"Fine," he grumbled. "Ricardo, you're coming with me. Carmen, stay in the car. Gilberto, when you get there, fill up with gas, we're nearly empty. If I'm still talking to Zapata, drive around the block until I call you."

"Why am I even here?" protested Carmen. "I would like to be taken home. You've already asked me everything."

Jacob turned his square jaw back to the woman. "Oh no. I've barely gotten any answers out of you yet. You get to go home once I'm satisfied you've truthfully told me everything I need to know."

He shouldered open his door and stepped out onto the roadway, copping a blast of horns and a barrage of earthy insults for his trouble. He held up both hands as if to say *Sorry*. *The people in this town are a lot friendlier when they're not behind the wheel*, he thought to himself.

As the two men marched down the sidewalk, Ricardo navigating with the GPS in his phone, Jacob asked him, "What do you know about the bug Carmen told me she planted in Brohman's apartment?"

"Nothing, jefe. I'm what they call analfabeto en computación. Gilberto knows more about that kind of–"

"No." Jacob cut him off, failing to disguise his irritation. "It's not about whether or not you're computer illiterate. I mean, do you know if Stynes himself is clever enough to do the listening in on his own, or would he need help with that kind of thing?"

A slow nod. "Yes, I get you. There's a small team of technical experts in the office. The main ones are an American, Marty James, and his assistant, a Puerto Rican dude called Juan Palacio. I guess they'd be the ones monitoring any signals coming through a listening device. Although maybe Stynes has the skills, who knows?"

Not the definitive answer Jacob was looking for. "One thing's been troubling me."

"Can you be more specific, jefe?"

They sidestepped a pile of rubbish. Jacob's nose itched as the smell of street garbage increased the closer they got to their destination. "If you were able to observe Carmen meeting up with Brohman and follow them to his apartment, how on earth did you miss him being lured away from Pepe's last week?"

Ricardo scratched the side of his nose. "You know, that's a very good question. The thing is, the night he went missing, we were reassigned to watch a warehouse where a big shipment of cocaine was supposed to be leaving from. We sat there all night waiting for something to happen. There were even Colombian cops stationed all around the precinct, ready for a big takedown. A complete waste of time—the place was quiet as a graveyard."

"Really?"

"Yeah. Stynes said he got a phone call with an anonymous tip. Untraceable, from a pay phone. Normally these tips are ignored, but the quantity was so huge, and other details from the caller seemed accurate...Anyway, turned out to be a big fat bust."

"You don't have to be Einstein to think this was probably a

diversion to get you and Gilberto out of the way so Brohman could be snatched without hindrance."

Ricardo pursed his lips. "Yeah, we raised that with Stynes, but he called us a couple of conspiracy theorists."

Jacob burst out laughing. "Did he just?"

"Si. Man, I was so close to accusing him of all kinds of shit..."

"I'm glad you didn't." Jacob stopped for a moment to allow a taxi to drive into the gas station. "If you had, I wouldn't have you and Gilberto helping me on this case. If Stynes is guilty of any crimes and I find out, there will be hell to pay!"

# ELEVEN

DRESSED IN GREASE AND OIL-STAINED OVERALLS, Zapata looked nothing like a rich magnate who owned a chain of gas stations. Well, five modest outlets under a franchise arrangement, as Jacob had recently learned.

Zapata wiped his grubby hands with a small rag and ushered the men into his tiny office. On the wall behind his creaky swivel chair, there was a calendar with an image of a buxom young woman in a thong looking over her shoulder and sticking out her tongue. "Buenas días, señores," he said in a voice made scratchy by years of smoking and tinged with mild curiosity. "What can I do for you? If you're selling something, I ain't buying."

Jacob and Ricardo were compelled to stand due to the lack of chairs for guests. Jacob handed over a business card, which Zapata read with darting eyes. He flipped it over in case there was something more interesting on the back. There wasn't. Gilberto had described him as being in his 60s but looking closer to 70. That was true: almost rheumy eyes, liver spots on the back of his hands (although, to be fair, it could have been engine oil), and well-wrinkled with sparse gray hair on top of an egg-shaped head. But no garish suit, no gold jewelry. He couldn't have looked any less like a gangster if he'd tried.

"I'm interested in talking to a friend of yours." Jacob stared directly into the old boy's eyes. "Paul Brohman."

Zapata didn't flinch. "Don't let me stop you. Give him a call."

"That's the problem," said Jacob, screwing up his cheeks. "He's not answering. We'd agreed to catch up this weekend for some hiking in the Santa Ana-La Aguadora. It's such a lovely time of the year for it."

"Your accent is weird," said Zapata, folding arms with faded tattoos that had probably been on the planet longer than Jacob. "Americano o inglés?"

Jacob shook his head, pleased he hadn't drifted into pure fluency. "Neither. I mean yes. Officially, I'm a US citizen. I was born in Spain, lived in Bogotá until I was eight, then moved to the United States. And that's how I know Paul Brohman. Through business. But I haven't seen him in years. I contacted him on social media, and he mentioned Pepe's nightclub. I spoke to the owner there, and he said you and he were friends and..." He paused, waiting for Zapata to add something, but the wily fox kept his silence.

"Look, I'll let you in on a little secret," Jacob said, as if doing the old dude a favor.

"Oh, yes?" Zapata leaned forward in his seat. To Jacob's left, Ricardo stood like a mute colossus; every now and then, Zapata's curious eyes would flick toward him, then back to Jacob.

"Paul was scared something might happen to him. Now he's disappeared, and I think his prediction might have come true."

The little man thrust out his chin. "And what do you want me to do about it?"

Perhaps a bribe might loosen Zapata's tongue. Better to use honey than vinegar with a man like this. Beating up old men might be an easy option, but it would only ever be a last resort. He tossed a bulging drawstring bag onto the desk. "I want you to tell me everything you know about a man called Adolfo Sanchez. You're both Mexican and arrived in Colombia within a year of each other, but no one can seem to find him in this country. I have a feeling you know him and that he's behind Brohman's disappearance. In return for your cooperation, you get to keep what's in the bag."

"Ha! Your information is pretty good, amigo. But the fact we came here at roughly the same time is pure coincidence."

"So you know he's here? It's not exactly reported in the press," said Ricardo.

"You never heard of the grapevine?"

"Where is he?" said Jacob sharply. "I haven't got all day."

Zapata shrugged. "I haven't seen that hijo de puta since I left Mexico City in 2014." Zapata opened a drawer and pulled out a crumpled packet of Marlboro. "I don't care if there's a cashier's check for a million dollars in that damned bag, I'm not getting involved in nothin' to do with Adolfo Sanchez."

"Are you that scared of him?" said Ricardo, massaging his fists. "I don't believe it. The fact an old man like yourself, an immigrant into our country, has set himself up with a bunch of gas stations tells me you've got cojones. Why not be honest?"

A cloud of smoke billowed from behind the chair. "Listen to me, kid. I've had two strokes, three heart attacks, and they recently found a shadow on my fucking lung." He placed the cigarette in a tin ashtray and pointed at it. "I'm more scared of Adolfo than I am of those fucking things."

Jacob sighed and reached across for the bag, but Zapata was quicker. "Not so hasty," said the old man. "Let me just satisfy my curiosity." Jacob and Ricardo looked on in amazement as he untied the drawstring and tipped the contents onto the table. There were ten bundles of US$100 bills, a hundred grand in total. Well short of the million that supposedly wouldn't get Zapata talking. Still, the man fondled each bundle, sniffed the cash, extracted one Ben Franklin, and held it up to the light.

"You know what?" He crushed out the cigarette. "This could buy me smokes for the rest of my life, which may or may not be that long after all. Maybe pay for some nice young Colombian hookers." He chuckled. "That's what drew me and Brohman together, our appreciation of the local beauties."

"So you've changed your mind? That fast?" said Jacob.

He swept the cash into the same drawer the Marlboros came from and slammed it shut. "Si! Money talks, after all."

Over the next five minutes, Zapata explained that ten years ago, Sanchez was dancing to *his* tune on the mean streets of Mexico City. But Sanchez was ambitious, fearless, and most of all, ruthless. Soon, he had replaced Zapata as leader of a small but respected street gang in one of the city's poorest neighborhoods. Sanchez recruited men fresh out of prison with nowhere to go and offered them a life of adventure, brotherhood, all that bull-shit, in return for unquestioning loyalty, a roof over their heads, and a sense of purpose. "And this"—Zapata pointed at his temple —"is where that asshole is smarter than everyone else. He understands the human brain. No, lemme put it another way; he understands emotions, the things that drive men. He can pick out a soldier who's gonna be loyal for the rest of his life, no matter if Sanchez abuses the guy's mother and sisters before his very eyes."

Then, with those loyal deputies and lieutenants— all of whom were still with him, except for those who died in battle— he took over the deadly neighborhood of Tepito. Rival gangs simply lacked the firepower and the will to resist. Having conquered his own backyard, Sanchez set his sights on the cradle of the cocaine world, a place where he wasn't known. Colombia. "He splits his time between the two countries, so it's impossible to catch him."

"A wonderful history lesson," said Jacob. "But how does any of that help us find where he is now?"

"My friend, there is an easy way to find him."

"I don't believe you."

He tapped the side of his nose. "I am the only one who knows this. It will cost you a plane ticket to Mexico City, and then a bus ride to the sticks." He burst out laughing, which morphed into a wracking cough. "I only have one favor to ask. Once you find Sanchez, for the sake of the world, you must kill him!" He lit another smoke and drew deeply. "Oh, and if you find Brohman, bring him here. That hijo de puta owes me fifty bucks."

# TWELVE

"I WANT TO GO HOME," SAID CARMEN. SHE SHRANK into herself, tucking her arm in to avoid the touch of Jacob's arm. "Why are you keeping me captive like this?" she whined. "Please, muchachos, just take me home." Jacob sensed her anxiety level rising. He took a good look at her now, studying her forensically. She had the body of a librarian too busy with books to find the time to eat or exercise properly— no muscle tone, limbs like twigs. Not the Rubenesque physique he imagined would appeal to a man like Brohman. But her face was angelic, like someone had taken the best features of the world's most beautiful women, shaken them up, and come up with Carmen Hererra. Not many red-blooded males could resist her.

Gorgeous as she was, the woman had taken a serious dislike to Jacob. It wasn't the first time, and it certainly wouldn't be the last. All in a day's work when your job is about manipulating people to get the answers you want.

"Are we taking her home, jefe?" said Gilberto from behind the wheel. "Because if we are, I have to make a decision about which of these exits to take. I miss the correct turnoff, it could add an hour to the trip."

Jacob considered for a moment how to play it with Carmen.

He was sure there was more information he could get out of her, but would it help find Brohman any quicker? Maybe. "I'm inclined to drop you back at work instead of taking you home. I'm sure you and Jim Stynes have got a lot to go over, right?"

"Fuck him!" she yelled. "I'm never going back to work for that creep."

*Better*, thought Jacob. Her anger directed toward Stynes gave him a chance to become the good guy in her eyes. "I understand how you feel. Like he's deeply betrayed you. I agree he's a creep, but maybe we should give him the benefit of the doubt? He may have had good reason to suspect Brohman of being a traitor."

Her eyes widened. "Benefit of the doubt? Are you joking? He gave me an ultimatum— sleep with Brohman, plant the bug, or lose my job."

"Didn't you just say you were going to quit?"

"No. I said I wouldn't work for him. You're the boss now. Fire his ass!"

She had plenty of spunk. Jacob twisted his lips. "It's only a temporary appointment, I'm afraid. I don't have the power to hire and fire staff. But I can make some recommendations—if you agree to be a hundred percent honest with me."

"I don't trust these guys." She pointed at the backs of Gilberto's and Ricardo's heads. "They do Stynes' dirty work without question."

The two men in front shook their heads slightly at her rebuke but knew better than to rise to the bait.

"Look, you've suffered a lot in a very short time." Jacob tapped Gilberto on the shoulder. "Let's take you home," he said, leaning slightly into her. Not so much pulling away this time as he felt a degree of tension leave her body.

"Good!" she said, crossing her arms petulantly. "My address is—"

Gilberto tilted his head back and laughed. "I know where you live, mi corazón. Stynes had us follow you as well as Brohman, don't forget." He turned around, giving her a smile of reassurance. "And, yes, we do what he says. But then again, so did you. We all do."

"What!" Her eyes bulged. "He threatened me."

"Okay, that's enough bickering," said Jacob. "Gilberto will drop you and me off at your place, where we will have a full and frank discussion about everything. In private. What you tell me could help track down Miguel as well as Brohman. Agreed?"

She gave a reluctant nod. "I guess."

"What do you want us to do while you're doing that, jefe?" said Ricardo from the passenger seat. "I think Zapata only gave us half the story. Let me go back and"—he cracked his knuckles—"convince him to open up a little more, huh?"

"No. I've got a better idea."

---

CARMEN HERERRA SHARED A SPACIOUS, modestly furnished apartment in the scruffy Fontibón district with two other women. The air inside was stuffy, the blinds drawn across a large window. A peek behind the blinds revealed a veranda covered in potted plants.

Carmen excused herself, the call of the bathroom urgent. "Make yourself comfortable," she insisted. In her absence, Jacob had a quick look around the apartment's living area. For a female-only household, there were few 'women's touches.' Not a picture on the wall, no knick-knacks or any kind of decoration except a couple of beige cushions on two olive-green leather sofas.

A small window in the kitchen overlooked an alleyway: graffiti-lined brick walls and a line of dumpsters overflowing with garbage. Snatches of animated conversation laden with religion-based expletives drifted up from the street. The thin windows looked like they would offer little resistance against the bitter cold at night.

Back from the bathroom, she told him her roomies were at work. Both the other women were eking out a living in dead-end retail jobs. Something to do with discount fashion, but she wasn't totally sure. They grabbed shifts when they could and might return home at any time. The women weren't really friends and only spoke to each other in passing or when it came to sorting out bills.

"You haven't tried to find work elsewhere? Maybe a safe retail position would suit you better than what you currently do." Jacob eyeballed her across the small kitchen table.

She shrugged. "Believe it or not, I earn twice what my roommates make." She offered a pallid smile. "At least they don't have to prostitute themselves at the direction of their boss."

Time was marching on. *Cut to the chase, Hunter.*

"What happened to the listening device, Carmen? My reading of the files tells me it failed to get any useful information."

"You don't waste time, do you?" She walked a couple feet to the tiny kitchen, poured herself a glass of water, and slammed it down. Back at the table, she said, "Like I told you back at the café, I hid it while he was talking a shower. I placed it under the coffee table in the middle of Brohman's lounge room."

Jacob tilted his head back and studied small spots of mold spreading in an arc across the ceiling. "And after that?"

"He got dressed, for work I guess because he was in a suit. I pretended that I'd enjoyed his company— the sex was gross, by the way. He's old enough to be my father. I said goodbye, he called me a cab, and I went home. That's the last I ever saw of him."

"Do you know who retrieved the listening device?"

"No." She laughed sarcastically. "For all I know, it's still there."

Many a true word is spoken in jest runs the old saying. Perhaps Carmen had inadvertently pointed them in the right direction. He held up a finger. "One moment."

He pulled out his burner cell operating with a local Tigo SIM and dialed one of ten preloaded contacts.

"Yes?"

"Are you at the nightclub?"

"No, jefe," said Gilberto. "Two blocks away. But we did break into Miguel's apartment like you asked. We found some stuff I think you're gonna find real interesting. Could lead us to Brohman."

"How far is Brohman's apartment from where you are?"

Silence.

"Well?"

"We have to backtrack. I know a few shortcuts. Maybe twenty minutes."

"Then do it! I'm heading there too. The nightclub can wait. Probably better to go tonight when it's full of customers. Who knows, we might even sniff out the kidnappers among the crowd."

He hung up, staring at Carmen. "What's the address of Brohman's apartment?"

She gave it and called a cab for him. He thanked a sobbing Carmen for her time and cooperation. To his surprise, she hugged him tightly.

"I don't care about that asshole Brohman," she said as he opened the door. "Just make sure you find Miguel."

# THIRTEEN

"GRANT. IT'S ME."

The sound of a can being popped came down the line as clearly as if Grant Fletcher was in the car next to him. A Miller Light, no doubt. "Please tell me you've found Brohman alive and well and you're at the airport waiting to board a flight home."

"I wish."

"Any closer? That Stynes prick has been calling me every five minutes. Wants to know what's happening. He tells me you've pulled your non-existent rank down there and put yourself in charge."

"Don't blame me. McDonald gave me the letter to do it." He watched a bunch of motorcyclists jockeying for front position at a crossroad. Jacob dropped his voice, even though, as a standard precaution, he'd swapped cabs at a shopping mall two blocks from where he was picked up outside Carmen's place. "I'm following a lead right now, but it's a tenuous one." He explained that the bug might still be in its original location.

"Of course it's not there, Jacob!" There was the sound of a deep swallow, then the inhalation of cigar smoke. "Stynes would have arranged for it to be retrieved."

"Not necessarily."

"Even if you find it, so what? These things transmit to agents in the back of vans with headphones where they record the sound. So you've–"

"You spend too much time with your damned goldfish or watching old spy films. Not enough time keeping up with what's going on in the real world."

"I beg your pardon?"

"Audio bugs these days have the capacity for storage. Some of them transmit audio in real-time and also record it for later retrieval. I'm hoping that's what's happened here." Jacob instinctively pushed his right foot to the floor as if to brake as the cab came to an abrupt halt.

A pair of unsmiling cops stood in the middle of the road. Tall, broad-shouldered officers with large weapons slung over their shoulders. From where he sat, the guns looked like H&K assault rifles.

*Damn it, not again*, he thought. "Wait a second, Grant. I'll call you back."

His eyes instinctively wandered to the officers' footwear. Regulation lace-up black boots, not sneakers. Still, that was no guarantee of anything. His hand involuntarily rested against the cold Glock under his jacket. A shootout in broad daylight was the last thing he wanted. He was outnumbered, and these cops looked like they could handle themselves. The uniforms exchanged a couple words with the anxious driver before turning their attention to Jacob. A woman had been raped in a nearby street earlier in the day. Was he in the vicinity?

"No, officers," Jacob said. "Just passing through on my way to visit a friend in the hospital."

The officers smiled sympathetically and waved them on.

"Señor," the driver stuttered as he crunched gears, "you told me you were going to Los Rosales. Now you want the hospital?"

"Rosales first. Now that I think of it, my friend was discharged yesterday." He made an exaggerated forehead slap. "I can be so forgetful!"

The taxi driver grinned sheepishly in the mirror. Jacob could tell the man was suspicious but wasn't about to cause any trouble. He raised Fletcher on the phone again for a quick rundown on what had happened so far, the impressions he had of the players, what he intended to do next.

"You've only just arrived in Bogotá. Now you wanna fly to Mexico City?"

"Yes. And I need some cooperation from the CIA embassy station. Stynes isn't trustworthy. Can you get McDonald to line that up for me?"

"What do you want?"

"Technical assistance. Like I got from brush-by man in Moscow, remember?"

"The guy who got you the...what was it again...some kind of explosives?"

"Correct. No explosives this time, though. I want three fake IDs. Make mine for a high-ranking police officer with the Policía Nacional de Colombia. And two more for a pair of guys under Stynes' command. I'll send you photos of my two men. You capable of handling that, or should I call Irina to help you?"

"Don't be insolent, Jacob. Of course I can handle that. But I thought you said Stynes' operation wasn't trustworthy?"

"No. I said Stynes wasn't trustworthy. The three people I've met who work for him seem to be solid. As for the rest, I haven't really met them, so I can't vouch for them."

"Is this your heart or your head making the call about these locals?"

Jacob sighed softly. "Neither. It's my gut."

"Señor," the driver said, the word sounding like a timid question. "We have arrived."

"Gotta go," he said into the phone as he nodded at the driver. "Get that organized for me, will you?"

"Sure thing. Someone from the embassy will call you."

*The irony*, thought Jacob as he alighted into the late afternoon sunshine. He'd recognized a couple of landmarks on the way here: Brohman's condo was a mere block away from his own.

The quiet side-street was deserted in both directions. Gilberto and Ricardo were yet to arrive; perhaps the traffic on the main arteries was worse than anticipated. Never mind. Jacob knew the number of the apartment.

Getting inside might take some time. Typical of security-conscious Bogotá, the lobby to this section of condos could only be accessed by a passcode. He paced the sidewalk, trying not to look too suspicious, waiting for a resident to turn up. Fifteen minutes later, the area was still as quiet as a graveyard except for the rustling of leaves in a light breeze. Patience wearing thin, he buzzed a random button on Brohman's floor repeatedly. No response. Rinse and repeat three more times until someone answered.

"Si?"

Caught off the hop for a second, Jacob scanned the name-plate. "Señora Alicia Fernández?"

"Si. Who is it? I'm not expecting any visitors today."

"Special delivery from Amazon."

"Must be some kind of mistake. I didn't order anything."

"The label says...ah...expensive jewelry. Maybe it's from a man in your life?"

"Ooh. Okay then. Come on up!"

A buzzing sound, then a click. Jacob pushed the door open and mentally apologized to the poor woman he'd just duped. She sounded like she was on the wrong side of seventy, probably dotty in her old age.

Inside the building, he was immediately confronted with another frustrating problem. He stepped into the elevator and pressed the button for the fourth floor. Nothing. The elevator car wouldn't go anywhere unless you first inserted some kind of card into a slot. Muttering under his breath, he stepped out and searched for the stairs. These couldn't be accessed from the outside without a special key either. Compared to Carmen's neighborhood, where there was no security apart from the feeble lock on her front door, this place was like Fort Knox.

Sweat forming on his brow, he dialed Gilberto. He'd have something in the car's tool box to get in here. A tire lever might do the trick. There was always the option of blasting a hole in the door with his Glock, but, lacking a suppressor, it didn't seem a smart thing to do in the confined space.

Gilberto's number rang out. He left a one-word message: Hurry.

As he was scratching his head and pacing back and forth, the sound of footsteps made Jacob raise his head. A middle-aged man in a yellow polo shirt had entered through the glass doors.

"Thank God you're here!" he said, trying to look like the most relieved man on the planet. "Do you know Señora Fernández? I'm her cousin Carlos from...Ecuador."

"Yes, I know Alicia. Lovely old lady. Her husband died last year. The poor dear hasn't been the same since."

"Yes, I know," Jacob lied. "I've come to give her some news that will cheer her up. The problem is"—he held up his phone—"my Ecuadorian SIM card isn't working here. Or maybe I've run out of credits, I don't know. Aunty Alicia let me inside, but now I'm stuck."

"No hay problema. *No problem*," said the friendly man, patting Jacob on the shoulder. "Anything for Alicia. Ride with me to the fifth floor, then you can take the stairs down to the fourth. You don't need a key, just lean on the bar and push."

Having wished the helpful resident a good day and trotted down to the fourth floor, he now stood in front of the door to Brohman's apartment. He cupped an ear to the door and listened hard. Silence. Next, he pulled out his trusty lock-picking tools. Compared to the hurdles he'd had to jump over to get to this point, opening the door would be a simple job. As usual, though, he turned the handle to see if it was unlocked. Just in case.

*Bingo.* It swung open, nice and easy.

Inside was total chaos. Furniture upended, drawers of a

polished walnut dresser flung open, debris all over the carpet. And that was only the living area. Heart beating fast, he examined the infamous coffee table from all angles, running his hand all over the underside. No listening device. It was a hail Mary, and, like most hail Marys, destined to fail.

A quick check of the other rooms revealed similar carnage and no listening device. Glinting silver cutlery littered the tiled kitchen floor, shards of broken glass were scattered from wall to wall. He checked inside the fridge and freezer, sometimes used as hiding places for important items. One half-consumed tub of ice cream. A dig around with a spoon came up empty.

Who had done this? The police, the CIA, the kidnappers, or someone else entirely? Maybe it was Miguel, getting even with Brohman for despoiling his sister. Such was the extent of the vandalism, Jacob guessed the perpetrator had either found what they'd been looking for or abandoned all hope and left a trail of destruction in angry frustration. Which meant going over it himself would be a waste of time. Still, he went through the motions, looking at random pieces of paper, flicking through books, tipping them upside down and shaking them in case something was tucked inside. Nada.

He plucked out his cell and dialed Gilberto once again. Same result.

Perhaps he and his sidekick had gone their separate ways. He called Ricardo's number. It also rang out until voicemail kicked in.

Dammit, Gilberto said they were 40 minutes away. That was 50 minutes ago.

Disheartened but not completely surprised at not finding the bug, he took a series of photographs to document the trashing, then turned for the door. Even though this expedition was a bust, he felt confident Zapata's Mexican lead would turn the tide. His phone jangled in his pocket. He ripped it out, placing it to his ear. "Gilberto. Where the fuck have you been?"

"Sorry, it's Peter Abraham from the embassy station. I'm

waiting for the photos of the guys you wanted the ID for. I had a call from our mutual friend stateside who told me he'd be sending them very soon. I thought I would have received them by now."

"So did I." Jacob rubbed his jaw.

"So this is a legit order?"

"Of course it fucking is! Don't you have interruptions to your schedule from time to time? You'll get them."

"I apologize, sir. I'll wait for the photos. Just checking that all was okay."

Jacob dabbed at his sweaty forehead with his shirt cuff. "No. It's me who should be apologizing. You did nothing wrong."

He disconnected the call and made his way back out onto the street. His eyes involuntarily flicked up to the fourth floor. Good, Alicia wasn't peeking through the curtains. The old dear had probably forgotten about it already. Another couple of calls to his buddies went the same way as all the others.

Something was off.

He decided to walk around the building, check in the garden beds. Another hail Mary. Another fail. A taxi with a vacant light glowing in the late afternoon gloom appeared from around a corner and slowed as Jacob raised his arm.

"Adónde? *Where to?*" said the driver, mashing gum in the corner of his mouth.

"Marriott Hotel." Once there, he would switch to another taxi, aware that this one had appeared a little too conveniently and could be part of a tail.

"We have to go the long way, if you don't mind." The driver couldn't hide the slight annoyance in his voice. "I just heard on the radio that Calle 74 is closed because of an accident."

A sick feeling gripped Jacob's stomach.

"What kind of accident?"

"I don't know. A bad one if they have to divert traffic."

"Get me as close to Calle 74 as you can, okay?"

"Sure," said the driver. "We'll be there in 10 minutes."

# FOURTEEN

Crime scene tape. Flashing red and blue lights. People in uniforms, face masks, white coveralls. Camera flashes in the descending evening light. Frenetic activity.

*No. No. No!*

His two soldiers cut down in the street. Sitting ducks in the Land Cruiser. He made the sign of the cross and whispered a quiet prayer for their souls. Good men gone.

He kept his distance, standing among the dozens of onlookers, cell phones held aloft. There was no way to brazen this out, to get close to the action without blowing his cover. Unless...

Jacob zigzagged a couple of blocks away from the tragic scene, coming to a busy street with an intersection. Yield signs but no traffic lights. He stood on the corner, pretending to be reading something on his cell phone and looking up every now and again to search the ubiquitous red-brick buildings that dominated this part of town. No security cameras as far as he could tell.

He watched patiently as a trickle of cars and motorcycles drove by, waiting for an ideal target to arrive. It wasn't long before a black-and-yellow Suzuki GN 125 slowed to give way to a truck already halfway across the intersection. What made this target ideal was the fact that this rider wore a full face-visor.

Concealing his body at the rear of the truck, Jacob held his Glock in a two-handed grip, aimed squarely at the chest of the rider. The motorcycle stopped, and the rider dismounted slowly.

"Get away from the bike! Hands in the air!" Jacob screamed, widening his eyes as much as he could. A crazy man waving a gun gets a ton of respect, especially in a city like Bogotá.

The man, body shaking, complied readily.

Jacob strode up to him and pressed the pistol hard into the printed tongue of his old-school Rolling Stones T-shirt. "Take off your helmet slowly. Place it on the ground, turn around, and calmly walk away." Then an empty and unenforceable threat but worth making nonetheless. "Describe me to the cops, and I will hunt you down! Got me?"

The black helmet rocked back and forth before the rider removed it. Jacob shook his head when he saw tears dripping down the cheeks of the young man who looked barely old enough to shave. Still, he jabbed the barrel of the gun at the kid's throat. "Do as I asked and walk away or I'll kill you on the spot."

Jacob sensed people approaching but backing off when confronted with the bike-jacking. A car honked behind him. He reached for the helmet and quickly donned it. The fit was snug, verging on tight, but at least it went on. He spun around and fired a bullet into the front left tire of the car that had tooted. The driver, a woman in her sixties, ducked for cover, as did her male passenger. Out of the corner of his eye, he observed maybe six people scattering in all directions.

Internally debating the sanity of this violent tactic, Jacob decided it was justified: only trusting his gut instinct would see this assignment come to a successful conclusion. He leapt on the bike, put it in gear, and took off up the hill toward the overlooking mountains. At the city's natural boundary, he pulled out his cell and engaged the GPS, punched in the US embassy's address, pressed the clutch, kicked into first gear, and ripped the throttle.

Navigating with a GPS while simultaneously operating a

clutch and throttle proved a lot more difficult than he'd predicted. In fact, it was impossible. Instead, he pulled over between two parked cars and plotted a course. He made a note of the street names, or rather numbers, as the designers of the city so intelligently decided, intersections he'd need to traverse, and the turns he would need to make. Satisfied he'd memorized the route to perfection, he gunned it down Carrera 11.

Twice he ran red lights, taking care as he watched for traffic going perpendicular on the green. He made a right onto Calle 64 as the Centro Commercial Cosmos shopping mall loomed ahead. A left onto Calle 15 after a couple hundred meters, a left at the Parqe de los Novios roundabout, a long stretch down Avenida Carrera 50, then a couple more turns until he roared up to Calle 24.

He stopped at a dilapidated cantina opposite the embassy and removed his helmet, sweat pouring down the back of his neck. He pulled out the key and approached a man with a gray beard and a combover who was engrossed in a newspaper. Four 100,000 peso banknotes, worth about $100, fluttered onto the table, making the man look up.

"I need someone trustworthy to keep an eye on that motorcycle and helmet while I attend to business." He gestured with his head toward the embassy. "Can you do that for me?"

The man folded the broadsheet and regarded Jacob with one eye closed.

Jacob peeled off another four notes, placed them on the pile. "Same again when I come to get it. Agreed?"

The man winked. "Pleased to be of service," he said before switching his attention back to the sports page.

# FIFTEEN

"You need an appointment, sir."

"I assure you, I do not. I'm expected."

"It's very busy right now, and we're closing soon." She nodded at the line of people sitting in plastic chairs up against a wall. "Visa processing, assisting US nationals in trouble, there's a lot going on here. What was the name of the person you wanted to speak with?" The curly-haired, matronly woman behind the counter spoke in a sing-song Minnesotan accent right out of the movie *Fargo*. Through a pair of round-rimmed glasses, she stared at the screen from a few inches away.

"Please." Jacob smiled, breathing almost tantrically to keep his cool. "You can speak to Peter Abraham himself." He plucked out his local cell phone, hit redial on the last number to call him, and slid the phone to her under the Perspex barrier.

She pushed it back, shaking her head. "Please, I'm not accepting some random phone shoved at me. Leave, or I will have you escorted from the building."

Jacob sucked in a deep breath. *The woman's just doing her job. Stay calm*. He grabbed the phone and listened as it rang and rang. He was just about to formulate another plan when the call was answered.

"Yes?"

"Peter Abraham? It's Montoya. Could you please come and fetch me from the lobby? Your super-efficient gatekeeper is doing a wonderful job."

A plastic chair was vacated as its occupant left, mumbling something under his breath about not having all day to wait. A side door opened within minutes. Peter Abraham, a short, swarthy man with blue stubble and a hobbling gait, approached with a chubby right hand outstretched. He unerringly homed in on Jacob, the only man in the line dressed like he was about to lead a boardroom discussion. "Please come with me." He looked back at the woman on reception, in her own world as she typed away. "Margaret, please make sure I'm not disturbed while I'm with this special guest, okay?"

She peered around the side of her monitor, eyes agog as Jacob looked back and gave her a benevolent smile.

Once inside Abraham's office, Jacob didn't waste time. "Scratch the two additional police IDs we wanted."

"Sure. Reason?"

"The men are dead. Well, I'm presuming they're dead. How fast can you work to get mine done?"

"Me personally?"

"I don't have time for jokes, Abraham. I mean your tech team."

"For the ID you requested, no time at all. We have templates, it's just a matter of sticking your photo on it. If we had more time, of course we could have made it look a bit aged and realistic."

"It is what it is," said Jacob, who normally hated that cliché. Abraham asked Jacob to take a seat while he called the person in charge of document creation. A minute later, Abraham ushered Jacob into an open-plan room where three employees were working behind computers, two wearing headphones. "I'll leave you in Jacqueline's capable hands."

The woman, a slim, heavily freckled redhead with angular features, asked Jacob to stand against a wall where his height could be measured in centimeters. She took a photo of him and pressed a couple of buttons on her computer, and a printer in the corner of the room spat out the document. She left him for a couple of minutes, returning with a laminated card.

"Lieutenant Colonel?" said Jacob, holding the still warm document by the edges. "Not bad."

On the way out, he stopped to quickly thank Abraham. "No need. Just doing what I've been told to do." He shook Jacob's hand firmly.

The ID was so obviously new, Jacob would have to flash it quickly and hope for the best. That's if he wasn't too late already.

---

HIS HEART POUNDED like a trip hammer as he contemplated the next episode in this nightmarish script. Getting caught impersonating a police officer anywhere was bad enough. In Colombia...shit, the consequences were unthinkable.

Light drizzle began to fall; he sensed the well-worn tires beneath him slip, struggling to grip the road. It wasn't like he could replace them; he could only keep going. It had become both a literal and figurative balancing act: ride fast but not so fast that he'd crash.

Under a kilometer to the scene now, a couple more annoying intersections to negotiate. Three down. Then two. One more to go, nearly there. Puddles were forming in potholes now that the drizzle had become heavier rain.

Last crossroad ahead. Cars all over the place now, barely any space to squeeze the motorcycle through. For a second he thought about switching to the sidewalk, but there were too many pedestrians, dense packs of workers and shoppers heading home.

Then a gap appeared between two cars traveling perpendicular to him, going with the green light. He revved the throttle, rpms in the red zone. In the middle of the crossing, for some reason, the idiot driver of the dark VW Golf decided to speed up, nudging the Suzuki on the back wheel. Jacob's heart pounded out of his chest as he barely managed to keep the wobbling bike upright. In another lifetime, he would have yelled a stream of abuse at the driver of the Volkswagen. Not today. There were more urgent things to do.

At last, through the curtain of gray mist, he made out a cordoned-off scene up ahead. He stepped off the bike and wheeled it down a narrow side street. Outside a closed shoe store, he engaged the kick-stand and clipped the helmet to the handlebars. There was no one to ask if they could watch the Suzuki this time. If someone took it, bad luck. He'd steal another if he had to.

As he neared the chaotic scene on foot, Jacob's head swam with possible scenarios, most of them bad. Hair and jacket wet from the rain, he pulled back his shoulders. Time to use the greatest skill in his arsenal. Bluff.

"Buenas, compañeros. Qué más? *Good afternoon, colleagues. How's it going?*" Employing Colombian slang from the outset earned a couple of nods from the officers nearest to him. He had to use every trick in the book: his almost Nordic appearance meant he had to work doubly hard to appear to be a local. At least no one was yelling at him to stop, leave, put his hands in the air, or get on the ground. A good start.

He ducked under police tape and looked at the six uniformed officers standing around the shot-up Land Cruiser. Even from the perimeter, he could see pools of blood among the glass fragments from the shattered windshield. One or more of these cops could be senior investigators from God only knew which of the numerous branches of the Policía Nacional. He brandished his bogus card in the air like a soccer referee sending a player off the field. "Qué coño pasó? *What the hell happened?*"

"Hola," said a burly man with plump lips and a thin mustache. He pushed his rifle to one side and hitched up his trousers as Jacob extended a hand. "And you are?"

"Lieutenant Colonel Esteban Moreno." He held out the phony card, inches from the man's eyes, pulling it back again before he had time to focus. The steady rain was now an asset. "On special deployment from the Grupo Antiterrorista. I received a call from my boss that two of our operatives didn't show for a meeting. When I heard on the police radio the description of the vehicle and the two occupants, I had a feeling it was our guys. Even from back here, I can safely assume that our valiant men have been gunned down in the line of duty. However, I need to officially identify the bodies and search the vehicle for sensitive evidence the men were collecting for an Interpol matter."

"Hang on a second. Let's just back it up for a minute. You said antiterrorism?" The man arched his eyebrow. "Initial observations suggest this was a random robbery. The men's wallets were stolen. Apart from that, there are no other signs of an alternative motive."

Jacob rubbed droplets of water from his eyes, focusing on the cop's nametag. The officer also had on a scannable badge that had everything about him on it: his biometric data, service record, all the jobs he'd been assigned to. The badges had been introduced to stop exactly what Jacob was doing—impersonating cops. By rights, as a Colombian officer of the law, Jacob should have one too, but there were limits to the CIA's technical capabilities. If ordered to produce his, he'd be toast. It must not come to that. "Officer Cortez," said Jacob, getting onto the front foot, "the enemy's motive was purely to liquidate these wonderful men, selfless servants of our country. To stop them from getting evidence to catch and put away a secretive paramilitary group plotting to overthrow the government."

Cortez chewed his bottom lip in thought, digesting the detailed nature of the false information being thrown at him.

"I guarantee that you've run a vehicle check and the registration comes up as something way out of the ordinary," said Jacob, hands on hips.

"You tell me." The man's suspicions were back on high alert.

"Okay." Jacob took a deep breath, drops of cold rain rolling into his mouth. "My bet is you found that vehicle over there"—he pointed at the car with a rigid arm for dramatic effect—"is registered to the Colombian National Intelligence Directorate. Or to one of its high-ranked operatives, Special Agent Gilberto Vicario."

"That's exactly what happened." Cortez wore the gaping-eyed expression of a kid wonderstruck by a magician's trick. "Will your department be taking over the investigation now?"

"That's not my decision to make. My job is simply to do as I've told you: ID the bodies and look for intelligence they've been gathering. My superior will be arriving in about an hour together with the national police director."

Cortez pressed a button on his two-way. "Vasquez, listen up. There's a guy called Moreno headed your way. Way over our level. Afford him every courtesy." He saluted as he waved Jacob toward the Land Cruiser.

Jacob shuddered as he looked into the dead eyes of Ricardo, whose body hung half out of the open door. Bullet holes pockmarked his throat and upper body. The black Uzi, its rapid firing power unable to save him and his colleague, lay on the ground in a puddle of black blood inches from his hand. "We won't move them until the coroner arrives," said Vasquez, a female officer. "I was first to arrive and contain the crime scene. Cortez's orders are to leave them in situ."

"Quite right," agreed Jacob, not knowing if it was right or wrong. "Yes, this is definitely our agent." He strolled around to the driver's side. Gilberto's body lay slumped across the steering wheel, face down. Three gaping exit wounds desecrated the back of his skull. "No need to turn him over. I recognize him, too." He made the sign of the cross, kissing the tips of his fingers.

"You want to see the shell cases we found?" She pointed at numbered yellow markers on the ground. "Talk to the forensics scientists?" said Vasquez.

"What?" Jacob spun around. "No. I need to search the car."

"Won't that be difficult with the bodies in the way?"

"Not if you help me."

"Ah." The woman sounded unsure all of a sudden. "Won't we be tampering with the crime scene evidence?"

"What I'm looking for trumps normal procedure. If you want to get bawled out, perhaps demoted or even fired, go and talk to Cortez." Jacob looked over to the senior cop. Another couple of men in uniform were stepping out of a shiny armored police vehicle, saluting like they were in a competition, and chatting animatedly with Cortez. Jacob had to move fast and get the fuck out of there or his cover would be blown.

He reached under Gilberto's chest, feeling around in the console for the man's iPhone. Not there. He could have sworn that's where he kept it. He used his shoulder to shove Gilberto back to a sitting position. "Here," he said to Vasquez. "Hold him back while I check his pockets."

The woman groaned as she struggled to find room to get close enough to the corpse with Jacob underneath her, then groaned even louder as she strained to hold the body in place. With no living muscle to engage the spine, a cadaver's natural inclination is to obey gravity and fall; Gilberto had a large build, and she had her work cut out for her. With sticky blood covering his hands, Jacob patted the inside of the jacket: a Beretta M9 in the right pocket, which he left in place; an iPhone in the left, which he deftly extracted and slipped into his own pants pocket.

"Are you done?" huffed Vasquez. "I can't hold him much longer."

"One second." Jacob had one last look in the console and on the floor around the pedals but found nothing of interest. He stood and helped Vasquez gently ease Gilberto down to his approximate post-mortem position.

He raced around to the passenger side, mentally apologized to poor Ricardo for leaning all over him, and popped the glove box. There was assorted debris inside, including a digital camera and some shopping receipts, which Jacob stuffed in his own jacket pocket. He found Ricardo's cell in the left-side pants pocket, which he also liberated and added to the growing collection. He turned to Vasquez and said, "Can you find me a large evidence bag? I'm running out of pockets to put everything in."

"Ah, one minute."

She quickly returned with an extra-large resealable bag, into which Jacob transferred the items he'd collected so far. It would look more legit walking away with this sealed bag than with pockets bulging like a professional street thief.

"One more thing I have to do before I leave the rest of the investigation in your team's professional hands," he said, smiling at Vasquez, who blushed. "Look in the cargo compartment."

Jacob strode to the rear of the vehicle and lifted the tailgate. Inside was a lockable strongbox. Dammit. Where was the key?

The new officers approaching had different uniforms than the ones who had already been here when Jacob arrived. Fancier, brighter color on the epaulets. He could almost smell that they were top brass. *Shit, shit, shit!*

Maybe he'd be lucky and the box was open, like Brohman's apartment.

He tried to lift the lid, but it was stuck fast. But the box slid under his hands; it wasn't drilled into the floor of the Land Cruiser as he thought it might be. He hefted the safe in both hands, and some items inside rattled around. It weighed about 10 pounds, 12 max. He could carry it and the evidence bag. In fact, with the big-wig local officers on their way to speak to him, it would actually be quicker to take the whole box and skedaddle than to waste time breaking into it.

With the strongbox tucked under one arm and the evidence bag clutched in his hand, he turned to see a delegation of three granite-faced uniformed officers marching toward the Land Cruiser. "Do me a favor, Vasquez," said Jacob, glancing at a bus pulling up at a stop outside the taped-off area, maybe fifty yards away.

"What?"

"Tell those officers that I've just received a message from an informant. Another attack is imminent. On a bigger scale this time, and involving the general public."

"Imminent? When?" Her big blue eyes seemed to double in size.

"Tomorrow, I think. I'm going to meet with the informant to find out the exact details."

"What, now?"

"Yes, now!" Jacob snapped. "If anyone follows me and this man figures out there's a tail on me, he'll vanish, and we won't find out the location of the attack. People will die."

"Mierda. *Shit.*" Vasquez strode across to the approaching officers with her jaw set determinedly. Too anxious to see the developments behind him, Jacob hustled his way to the bus stop. He held his breath and prayed his cock-and-bull story would be believed, at least for a while.

He broke into a power walk, the weight of the box starting to make his upper arm ache. No voices behind him. Good. A puff of smoke from the exhaust of the bus, a hiss of the hydraulic door closing. *No!* The bus started to move off, but stopped again; the door opened for an old man struggling along with a walker. Jacob gritted his teeth and broke into a jog. He waited as other passengers assisted the old man before he stepped onto the bus. The door squeezed closed behind him with a thunk. As the bus rumbled off up the street, he dared to glance back to the crime scene: Vasquez and the top brass were nodding approvingly as they looked in his direction.

He heaved a massive sigh of relief.

"Are you okay, señor?" said a woman seated near the door. "Would you like my seat? That box looks heavy."

"No thanks," he said. "I think I can manage."

He jumped out at a small, leafy park three stops from where he'd embarked and placed the box and evidence bag on a bench.

He pulled out his phone and called Carmen Hererra.

# SIXTEEN

Jacob watched the glowing small screen of the old-school Nokia 3310 as he waited for her to pick up. After four rings, he heard her small voice and placed the handset to his ear, which he realized was freezing— as was the rest of him. "Carmen, it's Carlos Iglesias. Listen, do you know where Parque República de Portugal is?"

"No idea."

"Google it. I'm sure you'll find it. It's a couple of kilometers away from the JW Marriott Hotel..."

He could hear her labored breathing. "Where the hell did this old phone come from that I'm talking into? It's not mine."

Jacob cleared his throat. "I left it in your apartment; it's an untraceable burner for me to call you on if I need to impart sensitive information. Or if I need to ask you something."

"You forgot to mention that. What if I'd popped out of the apartment for some reason? You should have told me."

"Yes, I should have." He chided himself for the oversight. He couldn't afford to make dumb slipups like that from here on in. *Focus, Hunter.*

"You said something about sensitive information. Did you...

Hostia! Have you found Miguel? Please tell me you've found him."

He waited as a man and a woman in floral outfits rode past on racing bicycles. "No, sorry...not yet. I'm still trying to piece it all together. I have to find Brohman first; that's my primary objective. When we locate him, we'll also find your brother, I'm sure of it."

Her breathing came in shallow puffs. "Why did you ask me if I knew where the park was?"

"I want you to come here. It's near where Gilberto and Ricardo were..."

"Were what? Has something happened to them? It has, hasn't it? I can tell by the tone of your voice that you're not being honest with me."

"I'll tell you when you get here."

"I'm not coming, so you may as well tell me now." He heard panting, heavy footsteps, a door slamming shut, more footsteps. She was descending stairs. "I'm going out onto the street in case someone's bugged my apartment. Okay, I'm right on the corner now. What's going on?"

There was no way to sugarcoat this. "They've both been killed, shot dead in the car."

"Mierda." There was a clunking sound, like she'd dropped the phone. Some white noise followed, then she blurted out, "We were riding around in that car earlier today. That could have been us!"

"Calm down. I spoke with the police, and they think it was a random robbery."

"Bullshit, Carlos. If that's even your name. Who the fuck are you?"

"Please. Grab a taxi and come to the gates at the front of the park. From there we'll drive to my company's office."

"Can't it wait until tomorrow? I've got a lot of work to catch up on."

Jacob checked his watch. Already 7:05 p.m. "No. It can't wait.

I'll explain my idea when we meet. All you need to know for now is that I want you on hand tonight. Every minute that goes by is lost time."

"What can I do?"

"I want you to help me go through material I've got hold of that could lead us to Brohman, and from there to Miguel. You'll have insights nobody else could."

"What material?"

"I don't know."

"You are fucking loco, man!"

"Look, I didn't want to tell you this now, but before they were murdered, Gilberto and Ricardo broke into Miguel's apartment. On my instruction. I don't know what they managed to find there, but in the last call he made to me, Gilberto said what they found was 'very interesting.'"

"Okay. But you're paying for the taxi. And dinner. I'm starving."

"Of course."

His shoulders stiffened as the same pair of cyclists went past again, laughing at each other's jokes. He was pretty sure they were innocuous Bogatanos enjoying some evening exercise, but with two dead agents a couple of blocks away, it paid to be vigilant, suspect everyone, and keep your weapon close.

"You still there?" she said impatiently.

"Yes." He felt a shiver run down his spine. Not paranoia—perhaps the beginning of a fever. The last thing he needed was to come down with some kind of illness. "Tell Stynes I've granted you extended leave until we find Miguel."

"Gracias. Oh, but will I still be paid my salary?"

"I'll make sure of it." With an extra bonus payment Fletcher would learn about later and not be in a position to refuse.

"I'll be there as soon as I can. Peak-hour traffic should have eased by now. Shouldn't take too long."

"Before you go, have you got a thermos at your place?"

"I think one of my roommates has one in the larder."

"Borrow it. Fill it with hot coffee. Lots of sugar. I'm absolutely freezing here."

She arrived in twenty-six minutes. Shivering, he clambered into the back of the taxi, placing the strongbox and evidence bag in the gap between him and Carmen.

"Is that the stuff I need to help you with? Cell phones and a safe?"

"Yes, but coffee first."

He guzzled the hot, strong brew from a plastic cup as she watched in wonder. "You're drenched. Why didn't you say? I could have brought you..."

"Women's clothes that are way too small for me?" he said, eyebrow arched.

"Actually, Juanita is a bit on the chubby side...but no, even her biggest poncho wouldn't go over your shoulders." She felt his right shoulder, giving it a squeeze. Whether she knew she was flirting with him or not, he wouldn't take the bait. "I'm organizing the food so we don't have to wait later, bien?"

"Bien."

Without asking what he wanted, she called a food delivery service and ordered two serves of bandeja paisa. He had no idea what it was and didn't care. He was so hungry at this point he'd eat his own leather belt.

---

THE NEON SIGN for the Gunderson Holdings SA company head office—and only office—outshone the other signs on the street by thousands of lumens, Jacob thought. The backroom boys had worked hard and fast to get the place looking realistic. They'd had to walk another four blocks in the rain when the taxi dropped them at a safe distance from the office. An uncomfortable inconvenience but a necessary one. Thankfully, Carmen had brought a large umbrella.

The shell of the front company had been organized in great

haste; nevertheless, Fletcher had assured him all backstops were in place and Gunderson's pedigree on paper was impeccable. Jacob pulled an old-fashioned Yale key from his pocket and opened the door. There was enough light coming in from the street to see where he was going but not enough to work in comfortably. He located a light switch near the door and flicked it on, and the space was instantly bathed in bright light.

Inside was a bare-bones office decked out with the minimum amount of furniture, a stationery cupboard, some audio-visual equipment, computers, and a fridge with cold drinks in it. The heady scents of a recent paint job and carpet underlay glue hung in the air. No commercial business of any kind was conducted here, although a couple of local CIA sleepers were on standby to front up if necessary to pretend to be employees.

"What kind of office is this?" Carmen forced a laugh. "It looks totally phony to me."

"You don't need to concern yourself with matters like that."

"Whatever," she said with more than a touch of sarcasm.

"You want to find your brother? You have to trust me. If you must know, this office was created as a bolt-hole for me, a place I can work alone and uninterrupted. This type of arrangement is perfect for doing the boring part of my job. Reading and analyzing, researching and planning. Unfortunately, when people go missing and my government wants them back, I have to do this boring work faster than I'd like to." He tugged at the sleeve of the brand-new green-and-white Adidas hoodie, paired with matching track-suit pants. The taxi had made a quick stop at a clothing store that was still open at this hour. It specialized in garish youth apparel, which meant Jacob looked more like a skateboarder than a businessman. He didn't care. He was dry and warm.

"Will this take long?" said Carmen, standing to open the door for the delivery driver. "Only I've had a think about your offer of me taking time off. Sorry, but I'm going to have to refuse. I've got a huge backlog of work to get through at the office."

Jacob waved away the concern. "Surely someone else can fill in for you."

She shrugged. "I guess."

"Then don't worry about it." He used his local phone to call Stynes, informing him that he'd granted Carmen time off, as much as she needed. Stynes grumbled about how hard it was to find good replacement admin staff at short notice, but Jacob wasn't listening. "Good-bye, Jim. Talk to you soon."

Carmen smiled broadly. "You have no idea how much it pleases me to hear that asshole being put in his place. Thank you. Now time to eat."

Carmen opened the cardboard box, letting out wisps of steam. Fragrant, spicy aromas filled the room. Jacob scrambled around in the makeshift kitchenette, finding cutlery and small plates. She did the honors of dishing up. The meal was an eclectic mix of red beans, rice, ground meat, pork belly, fried egg, plantains, chorizo sausage, blood sausage, avocado, and, to mop up sauce, a cornbread arepa. They devoured their food in silence, only stopping to wipe their mouths with paper towels.

When they were done eating, Jacob turned on a wall-mounted TV. "Can you find a channel showing the news?" he asked Carmen. "Maybe there's an update about the murders." She played with the remote, flicking through the stations.

"Stop there!" Jacob squinted as he approached the TV, even though he could see fine from where he stood fifteen feet away: A woman from the station Caracol Televisión was doing a live piece from the scene. "Can you turn up the volume?"

The glamorous reporter, with an assistant holding an umbrella over her head as the earlier rain had turned into a downpour, spoke animatedly about the horrific downtown double assassination. "Finally, in a surprising twist to this incident, embarrassed police have admitted that a man posing as a high-ranking officer has stolen what they think might be crucial evidence. They suspect him to be a member of the gang that murdered the victims, sent in to get rid of incriminating material.

The names of the victims, believed to be associated with international intelligence, have not been revealed. A short while ago, the chief of police released a photofit of the suspect."

Carmen gasped as a drawing appeared on the screen that looked somewhat like Jacob. "Carlos! That guy looks a bit like you. You told me you spoke with police, but this is, wow, what even is this? Did you impersonate a cop?"

Jacob puffed out his cheeks, concentrating on the unfolding drama on the television.

"Police have also released this CCTV footage," continued the breathless journalist. "However, the cameras are a long way from the scene, and the vision isn't clear. Nevertheless, it may assist in identifying this man. Finally, if you are able to help police locate the suspect, please call the number you see on the screen."

Jacob rubbed his temple. This was an unfortunate development but not an unexpected one. In fact, it was inevitable. He'd been up close and personal with Cortez and Vasquez. The police would be well trained in observing and describing people; no wonder the drawing was so close. Luckily the cops had been too busy with their tasks to take any photos of him at the scene, and they'd also done a great job keeping the public from stopping to gawk. Another plus—his accent was so convincing there was no doubt in Jacob's mind the cops would have thought he was a Colombian. Reverting to a heavily disguised US national might become an option if he wanted to stay in the country without the cops pinning the rap on him. The only problem with that was having to admit his deception to Carmen, that the persona of Carlos Iglesias was rolled-gold bullshit.

"What are you going to do now, genius? Anyone can see that's you." Carmen shook her head like Jacob was the biggest idiot on the planet. He'd shaved his head on the last mission, but he wasn't anxious to do that again. In Europe, sporting such a look might be okay, but here in South America, a tall, white skinhead, even a well-dressed one, could freak people out. He'd have to resort to old spy-craft methods: wigs, fake beards, sunglasses, and hats.

"I'll admit it looks like me, but there are significant differences. The nose is a lot wider in that photo, the eyebrows are too thick, the hairline and chin not as pronounced as mine. It's all wrong," he said with a half-smile. "You're only putting two and two together because I just told you I spoke to the police."

"Bullshit." She sounded unsure of herself.

Jacob shook his head. "People I've met here won't associate that photo with me. I guarantee it." He drew a sharp breath. "And if I'm wrong—which I'm not—it wouldn't be the first time the law was chasing my ass. To be on the safe side, though, I'll keep my head down, I promise."

"Why am I not surprised by all of this?" She seemed to have a lightbulb moment. "Wait a minute. You're a felon now. If I get caught up in this nightmare with you...shit!" She grabbed her handbag and headed for the door. "You're on your own, Carlos."

He stayed her with a firm hand on the elbow. "And the search for Miguel? Who's going to help you with that?"

"I'll find him on my own." Her breaths were coming in bursts, eyes staring wildly in all directions. "Whatever it takes."

Jacob shook his head. "I don't think so, mi corazón. The cops won't help you. Stynes? Forget it. Miguel's got himself involved with some really bad people. If you're serious about finding him, you're going to have to trust me."

She stood rooted to the spot, handbag dangling by her side. Jacob fetched her a glass of water and led her to a straight-backed chair. "You know I'm right. And you need to pull yourself together. I'll make sure nothing happens to you." He patted the pistol in his pocket as a punctuation mark. "In the meantime, I really need *you*, okay?"

She nodded slowly and took a sip of water.

"Let's start by examining the items I took from the Land Cruiser. Here." Jacob handed her Ricardo's Samsung, he then picked up Gilberto's iPhone. "See if you can get into that cell."

"Of course I can't," she pouted, holding it out in her extended arm. "It's got a fucking PIN."

"This one, too." Jacob scowled, placing Ricardo's Samsung back into the evidence bag along with the iPhone. "I'll need you to do something for me first thing tomorrow." He tore a page from a notebook and wrote on it. "Call a man called Peter Abraham and ask him to meet you somewhere you feel safe. Make sure you only use the burner, okay?"

She nodded slowly.

"His name and number are on this note." He scribbled on another piece of paper. "Tell him to send these phones via diplomatic pouch to this New York address." He tapped the second note for emphasis. "Can you do that?"

A cough into a fist. "Sounds easy."

"Good girl." He picked up the small digital camera. "While I'm working on the safe, I'd like you to flick through this." He passed the small digital camera. "Know how to operate it?"

She screwed up her face. "You insult me. I'm a millennial. I can figure out any gadget." She rested a hand on her hip. "I dabble in amateur photography, as it happens. This one is a Nikon Coolpix W150. I've got one the same, only a different color. It's okay, but there are better ones out there. I remember Miguel talked me into getting one because they're good for underwater photography. Still, even this one is much better than a cell phone for taking proper pictures."

"Really? I didn't think there was much difference anymore, what with the advances in mobile phone technology."

"You see many sports photographers at the big game taking pictures with their cell phones?"

"I get your point."

"Is it Miguel's camera? I haven't seen it before."

Jacob shrugged. "Don't know. Either they found it in his apartment or it belongs to one of them. Or any number of scenarios."

"Problem is, it's also password protected."

"What?" Jacob couldn't believe it. "Who password protects a damn camera?"

"Lots of people. Especially if they take, you know, erotic photos, things like that."

Jacob inhaled sharply. "Let's assume it is Miguel's and that there are no erotic pictures on it. Try a few combinations he might use. If they don't work, the camera will have to go to New York, too."

"No need," she said triumphantly. "His birthday didn't work, so I tried mine. It worked! Which tells me it's definitely his camera."

While she began to peruse the dozens of images, Jacob attacked the steel strongbox with the lockpicking tools he was never without. This safe proved trickier than usual, but after three minutes wrestling with the rake and short hook, the lid popped open.

Inside were a Colombian-manufactured a 9-mm semiautomatic Córdova handgun and two full magazines, $100 cash in US dollars and the equivalent in local tender, about 400,000 Colombian pesos, and a handwritten document inside a plastic cover. With thumb and forefinger, he slid the paper out of the sheath and eagerly began to read. The content was mind-blowing. As his darting eyes locked on to the first word of the second paragraph, Carmen let out a piercing scream so loud Jacob's head shrank into his shoulders.

# SEVENTEEN

"Another drink, Pablo?" said Adolfo Sanchez, leaning back in his outdoor lounge chair. "I've got a fridge full of them inside."

Brohman placed his empty bottle of Corona on a glass-topped table, squinting as he looked back at his captor. "Sure. Why not?" He'd sipped the beer slowly, finishing one in the time Sanchez had bowled over two. Who knew what the bastard had planned for him next: the beer you said no to could be the last beer you ever got to enjoy.

He wasn't able to hold the man's gaze for long, however. There was something telling in Sanchez's eyes, deep and obsidian, that Brohman had never seen before in another human being. It was more than simply a glimmer of badness and cruelty. He'd seen that in plenty of people. In Brohman's world view, bad men were as common as mud; often they were just weak men who couldn't control their weaknesses. He should know: He was one himself. His weakness for young women made him 'bad' according to commonly held standards of good taste and decorum. But he wasn't bad at all: Every woman he'd ever been with was of legal age, and he never coerced, cajoled, or even coaxed. They all submitted willingly to him, and that was that. Still, the whispers reached his ears. And those whispers said he was a pervert and worse.

However, with Adolfo Sanchez, the abyss behind his eyes was something terrifying. A window into the soul of indescribable evil. His parents had chosen the first name well.

"Excellent." He beckoned with a flick of the fingers, and a young man called José wearing a long-sleeved white shirt and black pants skipped across from his position by the door into the house. He leaned in close as his boss gave the order, then scurried away with his head down.

Brohman stood and walked to the edge of the slate-tiled patio the size of a basketball court. He rested his forearms on the railing, staring across an expansive, perfectly manicured lawn. Around the edges of the lawn were bright tropical flowers: birds of paradise, hibiscus, frangipani. Behind the garden beds was a thick wall of jungle, a number of paths leading who knew where. The mid-morning air was redolent of the scents of the jungle, rich and earthy and sweet, humid but not sticky, warm like an embrace.

But it wasn't those pleasant features that occupied Paul Brohman's thoughts. Rather, it was the four bikini-clad brunettes frolicking in the huge kidney-shaped swimming pool that occupied a vast section of the lawn.

"Like what you see?" said Sanchez.

Brohman turned to observe him lighting a large cigar with a red band around it. "Sure." Again, he couldn't look at the man for more than a couple of seconds. Was it disdain or fear, or a combination of both?

Sanchez laughed loudly. "Of course you do, gringo." He sucked wetly on the end of the cigar, the sloppy sound making Brohman cringe. "You'll be pleased to know that Carolina, remember the young lady who tricked you at the nightclub? Well, she's not here at my villa."

"Great." Brohman was unable to formulate answers beyond one-word reflexive responses.

"Her being here wouldn't be very pleasant for you, now, would it, Pablo?"

This time not even a one-word response, just a grunt.

"You're not being very talkative, my friend. From what people told me, I was expecting a party animal, not some shy boy." More sloppy interaction with his cigar. "Oh, I should tell you, in case you were wondering. The reason Carolina isn't here is because she's dead." He chuckled. "Such a shame. I really liked her. But for some reason, last night she decided to wander off into the jungle by herself. Javi, the man who was a little rough with you—but don't worry, I've told him no more of that—found her a little while ago with her arms and legs, even her head, cut off. While you were having a shower, in fact. Less than a hundred meters from the boundary fence, can you believe it?"

"Oh my God," Brohman whispered under his breath, his heart racing a million miles an hour. The poor woman had done a job for Sanchez, a dirty job, and once she was of no further use, dismembered and decapitated. *Jesus.*

"I know, you're lost for words, but she shouldn't have been rude to Javi."

"I thought you said he found her, not that he killed her."

The sound of air being sucked contemplatively through teeth. "Let's not argue over semantics." Brohman's curiosity won over his disgust and fear. He looked sideways at Sanchez, making a balancing-the-scales gesture with his large hands. "Found, killed, what does it matter? Point is"—he stabbed the cigar toward Brohman—"she shouldn't have been rude to Javi. In my mind, a woman should know her place and never be rude to a man. There is never any excuse unless that woman is your mother. Am I right, Paul?"

"Of course." Brohman's mind was turning to mush, his stomach churning like a washing machine. He shifted his gaze back to the buxom women, all lip-filler and implants. Brohman abhorred the fakeness of modern fashion, but who could stop the tsunami? They splashed about with an oversized beach ball, stopping only to sip from champagne flutes resting on the side of the pool, to sniff lines of coke from small mirrors. They giggled uncontrollably, shouting in their incoherent thousand-mile-an-hour Spanish. The scene reminded him of a corny '80s TV ad for a famous cola. It was all so frivolous. No doubt staged by Sanchez in an effort to get Brohman excited, primed to give extra information he hadn't already. Maybe one or all of them were expected to service him in return for information.

But that made little sense: Sanchez could always torture Brohman until he spilled his guts. No doubt his truth-extraction methods were state of the art. Brohman wasn't that naïve to think he'd be stoic enough to resist. And he'd also just given him the Carolina horror story. The strategy now made sense: he was fucking with Brohman's mind.

He heard the clanking of glass on glass. "Come, sit with me."

Brohman took a seat, deliberately choosing a chair facing away from the pool to demonstrate he had no interest in the pussy party.

José fussed about slicing lemons and stuffing wedges into the necks of the bottles. The imagery of it made Brohman shudder: disposable Carolina being dissected in the bushes.

"Where am I?" said Brohman, figuring the question innocuous enough.

Sanchez scratched his chin, cobalt with stubble. "Now this is the Paul Brohman I've heard about. Decisive, to the point." He sipped his beer, burped, and made a face like a child guilty of farting at the dinner table. "Oops. Where are we, you ask? Well, I've given you a massive clue." He raised his bottle in the air like he'd won the world cup.

"Mexico?" said Brohman.

"Very astute." He snapped his fingers twice, and José appeared by his side as if by magic. The servant wore the look of someone perpetually afraid of making a mistake and paying the price. Perhaps he, too, was aware of the fate that had befallen Carolina.

Sanchez asked the boy to bring an assortment of tasty dishes, all Mexican, as if to drive the point home.

"Why are we in Mexico?" said Brohman, savoring the beer like it was the last he would ever drink.

"Because it's my home, and"—his voice rose a couple of octaves—"thanks to a couple of busybodies, it's safer right now for me to be here than in Colombia." On the last word, his fist smashed into the tabletop.

Brohman pushed his beer away, placed his hands on his lap, and adjusted himself under the table. The white polo shirt he'd found in the guest bedroom was a perfect fit, but the chinos, like all the other pants hanging in the closet, were a size too small. They pinched in the crotch. He couldn't be sure, but he thought he detected Sanchez smirking at his mild discomfort. "I'm glad you're safe now." Brohman's lie was so big you could see it from the Space Station.

"Not safe. Saf-*er*." He drank greedily from the bottle and wiped his mouth with the back of his hand. "In this business, 100 percent safety is a pipedream." He paused for a few moments, then said, "You need to start talking if we're going to be friends instead of enemies."

"Why should I?" Brohman's head was starting to shed some of the fuzziness. Either that or the beer was giving him mild Dutch courage. "You're going to kill me whether I speak to you or not."

Sanchez shook his head slowly. "I have no intention of killing you—if you cooperate. You are worth much more to me alive than dead, believe me."

He decided to test him. "Yeah, but for how long? Carolina outlived her usefulness, had her pretty head separated from her shoulders. I cannot be of value to you forever."

"Believe it or not, I am a man of honor. My word is my bond." He stood and walked to the railing. "I'm really sorry about what happened to Miguel, but you know, he wasn't acting in your best interests, despite what he may have told you."

A flash of lightning over the top of the canopy of trees seemed to underscore Sanchez's words.

"And what did he tell me?"

"That he was going to hand this over to you..." He reached into a pocket and waved a bright blue USB flash drive in the air. "Unfortunately, you'll never get to see this, but you don't have to. I can simply tell you what it is. The little rat Hererra is smarter than he looks— or should I say looked." An evil chuckle followed the macabre remark. "Somehow, he managed to hack into the private email account of someone working for me. A person inside the CIA's Clandestine Operations department." He laughed, sipped beer, and let rip with another burp. "Hererra downloaded and copied correspondence between my...representative...and my little mole, plus other messages on the mole's account.

"You were going to be the conduit, the person to hand over this device to the American embassy. To a man called Peter Abraham. We also have Hererra's laptop, phone, everything he could have stored the incriminating data on." Sanchez tilted back his head and roared with laughter. "The little sneak thought he could store it on the cloud and we'd never find it. But Javi..." Sanchez offered a half smile through pursed lips. "...He's a special boy. Very talented. He managed to get Herrera to log onto his cloud account and show Javi where the information was lurking in cyberspace, and then Javi, bless him, knew exactly what to do to get Hererra to delete it all. And then, well, as the old cliché goes, Miguel simply knew too much to live."

"I have no idea what you are talking about."

"That's exactly how I expected you to respond, Pablo. And I know you are not telling a complete lie. Just a partial one. Miguel Hererra wanted something in return for this information, didn't he? That's why you have no idea who the mole is. Hererra kept it up his sleeve as a bargaining chip."

Brohman blinked as the sun broke through the dispersing dark storm clouds. The weather gods had decided today wasn't the day for spoiling the weird little garden party in the middle of the jungle in Mexico. "If you say so."

"Oh, I do. He admitted as much. Said he wanted a million dollars from you in exchange for information that would rock the Hannah McIvor presidential campaign."

"You're fucking kidding me!" said Brohman, shaking his head, fully aware that this was indeed the case. He didn't know exactly what that information was; he presumed it had something to do with Stynes, that he was cooking something up to help derail Claxton's re-election chances.

"He didn't want a million dollars?"

Brohman tried to gather his thoughts: not easy under the circumstances. "That part, yes. But I thought it was something to do with...the station chief, Jim Stynes."

Sanchez cradled his chin in his thumb and forefinger. "Hmm, yes, I can see why you would think that. He is, as they say in English, a total creep. Even worse than you! Imagine forcing his secretary to fuck you, a man old enough to be her father, to get compromising information on you." He extracted another cigar from the box and sniffed it deeply. "That's the value of a clever mole, you see. He sowed the idea in Stynes' head that you were suspect."

"Who is this fucking mole then?" Brohman's curiosity got the better of his caution.

"Does it matter?"

"I guess not."

"Of course not. Imagine, heaven forbid, you managed to escape my impregnable and inescapable compound, made your way back to Bogotá, and pointed the finger at my informant. All of my groundwork would have been for nothing."

Brohman pushed away from the table and retook his previous position overlooking the pool. The women were out of the water, sunbathing on banana lounges, damp cloths over their faces. Without looking back at Sanchez, he said in a resigned tone, "What is it you want to know?"

"A man called Carlos Iglesias has been sniffing around CIA Clandestine Operations, asking a lot of questions since we ah... brought you on a Mexican vacation. I think you know about this person. Tell me, please, Pablo. Who is he?"

Brohman's heart beat like a marching band's drummer on speed. Not because he knew who Iglesias was but because he had no fucking idea whatsoever.

# EIGHTEEN

The transfer of all of the images from the 64GB SD card in Miguel's camera to the laptop provided in the office took a little over two minutes. Jacob then transferred the images onto a USB flash drive and finally dropped them via cloud technology into his little corner of Skia cyberspace. While Carmen was curled up in a ball, crying on the floor in the corner, he put in a call to Peter Abraham at the embassy. After five rings, he realized the stupidity of what he was doing: the embassy staff had long gone home. He called Fletcher instead.

"Jacob. What's happening? Have you–?"

"No!" Jacob growled. "Not yet. I've uploaded a shit-ton of photos to the Skia cloud drive. They're in my folder and yours. I want you to get Irina to take a look at them."

"Firstly, how many is a shit-ton?"

"Around 2,000."

"What the hell! And how is she supposed to analyze all of them? Sounds like a monumental task."

"She'll have some kind of program to do that for her. Probably group them thematically or something, I don't know. The woman's a genius." He turned to look at Carmen, still in the fetal position, rocking back and forth and sobbing inconsolably. "In all probability, the most recent images are the ones she's going to want to look at the closest." He exited the main room and took refuge in the bathroom, out of earshot. "Look, I've got a bad feeling. I think something terrible may have happened to a man who's critical to me finding Brohman."

"Who?"

"No time to explain. I have to get out of Colombia. I've got a lead from a key figure. I think Sanchez might have outsmarted everyone and holed himself up somewhere in Mexico."

"What the fuck's going on, Jacob? I've just opened an email from Peter Abraham. He tells me a face very similar to yours has been plastered all over the television down there."

"Like I said, explaining will take too long. Once I'm on the road, I'll call you, fill you in on everything."

"Okay, and...one second. I've logged onto the cloud system." A short pause. "Just opened the first image. A close up of a boot. Second one, the same. What gives? Hang on...oh my God!"

Jacob bit his bottom lip. Fletcher must have opened the image of Miguel Herrera, giant knife pressed hard against his neck, blood streaming. "I'm with that man's sister right now, boss. He's the one I told you was the link to Brohman. And she's the one who found the picture on his camera and some others that will make you sick. Men in ski masks taking selfies with a man who's about to die. As you can imagine, the woman's a wreck. I shouldn't have let her have the camera, dammit. We've been clinging to the vain hope the guy was still alive."

"But who is 'the guy,' Jacob?"

"Like I said, a link to Brohman. Miguel sniffed something out and was probably going to dish off information to Brohman, but someone else found out first."

"What's with the close-ups of the boots?"

"I'd say the last two pictures were taken accidentally by one of the killers. Perhaps in too much of a hurry to check the reel before they dropped the device. My gut tells me they left the camera behind on purpose, hoping someone would find it and see the shocking image of Miguel with his throat bleeding. Rubbing it in, as it were. That's why I want Irina to look at it—and whatever else is on that camera. There could be something that will point me in the right direction. I also want her to go over a couple of cell phones I'm sending to you via diplomatic bag."

"Let's leave the why out of it for a minute. *How* are you planning on getting to Mexico now that you're a wanted man in Colombia?"

"I'm not a wanted man. There's a resemblance between me and the man the cops are looking for, but it's not a conclusive likeness. To be on the safe side, Abraham can source me a car, perhaps a driver."

"Scratch that. The tone of his email tells me he's getting antsy. That stunt with the crime scene's rattled him."

"Tough shit. The man as good as handed me the fake police ID himself. Did he not anticipate I'd actually use it? Gimme a break. Besides, he's answerable to the president, just like us. Email him back and tell him I expect to see a driver at Parque República de Portugal tomorrow morning at daybreak. I'll email a list of things I'd like their tech department to provide me for the journey."

"Is this chauffer gonna drive you all the way to fucking Mexico?"

"Don't be ridiculous, Grant. I know geography's not your strong point, but I'd have to traverse the entirety of Central America to get to the Mexican border. No. I want a flight. If that British pilot's got some spare time on her hands, send her to fetch me."

"Listen, Jacob. Why don't you liaise all of this with Stynes? He can get onto Laura Torres from the Colombian National Intelligence Directorate. Surely she can do something to take the heat off you for pretending to be a Colombian cop. Get them to look the other way."

"Maybe she can, and maybe she can't. I'm not familiar with how the police and the main secret service agency get along in this country. Maybe deep down they don't like each other, like the FBI and the CIA have their historical animosity. How the fuck would I know?"

"Easy, Jacob."

"Sorry for that." Jacob could feel beads of sweat forming on his brow. "One second." He went back to quickly check on Carmen. No change, still rocking and sobbing, almost catatonic. Back to Fletcher. "The thing is, I don't trust Stynes, and I don't trust his employees, apart from the two who are dead—and poor Carmen, who's going to need psychological intervention." He rubbed his face rapidly as he paced back and forth. "Can I even 100 precent trust Abraham? I mean, this country seems to toss up temptations left, right, and center. Incentives to do the wrong thing, look the other way for money. Maybe he's on the take too."

"This is paranoia talking, Jacob. At the end of the day, you can't do this alone, or rely purely on unvetted locals. Have some faith in our side, in Abraham, at least. He's got a good reputation, been in his post for nearly a decade. Never set a foot wrong."

"You're right, Grant. Abraham's delivered so far for me. I'm still rattled by what's happened tonight and what I saw on the camera."

"That's better. Send me that email with the list of things you need, and I'll tell Abraham to get his ass into gear."

"Have you got his personal number? It's after hours."

"Fuck it! No, I don't."

"What about Joel McDonald? You've got his number, right?"

"Good thinking. Hang on while I put the wheels in motion. Hey, there's another file you've dropped in the folder separately. What's that?"

"A photo I took of a document. A handwritten agreement between Miguel Hererra and Brohman."

"What?"

"I'll summarize it for you. Brohman agreed to hand over a million dollars to Hererra in return for a USB flash drive containing compromising material on someone under Stynes' command who was leaking information to Sanchez. The name of that person isn't given in the agreement. I guess Hererra was using that knowledge as extra leverage. The date for handing over the USB drive was the day after Brohman was snatched."

"Holy shit!"

"Yeah. It's the smoking gun. Sanchez must've known his informant was about to be exposed, killed Hererra, and took Brohman as extra insurance."

"You said Brohman's place was trashed, searched. How did they miss this, and the other stuff your dead friends found subsequently?"

"I've got a theory on that. Sanchez's people were ransacking the place at the very time Gilberto and Ricardo were on their way. The bad guys stood aside, then chased them down in the street and assassinated them."

"Poor bastards."

"Yeah. Anyway, wish me luck on my Mexican leg of the magical mystery tour."

"Break a leg."

Jacob disconnected the call. He prayed the stars would align and he'd get what he needed from Abraham. He cobbled together a short message with his wish-list: a driver with a fast car; a pilot to fly him from the elevated city of Tunja to Tuxtla, Mexico; and a bag full of disguise material. He considered asking for fresh clothing to avoid returning to his apartment. But that short trip was a risk he was prepared to take. If he later ended up in the jungle, his Sig Sauer P320 and pair of well-worn boots were valuable assets he would be a fool to leave behind.

Email sent, he returned to Carmen, daring to place his hand on top of her head. He waited for the flinch, but none came. He rested his back against the wall and slid down until he was sitting cross-legged on the floor next to her. He began to stroke her hair, like he was comforting a scared animal, quaking with fear in a thunderstorm. She made no protest; instead, she sat up straight, rubbed her eyes with the sleeve of her blouse, and forced herself to look at Jacob. "You and I, we're going to get whoever did this to my brother!"

"Yes, we are. Can I ask you to be my eyes and ears here in Bogotá while I'm in Mexico?"

"What, where?"

"Mexico. There's someone I have to talk to."

"Who?"

"Adolfo Sanchez's mother."

# NINETEEN

His bones ached after a night sleeping fitfully on the hard floor, his rolled-up hoodie for a pillow, no sheets or blankets. Thankfully, the heating system in the office was brand-new and threw out enough warmth for Jacob to sleep without shivering. The fever he feared was looming failed to develop into anything serious, not even a sniffle. His main gripe about the conditions was the thin carpet, barely thicker than linoleum. Fair enough, though, he reasoned. It wasn't designed for people to hide out in. Jacob filed away an idea to bring up later with Fletcher: when the experts were designing workplace bolt holes, make sure they include a fold-out bed somewhere in the joint.

The morning was crisp and clear. A quick browse on the Internet confirmed there was no rain forecast for today in the Bogotá area. Which meant his garish green tracksuit would remain warm and dry.

A quick call to Carmen, whom he'd sent home in a taxi once she'd calmed down sufficiently after the shocking discovery. "You okay?"

"No! I'm devasted." Not a trace of tiredness in her voice despite the fact it was still dark outside. She obviously hadn't slept a wink. She stifled a sob before gathering herself. "You know, I have to tell my mother about what's happened."

"No!" Jacob blurted. "Please don't do that. Wait until everything's cleared up."

"Are you fucking serious? A mother deserves to know when her child dies."

"Believe me, Carmen. The fewer people who know about this, the better." He wracked his brain for a reason— a real reason—why she should keep her mother in the dark. "There's still a chance we can recover his body. If the killers are alerted, they may try to make sure that he's never found."

She breathed heavily and didn't answer for some time. Finally: "That kind of makes sense. Mamma wouldn't like his remains to be lost, I guess. She's a devout Catholic, and burial is important."

Jacob sighed. "Do you need someone to be with you today?"

"No. I think I'll be best left alone."

"Good." A person on hand would be the default setting under normal circumstances of bereavement. These were not normal circumstances. "Don't even bother calling Stynes. I'll take care of that for you. But keep your burner phone handy. I'm gonna need you on stand-by to let me know what's going on in Clandestine Operations. Agreed?"

"Si. De acuerdo. *Agreed.*"

Exiting the office, Jacob switched off the lights, locked the door, and power-walked his way to the small and discreet Parque República de Portugal. It sat on a rise, surrounded by low-set brick buildings. The hood of his sweater was pulled down to half cover his face, and he affected a loping gait, like he owned the streets. At a glance, no one would suspect he was the bogus police officer, more like a violent thug best left alone. He was ready for any trouble; in addition to the evidence bag, the small sports bag slung over his shoulder contained his fully-loaded Glock 19.

Getting to the embassy pre-dawn presented no problems in a kick-ass Jeep. The driver was a taciturn, gum-chewing brute called Mateo. He answered Jacob's small-talk questions with monosyllabic answers; clearly, he wouldn't provide much in the way of sparkling conversation on the two-hour drive along Highway 55 to the high-elevation city of Tunja. On the positive side, Mateo's driving skills and attention to the road in front of him were impeccable.

Passing the now empty crossroads where he'd perpetrated the motorcycle jacking yesterday, Jacob intoned a little prayer, asked that the good Lord would make sure the owner of the stolen Suzuki got his property back. And that he didn't suffer recurring nightmares after being held up at gunpoint. He wished the same for the driver and passengers of the car whose tire he'd shot out.

A sleepy-eyed Peter Abraham met Jacob at the embassy gate. Those tired eyes widened and elevated when he copped an eyeful of Jacob's attire. However, he said nothing about it. "Thanks for coming so early," said Jacob. "Appreciate it at short notice. Make sure all of this stuff goes in the dip pouch and send it to this address." He handed the diplomat a note. "Like, yesterday."

"Sure thing." He handed Jacob a clutch bag, twice the size of the one he already had. "There's more disguises in there than you'd need for a one-man variety performance at Carnegie Hall." He smiled, but Jacob found little humor in the words.

"Thanks." He gestured with a backwards head flick to where Mateo stood by the Jeep, sucking the life out of a cigarette. "This guy's giving me the silent treatment. He's solid?"

"Been on the payroll since he left high school. Solid as a rock. Good in a scrap and an excellent shot on the range."

"What about in real life?"

Abraham shrugged. "As far as I'm aware, he's never discharged his weapon while on the job."

Jacob nodded. "Let's hope this isn't the first time he has to."

A final confirmation the Gulf Stream would be waiting at the airport in Tunja. "Flight's scheduled to arrive at 9:00 a.m.. The pilot's a woman," said Abraham with a slight twist of the mouth. "Not a problem?"

Jacob slapped the man on the shoulder. "You're a dinosaur, Abraham. Ever heard of Amelia Earhart or Amy Johnson?"

"Didn't they both disappear?"

*Smart ass.* "They were braver than you and I will ever be. They were basically flying wooden crates with lawn-mower engines. Women are actually the best pilots. No macho or ego gets in the way of the job. And if it's the same one that brought me here, I'd wish her in the cockpit of every plane I ever flew in."

---

AFTER NEGOTIATING a multi-lane toll station to get onto the main highway, Jacob wasted no time donning the fake beard. The quality was excellent: not even Irina would believe he hadn't grown it out naturally. Windows tinted to within an inch of legality made the task of putting it on a less nerve-wracking experience, as did the relative sparseness of Bogotá traffic at 6:00 a.m.

Five miles beyond the city limits, Mateo swore as they were confronted by a police check. Jacob was getting sick of these stops; there were stricter government controls in Colombia than in authoritarian Russia. Luckily, Mateo's ID that showed him as an employee of Uncle Sam got them in a cooperative mood. To Jacob's surprise, Mateo transformed from the shy and quiet type into an animated talker. He laughed and shared a couple of jokes with the cops, explained that Jacob was the important American businessman Carlos Iglesias on his way to conduct important trade talks with the Tunja chamber of commerce.

"No offence, Señor Iglesias," said the younger of the two officers, regarding Jacob through the passenger-side window. "But my commanding officer over there"—he jerked his head toward the overweight, middle-aged lieutenant on the opposite side of the car —"is testing me in the field. I only just graduated the academy, you see, and I'm under the microscope." He lowered his tone. "You're probably aware there was a serious shooting in the city yesterday, and the chief of police has been cracking the whip. I promise, this won't take a minute."

Jacob nonchalantly shifted his sunglasses onto the top of his head and handed over his fake passport. "You're doing a great job," he said, ensuring to maintain his twangy American accent as he spoke Spanish. "I'm lucky not to get tasered by a cop just for jay-walking back in New York. So it's a treat for me to come across such a well-mannered person in uniform."

The young man blushed and stammered something unintelligible. He glanced at the passport, studied it for a moment, then looked back to Jacob. A frown furrowed his brow, and for a second, Jacob's heart was in his mouth. No doubt he'd been shown the drawing of the fake police officer. Then the frown straightened out before forming a smile. He tapped the cover of the passport as he handed it back. "I really like the beard you've grown since that photo was taken. Makes you look very distinguished."

Jacob heard the commanding officer sigh deeply as his charge fawned to the foreign guest. "Basta, Diego," he growled. "The man's probably thinking you want to ask him out on a damned date. Let's allow these good people to continue their journey without getting their buttholes licked clean."

Mateo burst out laughing. "Good one!"

The young cop looked down at the ground, perhaps seeking a hole to crawl into. Jacob reassured him. "It's all right, Diego. Keep up the good work."

The rest of the journey to the ancient city of Tunja was uneventful. The Jeep gobbled up the road, handling the continual climb toward the elevation of around 9,000 feet above sea level with ease. The numerous brave cyclists ascending the mountain had a much tougher task; Jacob imagined their thighs would be jelly at the end of the ride. If he'd had more time up his sleeve, this attractive and reputedly very safe (by Mexican standards) city would have been perfect for relaxing sightseeing.

But not today.

Today he had a plane to catch.

Some manly charm from Mateo to a middle-aged female airport official wearing an outmoded perm was all it took to clear a path. *The man's a chameleon*, Jacob observed: from barely a word to talkative and now positively garrulous. Skipping the line thanks to Mateo's magic, Jacob shoved his passport under the barrier. The customs official flashed a genial grin before going clack-clack with his trusty stamp. Within minutes, Jacob was striding across the tarmac, up the stairs, and back into the private jet.

Once the attendant had ensured Jacob was comfortable in his seat, a familiar voice jolted him from his contemplative state as he stared out the window. "Señor Iglesias," she said in her rounded British vowels. "I didn't expect to see you again so soon."

"Neither did I," he said.

"Mexico this time, huh?"

"My job takes me to the most unexpected of places," he laughed. "Much like yours, I guess."

"Indeed. However, I've been warned not to ask you too many questions. Not even about the instant beard, because–"

"Because if I told you, I'd have to kill you." He kept his voice low and made a firing-a-pistol gesture with thumb and forefinger.

She tipped him a salute and headed for the cockpit, a little extra zing in her step.

"Only kidding," he called in her wake, fearing she'd taken his joke literally.

"I know!" she said but didn't turn around to look at him before opening the cockpit door.

Looking out across the barren hills, he sensed a yearning for Irina that made his heart ache. Things had been developing so fast, he's only been thinking about her in terms of her utility to the operation. Analyzing data, checking information. She'd be at her desk at the bank now. He called her number.

"Zaichik!" she exclaimed. "Are you okay? What's happening?"

She spoke in Russian, her previous commitment to the language of her adoptive country forgotten for the moment.

"I'm fine. On a plane, about to take off."

"You coming home?" She sounded hopeful.

"Not yet. Still got things to do."

"Damn. I miss you, even though it's only been a couple of days."

He watched people, small as ants behind the glass of the terminal, wondering how many were cursing him for the special treatment he got. "I miss you, too. And I've got good news."

He heard the sounds of a busy office in the background: snatches of conversation and laughter, electronic equipment. "Can you be quick, zaichik? I've got a planning meeting in ten minutes." She lowered her voice. "I think I might be in line for a special appointment." There was sunshine in her voice.

"I need you to help me out on this case."

"Aha!" Her cry was an obvious 'I-told-you-so.' Her way of saying *you can't get things done without me*. And she'd be right in thinking that way. "So much for keeping it all secret."

He smiled but wouldn't rise to the bait. "Fletcher's going to call you when a special delivery arrives. I've got my fingers crossed it will be tonight, but there's always a chance of a delay."

"What should I say to him when he calls?"

"Nothing. He'll give you instructions, probably send a car to bring you to Tribeca."

"Jacob," she whispered. "I'm dying of curiosity."

The turbo engines began to whir; soon he'd be in the air. The flight to Chiapas in Mexico would only take about two and a half hours. "I can't tell you any more details. Suffice to say, I'll need you to put your analytical hat on."

"I can't wait." He could almost picture her rubbing her hands together in excited anticipation.

"How's Vova doing? Any update on what the school is going to do about the bullying?" He wanted to hear that she'd decided he was right and it was time to move to the countryside.

"Um, I gotta go. Everyone's heading for the meeting." It was a topic she was anxious to avoid. And she was doing it again. That damned pride of hers about her job meant she'd be staying in NYC for the time being.

"I'll call you when I land. Around 3:00 p.m. your time. Good luck on getting that appointment."

"Bah. It's nothing special."

"Come on, what is it? You sounded pretty excited about it a minute ago."

"You know what, Yakov? If you can have secrets, so can I."

*Touché*, he thought as he told her he loved her before reluctantly disconnecting the call. He could not argue with that.

---

AN HOUR LATER, with the plane carving up clouds, he could barely concentrate on the background information on his destination, the Mexican state of Chiapas. Two women occupied his mind: Irina and Carmen Hererra.

And, if he was going to be totally honest with himself, Carmen was dominating his thoughts. Not because of a misplaced romantic attraction; there was none. He genuinely feared for her on many levels. Her mental and emotional health, but even more, her physical safety. Whoever had snatched Brohman and killed Miguel—and after his pow-wow with Zapata he was almost certain Adolfo Sanchez was behind the crimes—could be watching Carmen closely, too. Had someone followed her to the Parque República de Portugal last night?

Then there was her boss. Jacob's gut told him Stynes was an idiot, but worse than that, he lacked the number-one quality a man in his position needs. People skills. But he was almost certainly no mole. The traitor was working under him, though, and now Jacob was throwing Carmen back into the lion's den. If this mission ended in success but something bad happened to

Carmen along the way, he'd be blaming himself for the rest of his life.

He made the promised call to Stynes. "Jim. Carlos Iglesias. "

"Yes?" It was clear by the tone of his voice that 'Carlos' was the last person in the world Stynes wanted to talk to.

"I'm calling to let you know that Carmen's not coming into the office today. She's had some rather shocking news. She needs a day or two to get over it."

"Oh my God. What's happened? Is she sick?" The man sounded worried. Jacob didn't buy it; it was a superficial concern.

"As you're probably aware, her brother's gone missing."

"Yes, I know. She's very worried. But the kid's been known to take off at a moment's notice. He likes to surf up north, where it's warmer. Can't say I blame him."

"I don't think he's gone surfing."

"No?"

"I think something terrible has happened to him." *Stay close to the truth without giving the game away.* "Carmen heard a rumor he's been kidnapped by the cartel, and she's not handling it well."

"What rumor? Where did she hear it?"

"I'm chasing up some leads. I'll let you know if I find anything. In the meantime, do not harass Carmen. Understood?" He hung up before Stynes could reply. Let him stew.

# TWENTY

Mexico was a place he was quite familiar with, having run a handful of missions there over the last five years or so. But they were all in the northern and central parts of the country. The deep south remained an exotic mystery. But this was where he needed to start looking.

According to old man Zapata, whose enmity for Sanchez thankfully outweighed his fear of the man, the key to finding Sanchez was via the man's mother. The old dear was supposedly residing in a care facility in this part of Mexico. A long way from Sanchez's home turf, but it made sense. The state of Chiapas was rich in rugged terrain, mountains and heavily forested territory. Thick jungle where a sharp machete was as important for hiking as a compass. The perfect place for Sanchez to set up a base. And to hide away his dear old mom.

Another regional airport, another round of formalities to go through. He was heartily sick of the constant changes of environment: something told him this would not be the last stage of the journey. Jacob's heart leapt into his mouth as he approached the scanner, suddenly realizing he had no special status here. If they found his guns, they'd arrest him on the spot. He dropped the heavy bag and slung it over the other shoulder, ready to head back to a bathroom and reluctantly part ways with his pistols. Out of the corner of his eye, he saw the words he could only have wished for. He smiled in disbelief when he saw the handwritten signs taped to the two scanning machines: *Fuera de servicio.* Out of order.

As he stood close behind a young woman bobbing her head to music pouring through headphones, Jacob observed how the passengers were being processed. In one line, an obese airport employee stopped and patted down every tenth or so person. Her sidekick in the second line peeked into random bags; however, he too showed little enthusiasm for his work. When it was Jacob's turn, the security guard's expression changed: the raised eyebrows and slight tilt of the head told Jacob the woman was simply checking him out as a male specimen. She gave a sultry smile that boosted her attractiveness and wished him a nice day.

At a bureau de change, he swapped a couple hundred US dollars for local currency, purchased a local SIM card, a cheap burner, and a fold-out map of the region, plus a bigger one of the entire country. He had plenty of resources downloaded onto his primary phone and electronic notebook, but, as he knew well from experience, you can't beat hard copies for those times when technology fails. At the last second, he bought a bottle of chilled water: it was going to be mighty hot out on the streets.

With no checked luggage to retrieve from the carousel, he headed for the nearest bathroom in the arrivals hall, waiting for two other men to leave. With the mercury outside through the roof, he decided to ditch the fake beard. The odds of anyone in this backwater having seen the drawing from reports about the Bogotá shooting was infinitesimal.

He exited the automatic doors of the Tuxtla Gutiérrez International Airport, whistling as he appreciated the 85-degree temperature against his skin. After the chill of Bogotá, it felt way more brutal than warm; the fingers of his right hand clumsily undid the top button of his collared shirt as the high humidity kicked in. Shielding his eyes from the blazing sun, he scanned the long line of taxis. Someone had been ordered to pick him up, but no candidates stood out among the crowd. Due to some choppy weather at altitude, Cynthia hadn't been able to get the Gulf Stream on the ground at the estimated time. Another thirty minutes had been added to the flight. *So sorry*, she said. *I hate not getting my passengers to their destinations on time.* Jacob consoled her with the truism: *Better late than crashing*. Maybe the driver didn't share that philosophy and took off when his passenger didn't show up on time.

A man in a broad-brimmed cowboy hat puffing away on a rancid roll-up cigarette you could smell from a distance of a hundred yards caught Jacob's eye for a moment. A wave and a smile in his direction and Jacob picked up the pace, smiling back amiably. The stench in the taxi would be hard to cope with, but not as hard as the heat and humidity. He was soon overtaken by a running woman who dragged along two small children. The reunited family kissed and embraced like they hadn't seen each other for years and then walked away toward the parking lot. Jacob grimaced. Someone had fucked up, and now he was stranded with no ride into town.

Nothing for it but to grit one's teeth and join the line with the common folk. The line seemed to crawl, little shuffles of a couple of inches, then a stop. When he finally got to the head of the line, his armpits were drenched, sweat dripping from every pore on his head.

"Adónde, amigo? *Where to, buddy*?"

"No se. *I don't know*. Just head for the center." He placed the bags by his side in the back seat and greedily sucked on the water bottle. The air conditioning in the late model Toyota was cranked up high. Bliss. It was twenty miles to the city, plenty of time to cool down, but also to bend the driver's ear for local tips.

"Bien. You are the boss!" The man, who reeked of stale body odor, took off gently before accelerating like an F1 driver with a lap to go in the race. Jacob had traveled around the world enough not to comment on the driving culture of other countries. Rubbing his neck, he turned and looked back, the gleaming glass and white-metal terminal building impressive for what he was expecting to be a backwater of a place.

"Can you recommend a decent hotel to stay at?" For once, Jacob was glad little had been planned in advance, mainly due to the rapidly evolving situation. The only booking had been the no-show driver, organized, once again hopelessly, by Fletcher's useless secretary. Perhaps it was a blessing in disguise. He was beginning to think that playing everything by ear from now on was going to be the best way forward. Harder for enemies to intercept information on itineraries, people, and locations. After being jumped only minutes into his stay in Colombia, and then the brazen broad-daylight slaughter of Gilberto and Ricardo, he believed that he had been closely watched. He was sure his cover was intact, but the persona of Carlos Iglesias was attracting attention he didn't want.

"It depends, señor. Hey, your Spanish is pretty good for a gringo."

"Gracias. Now about the hotel?"

"How much money you got?"

Jacob laughed. "You gonna get your friends to rob me when I tell you I got a bundle?"

The cabbie thought this was the greatest joke he'd ever heard, leaving Jacob wishing he had a pair of earplugs as the laughter boomed off the windows. "No," he snickered. "Tuxtla is not dangerous like Mexico City. I mean there's all kinds of accommodation here. Cheap, mid-range, expensive. You got a nice suit on, so I guess you want a fancy hotel?"

"That's where you're wrong. The suit's borrowed. I needed it for a court appearance." He'd eagerly changed out of the skater gear in the Gulf Stream, but he'd kept hold of it. An accidental disguise that was probably the equal of anything the tech team could invent. "The court case didn't go my way. It's always the women winning, am I right?"

"Si, señor."

"Now I'm running away from my Colombian wife and her greedy lawyers, looking to make a new start in Mexico, transfer my money to a Mexican bank. But first I need somewhere to put my head down. I'm looking for a modest place that's clean, near the city so I can hop on a bus out of town if I have to."

The driver nodded, lips pursed seriously, as if he understood this scenario of domestic disaster all too well. His words confirmed it. He pointed as his chest. "Me? Also divorced. Three times. And poorer after each round. But you did the right thing coming to Mexico, señor. It's a great place to hide away and never be found."

"Great." Those were exactly the words Jacob wanted to hear and, paradoxically, didn't want to hear. Hiding himself from tails — positive. Sanchez bunkering down somewhere no one could ever find him— a big fucking negative.

"Listen," said the driver cheerily. "My cousin, Manuel, he has a small hotel in town. Not right in the center, but it's nice and quiet. Safe, too." He let rip with a long chuckle. "Believe it or not, that cheap-ass cabrón even has Wi-Fi there for his guests to use." More sniggering. "Sometimes I park outside his premises, log on, and watch soccer videos."

Jacob's internal alarm bells would normally be going off like there was a terrorist attack happening, but not this time. He glanced at the driver's photograph under the rearview mirror. Justino Aguilera. Middle-aged, weathered face, twinkle of mischief in the eye. Gone slightly to flab around the belly. Everyone's favorite uncle. He was blathering on with so much mundane detail he had to be on the level. "How much does he charge for a room?"

An exaggerated shrug with hands off the wheel but foot still firmly grinding into the gas pedal. "I have no idea. Want me to call him and ask?"

"You know what, Justino? Just take me there. If I don't like it, we can try somewhere else. Don't turn off the meter until I'm done negotiating a fair price with Manuel."

"As you wish."

---

The resemblance was strong. Same hooded, hazel eyes, even the slight hook in the nose. He also shared the same ebullient personality. He talked up the qualities of the hotel like he was trying to sell the entire establishment. "We aren't on any of those big aggregate websites," he declared. "No need because we have such a good reputation in the tourism industry. Most of our guests are from nearby towns and villages, coming into Tuxtla on business. To complain to city hall about the state of the roads, ha ha! And, if you ask me–"

"I have to stop you there, Manuel."

"Oh, I'm sorry. I do tend to ramble. You were asking about price? For an extended stay, say, one month, I can offer you 420 pesos per night. Is that okay with you?"

Jacob puffed out his cheeks, pretending to be concerned by the exorbitant cost, which was only about the equivalent of $25. If he got lucky, he'd only be here for a short while, but cultivating the owner made sense. "I don't know. You see, my wife's extorting me and..." He folded his arms across his chest and sighed. "I've got plenty of savings, but they are not infinite, if you get my meaning. I'll have to start looking for a job."

"Tell you what, I'll knock it down to 400 even."

A quick handshake sealed the deal.

"What kind of work are you looking for?"

Jacob winked and said, "The kind that pays well."

Manuel slapped him on the shoulder and said, "You and I will get along perfectly!"

The room was small but not cramped, clean but not spotless. Well worth the modest tariff, which he paid in cash. He checked the Wi-Fi signal, excellent. A sign on the door provided the longest passcode he'd ever seen— the maximum possible 63 characters. He took his time to get the code correct and logged his burner smart phone onto the network. He then searched the Internet for care homes for the elderly in the region of Tuxtla. To his surprise, there were a good many of them. Question was, which one was Mamma Sanchez in?

# TWENTY-ONE

"THE ROOM IS PERFECT," JACOB ENTHUSED. "I couldn't have asked for better."

Manuel was fussing about with paperwork behind the reception counter, a small electric fan blowing gently onto the back of his head. He looked up and beamed at his new guest. "I'm so glad, Señor Iglesias. Anything I can help you with, don't hesitate to yell out. Oh." He rummaged about in his pants pockets and extracted a business card. "Here's my contact details. I live on the ground floor with my wife." He pointed at a green door bearing a black number 01 on it. "But we don't go to bed until very late most nights. Just call my number or knock on the door. Doesn't matter what time."

The images and figurines of Jesus and Mary spread all over the small lobby instilled a sense of peace in Jacob. On a shelf behind him was an enormous leather-bound Bible. The religious paraphernalia pointed to a possible reason why Manuel was being so helpful, even though Jacob had talked him down on the rate. Manuel was a true man of God. Maybe Jacob could leverage those Christian values to track down Sanchez's mother. "Thanks for the offer, but I promise I won't be bothering you with my dramas."

"Look, I can see you're going through tough times. My cousin couldn't help himself. He probably shouldn't have, but he told me about your marriage problems."

Jacob leaned on the counter, screwed up his lips, then said, "Ten years of happiness down the drain. I wish..."

"You wish what, Señor Iglesias?"

"No." He shook his head slowly. "This is my mess. I have to sort it out."

Manuel closed the cover of a big black book; Jacob noticed the lack of modern equipment in the reception area. Good old-fashioned registers and accounts ledgers. "The family unit is the most important thing society has, the foundation stone. We must do everything we can to stop that wonderful institution from being eroded. Do you have children?"

He nodded. "One daughter. Carmen." He winced as he used the first name that popped into his head. "She's a sensitive soul." Lying to a decent, devout man like this would require much seeking of forgiveness later. Although a believer of sorts, Jacob was by no means religious. His prayers for the men he killed were genuine enough. He summoned the memory of the last time he dispatched an enemy and ask the Lord to forgive him, hoping it would give him an air of piousness. "What you say about family is true. I should try to find a way to patch things up."

"Si! Exactamente. That's the spirit."

"I'll call my wife later tonight, see if she'll listen to me."

"Speak with your heart." Manuel melodramatically touched his breastbone. "God will do the rest."

"You sure?"

"Por supuesto. *Of course.*" He beckoned his new guest to come closer to the Perspex pane. "Later tonight, we can take a walk to the local church, light some candles, and ask for guidance. Would you like to do that?"

"Oh, yes!" Jacob tapped the wooden counter. "But right now, I need to earn some pesos so I can pay my way. If I don't find a job, my small savings will soon dwindle away. Can you point me in the direction of the nearest labor hire company?"

Manuel scribbled an address on a piece of paper. "This firm is always looking for farmworkers. But"—he made a face like he'd sucked a lemon—"a gringo like you might find it a bit...weird. You arrived here in a suit, not overalls."

"A borrowed one, like I told your cousin." Jacob shrugged. "Anyway, I have no pride when it comes to work. I've had jobs in offices, factories, you name it." He went to the doorway, his stomach screaming for something to eat, then turned around as if he'd just remembered something vitally important. "Actually, I forgot to say. The main reason I came to Tuxtla, of all places, is because my wife's mother is here."

"What?"

"Yes. You must have known, instinctively, that I wanted to get back with my wife"—he searched his brain for a name—"... Juanita."

"How could I have known that? You overestimate my abilities, my friend."

Jacob held up a clenched hand. "No. You have a gift. I can feel it. Anyway, I'm here to talk to Juanita's mamma, Maria, to see if she can talk sense into her stubborn daughter."

Manuel scratched his stubbly beard for a moment. "So go there now! You can look for work later. Perhaps if you sort out your relationship, you can go back to your old life in Colombia."

Jacob affected a look of exasperation. He sighed and said, "That's the problem. I don't know exactly where she is. All I know is that she's in some kind of care facility. Juanita refuses to tell me which one."

"Why don't you try them all until you find the right place?"

"I'm worried if I make enquiries, word will get to Juanita, and she'll think I'm a stalker or something."

Manuel stepped out of his booth and called his wife to substitute for him for a while. "Let's walk. Maybe together we can come up with some ideas."

Out in the steamy midday weather, delicious odors of cooking food wafted from restaurants, triggering a flood of saliva inside

Jacob's mouth. "Listen, Manuel. How about I treat you to some tacos or something? For being so kind."

The godly landlord would have none of it, insisting he be the one to pay for lunch. Jacob humbly accepted, making a mental note to repay the man, with interest, once he got back stateside. Inside a small cantina, chowing down on delicious burritos with beef and refried black beans, Jacob formulated a plan and somehow made Manuel think that *he'd* thought of it.

But first, they had to go back to the hotel and print out some documents.

"You do have a printer, don't you?" said Jacob hopefully.

"Por supuesto! Ah, I think my wife knows how to operate it."

"Excellente. Let's go."

# TWENTY-TWO

He leaned up against the brick garden wall of the Villa Serenidad, the oppressive sun shaded by an enormous old jacaranda tree. The lush gardens of the casa geriátrica boasted masses of orange and red geraniums, azaleas and, as Jacob would have expected in this country, flowering cactus with evil-looking thorns.

He flicked through his phone to kill time, wondering whether the Wi-Fi signal from the casa geriátrica reached the perimeter of the facility. It did, but it also required a password to use it. With no data on his local SIM, the phone went back in his pocket. Nothing for it but to wait.

As more minutes dragged by, he began to worry Manuel had been rumbled. He shifted to a wooden bench seat, where he sucked greedily on a bottle of water. He smiled at a couple of visitors coming along the path toward him, pushing their elderly relatives in wheelchairs. The residents wore vacant stares. He prayed Maria was a bit livelier than that. If she was even here. They had already canvassed seven care homes. This was the second-last one in the area. Jacob had a good feeling: this one, from the outside at least, was far superior in quality to the others they'd visited.

Adolfo Sanchez would surely spend whatever it took for his dear old mom to get the best possible accommodation.

As the tide continued to go out on Jacob's bottle of ever-warming water, Manuel's smiling face appeared at the end of the pathway. He ambled up with a rolling gait, nodding as he got closer.

"And?"

"You can go and see her."

"The administration was okay with it?" Jacob cleared his throat. "With the scenario you so cleverly came up with?"

"Si. Like we agreed, I told the manager we were sent by the government to urgently check out their security protocols and that my boss would be along shortly. I said there was an identified threat to a very important resident, the mother of a client who paid them extra. You know, you must have been right about your wife Juanita spoiling her mom because the manager's eyes lit up, and she said *I know exactly who you are talking about.*" He looked up at the sky and closed his eyes. "Dear Lord, this is to help reunite Carlos with his wife. Forgive me for deceiving the manager of this facility."

Jacob slapped him on the shoulder. "That's what I like about Catholicism. The ability to ask for forgiveness when you commit a sin."

"Hmmm," muttered Manuel. "It's not something to be taken advantage of, you know. Only for emergencies."

"Oh, yes. Of course. My bad. But like you said, this is an emergency."

"You want me to come with you?" said Manuel, his tone leaving no doubt he wanted nothing to do with this subversion while 'Carlos' did his thing.

"No, it's okay, I can manage on my own. I was an actor in amateur productions back in America." He rolled his shoulders like a boxer before a bout. "I just hope Maria doesn't get mad when she sees me. She's so close to Juanita and...anyway...wish me luck!"

"Buena suerte!"

---

WITH MANUEL SITTING in Justino's taxi around the corner, Jacob took a deep breath, tightened his necktie, and marched up the path. Tucked under his arm were hastily typed sheets of paper, peppered with gobbledygook taken straight from the Internet.

A reception committee welcomed him at the door. Jacob thrust out his clammy palm; an attractive woman in a crisp white blouse and tight-fitting pencil dress shook it.

"Carlos Iglesias, chief of logistics at Protección Total Seguridad." No American twang anymore; his made his accent sound like he had been born and raised in Mexico and had never left. "We contract to the Mexican government at the federal and state level."

"Margarita Alvarez," she said in a halting voice. "I've never heard of your company. We deal with another one, have done for many years. Fortaleza Segura is the top agency in the state of Chiapas."

"We are a semi-autonomous government agency."

"A what? Where is your identification?"

He was ready for this, but it could get ugly if she was a hard-ass. "Here's an official letter from the highest authority, the Ministry of Public Security. It demands you grant me access to every part of this facility and states that any obstruction from you will be looked upon very unfavorably." Jacob pulled out a piece of paper bearing the letterhead of a fake government department and the Mexican coat of arms. She read it thoroughly and, seemingly convinced of its authenticity, handed it back to Jacob, who returned it hastily to the folder. "The company you refer to has been under investigation for several months," he said. "Faulty and unreliable equipment, mainly, but there have been all kinds of breaches."

"We've had no problems that I can recall," she said a little unsurely. He breathed an inward sigh of relief. She was no hard-ass. Continued alpha male behavior by him should keep her compliant, but in this game there were no guarantees.

"Aha. But you wouldn't necessarily know about any problems. A lot of stuff happens in the background, so to speak. The alarm systems, for example, send regular signals back to the security company's base to show that the units are functioning. Our audits show that this has not been happening in the proper manner. Which means someone could break in and murder all the residents, and no one would know until the next morning."

"Dios mío. *My God*," she muttered. "I had no idea."

"Indeed you didn't." He flashed a sarcastic grin. "And that's just the tip of the iceberg, I'm afraid. There are also clouds over the company in terms of embezzlement by senior staff. It's possible we will have to shut them down. People may go to prison."

"Are you sure there hasn't been some kind of mistake?" He looked down to see her hands shaking by her sides.

"None whatsoever." He smiled like a complete smart-ass. "I'm the one heading up the investigation." He pulled the folders close against his chest, like he was protecting his young. "It would be in your best interests, and those of every resident in this home, that you grant me unrestricted access to every inch of the place."

"Would you like a cup of coffee first?" Now she seemed intent on ingratiating herself. Jacob's initial thought was that Alvarez herself might be up to a spot of small-scale larceny, ripping off the home. He thought he'd test that theory.

"No thank you. I might also be sending a financial auditor to look at your books. So I'd ask you to be prepared to hand those records over, too."

A look of abject terror froze her expression. "Um...Okay," she said slowly. "Please follow me."

She led him down a corridor, past a noisy kitchen, to a utilities room. Inside was the back end of a security system Jacob was totally unfamiliar with. There were keypads and a couple of CCTV monitors flashing red and green lights reminiscent of an Internet router. "If you don't mind, I'd like to run some checks on this equipment."

She stood in the threshold, watching closely. "Be my guest."

"I'd prefer not to have you gawking at me. I need to check the codes and settings for all the sensors, the calibrations and configurations." The randomly chosen geek-speak seemed to be having the desired effect on Alvarez, who was quickly uncrossing her arms. "To do this job properly, I have to focus like a brain surgeon. Any mistakes, and the entire trip will have been a waste of time. And I'd hate to have to put your name in my report to the minister of public security and say that you didn't comply with my requests."

"I understand. I...I'll wait in my office, shall I?"

"I think that's a brilliant idea. This shouldn't take too long."

He waited inside patiently for five minutes, going over in his mind how he was going to approach the meeting with Sanchez's mother. It largely depended on her mental faculties. The more feeble, the better. He checked his watch. Time enough. One last important job: he erased all footage the external and internal security cameras had taken today, then switched the cameras off altogether. He returned to the manager's office, making sure his footfalls were heavy. He'd thought about straight-up demanding to see Maria first, but for the charade to be as authentic as possible, he knew he mustn't rush or act recklessly.

After a tap on Alvarez's door that was more like a bash, he heard a chair scrape; he'd startled her. Excellent. "Come in," she said meekly.

"As I suspected, not functioning properly. I'll be sending a technician to recalibrate the motions detectors, which aren't working to their full capacity. Your current security company will be issued with an official warning in terms of their substandard equipment."

She nodded, rolling her fingers in her lap. Clearly, she was worried about the potential for an upcoming financial audit. "You mentioned a coffee before?" said Jacob, who realized a strong brew wouldn't go astray.

"Yes, of course. I'll go and get us one."

She returned with two shots of espresso the thickness of mud. "If you don't mind, I'd like to take mine in the company of Señora Maria Sanchez. And organize for something special to be brought for her, too, please. I've got a feeling she's going to be a little upset when she hears the news."

"Oh, yes! Of course. Your colleague mentioned she might be" —she whispered the next part—"under some kind of threat?"

"It's a very real concern. Her son is an outlaw; however, his mother is innocent. We've had word a Colombian cartel is looking to kidnap her and demand that her son pay a huge ransom and desist from his own activities or his mother will be killed."

"Oh dear." Alvarez looked like she was about to faint. "That's terrible!"

"And for that reason, we need to evacuate Señora Sanchez to a secure government facility." Jacob chewed the inside of his cheek for a moment. "In fact, we also know the owners of Villa Serenidad— your employers— have been taking kickbacks to hide the source of payments for Señora Sanchez's accommodation here."

"That's got nothing to do with me," Alvarez protested.

"Of course not," Jacob consoled. "You just work here, right?"

A vigorous nod. "Si! I know nothing about where the money comes from..."

"Even though you are...and it's even on your nametag...the manager?"

Her mouth opened and closed like one of Grant Fletcher's precious aquarium fish. Jacob touched her lightly on the forearm. "Listen. For now, all I want to do is have a chat with old Maria, give her fair warning that we are going to move her from here to a safer location later in the week. It's only fair she hears it now so she's not frightened when the van rolls in on Friday to whisk her away. Don't you agree?"

Again, Alvarez could only communicate by nodding.

"Muy bien. *Very good.*" He stood and gestured toward the door. "Let's go."

---

HIS PHONE LAY on the small wooden table in Maria's kitchenette, switched on to capture her every word. "What do you mean I have to leave? I love it here."

"We understand your reluctance to move out, Señora Sanchez, but it's a matter of your safety. If we can establish later that it is again safe for you to return, then you certainly can. For now, though, even your son mustn't know about this." He set his small china cup next to his bogus paperwork, crossed his legs, and then steepled his fingers. Despite manufacturing a calm façade, his heart thumped. Surely Alvarez would get curious, make some phone calls, search the Internet, and find out his entire story was hogwash. With every passing minute, the risk the penny would drop increased. He had to get the job done, and fast.

"Mi hijo? My son? What does he have to do with it?" The old lady's voice was strong and steady. The skin was only mottled slightly on her hands; on her largely smooth and ruddy face only a couple of thin crow's feet. Her sparkling violet eyes bespoke of a woman with her faculties well and truly intact. As did the almost completed 1,000-piece jigsaw puzzle and selection of crossword books on a shelf. Not what he was hoping for.

Did she even know what her precious son was involved in? "There are rumors that Adolfo has made some enemies in recent years. These are evil people, and we have obtained intelligence that they are planning to launch an assault on this rest home and kidnap you. They are prepared to kill anyone who gets in their way."

"But my son is a good boy. He was a wild one in his youth, I'll admit. But not anymore. Why would anyone...?"

This was the chance. Get her talking, record as much of her voice as possible. "What can you tell me about Adolfo? Do you know where we can find him? The government would like to offer him the same kind of protection we are extending to you."

She coughed into a lace handkerchief, the rattling sound of her lungs the first indicator that this was an old person. She wasn't doing herself any favors: on a coffee table in front of the television lay a packet of Marlboros and an ashtray with six lipstick-ringed cigarette butts. According to Zapata, she'd given birth to Adolfo when she was 46 years old, which meant she must be 81 now, give or take a year or two.

"He's the best son a mother could hope for. He took me from the noise and the filth of Mexico City and brought me to live in this peaceful, tropical paradise. Sadly, because of the nature of his work, I'm not able to say for certain where he is. I haven't even laid eyes on him myself since 2019."

There was a quiver in her bottom lip, then a prolonged look up and to the left. Was it a tell? Was she lying? Common wisdom said that she was; then Jacob remembered a psychological study he'd read. It dispelled the myth, proving that 70 percent of liars actually held eye contact with the person they were deceiving.

Press on.

"And what do you believe the nature of his work is, Señora Sanchez?"

"I don't believe. I know. He's in the military. Special forces." A deep maternal pride sounded through her words, her eyes glinting with moisture. "They get shipped from place to place. Last I heard from him, he was on a training mission out in the desert."

The conversation was interrupted when a young woman brought in a tray of tea and cookies. Maria thanked the woman as Jacob poured from the teapot.

"Hmmm. Special forces, you say? Do you have any photos of Adolfo in his uniform?"

She shook her head before taking a noisy slurp. "Oh, no. I've only got photos of when he was a boy. Nothing current. It's sad for me, but his army unit is top secret." She touched the side of her nose. "All I know is they must pay him well, because I get everything I need here. Back in the capital, we lived very poor. You know"—she dropped her voice so low there was no way Jacob's phone would pick it up—"things were so desperate that sometimes he had to sell drugs just so we had enough to eat. But he stopped all that so he could join the army."

"Very admirable." He picked up his phone and turned off the voice recorder app. He had enough audio material now. "If you don't mind, I'd like to take a picture of you to prove to my bosses that I actually came to see you. They are very demanding."

She frowned. "Are you sure it's necessary?"

"Absolutely."

The old woman reluctantly posed, even put on a smile as he snapped off six shots. "That's wonderful," he said, overegging it a little. "Gracias."

She gripped the armrests of her recliner and stood on a pair of wonky legs. "I apologize. This tea has an immediate effect on me. Please, I won't be a moment."

"Of course."

This was his chance. She moved slowly toward a corridor, presumably leading to a bathroom. He heard a door close, and he was up on his feet.

First, he removed the SIM from Maria's phone and stuck it in his pocket. Next, he began rifling through drawers. A chestnut dresser displaying decorative plates contained a treasure trove of letters and cards. He heard a toilet flush just as his eyes descended upon a small, black leather-bound address book.

Indexed alphabetically. Jacob was delighted the man's mother had named her son Adolfo.

And there it was, the prize he sought. In neat, feminine handwriting, Adolfo Sanchez's Mexican cell phone number, as well as a Colombian one. No physical addresses, but a post office box in Ocosingo, wherever that was. He memorized the numbers, but just in case he fished out his cell and captured a close-up image of the page. No, that wasn't enough. He tore the page out of the book. If the numbers were written down, that could mean the old woman hadn't memorized them. The chances of her contacting her son and vice versa were now greatly reduced.

"What day will they come for me? I need to say good-bye to my friends," said Maria as she entered the living room, tears in her eyes. She smoothed down the front of her dress and resumed her seat. Jacob pushed a box of tissue towards her; she plucked one and dabbed away the tears.

"You're not going to believe this, Señora Sanchez," said Jacob, rising from his seat. "But I've just received a text message from my boss. It appears the information we had was completely wrong. You are not in any danger here at all. Someone's going to be in big trouble at the office!"

Maria's body visibly relaxed as she sank into her plush armchair recliner. "Oh, my. That is good news."

"The best." Jacob smiled warmly, gathered his props, said good-bye, and headed for the exit. "You can relax in the knowledge that you are in good hands here."

Gripping the push bar on the door leading to the garden path, he heard Alvarez behind him, calling his name. "I'd like a word before you go, Señor Iglesias, if you don't mind."

She'd rumbled him but spoke in a way so as not to scare him off. Jacob saw through it, waved his hand at her backwards, and said, "No time. Adios!"

# TWENTY-THREE

"Did that work out the way you wanted?" Manuel sat in the front passenger seat, licking a dripping chocolate ice-cream; his brother was behind the wheel, scrolling through his cell phone. It looked like Instagram photographs of ornate wedding cakes. You never know what people are into, Jacob mused as he clunked the back door closed.

"Sure did," he said, puffing. "But we gotta go. I think the manager smelled a rat."

"You heard the man, Justino." Manuel tapped his brother on the shoulder. "Put that phone down."

"Juanita will definitely want to talk to me after Maria's given her a call," said Jacob. "I can't thank you enough for your help. You, too, Justino."

The taxi driver twisted his neck, smiling benevolently. "I'm not a devout Christian like my brother, but I also wish you luck." He chuckled. "Even though, personally, I think you'd be better off..."

"Enough!" said Manuel. "You are paid to drive, not offer marriage advice."

"But..."

"But nothing. Vamonos. *Let's go.*"

---

THE FAN-SHAPED Wi-Fi symbol reappeared on the top of his phone's home screen. He attached the images he'd taken on the cell phone and emailed them to Fletcher, then resumed the call. "Did you get that?"

"Wait...yes. It's arrived. What am I looking at here? I don't read Spanish, remember?"

"Gold, Grant, absolute gold. Information you'd never get in a year of surveillance and hacking. Sanchez was a fool making an enemy out of old Felipe Zapata."

"The gas station proprietor?"

"Yep. The old man used to rule the roost back in Mexico City, but Sanchez got all ambitious, took over, and put Zapata in his place. But Zapata knew something vital: the man is a mother's boy. He suggested I try and track down the Cartel Moderno via her. And now we have the best lead so far."

Fletcher cleared his throat. "Are you sure about that? We have, what, a couple of phone numbers and a post office box. What are we going to do with this information? The numbers will likely be as untraceable as Jack the Ripper."

"Correct. No doubt he's chosen providers that offer 100 percent anonymity and all kinds of security features, for both the Mexican and Colombian numbers."

"Can't the respective police forces compel the providers to offer up the information we need?"

With his amateur lawyer's hat on, Jacob said, "Without prima facie evidence that the owner of that cell number has committed a crime, the cops will tell us to fuck off. Besides, we don't get to call the tune with the Colombian and Mexican police. That's for their DAs or whatever the equivalent is."

"Then how do we proceed with this so-called gold?"

"No need for sarcasm, Grant. It is gold, we just have to melt it down give it some shape." Jacob fingered open the venetian blinds in his third floor room and looked down at a couple of kids in shorts and singlets kicking a soccer ball around, bouncing it off the brick wall of a block of apartments. A fat lizard scrambled its way along the wall, eager to get out of the firing line. "We simply send Sanchez a couple of messages."

"What?" There was the sound of a cigar being lit. "We tell him he'd better surrender or else?"

"Not quite. Here's my idea."

As Jacob outlined his scheme, the sounds of the puffs on the Cuban cigar back in Tribeca came thicker and faster. When Jacob had finished speaking, Fletcher said, "You're a damn genius, my boy!"

"Let's not get too ahead of ourselves." He undid his shirt, threw it on the floor, and opened the blinds fully and then the French doors. An afternoon breeze had sprung up; he stood close to the Juliet balcony, letting the air cool his body as it blew over evaporating sweat. "Irina still has to do her thing."

"What about the PO box?"

"My hunch is it belongs to Sanchez. I can't think of any other scenario. The city of Ocosingo isn't far from Tuxtla, where Mom lives. Ninety-four miles by road. If Sanchez collects his mail from Ocosingo, then perhaps his base isn't far away from there either."

"I'm just bringing it up online. Christ, there's a shitload of thick-ass jungle out there. If he's holed up in it, the odds of us finding his hideout aren't good. Needle in a haystack."

"Yes, I've had a quick look, too. The Lacandón jungle is vast. And there are protected areas you'd think were off-limits, but for a criminal like Sanchez, I wouldn't put it past him to pay off government officials to let him build whatever he wanted there. So"—Jacob turned the air-conditioner up; the breeze had died as quickly as it had sprung up. "I suggest we get some remote sensing experts to analyze satellite photos of an area of at least 100 miles radius from Ocosingo."

"Not more?"

"I figure even that's a stretch. How far would you drive to pick up your mail?"

"Not that far!"

"Precisely." Jacob put Fletcher on loud speaker, pulled a fresh T-shirt from his travel bag, and wriggled it on. "Did you receive the parcel from the embassy?"

"Yeah, I got it. Just waiting for Irina to get here so she can trawl through the devices. And create the magic video you told me about. She should have been here twenty minutes ago. I sent a driver over to fetch her from Harlem, but traffic's a bitch."

"Let me know if she finds anything. I'll be looking at Google Earth."

"I thought you wanted to get the experts looking at it?"

"Yeah, but I booked a restaurant for dinner, and I've got two hours to kill. Who knows, I might stumble across something."

Fifteen minutes before Justino was due to pick him up and drive him to a cantina that reputedly made the best tamales in town, Jacob reluctantly threw in the towel. Staring at a bird's eye view of the dense Mexican jungle had yielded precisely zero results.

Still time to call Carmen before heading out.

"How are you?"

"Fine."

"You sure about that?"

She burst into tears. "No. But what can I do?"

He was tempted to tell her to hold out hope. That maybe the images on the camera were fake, set-up shots to make people think Miguel was dead. But, after wracking his brain, he couldn't think of a single legitimate reason Sanchez would do that. Miguel knew too much and they killed him, pure and simple.

"You can take medication to help you get through this. Maybe you should have a talk with your doctor."

She blew her nose like a trumpet. "Sorry." A half-apologetic, forced laugh. "I don't want to turn myself into a zombie. Like you said, I can be your eyes and ears at the office." Her access to sensitive information was limited, but Jacob trusted in the power of HUMINT, the kind he got from Zapata. An incautious word around the water cooler about a colleague, her observation of out-of-character behavior: these things could help turn the tide. Although, he reasoned, her simply having useful jobs to do—even if in vain— at least kept her mind focused on something other than thoughts of her dead brother.

"And that's great. Of course I want you to do that for me. But your mental health right now is paramount. Promise me you'll check in with your doctor before you return to the office."

"I promise."

An hour and thirty minutes later, he tried to push all thoughts about the case from his mind. Not easy to do, but the white noise in his brain had to be let out. The opportunity of a normal dinner with normal people was the release valve. Sitting at the table, where an attentive waiter hovered like a humming bird, and listening to the animated chatter of other diners, he just about managed to achieve his goal.

"A toast to our new friend," said Manuel, raising a glass of red wine. "May he find love again with his estranged wife, Juanita. To Carlos!"

"To Carlos!" echoed across the table.

Jacob felt himself blushing, as if he really were Carlos. The deception perpetrated on these well-meaning folks made him uncomfortable, but looking at it logically, if they never found out the truth, they'd be none the wiser. On the contrary, they'd be filled with that warm feeling kind people get when they help others in need.

In the unexpected good company of Manuel and his wife, Justino, and a flighty woman he'd met on a dating app, Jacob relaxed for the first time in a while. The only thing he cared about right now was getting stuck into the tamales, guacamole, jalapeño poppers and Mexican salad spread out before him. He raised his glass. "To me!"

From two tables across came an almighty BANG! Jacob's heart began to beat at a thousand miles an hours, adrenaline coursing through his veins. His hand reached automatically inside his jacket pocket for his weapon, only there was no jacket. It was hanging over the back of his chair on account of the heat. And he'd left the Glock in his room, knowing it would be on show when he inevitably took off his jacket at the restaurant. He looked around. No gunman, no dead bodies, no panic. Sweat beaded on his brow as he gulped down a glass of water.

"You all right, Carlos?" said Manuel, concern furrowing his brow. "It's just a champagne cork. This isn't Mexico City, you know. Shoot-ups don't happen here."

"I'm sorry. I've spent too long living in Bogotá, my friends. Where shoot-ups happen far too often."

The Mexicans roared with laughter. Jacob tucked a big napkin under his chin and, calm restored, went about eating his meal.

By the time the check came, with Manuel generously taking care of the entire bill, Jacob realized something obvious that had been staring him in the face the entire time. From the moment he set foot in Jim Stynes' office, not one person had stood up and offered him any pro-active assistance in his quest to track Paul Brohman.

Were they all in on it?

# TWENTY-FOUR

JACOB HAD TOLD HER—ON PROMISE OF SECRECY TO THE grave that she never repeat it—that Fletcher liked to take Susan Stonehouse into the back office for extra-curricular activities of an erotic nature. That's why Irina baulked when the Skia boss directed her to do her work there. "Ah, maybe I could stay out here in the open-plan area?"

"Certainly not," Fletcher objected. He pressed a button, and a giant monitor descended from the ceiling. "I'm watching the Jets play tonight."

"Is that more important than helping Jacob success with his mission—whatever it is?"

Sudden understanding drew his lips into a knowing smile. "I can guess what's going on in your head." A waggle of the index finger. "Jacob's told you something about me and Susan, right? I see you're blushing. There's no need, because Susan is not interested in me in the slightest. I think she prefers women over men. I don't know where your boyfriend got this notion, but it's total nonsense."

She sighed, relieved she'd be working in an environment unsullied by bare buttocks, and worse, slapping on tabletops. And she wondered why Jacob had made the claim about his boss: his instincts were generally pretty good. Moreover, Fletcher didn't seem to be lying. "I'll be happy to work wherever you say, Mr. Fletcher."

"Grant, please."

"Sure."

He waved the remote control around like the conductor of a swing orchestra. "Believe me, you will find it a lot more comfortable in the dedicated research room. It's soundproofed, so you won't be disturbed if I start yelling at the players and officials on the screen."

She gave a tiny head shake, finding it hard to believe he could watch a football game when his number-one agent was in the field, crying out for assistance from home.

"There's all kinds of equipment in there that you'll have at your fingertips. Wouldn't you prefer that to dashing in and out of there all night, fetching printouts and whatnot?"

"All night? Nobody said anything about all night." She readjusted the bag hanging over her right shoulder. "And what exactly is my job? I'm in the dark here. Jacob didn't give me any specific details."

"In a nutshell, we want you to look for clues that will help us track down whoever is involved in the kidnapping of a US citizen from Bogotá, Colombia."

"What kind of clues?"

He shrugged his broad shoulders. "That's the thing. We don't know. Now Jacob might give you the impression I'm a dull-headed bureaucrat— and sometimes that might be true— but I'm pretty good at summarizing information to make it more digestible." He handed her a manila folder. "Shouldn't take you more than fifteen minutes to get through that. In there is a basic rundown of what we know, including the key figures in this saga. It includes the latest intel Jacob's managed to give me over the phone. Things are moving rapidly, although Jacob thinks he knows the general vicinity of the person we are looking for."

"Then why do you need me?"

"Because we believe there's a mole inside the Clandestine Operations unit, headed up by a man called Jim Stynes." He gestured toward the folder in Irina's hand. "As I said, it's all summarized in there. Knowing your skill and aptitude, I'm sure that if there's any useful material on those devices, you'll spot it. You'll be remunerated for your efforts, whether you find anything or not."

"How much?" She would have helped Jacob for free, but she wouldn't protest.

"A lot. Anyway, I'm sure you'll be done in a couple of hours." He led her a hundred feet to the end of the open-plan space, along a caged gantry, down a level, and into the tech room. She knew that's what it was because there was a huge sign hanging on the door that said *TECH ROOM*. Fletcher flicked on a switch that flooded the vast room in a bright, clinical light. It reminded her of a laboratory she'd often used at Moscow State University. "If you don't mind me asking, why is this room even here? Jacob tells me you aren't, and I don't mean to be rude, technically minded."

"No offense taken. We have an identical facility off-site where a number of employees work. It's practically a mirror image of this one. I can't tell you where it is, but this one here is a backup. Hardly ever used. Someone with high clearance comes in a couple of times a month to make sure everything's working fine. We could use our own people for this, but when Jacob says you are the only person for the job, I listen to him."

She felt the heat of embarrassment prickling the back of her neck. She was basically allergic to praise and flattery; all she wanted to know was the specifics of the task and for Fletcher to leave her to get on with it. Perhaps sensing her discomfort, he got to the point quickly. "On the central bench you'll see three devices: two cell phones and a digital camera. Go through all the data on them and see what you can find that might help us flush out the mole. If you stumble upon proof of the location of Adolfo Sanchez, come and tell me. I don't care if the scores are tied and there's one play left. Interrupt me." He pointed at a row of glass shelving. "Over there, you will find every conceivable type of battery, charger, connector, cable, SD card, tool, anything to assist with getting into nearly every brand of device on the market and copying content."

She extracted the three devices, turning them over in her hands. "Shouldn't be a problem. iPhone, Samsung and Nikon."

"Even if it was some obscure North Korean brand, we've got that covered, too." He laughed. "Not quite, but you get my meaning. Now, the images on the camera have already been copied, but for some reason, Jacob wants you to go through everything from scratch, as if you are a detective who found the devices herself."

She nodded. This was going to be a challenge with a lot of responsibility attached, but one she would thoroughly enjoy.

"Maybe there's something on the camera itself that's going to offer up a lead," added Fletcher.

"I brought my own laptop to use. Is that okay?"

"No. Unfortunately, I can't allow that. Please restrict yourself to the PC and other equipment at your disposal in the lab. You've already got a guest email account." He handed her a very low-tech yellow Post-It. "Here are your log-in credentials. Also a contact number to call Nate, the head of IT, if you get stuck with any of our proprietary software. Which I'm sure you won't." He paused as he sucked in a breath, then said dramatically: "I'm going on trust here, Irina. If something goes wrong or you email yourself something you shouldn't and it comes out later, I could go to prison." She'd never seen the man so serious. On the few occasions she'd met him, he'd acted almost nonchalantly, even frivolously.

"And Yakov?"

"Yakov, too." He nodded, grinning slightly as he used the unfamiliar Russian form of his ace employee's name. "Since he vouched for you."

"In that case, I'll be on my best behavior."

With Fletcher gone, she realized he might not have been straight-up about Susan Stonehouse. She remembered Jacob had referred to the 'side office,' and the tech lab was, at least geographically, the 'back office.' The sly dog had most likely fobbed her off but, she shrugged as she told herself, it was Fletcher's business who he fooled around with, not Jacob's and not hers.

Now to work.

She pulled out a thermos of strong coffee and a bag of potato chips. Sustenance sorted out, she read Fletcher's summary. He wasn't lying about his summary-writing prowess. It was as good as the best plot description for a book or movie she'd ever read. Smiling appreciatively, she then picked up the vivid blue digital camera, found the on button, and pressed it. Charge was low: she quickly plugged in a micro USB cable to power it up. The menu was super simple: it appeared to be a cheaply made yet functional camera made for complete amateurs. Looking via the small viewer screen was going to be a problem: out popped the SD card, and she transferred the contents via the cable onto the hard drive of the PC. In no time at all, the items were available to view on a bigger screen. She took a deep breath, arranged the files by date, most recent at the top, and clicked on the first image, taken October 14. Four days ago.

Not what she expected.

A pair of leather boots. Out of focus. Obviously an accidental shot. Which meant it could be laden with unintended clues. She zoomed in, looking for a label, something to indicate a manufacturer. Nothing.

Next, same boots. Slightly better focus. Brown leather, maybe snakeskin, an intricate pattern, pointy toes. She loaded this picture onto Google image search and came up with thousands of results. She popped open the bag of chips, munched a handful, wiped her hands on a napkin. Dammit, this really could take all night.

She poured a cupful of steaming coffee, clicked on image number three, and nearly spat out a mouthful of soggy chips. She averted her eyes, then forced herself to look back. A terrified man, masses of thick black curly hair, eyes as wide as they could possibly be, the whites showing bright like sun against snow. A line of blood trickled from his throat, against which was pressed a massive steel knife. Where they cigarette burns on his cheeks? Yob tvoyu mat'! Fucking hell!

Next, the same man, more blood, almost a stream now.

Twenty more photographs featuring the same man, but these included other subjects. Two men in ski masks, tormenting and torturing the curly-headed one. They grinned under their masks in a number of selfies, peace signs, tongues protruding.

Would just eyes and mouths be enough to find a match in a database? She found an icon for a facial recognition program that combined a large number of international databases and uploaded all the images featuring the masked men and the man she presumed to be Miguel Hererra. The cursor turned into a whirling circle and the program spat out some possible matches. None of them seemed likely.

She continued scrolling through the images. There were several of a man, tall and blond, well dressed, seemingly taken in a clandestine fashion. Fletcher's report appended photographs of some of the main figures in the case, so she could see straight-up this was the missing businessman, Paul Brohman. The man the president wanted rescued. Among the Brohman-themed shots taken on the Nikon were three of him with a young woman, both heading for the entrance of a block of apartments. The woman was Carmen Hererra. Having been a victim of sexual predation in the context of power imbalance back in Moscow, Irina could only shake her head in revulsion. The zoom quality of the Nikon cheapie was remarkably high— good enough to capture the look of disgust on Carmen's face as she followed Brohman, two steps behind him, through the door of the building.

These photos would make more sense if they were attached to some kind of document, with annotations. Knowing what was in Miguel Hererra's mind, what his plans were, and most importantly, whom he suspected of being a rat, would make her job so much easier.

Next were photographs of four different people— two men and two women— entering and leaving a three-floor office building. The shots were taken on an oblique angle, several hundred feet from the entrance, perhaps due to the narrowness of the street and Miguel's need to stay undetected. None of these people were in Fletcher's report. She fed the images of the four unknowns into the same facial recognition software.

Hits for each. All employees of the CIA, attached to Jim Stynes' Bogotá team. In-house IT guru and MIT graduate Marty James and his assistant, Puerto Rico-born Juan Palacio. The females were US nationals: analysts Fiona Giles and Amanda Costello. How much time did she have to research all of these people, and in what direction should she look?

She fed the names into a global crime database, but she already knew what would happen. Exactly as she expected: all one hundred percent clean skins. On a whim and going in alphabetical order, she typed the name 'Amanda Costello' into Google together with +Bogotá. A couple pages of returns. Each result was for a totally different woman. A Scottish travel blogger who'd visited Colombia three years ago. A YouTube video and some articles. She tried 'Mandy' instead of Amanda. This time another tourist. She then switched to image search. She plucked more chips out of the packet and wriggled into her seat, prepared to spend a maximum of half an hour on each person. After that, she'd turn her attention to the cell phones. They likely needed PINs to unlock them, so she wasn't hopeful. Then home to her son Vova.

Pouring a second coffee, an alert told her a message had landed in her temporary Skia email account. A split second later, her phone rang.

"Zaichik! What have you sent me? A love poem?"

A stifled laugh came down the line. "I'm still working on that. No, this one's a challenge. One I'm sure you can handle."

"Good. Because the challenge I'm working on now is proving very tough. I'm getting nowhere with the photographs, apart from learning the names of the people working for Jim Stynes. And I don't think I'll be able to get into the phones unless you can get the Colombian provider to unlock them for me."

"Leave that for now. Uncovering the mole is secondary. I have to find Brohman."

"Okay. So what can I do?"

"Open the attachment I sent you."

*Click.*

"A photograph of someone's babushka?"

"It's Adolfo Sanchez's elderly mother. I took the photo."

"Excuse me, Yakov? You met the mother of the leader of this new drug cartel? How..."

"You want me to give away all my trade secrets?"

"Ah..."

"Listen. There's also an audio file on there. What she says is completely unimportant."

"Well, that's good news. I don't speak Spanish, remember. You're the genius linguist who can learn any language, not me."

"Irrelevant. What I want you to do is create a deep fake video that I'm going to send to Sanchez."

"What, his mom obligingly gave you his email address?"

"No. I found his phone number while she was in the bathroom. I imagine the file will be too big for an MMS."

"I'll compress it, don't worry."

"Excellent."

"There also the option of sharing it to a secure server where the video will sit. We create a password for him to access it. But if the clip is short enough and to the point, compression will do the trick."

"In the body of the email I've typed out a message that fake Mom is going to say to her son. Think you can handle it?"

"Govno vopros! *Sure as shit!*"

Thirty-seven minutes later, the video was complete. She watched it replay a couple of times. The AI program had created a remarkably realistic clip. The question was, would her son be convinced by the deception?

She called Jacob. "It's done. Should be sitting in your inbox. Let me know if it needs modification."

She waited on the line, crunching the last of the potato chips and washing it down with a Diet Pepsi she found in a two-door fridge that was fully stocked with soft drinks and snacks.

"Perfect," he said. "I like how there's even some slight hand movements, rise and fall of the shoulders, change in facial expressions and intonation according to the words. I was worried it'd just be her mouth moving."

"Need anything more?"

"It's late, Irochka. Go home, be with your son. You've done a great job on the video. It's a shame about the camera, but it was a long shot."

They bade each other good night, and she booked an Uber to pick her up in thirty minutes. She wanted to have one more look at those ancillary staff members.

Back to the Internet, image search using their names. The first three were all busts. Social media accounts also bore no fruit. Not surprising, given who they worked for.

Then came the IT gopher in the office, Juan Palacio. Unlike the others, he did have an online presence, albeit a rather innocuous one. The kid played indoor soccer, was quite a star in his amateur competition. Top goal scorer three seasons ago. The last entry for him was in 2020. He won an award for his goal-scoring ability. Yawning, Irina clicked on the photograph of Juan standing on a stage with a group of other young men, arms around each other's shoulders, smiling like they'd won the lottery.

Just about to click out and shut everything down, a detail caught her eye.

A pair of brown, snakeskin boots with pointy toes.

# TWENTY-FIVE

"Yes, I agree. The boots are very similar." Joel McDonald, Deputy Director of the CIA Directorate of Operations, held the printouts from the camera and the Internet side by side a couple of inches from his face. One of those guys who needs glasses but is too vain to get them, Fletcher thought as the man squinted. "But there's no guarantee they're the same pair."

"Are you kidding me?" said Fletcher. "They're virtually identical."

The red-eyed CIA chief, who'd once again flown at the crack of dawn from Langley to parley with Fletcher, hummed through pursed lips. "I'm reluctant to push ahead with any action against the young man without further evidence he's linked to the kidnapping of Paul Brohman." He leaned forward, taking another look at the photos. "Get me something more convincing, and I'll open up the entire office for a purge. Unfortunately, at this stage there's nothing proving there's a mole in Stynes' team." He ran a reptilian tongue across his top lip. "Show me some real proof and maybe we can open up the books, so to speak."

Fletcher fought hard to control his breathing. "What else do you need?" He started enumerating points on his fingers. "The brother of employee Carmen Hererra, whom Jim Stynes unconscionably used to find out if *your* man—the *president's* man, for fuck's sake—was actually a mole, is missing. We have images of Carmen's brother being terrorized and cut with a knife, burned with cigarette butts. There are photographs of unusual leather boots on the camera, right after the pictures of Hererra and the hooded men, and the same boots appear on a photo of Juan Palacio taken three years ago."

"I'm afraid that's circumstantial, and barely that. The boots, well, anyone could be wearing them."

Fletcher shook his head. "Look at the timestamp of the metadata. The accidental shots of the boots were taken literally minutes after the ones with the mask-wearers who were tormenting Hererra."

McDonald would not be swayed. "Listen. If you are right, and you very well may be, and Palacio is the mole, now is not the time to go in, excuse the term, boots and all."

"Why not?"

"We spook the guy and he—or someone working with him—alerts Sanchez that we're on to him, and it's curtains for Brohman."

Fletcher felt the heat rise under his collar. "We don't even know that Brohman's still alive! Two operatives assisting my man were slaughtered in broad daylight."

"Those men could have been murdered in a random robbery."

"A bit extreme to riddle people with bullets to lift a couple of wallets, don't you think?"

McDonald waved the concern away, absently tugging his cuffs. "Whatever. We must, however, proceed from the assumption that Brohman is alive. The president is frantic right now. The polls are getting away from him and McIvor's almost caught up. Some of the polls have her ahead. He needs Brohman's money to drive the campaign."

"You do realize, Joel, that if she wins, she becomes your boss."

McDonald refused to be drawn by the comment. "On the

plus side, he's impressed with this other intel you have about the possible general area of Sanchez's base." He smiled broadly and tapped the top of the coffee table. "On that front, you've done very well."

"Have you read my suggested course of action?" Fletcher chewed the end of a cigar; he would refrain from lighting it until McDonald was out of his hair. "The ideas I emailed you?"

"Indeed, and I largely agree with you. We are onto the task. Our best remote sensing experts are looking at the Lacandón jungle area. Comparisons over time show several areas where irregular forest clearance has taken place over the last couple of years. We're hopeful analysis of close-up satellite images will reveal Sanchez's base within the next 24 hours."

"Impressive." Fletcher nodded. "What about the PO box in that fly-speck town? Maybe Sanchez will show his face when he comes to pick up his Dominoes flyers."

McDonald took a sip from a coffee by now stone cold. "I doubt it. A couple of guys down the food chain have been assigned to stake it out, but it won't be for long. I'm confident the analysts will pinpoint the base, and we can engage the Mexican government to organize a raid. Their president is a close friend of ours; large-scale material and manpower cooperation is practically a *fait accompli*."

Fletcher coughed into his fist. "I'm not completely in agreement here about a raid. Don't you want to ensure Brohman's safety? First sign of trouble and Sanchez will have a knife to his throat or a gun to his head. You need Brohman alive to unfreeze the bank accounts, right?"

A dark shadow passed over McDonald's face. "I'm a professional, Grant. Been in this job longer than you've been in yours. You don't think I haven't considered that?"

"Well...I—"

McDonald pointed a finger in the general direction of Fletcher's chest. "That's a job for your guy. He's being paid a fortune, or so the rumor goes. Tell him he's gotta somehow get inside undetected, rescue Brohman. Then we go in en masse, all guns blazing, and take the motherfuckers down."

Fletcher rubbed his wrinkled brow. If it wasn't bad enough the Jets got their collective ass kicked last night, now he had to inform Jacob of the monumental task before him. The man would find a way. He always did. "We may get a bead on the location of the hideout before the remote sensing guys find it. In fact, Hunter's idea could be an even more precise method."

"How so?"

Fletcher described the AI video Irina had created using the material Jacob supplied, how it was going to be used to force a response from Sanchez, make him show his hand.

"Sounds like a long shot to me. Sanchez will smell a rat straight away."

Fletcher shook his head. "Yeah. That's what I thought." He paused. "At first. I've seen some of these deep fake videos on the Internet, and even the best efforts aren't a hundred percent convincing. But this...this is special. Our Skia coders have come up with something you at the CIA might want to think about purchasing."

"Purchasing? Are you fucking serious? We're supposed to be on the same side."

"True, but we've all got our budgets to work under."

"Fuck off, Grant. Your budget is limitless."

"Don't believe every rumor you hear. Anyway, you want to see the video?"

"I'll admit, I'm curious."

Fletcher pressed a button, and the big screen descended.

"It looks and sounds real," McDonald admitted when the short clip ended. "I'm not sure her son, who knows her better than most people, will be convinced. She may have certain speech mannerisms, other tell-tale behaviors, that your video gets wrong."

"True," admitted Fletcher. "In which case we throw everything we have at the satellite images."

As the men parted, with McDonald expressing his frustration at early-morning flights and a wish that future meetings be held via Zoom, Fletcher shook his head. "You know the rules. Only in-person meetings are allowed between us on joint operations, unless there's extraordinary force majeure reasons to do otherwise." He had a sudden thought. "However, if you give me the encryption protocols to access Stynes' data systems in Bogotá, I might be prepared to bend those rules and spare you the worry of flying."

"Certainly not! If I wanted to go down the path of hacking into Bogotá, we would have done it from here without Skia's involvement."

Fletcher nodded. "Yeah, that sounds logical. Although if you let us do it, there would be no comeback on you for mistrusting your people if they all turn out to be clean."

"I'm sorry, Grant, but no. It's a step too far."

"We can get in anyway," Fletcher said with an undertone of threat. "In and out and no one would be any the wiser. Skia has the best hackers in the world at its disposal. It would just take a little longer than if you played ball, that's all."

"You really are an asshole, Fletcher, did you know that?"

"Besides, resolving this matter satisfactorily would help ensure Hannah McIvor doesn't become the next president. And I know how much you fear that scenario."

McDonald closed his eyes and tilted his head backwards, grasping the bridge of his nose as if he had a crushing headache.

"Very well, but only this once, and I want your word on your mother's grave that this stays between us and the relevant officers. Waivers will be drafted by my top legal guy."

Fletcher extended his arms to the sides. "Of course, Joel. Whatever you want." He could readily agree to any demand or condition McDonald liked even if it was unlawful: unknown to everyone bar his two predecessors in the role, he enjoyed complete immunity from prosecution for anything he did in the line of duty.

Fletcher consulted the balance of the account for "consultants." Absolutely swollen with funds. He'd promised Irina $50K for her work on the AI video, which made her eyes almost pop out of her head. It was an absolute masterpiece and worth every penny, even if it failed to get the desired result. If it did, and he hadn't told her this, he'd pay her the same again. And if she could find the mole inside Bogotá Clandestine Operations section, she'd get another $50K and an offer of a full-time job at double whatever the bank was paying her.

He fired up a stogey, picked up the phone, and dialed her number.

# TWENTY-SIX

The fake Maria on his laptop screen gave a heart-wrenching, Oscar-worthy performance. Truly, Irina had done a superb job. It was easily the most convincing example of a deep fake video he'd ever seen. Before sending it, though, he wanted to vet it thoroughly. Convince himself it would do the job it was designed to do.

Tucked away in his room in Manuel's hotel, he noticed his laptop's power level dropping. He plugged it into the wall socket and settled down to review the short clip as many times as necessary before clicking send. He increased the size of the viewer on his screen, looking for tell-tale signs of manipulation, excessive pixelation, jumpiness. Nothing. It was, to his non-expert's eye, a beautiful, high-resolution, high-definition video.

Next, he increased and decreased the volume. Played it at increased and decreased speeds. The intonation of fake Mamma Maria was perfect. Or so it seemed to Jacob.

Question was, would it get the desired result?

A glance at the clock icon. 10:32 a.m. He called Irina.

"You free?"

A stifled yawn then a whisper. "For you, zaichik, nearly always."

"Nearly?"

"Yes. But not now. I'm attending a presentation on social media trends and people are giving me dirty looks. I'll call you back."

Forty-six minutes later, the return call came. He'd had time to shower and remove a layer of dust and another of stubble. "I'm about to send this video," he said. "I watched it on my laptop as well as my phone screen. I wanna check it's compressed enough to get through from my cheap burner to another cell. Ready?"

"Da. Send it to me now."

File attached and sent. "Done."

"Might take a couple of...no...wow, quicker delivery than I expected from Mexico."

"This *is* the home of Speedy Gonzalez."

"Who?" Genuine mystification as the cultural reference was lost on a Russian immigrant.

"Never mind. Can you play the video?"

"One second...yes, it's working. Looks as realistic as it did when I made it. The sound is clear, too."

"Excellent, thanks."

"Uh, Yakov..."

He sensed something bad was coming.

"I've been asked by your boss to do something I have a fundamental problem with."

"What?" He knew her ethics were generally strong. Not a positive trait in the spying game, but technically she wasn't a spy: rather a guest star on the Jacob Hunter show. The only reason she'd agreed to make the video was to save a man's life and because Jacob promised there would be no blow-back for poor old Maria.

"He wants me to hack into a private database. It won't be hard because the encryption protocols are going to be handed to me on a plate."

Jacob rubbed his chin hard. "What are you talking about? You've done this kind of thing before. Back in Moscow you overrode the alarm system of a federal ministry, remember?"

"That was against a regime of criminals. This is against"—her voice dropped to a faint whisper—"...the CIA."

He walked to the window and opened it wide. The heat was still bearable, and he was tired of the AC running. Mainly because of the knocking noise it made. If the video had the desired effect, he'd be out of this room before lunch time, making his way to the small town of Ocosingo. "Listen. The CIA has bad guys in it, rogue elements, just like the FSB and the SVR in Russia. Without the CIA, the USA and the West in general would be screwed, even if some people think it's the embodiment of evil, run by illuminati, Freemasons, and such like."

"Is it?"

"Honestly, Irochka? I don't know, but I highly doubt it. I know Skia isn't, and that's who you're working for on this case. For all Fletcher's faults, he's a man of integrity. He wouldn't ask you to do this—and I wouldn't back him up—unless there was a damned good reason."

"I guess it would be rude after he paid me so much for the job."

"How much?" he asked as casually as he could.

"Enough to buy you dinner at your favorite restaurant when you get back."

He laughed but wouldn't push her on the amount. Knowing Fletcher as he did, it would have been a generous sum. "How about a steak dinner with vintage wine at Gallagher's on 52$^{nd}$ Street?"

"Never heard of it."

He smiled. She didn't go out much, preferring to cook at home for herself and Vova, Jacob too when they got the chance for a meal together. "The place has a lot of history. Goes back to 1927. It was the place to be for all the Broadway stars, high-roller gamblers and sports legends. Not to mention the biggest and baddest crooks in the history of America."

"Baddest is not a word. I thought you were a linguistic genius."

"Poetic license. Anyway, it's my favorite eatery in Manhattan. You'll love it. But I gotta warn you, a rib steak there costs nearly eighty bucks."

He heard a gasp. "Are you serious?"

"Dead serious."

"Then the food must be great. You got yourself a deal, zaichik."

---

THE MOMENT of truth had arrived.

Sitting on the edge of the single bed in only a pair of jockey shorts and flip-flops, he cracked the top of a Dos Equis beer, flicked the cap into a waste-paper basket, and took a long slug. He pressed the cold bottle against his forehead, the heat of the afternoon having become enervating. Manuel and his support, well intended and totally misguided, were great, but the conditions in his establishment warranted only a short stay. There was no cross breeze in the small room, and, to make matters worse, the clunky air-conditioning unit had let out a mechanical groan before deciding to stop working altogether. He finished the beer in two more gulps and turned his attention to the job at hand.

The hard technical work had been done by Irina, now it was time for Jacob to get creative with the accompanying text. The style would be a lot more formal than the script he'd composed for AI Maria but no less challenging. He swapped out his own SIM for Maria's and began to carefully composed the SMS message that would be sent prior to the video.

*Attention Adolfo 'Hitler' Sanchez. Read this SMS very carefully. After you have read it, read it again.*

*We have recently learned that you have kidnapped an ally of ours, an influential American businessman. A very foolish move, Adolfo. What you have done has not only pissed us off greatly, it has angered the American president. He has authorized all and every means to get Mr. Brohman back on US soil. To secure the prompt and safe release of Mr. Brohman, we have kidnapped your mother, Maria Isabel Sanchez. Until advised otherwise, all your communications with us will be conducted via her cell phone. Do not call Villa Serenidad! We are monitoring all numbers associated with the facility. You call them, Mamma dies. Simple.*

*A short video clip will follow this message, in which your mother appears for exactly 1 minute and 38 seconds. You will observe that she is very frightened, and she has every reason to be. She has some well-chosen words for you. Words you must take very seriously if you don't want us to kill Maria in cold blood. We are prepared to take this unfortunate step should you fail to carry out our instructions, to the letter. By the way, we will send you a video of the murder taking place, and be assured, it will not be quick and it will not be humane. She will suffer.*

*But it doesn't have to go that way, Señor Sanchez.*

*While she has been in our custody, your mother has demonstrated great humor and courage. Indeed, we have quickly grown to like her, and we are amazed a lovely woman like her gave birth to a monster like you. Killing her will cause us a great deal of emotional pain if you don't do exactly as we demand, but we are sure it will cause you even greater pain.*

*You must release the man you have kidnapped, Paul Brohman, into the custody of the Mexican police.*

Jacob gritted his teeth at this point. He had not secured the cooperation of said Mexican forces; however, according to Fletcher, it was a mere formality to get them onside.

*We are currently working out the logistics of the handover and will contact you soon with precise instructions. You and everyone who works for you at your headquarters will also be expected to surrender to the police. For now, though, please enjoy the video. Do not respond to this message. I will tell you when it's time for us to talk. One last thing. Keep your cell phone handy and operable at all times. If you don't respond quickly, well, you know what will happen. Ciao.*

Jacob made the sign of the cross over his bare chest. He

double-checked that everything was spelled correctly and expressed in a form of Spanish that a criminal from the slums of Mexico City would understand meant business. Right at the end of the text he spotted an error and changed the standard Italian spelling of ciao to the Spanish *chao*. Then he hit send.

# TWENTY-SEVEN

"I don't care!" Sanchez roared. "Don't get sidetracked by things that don't matter. If someone pretended to be a cop, so what? The pair of troublesome CIA operatives were liquidated, were they not?"

"Yes," said Laura Torres, NID liaison officer. "But...I fear compromising material may have been taken from the vehicle."

"What compromising material? The boys who snatched Miguel Hererra told me they turned that fucking place upside down and inside out. Tortured him within an inch of his life, and all he admitted to was the laptop, the USB with all the shit he copied from Stynes' office, and a bunch of gay jerk-off magazines." He strode back and forth, aware of Brohman's glowing eyes following him along the patio. He adjusted the silk robe he always wore at the swimming pool, the ties annoyingly tangling between his legs. "If anything points to me involved in this ludicrous scheme—and I question my sanity about even agreeing to it—I'll make sure you and your family suffer in ways you can barely imagine."

Sanchez stopped, shielding his eye as a medium-sized drone flew past the boundary of his compound. He'd never seen one out here before. Probably a tourist trekking through the edge of the jungle. There were resorts not too far away, so it was a possibility. And yet it looked too large for a hobby drone. He'd paid the local mayor and a bunch of his underlings shitloads to be left in peace to build his hideaway out here in the wilderness. Jesus, this could be bad news. Very bad news.

"One of the Bogotá uniforms assisted him," Torres explained, rousing Sanchez from his musings. "He was very convincing, apparently. Had an ID that looked exactly like the real deal. My intel is that the poor woman who was deceived was put on unpaid leave. Even though her superior officer was the one who gave the man access to the fucking car."

He thought he was going to have a stroke as she rambled on. "Too much detail, Torres. What the hell do I care about some Colombian cops?"

"The impersonator scurried away from the scene with what looked like a small safe and a plastic bag containing electronic devices." Torres maintained her authoritative tone, much to Sanchez's chagrin. Being an ex-forces recruit to the NID, the woman was hard to intimidate. "Items your stooges missed."

Sanchez squeezed the top of his nose; a migraine was threatening to erupt inside his head. "It's probably nothing. We worked Hererra over so thoroughly those items were only left behind because they're of no value. I wouldn't be surprised if the safe was empty and the bag contained a couple of old cell phones destined for the recycling bin."

"Maybe Hererra had more guts than you gave him credit for. Anyway, the point is"—she ramped up her serious-tone dial—"the realistic bogus identification means the guy's probably a spy."

"You're a damned spy!" *Is the woman a complete idiot?* "And you are surrounded by spies. From moment you wake until you go to sleep. What I don't want is fucking excuses. I want you to do something about it!"

"I am. I have a hunch I know who this might be. A mysterious businessman lobbed into Bogotá the other day. I was meant to be having a meeting with him, organized by Stynes and—"

"By Stynes? Fucking hell, Laura. Find this man and deal with it. He's getting too damned close for my comfort!" He disconnected the phone and threw it over the side of the patio railing. It spun through the air like a spiraling football before plopping into the lush grass a foot from the edge of the pool.

"I knew you were full of shit." Brohman's voice echoed in the amphitheater created by Sanchez's villa and three sides of thick jungle surrounding it. "Telling me you're not a cruel man. That if you were going to kill me, you'd do it quick. Then I hear you virtually bragging about torture to that Laura Torres— yes, you look surprised. I know her very well. We've had dinner together. Rather attractive, charming too. She had me completely fooled. I couldn't hear her side of the conversation, but the Spanish you spoke that I could figure out was enough to tell me she's a dirty rotten traitor to her country."

The blood rose in his chest, crawled up his neck, and pushed against his cheeks. The temptation to fetch his AK-12 and turn this idiot American, a serial sex-offender, into a colander was strong, but it must be quelled for now. The man might be needed for collateral, a bargaining chip if Torres's words carried any weight. He spun around and confronted him, fists bunching by his sides.

"I'm not a monster who hurts people indiscriminately," he spat. "But if there is a reason, oh yes, I can indeed be cruel. So far, you've behaved nicely. But"—his finger wagged like a metronome —"do not. Ever. Insult me!" He strode the three yards to where Brohman sat under an umbrella, walking with a swagger, as if he were itching to take a couple of swings. The captive American simply stared, did not move a muscle, challenging Sanchez to try something. Sanchez pulled up, blinking hard a couple of times as if coming out of a dream.

"I won't punish you this time, gringo. Now take your things and fuck off back to your room before I change my mind and empty a magazine into you." He barked rapid-fired Spanish instructions to two goons dressed in jungle fatigues who were loitering by a set of sliding doors. They were upon Brohman in an instant, frog-marching him away from the seething Sanchez.

The American was like one of those troublesome skin-tags: you toy with it, unable to leave it alone, yet at the same time it torments you with its insistent presence; you despise it and want to get rid of it more than anything in the world.

Brohman's personality type was complex, hard for Sanchez to get a proper read on. Yes, his treatment of women was appalling, and that angered Sanchez. However, that wasn't the aspect of his behavior that Sanchez found so infuriating. It was the way the big blond oaf just sat there, barely offering up any contribution to their conversations. God knew Sanchez was simply trying to be civilized, yet his guest didn't appreciate it.

Perhaps it was the gringo's military training coming to the fore: stoic in the face of adversity. For all intents and purposes, Brohman was a prisoner of war. Sanchez himself had spent no time in the military, although the weapons training would have been fun. Sadly, the army would never have allowed him to join their ranks. Too much bad shit on his record. But this 'silent' behavior of Brohman's was exactly the same with the ex-soldiers he recruited to the cartel. It had been drilled into them—don't speak unless spoken to. And to be honest, it was a great character trait for an employee in the organization.

But Brohman wasn't an employee; he was a guest, and guests should make an effort. This ongoing silence was starting to irk Sanchez more than he knew it should. On the other hand, he'd never had a guest like this one: a trusted confidante of el presidente of los Estados Unidos. A businessman worth as much as Sanchez himself but perhaps not enjoying the same degree of liquidity in terms of his assets. So yeah. The rules for this guy were a little different and subject to change without warning.

And, of course, Brohman was never going to be killed. Sanchez kept the unspoken threat hovering over Brohman like an annoying mosquito, but there was no benefit to be gained by killing this man. Sanchez had never murdered another human being without there being an overwhelmingly justifiable reason. And there was no such reason in the case of Brohman. Sure, the man had said Sanchez was 'full of shit,' but that wasn't even close to justifiable. Heck, even young Javi let loose with ill-chosen phrases like that sometimes. Sanchez actually took pride in the fact his skin was a lot thicker than that of many of his rivals. Their stupid vanity was one of the main reasons he was going to make history by putting all of those hijos de putas, those sons of bitches, in their graves, leaving him in charge of one mega cartel. He knew it was just a matter of time.

Another piece of the puzzle that would lead to his monopolization of the narcotics landscape was the upcoming Big Dump, the start of the rollout scheduled for 29 October, exactly a week before election day. The realization of the grand conspiracy with Laura Torres and the other actors that would net him close to a billion dollars.

The hard work was done. Now all he had to do was keep Brohman separated from his bank accounts long enough for the election to come and go. Hannah McIvor would make a cake walk of it thanks to her financial advantage. Victory would be mainly due to the massive swing to her from Claxton's traditional base; when the streets in key constituencies were flooded with vast amounts of cheap, impure heroin, her hardline appeal would be impossible for many undecideds to resist. Crime in many cities, already high, would surge. More people would be mugged and murdered by crazed junkies, more properties damaged and destroyed. The perfect storm. Fed-up common folk would desert Claxton with his wishy-washy soft-on-crime policies and flock to the hard-liner McIvor. All was set to roll on time and without a hitch.

When Hannah McIvor was announced as the next president of the United States, his colossal bonus payment would hit his account within 24 hours.

He drank deeply from a double shot of cognac that had been thawing ice cubes for the last twenty minutes. A hand reached out and raked his smokes in. There really was no need to panic, he thought as he sparked up the cigarette. No more drones— obviously that one belonged to ecotourists with enough money to buy serious equipment.

This so-called spy at the Bogotá shooting, that was a concern. He hated unknowns, things he couldn't control. Torres was a good operator, though; she'd take care of it.

He flipped open the lid of his laptop, navigating his way to the folder containing everything on the Big Dump. He double-checked the times, the amounts of narcotics going to each locality, and the names of the key distributors. Number, numbers, numbers. Sanchez thrived on the numbers. The most important number of all was the gargantuan sum of money heading into his Panamanian bank account the day after the election.

And the best part?

The consignments were already sitting inside the United States, a large portion of it smuggled across the border by hundreds of trusted men. Undetectable, they blended deep inside the hordes of 'undocumented migrants' who last week breached the border fences at El Paso-Ciudad Juárez and a number of other crossing points in Arizona and New Mexico. Once past the paper-thin defenses, these men had handed over their packages to drivers, who transported the drugs to their nominated destinations. All of the small packages together combined into many hundreds of kilos of bad-quality, cheap smack.

This time it wasn't the value of the drugs that was going to add to his already huge fortune; it was their purpose. Fucking up key cities Hannah McIvor needed to swing her way to win the presidency. Hers had been an unlikely rise to power, a shrieking populist the like of which the country had never seen. A divorcee, single mother to boot! The chaos about to unfold would be the tipping point required to ensure her victory, once thought unlikely but now almost a certainty.

Seeking a boost to his mood, dented by Laura Torres's damned eternal pessimism, he logged on to a video-streaming website. It wasn't quite the dark web, but it hosted clips that were so controversial they often got banned on the mainstream. The grainy and jerky footage, taken and uploaded by an anonymous and disgruntled Homeland Security officer who had decided he had to document the migrant invasion, brought a huge smile to Sanchez's face. The border guards, in every instance and in every state, instead of shooting or at least restraining the invaders, had simply stepped aside and let the masses of men (no women at all) roll in. A deadly crush ensued at the El Paso site, with a number of men turned to bone meal under the weight of those pushing from behind. A couple of his own guys had perished, but there was always going to be collateral damage in an operation like this. Over 95 percent of the mules got through, and that meant bad news for President Claxton. Sanchez had nothing against the man —politically, he actually leant in his direction and thought McIvor was a whining harridan. But at the end of the day, business is business.

Smiling like a child at a magic show, Sanchez switched to another website to enjoy more of the glorious border mayhem. This site aggregated the most popular links to videos available on the main news sites: These also showed the scenes at the border but from a greater distance and without the closeups of the crushed bodies. Hysteria light. Whether the images were graphic or muted, though, it didn't matter. The result was the same. A big fucking win to Adolfo Sanchez!

Once he'd had his fill of watching videos, a nagging thought came into his mind about that pesky drone. He remembered reading recently that the Fuerzas Especiales, the Mexican Special Forces, had invested heavily in drone technology over the last couple of years. Sanchez's own surveillance camera would have picked up the one that flew by not long ago. He checked the footage via a Bluetooth connection on his computer. He then pulled up some Googled images of the ones the cops were reportedly using, compared them, and heaved a sigh of relief. Not a match with any of them. Must have been tourists after all.

Closing the lid of the laptop, he figured on enjoying X-box games to pass a couple of hours: just the thing to rev him up before hitting the gym for his second workout of the day. Leg day, dammit. As he tied the belt of his silk robe, he cast his thoughts to Brohman again. Prior to his capture, Brohman had been about to receive a massive cache of information from Miguel Hererra, but the billionaire didn't know what was on it. He was just a dumb mule, trying to help out his pal, Claxton, and as such probably deserved to be set free once the operation turned out to be a resounding success. On the other hand, perhaps it *would* be best to put him out of his misery, after all. If McIvor lost...well...a living Brohman, with Claxton as an ally, would be a big, dangerous thorn in Sanchez's side. Besides, the longer Brohman remained missing with no proof of life or ransom demands issued, the more antsy Claxton would get. No doubt he was already throwing every possible resource he could at finding the man. And as a financial backer of the president, there was far more than friendship at stake.

He placed the laptop in its bag. Leaving it out on the patio wouldn't be smart with heavy rain predicted for the afternoon. You didn't have to have read the forecast to know what was coming— you only had to look at the sky. Dark and menacing.

And there it was again! Closer this time; maybe a meter or so inside the northern perimeter of his compound. He jumped on the phone. "Javi. Bring me my long-range rifle. Quick."

Javi arrived as the drone changed course at the northeastern corner and began to track south. Sanchez snatched the gun, a Christensen Arms MPR, rested the stock on the top of the panel glass railing, took aim, and let fire. The crack echoed around the jungle; colorful birds squawked and scattered in all directions. The shot was wide, and the drone continued on its way.

"Man!" hollered Javi, wiping a trace of white powder from

under his top lip. "Look at that sucker. Never mind that you missed, jefe. You got it next shot."

Sanchez spat on the ground, lined up the buzzing flying object in the sights, and squeezed off another shot. Right on target. A fireball exploded above the tree line, burning brightly against the dull gray clouds. Amidst a pall of black smoke, debris scattered in all directions before what was left of the spinning machine's body came crashing down to earth. Sanchez glared at his bug-eyed charge. "Why are you snorting coke in the middle of the day?"

"I...uh..."

"I don't want to hear it! Get Fernando, if he's not out of it like you. Go gather the remains of that fucking drone and bring it to me. I wanna take a good look at it."

"Si, jefe."

He shouldn't be too hard on the boys: Partying in anticipation of the Big Dump was understandable. The business was so beautifully fine-tuned by Sanchez and his trusted lieutenants scattered around Mexico, Colombia and the United States that it was no crime for his inner circle to let their hair down on occasion. They would die for him, he had no doubt.

Pacing the patio, he looked down at the pool, earlier the scene of female frolicking. The women he kept in his stable would now be at the indoor bar that was as big as a nightclub, waiting with his other henchmen for Javi and Fernando to return from whatever job they were doing for the boss. Between the steel wall pockmarked with oversized rivets and a row of hibiscus, he saw the tops of Javi's and Fernando's heads as they searched the ground for the wreckage.

Just then, his cell phone jangled in the pocket of his robe.

A number he knew as well as his own birthday. The preview of the message showed on the home screen.

Sent from his mother's number, but the words were not hers.

# TWENTY-EIGHT

His hand shook violently as he read the horrific words, barely comprehending their unambiguous meaning. Not Mamma. *No, no, no!*

The phone call from Laura Torres, the strange drone, now this fucking nightmare? His hand was inches away from a billion dollar payday. Now jeopardized by some fuckers who *dared* to kidnap his mother? As his favorite British thriller writer would say, what an absolute clusterfuck.

*No. Do not panic.* He would find a way to solve this problem. He'd get to keep the money and secure the safety of his dear mother.

One hand shot to the side of his head as hot tears sprang forth in his eyes. He slapped his hand repeatedly and viciously on the top of the outdoor table. He glanced at his palm, bright red like he'd been whacked with a rattan cane, yet he felt nothing.

"Boss, here's what we found." Fernando Carriga, ten years older than Javi and in many ways a mentor to the tearaway youngster, held out a metal box containing smoldering and bent pieces of metal.

"Go away, you pair of cretins!" Sanchez roared. "Leave me in peace for a moment, will you?"

The men scampered away into the bowels of the compound, no word of protest. They knew that when el jefe said he wanted to be alone, he damn well meant it.

The words of the SMS swam before his eyes. Was that bitch Torres right after all? Someone had sniffed out the conspiracy and was now using his own precious mother as collateral. How dare they! He tucked the tail of his robe under his buttocks, sat down, and unscrewed the cork of the bottle of cognac. This horrific turn of events required an extra dose of the good stuff before he made any decisions.

Then—*ping*.

Hostia! The video had landed. He clenched the muscles around his cheeks and eyes, breathing hard through flared nostrils. His finger hovered over the message; he was tempted to send it to the trash. What would be the worst that could happen if he didn't watch? He didn't need to see it. The thrust of what the kidnappers wanted was in the text. The video was just salt to rub into the wound.

But he couldn't delete it. It would be like deleting *her*. He simply had to see what these assholes had done to his beloved mother.

She sat in her lounge room at the Villa Serenidad, on her favorite armchair, the one he'd bought for her in Acapulco. He'd seen it in a rundown furniture store and had to buy it—it was identical to one she had owned many years ago but lost when their shantytown hovel was burned to the ground. By people Sanchez had pissed off. The replacement piece of furniture was an apology of sorts. She'd wept with joy the day it was delivered. That's what she'd told him, anyway. He wasn't there to witness her receiving the gift. By a twist of fate, he'd had to flee Mexico altogether just a few short hours after he bought the chair and hide out in Bogotá for a while. That while turned into two long years. He learned later that some stooge from a rival gang had spotted him on vacation in Acapulco and informed the Mexican Federal Police. Later,

Sanchez learned who the informant was and paid someone to hack off the man's hands and feet with a rusty machete.

He snapped his attention back to the small screen in his hand. Now suddenly, the scene had changed. *Madre* was in a different place. A darkened room, with the faintest halo of light radiating from behind her head. She opened her mouth and began to speak.

"Mi hijo. *My son*," she stammered. *Dammit, her voice is shaking more than my fucking hand!* "Please do exactly as the man who wrote the message asked you to do. He said you mustn't [she shook her head for emphasis] do anything differently to what he wrote. Don't panic, I have not been harmed, and the people who have taken me are treating me well so far." Her eyes darted to the right, alarmed. Was someone aiming a gun at her, forcing her to say the words? She gave a nod of understanding and clasped her hands together, as if in supplication. "Please, please, please, mi amor," she pleaded, her eyes moist and blinking rapidly, "just comply with their wishes, or they..."—she choked off tears—"... they will kill me." She blew him a kiss. "Te quiero, mi hijo. Adios. *I love you, my son. Good-bye.*"

Two large cognacs down, his heart rate no slower but his brain marginally sharper, he called the only person he knew who might have an idea about where the hell this fucking curve ball had come from.

The Puerto Rican IT guy spying on Stynes and his crew, Juan Palacio.

---

"Juanito, soy yo. Eres libre de hablar? *Juan, it's me. Are you free to speak?*"

"One second." Palacio shot glances over both shoulders, his pulse quickening. This was only the second call Sanchez had ever made to him. The other time was through an intermediary, giving the order to snatch Hererra. There was a distinct edge to the man's voice. Something was definitely up. "I'll call you back," said Palacio in a half-whisper. "I'm with people."

"You can't call me back, estúpido. You can't see the number I'm calling from."

Palacio twisted the cell round to see the screen. Of course: number withheld. "Call me back in ten. I'll be waiting."

He brushed past his immediate supervisor, Marty James. "Just going outside for a smoke. Back soon."

James grinned, looking up from his bright-red gamer's chair. "Finished ironing out the bugs in the staff roster software?"

Palacio frowned. "Not quite, boss. Another couple of hours and I'll have it all sorted."

"You'd better. I've got Stynes on my ass hounding me about it. He's all up in the air with Carmen talking time off with her brother missing. He's worried she'll resign and he'll need to juggle things until we get a replacement."

"I thought that Iglesias dude was in charge now?"

James shrugged. "Stynes told me it's only a temporary arrangement. Seems Iglesias took off somewhere to investigate this Brohman disappearance. Thinks we're incapable of doing anything." He chuckled as he reached for a coffee mug.

Palacio gave an apologetic smile and pointed at his phone. "Actually, I've got to make an urgent call."

"Who to?"

"Come on, man, it's personal."

Without waiting for the uppity asshole to reply, Palacio grabbed his coat and headed for a coffee shop two blocks from work. The second call from Sanchez came exactly ten minutes after the first, just as a waiter placed an espresso and croissant on the outdoor table. It was cold, and Palacio was alone on the sidewalk.

"What the fuck's going on?" said Sanchez with no preamble.

"I'm sorry," Palacio gulped. "But can you please be more specific?"

"Something fishy's going on. Tell me if anything unusual has caught your eye in the last couple of days. You're supposed to be monitoring all the email traffic going through that office."

"I haven't heard from you or Laura Torres for a while. I thought my job was done after me and my pal handed over Hererra."

"Well, it isn't. Have you noticed any changes to routine at Clandestine Operations?"

"Hmmm." He stirred two sugars into the thick black brew. "There's been a bit of upheaval, now that you mention it."

"Upheaval? What do you mean?"

Palacio's heart was really racing now, pounding like a steam-train. Even as he drank the strong coffee, he questioned the wisdom of ordering a double shot. "A guy came in from America. Speaks perfect Spanish but with a weird accent. Took over from Stynes and–"

"What? Why haven't I heard about this? You are supposed to keep me in the loop."

"I...I..."A giant ball of fear lodged in his throat. "I have to wait to be contacted by you, señor. Like you've done today. Like you did when you wanted me to keep an eye on Brohman and to abduct Hererra." He lit a Camel and sucked in the soothing smoke.

"Ahh! Dammit. I should have trusted you more."

The temptation was to say 'yes, you should have,' but he kept his mouth shut tight. Much safer that way.

"Are you still there, Juanito?"

"Yes, I'm here."

"Who's this guy? What did you say his name was?"

"I didn't. He's called Iglesias. First name Carlos."

"Who the hell is he?"

"Like I said, he came in to take over from Stynes for a couple of days. If he's got some other assignment, I don't know what it is. All I did when he came in was set him up a guest account so he could log on to our system, go over some data."

"Can you check his emails?"

"There was no email account created for him. Just log-in credentials. Like I said, I have no idea what he was doing on the system."

"Can you check?"

Palacio crushed out the cigarette and immediately lit another. "The account is still active, so I guess I could retrace his searches quite easily."

"No *I could*, no *I guess*. Just do it, okay? He's obviously been sent here to find Brohman. The guy's a friend of the US president, for fuck's sake. What other reason could there be?"

"You're probably right. Let me go back to the office and find out what I can about this man Iglesias."

"Excellent. When do you finish work for the day?"

"In an hour. Doesn't give me much time."

"Can't you hack in from outside, from your home? You're an IT guru, aren't you?"

He choked off a sarcastic laugh. "Clandestine Operations is impenetrable from outside. This is the CIA we're talking about. The man who's in charge here, Marty, he's a genius-level programmer. He set up firewalls that are virtually unhackable. No one can get inside without having the encryption protocols and a bunch of algorithms, esoteric stuff I can't get my head around."

"Very well. Just do what you can. I'll call you at 7:15 p.m., give you time to get away from the office, digest what you've found, and make sense of it. Remember, I'm paying you a shit-load of money to do as I ask. Bringing Hererra to the attention of my deputies was important. He could have brought the whole thing crashing down around our ears. Your help there was crucial to the whole operation, in fact. This could be equally vital, if not more so."

"Understood."

"One more thing. Since you're on the ground there, have you heard about a man impersonating a police officer at the scene of a murder in downtown Bogotá? He apparently took some stuff that belonged to Hererra."

"We made Hererra spill his guts. He was terrified. No way he withheld information from us." He shuddered at the memory of him and his amigo torturing Hererra. He was having trouble sleeping; nightmares about it haunted him.

"I'm not blaming you. A tiny number of people hold out even under the most horrible duress when they set their mind to it. Hererra was obviously one such person. When you've got spare time, look up the name Irena Sendler. She withstood the worst the Gestapo could throw at her during World War II." A deep intake of breath. "Anyway, I'm rambling. Do you know about the bogus police officer?"

He crushed out the second cigarette, anxious for this conversation to end so he could do as Sanchez requested in the short time frame available. "I'm sorry. I don't read papers or watch the news. Why do you ask?"

"I can't say exactly. But I think it may have something to do with me. Look into it for me, will you?"

"Is this before or after I run a check on Iglesias's activity at work?"

"Hostia!" Sanchez roared. "Use your initiative. I expect results!"

People walked by, bundled up against the cold, biting wind, staring at the crazy dude at the outdoor table. Palacio, unlike those passersby, was feeling the heat.

---

A HUNDRED YARDS from the front door, his phone buzzed. A text from an unknown number. Had to be Sanchez. The message contained the address and email details for a retirement home called Villa Serenidad. The instruction: *Find out whatever you can about a Maria Sanchez who lives at the facility WITHOUT alerting the retirement home. Exercise extreme caution in your enquiries. You fuck up, and the entire deal is off. Get me the information I need, and your fee doubles.*

*Shit*, thought Palacio, *talk about pressure. And on top of everything else, now he thinks I've got the skills of a damned private eye. The joint he wants me to investigate isn't even in Colombia.*

"That was a long phone call," snarled James as Palacio hung his jacket on a hook on the back of the door. "Everything all right?"

"Yes. Some family issues. All resolved now."

"Good. Because we're late with the roster rebuild I put you in charge of. I'm going to need you to stay back to catch up on the forty minutes you've stolen from the agency."

Palacio shrugged. "Fine by me." In fact, it was a gift. He'd be left alone to make his checks for the Mexican narcobaron without the ugly, preppy asshole looking over his shoulder constantly. "I'll stay as long as it takes."

"You're not getting overtime for it, you understand?"

Palacio made a face in mock protest. In truth, he didn't give a shit. The money Sanchez would pay him after the US election would more than make up for any lousy overtime bonus.

---

THE WHITE, clean, and clinical office seemed a lot creepier with the other staff gone. His footsteps, the hum of the electronic equipment, all the sounds were louder. The place reminded him of a hospital at night.

Retracing Iglesias's searches was a piece of cake. A simple matter of logging on with the credentials he'd provided the American, plugging in the app that he'd pre-installed to record every single key-stroke, then aggregate the results and home in on the drives and folders visited.

Palacio wriggled into the seat so well worn it fit like a glove. His eyes darted back and forth across the monitor as he retraced Iglesias's steps. He smiled for a moment—he really was feeling like a detective. *Right, let's see.* Iglesias had been extremely thorough in his investigation of the Brohman disappearance using Clandestine

Operations resources, that was for sure. He'd watched the CCTV from Pepe's—where the Venezuelan beauty recruited by Palacio from the desperate-for-money ex-pat community, Carolina, had lured Brohman to his doom. Or whatever happened to him—Palacio had no idea and didn't want to know. He shuddered as he recalled how he and another Venezuelan from indoor soccer had snatched Hererra and bullied the living shit out of him before handing the poor fellow over to men in ski masks on the outskirts of town. His friend was a little too gleeful when he applied the glowing cigarette ends to Hererra's face; Palacio would have to seriously rethink that friendship.

Iglesias then went through the video footage shared by the National Police. Also trawled through the reports on the abduction submitted by the cops and the one compiled by the dearly departed Gilberto and Ricardo. None of the office staff had met those men, who had worked in the shadows and kept away from the office as if it contained people contaminated with the plague. Their sensational deaths were brushed off by Stynes, who said the local police would handle it. "They were contractors, not staff," he'd said, not a trace of sadness in his voice. "They were good operators but not irreplaceable."

He looked at his watch. Another twenty minutes before Sanchez would call. So far, nothing to tell about what Iglesias was up to. Then a thought. Research the man, not what he had done.

A Google search turned up a couple of American businessmen called Carlos Iglesias. One ran a Tesla dealership in Michigan, another a supermarket in upstate Oregon. Neither looked anything like the man Palacio had met. Social media was also a barren path. He accessed the security camera images from the offices, created a still from the video that captured Iglesias's face, and ran an Internet image search. Nada.

Then the entire menu of international face recognition databases. He whistled through pursed lips as a couple of matches came up. The one that blew his mind was a match with 65 percent certainty. A heavily disguised bank robber in Switzerland.

He expanded the image. The eyes were very similar to Iglesias's. The height and build of the man were also exactly right. Other than that, nothing.

The man was a phantom. Sanchez wouldn't be thrilled to hear the news, but what could he do about it? Palacio had exhausted every possibility.

Next task: the Villa Serenidad. Who was Maria Sanchez? Adolfo didn't say: his gut told him it was either his mamma or grandmother. Or maybe an aunt. The important thing was get in and out without being detected. And that was always a problem. Another problem was time. He could send a phishing email to get inside their system, but that could take days, or his own bait could be immediately deleted. And if they opened it, someone would have to click on the link he'd created to gain backdoor access to their mail account.

Not. Going. To happen.

He sat there for a while, drinking a flat cola from a can he'd left on his desk all day. He googled the name of the nursing home. Lots of contact details, the name of the manager. How easy would it be to track down Margarita Alvarez in a town like Tuxtla?

He remembered a trick his cousin the debt collector revealed to him about finding information on people. Talk to the neighbors. "It's easy," Vicente told him over a couple of beers back in Puerto Rico. "You pretend you're some long-lost relative, school friend, whatever, and you're desperate to catch up with so-and-so. Doesn't always work, but sometimes you strike gold."

Great idea in theory. He checked Google Earth, zeroing in on a couple of houses next door to the retirement village. He figured out a couple of addresses, did a reverse search on the CIA database, and came up with a couple of phone numbers. Problem was, the village was gated, and it was unlikely the residents would associate with the folks in surrounding homes. But hang on a second. There appeared to be a small grocery store on the corner. Maybe it was still open. He zoomed in on street view, maneuvering the cursor. The sign above the mini mercado said the store was open until 9:00 p.m. Even the phone number was on display.

Two rings and a woman answered.

"Sorry to bother you. My name is Juan (true) Marrón (lie). I've been trying to get in touch with a lady that I think lives in your neighborhood, but I only have an old phone number." He quickly explained he was calling from Bogotá, and that he needed to speak to the lady in question about a legal matter (his cousin had told him that phrase always got people's attention).

"Oh yes? And who would that be?"

"Maria Sanchez."

The woman laughed. "Dios mío! Are you kidding me? That's a very common name. There are three of them I know who buy produce here."

"Oh."

"Which one do you want?"

He hesitated. "I...think she might be in one of the nursing homes in the area."

"Which one?"

"I don't know."

"Well—" The woman sounded a little uncertain. "There's Maria from the Villa Serenidad. Lovely, she is. Always smiling, talking about her son in the army. In fact, she was in just an hour ago. Bought a bottle of tequila and some peanuts. You want me to..."

"No. That's fine. You've been a great help." That was enough with this conversation. He couldn't risk word filtering back to the nursing home administrators. Sanchez expressly said in his text that must not happen.

He looked at the clock icon in the bottom of the screen. Sanchez would be calling back soon. Time to make a start on the stupid roster rebuild. He had to have at least some of the work done to show that prick James tomorrow or his life would be misery all day.

The job for James was surprisingly easy: done in under 20

minutes. He decided to kill time with an online video game until the call came. Up 2 to 0 against the robot in an online soccer tournament, his phone rang.

Palacio's nerves jangled as he answered Sanchez's insistent questions with answers that didn't create joy on the Mexican end. Thankfully, Sanchez was calm about it all, not blaming the messenger as Palacio had feared might happen.

"And the Villa Serenidad?"

"I had no hope of cracking their emails with the amount of time at my disposal. I would've needed at least–"

"Never mind. Thanks for trying."

"Wait!" He explained how he'd managed to fool the storekeeper.

"No! Impossible."

"I swear. She said Maria had been in the store an hour ago. A little more than that now."

Palacio had no idea how Sanchez felt about that piece of news. The call disconnected, and that was that.

# TWENTY-NINE

She held her tongue just so; slightly poking out of the right side of her mouth. It was her signature concentration pose, and it often earned plenty of laughs from those around her. A colleague back in Moscow at the Ministry of Finance had christened her with the unflattering nickname of *Yascheritsa*, which she hated, although the English translation of *lizard* sounded pretty to her ears.

No amount of tongue gymnastics was helping. The amount of effort the CIA had gone to in terms of protecting itself from cyber attacks was no surprise. The real surprise would come if she had any success at all in breaching the firewall.

Again she ran through the code of the Trojan horse she'd created. Not perfect, but it might do the trick.

She called Jacob on his new Mexican burner. "Hey. Busy?"

"I'm getting ready to disappear from Tuxtla. I'm taking a bus to Mexico City as planned. When I get to the embassy, I'm going to call him, see if the tech guys there can help me get a location on Sanchez via his cell."

"Don't hold your breath. Like we assumed already, he'll be covering his ass."

"Yeah, well, until we get something from the remote sensing

experts, I have to at least do something. I can't sit around twiddling my thumbs."

She couldn't argue with that, although she'd rather he was home and not sticking his neck on the line to protect a president she felt no loyalty toward. If anything happened to Jacob, Claxton could rot in hell. She pushed the thoughts of danger out of her mind. He was in the lion's den, and she would do absolutely anything she could do to help him get the job done and out of there as fast as possible. She'd called in sick this morning after undertaking to prepare a seminar for a coterie of specialists, and her boss was furious. And, she sensed, not totally convinced she was on the level. If she couldn't crack Bogotá today, she had a feeling unpleasant things awaited her at the bank tomorrow.

"Listen, here's my idea. Did you have an email address created for you in Bogotá?"

"No. Didn't need one."

"Okay. Let's rectify that. Call the IT boss there"—she paused as she wracked her brain before remembering his name—"Marty James. Tell him you need one set up straight away. Make sure he does it personally, doesn't delegate it to Juan Palacio. Make it something simple. jiglesias@cia.gov."

"On what pretext? Why would I need a CIA email address?"

She spun a pen around on the desk in Fletcher's tech room. Not her preferred environment to work in, but the resources were virtually unlimited. In addition to herself, there was a team in another location banging their heads together to try and find a way into the Bogotá citadel. "You were put in charge of the office there. Even if you aren't physically there, you've got the authority. It's not for James to question why. Just demand it. If he asks why, tell him you need to keep this case entirely separate from everything else and...shit, just tell him it's an order from the White House and it's his top priority."

"You're not just a pretty face, Irochka. Normally that kind of name dropping gets results."

"Only, could you do it now, please? Once you've got an

account you can log into remotely, do it. Send me the log in details, and I'll be you. After that, your Skia pals and I should be able to figure out how to get in the back door."

Twenty minutes later, the call came. Jacob gave her the URL for the email server, the username and password and wished her luck. And, just like that, Irina was him.

She contacted the three other IT specialists assisting her. They took a vote on the four possible Trojan horse viruses to embed in an email 'Jacob' would send to himself with the word TEST in the subject line and code hidden in the body of the message. Four to zero they voted in favor of deploying the Trojan software Irina had developed. She had a hunch they wanted her to go with her own baby in case it was detected at the other end. That way, they'd all have a better chance of keeping their jobs if it led to a major snafu. Which was always a possibility. Especially in this instance, where Marty James was one of the top programmers ever to come out of MIT and quite capable of detecting if a thief had crept into the inner sanctum.

A swig of cold coffee, a crack of the knuckles, lizard tongue out. A quick intake of breath and a squint of the eyes. Intense concentration. Like an orchestra conductor about to wave the baton and get the symphony underway, her index finger made the first, confident key stroke.

Within thirty minutes, she'd found and copied everything she possibly could— emails as well as the contents of Palacio's hard drive. The temptation to access every computer on the network gripped her. Yes, they were primarily interested in Palacio, but who knew who else was implicated in whatever was going down? So she did just that. Ripped the individual hard drives of every employee on the system, plus a couple of shared drives. Heart racing—although she was at no risk personally, according to Fletcher—she jumped out of the system and obliterated every trace that 'Jacob' had even been there.

---

HER EYES BULGED as she forked over the harvest. There were numerous emails between Palacio and NID liaison director Laura Torres. Going back several months, at least one a week and sometimes two or three. The content was wrapped up in code—when she transferred the email texts into Skia's proprietary universal translation machine, it made no sense whatsoever in English: random, unconnected words.

"It doesn't matter," said Fletcher, hovering over her like a dragonfly. "We'll get it decoded eventually. What's important is the fact the two were directly corresponding. He's a lowly IT assistant, she's a high-ranking officer of Colombia's top intelligence organization. I can't see any reason for such regular correspondence."

"Should we send the texts to Jacob?"

Fletcher shook his head. "It will be just as meaningless to him in Spanish. Our translation machine is better than any in existence. Can you try and decode it?"

Irina shrugged. "If I were you, I'd get a Spanish-speaking equivalent of me onto it. There could be some cultural nuances in the exchanges only a human would pick up on."

"Good idea." He scratched stubble he'd missed during his morning shave. "You know, I can't believe how careless Palacio was here," said Fletcher, arms crossed as he paced the floor. He was so absorbed in the revelations, he didn't hear his phone blaring out Colonel Bogey in his trouser pocket. "Using the work email for stuff like this instead of his private one seems the height of stupidity."

"Arrogant, more like it," said Irina. "It's often the way with people who think they know everything, that they are smarter than everyone else. By the way, your cell phone?" She nodded at the source of the ringing.

Fletcher snatched at the device and placed it to his ear. Even from a distance, Irina heard the immediate ranting on the other end of the line. Fletcher paced as he listened with a pained expression and a palm pressed firmly to his brow. After a few moments, he interrupted. "We have made substantial progress on our end, Joel. Thanks to Hunter, we're getting closer to finding Brohman. He's chasing a lead in Mexico, where Sanchez comes from, and... Please don't raise your voice to me. No, no, let me finish." He sighed deeply. "Listen, I'm putting you on loudspeaker, so you'd better mind your manners." He flashed a grin at Irina, reveling in his superior rank over the angry CIA man.

"Who's listening in, Grant?" McDonald blurted in his feminine tone. "I have a right to know."

"A trusted colleague who has done the impossible. Even without the encryption codes that you sent eventually got here." Fletcher laid heavy sarcastic stress on the word *eventually*.

McDonald mumbled something unintelligible, then: "Tell me more about this progress."

"Like I said, Hunter's in Mexico, we believe in an area where Sanchez has his base. We've got our own remote sensing experts combing through a vast archive of satellite images because your guys are taking so long. I believe a breakthrough is imminent."

"We're all doing the best we can." McDonald sounded pissed and disingenuous. "That's encouraging. I'll forward the news to Claxton."

"Additionally, we have 100 precent positively identified the mole inside the Clandestine Operations office. As we told you already, it's Juan Palacio."

"It better be something better than a pair of fucking boots."

"Much better, although the boots were enough, in my opinion. Our officer infiltrated the Bogotá system, got into every nook and cranny." He explained the encoded email correspondence between Palacio and Torres. "Palacio is the rat, but to what extent remains to be seen."

"Hey!" shouted Irina, who'd been digging further into the digital treasure trove, barely registering the heated discussion between the two men. "Come and look at this."

"Hang on a second, Joel."

Irina pointed at her screen. There was a collection of images of Carmen's brother talking to Paul Brohman taken during the day on the streets of the city with a couple at night outside Pepe's nightclub. In three images, Hererra and Brohman were shaking hands, smiling, in one even laughing.

"I'm calling you back on video link," he barked into the phone. Seconds later, he was waving the cell in front of the images on the monitor for McDonald's benefit. "Do you have any idea why a lowly IT assistant would be tailing and photographing the president's friend?" He laid on the sarcasm for the next part. "You think Stynes couldn't find someone among the highly trained Langley graduates and plumped for this dude?"

Irina sat back in bewilderment. The men were supposed to be on the same team, yet they were acting like rivals. She chipped into the conversation. "There are annotated Word documents that I think might go with these pictures. Like with the emails, I copied the text into your translation engine, but this time—no coding. Look." She pointed at another part of the huge monitor. "Dates, times, even information about where the pair met and whether items were exchanged. In fact, in one case, it's recorded that Brohman handed what appeared to be an unknown amount of cash to Hererra."

"I agree," said McDonald. "It looks very suspicious."

"Joel! Don't be fucking obtuse! You have to move now. Two men are missing, there's encoded material in emails, and this Palacio guy is implicated up to his neck."

"All right, all right. I'll move on it."

"About time you started talking sense, Joel." Fletcher sighed. "Irina, I'll leave you to keep searching for evidence. You okay with that?"

She nodded. The excitement of what she was discovering, piece by piece, gave her an adrenaline rush like she'd rarely experienced before.

"Good. I need to speak with Joel in private now. It's time for him to decide what he's going to do next."

“This is all well and good,” said McDonald. “But we still haven’t found Brohman. The clock’s ticking.”

“With this link to Laura Torres, I have a feeling we are very close to…” The rest of what Fletcher said grew fainter and fainter until he closed the door to the tech room behind him, leaving Irina to plow on.

With another diet soda on the desk and no more obvious secrets to be unraveled from Palacio’s drive, she clicked on the icon representing the working (and perhaps more) life of Jim Stynes and started reading.

# THIRTY

THE OLD TOOTHLESS MAN NEXT TO HIM STANK AND could use a long, hot shower. With luck, he would get off well before Mexico City. The man undid the zipper of a bag between his legs on the floor and pulled out a spotty banana. "Have one, señor. This is the only food I can eat with no teeth. And they have to be real ripe ones at that. You have very few supplies, I see."

That was an understatement. He had no supplies. Just a wallet full of money stuffed down the front pocket of his jeans to buy food at rest stops. "I'll be okay." He smiled. "My plan is to sleep most of the way, maybe buy something at roadside cantinas."

"You a gringo?"

"Si. Is my Spanish that bad?" He laughed.

"No. Perfecto. You just look like one." He cackled a crazy old-man laugh. "John Wayne!"

Jacob couldn't help but join in with the infectious laughter. God knew he'd had precious little to laugh about over the last four days.

The old man nodded sagely. "Good idea to sleep, gringo. Half a day on the bus is a long time to be sitting in one spot." He gave Jacob a once-over, paying attention to his polo shirt bearing the

Ralph Lauren label. "You look like you can afford a plane ticket. Why aren't you flying?"

Good and reasonable question. Truth was, Fletcher was unable to get a private plane to fly to this airport. Cynthia was busy on a job in the Middle East, and there were no spare Gulf Streams available. Even if the boss had managed to score a plane at short notice, Jacob didn't fancy trying to smuggling his guns through security. He'd been extremely lucky at Tunja; best not to push that luck any further. His heart had leapt into his mouth when he saw the random bag checks as the passengers lined up to board the coach. As a standout in appearance among the locals, he was sure he'd be selected for a thorough vetting. Nope. The transport official looked at his ticket and waved him through. She even gave him a big smile and wished him a pleasant journey.

Jacob shrugged and said to the old man, "I choose the bus because I'm scared of flying, simple as that. So I have to take the long way every time."

"I've never been on a plane," the old man admitted with a tinge of regret. "Different reason to you. No fucking money!" Another hysterical laugh, accompanied by some knee slapping. As enchanting as the stinky little old man was, his antics would wear thin quickly. And the odor would become unbearable. Jacob excused himself and found a woman sitting on her own in an aisle seat, two spots back from the WC. For 1,000 pesos— around $60 —she willingly swapped seats. "I ate something that didn't agree with me last night," said Jacob. "So I...ah...need to be near the bathroom." Needing no extra persuasion, she grabbed her bag and headed for the seat Jacob had vacated. No one occupied the window seat, but passengers were still boarding. As the bus pulled out of the terminal, he still had no neighbor.

The pitch blackness outside and the trundling of the bus, combined with a tired body and mind, meant sleep came easily. Dreamless, uninterrupted sleep until the first scheduled stop, three and a half hours later at the Coatzacoalcos Bus Depot near the oil refinery city of Minatitlán on the Gulf of Mexico. Out into the humid night with the other zombies, a stretch of the legs, a hot dog and fries and a soda, then back for the next ass-numbing leg of the trek.

More solid sleep until Veracruz. Replay the routine of the first stop. Five hours and forty minutes left to the capital city. The free seat remained blissfully unoccupied for the rest of the trip until the sleek red-and-white coach pulled gently into the Eastern Bus Station in Mexico City at 8:25 the following morning.

At one point in the middle of the night, a burly male passenger woke him up with a firm shake of the shoulder. Jacob leapt to his feet, ready to repel the attacker with his fists, an eye on his bag containing the Glock and the Sig Sauer should fists not prove up to the task. "What the fuck do you want, asshole?" he hissed in Spanish.

"You got some spare change, señor? I saw you give that woman"—he pointed up the aisle—"some money. Sat down with a big smile on her face, so I figure it was a lot." He laughed softly like a lunatic escaped from the asylum.

"I owed it to her." Jacob kept his voice calm and even. "Do not disturb me again, or I'll have you thrown off the bus and handed over to the police. Entiendes? *Got it?*"

The strange man, pupils like pinholes and darting all over the place, placed his hands up as if in surrender and barked like a dog. Jacob stared him down before the man spun unsteadily on his heel and shuffled back to his seat. *Drugs*, Jacob thought. *This is the end result of what I'm fighting against.*

Sunlight woke him. That and the hiss of the air brakes.

Out in the bus waiting hall, a representative of the Embassy of the United States awaited him. Turned out it was two representatives: a veritable welcoming committee. One held up a sign bearing the name *Carlos Iglesias.*

"I guess you fellas are here to take me to see the station chief?"

"Correct. Follow me, please, sir," said the shorter of the two.

No pleasantries on the long walk to the vehicle. The escorts gave the impression they were in a desperate hurry to get out of the lot. He remembered the jolly banter with Gilberto and Ricardo, God rest their souls, when they fetched him in Bogotá. These CIA men were soulless automatons by comparison.

And that suited Jacob just fine. It gave him time in the back of the black town car to compose his second message to Adolfo Sanchez. It simply said, *Call back on this number within fifteen minutes or we slit Mamma's throat.*

Two more SMS messages to send. To Carmen on the local cell he'd bought in Tuxtla. *I'm in Mexico. Any news, text me on this burner.* To Irina. The exact same message, with an *I love you* tacked on the end. He kissed the screen and slid the phone back into his pocket.

---

THE AMBASSADOR, a distinguished silver-haired gentleman called Mark Roffey, greeted Jacob at the reception with a twinkle in his eye. There was none of the attitude he experienced from the frontline staff in Bogotá. Overall, it seemed a slicker outfit in Mexico City. The building was vastly more appealing aesthetically, reflecting the greater geopolitical importance of Mexico than its poorer and more distant cousin Colombia.

The complex sprawled over a large territory, and the CIA station, which didn't officially exist, occupied but a tiny part of it. The FBI didn't hide its presence here, and it was a mystery to Jacob why the Feebies weren't working on this case. It seemed exactly the kind of operation they'd be involved in. Them and/or the DEA.

Roffey handed Jacob over to a female with a severe ponytail and the reddest lipstick he's ever seen, who took him down a maze of corridors and down a short flight of stairs into a bunker. She asked him to take a seat in a small waiting room with dark walls. He sat still on a shiny wooden bench, meditating and wondering in what direction this bizarre case would head next.

"Mr. Iglesias?" A lean and sinewy man with horn-rimmed

glasses and thinning brown hair approached confidently. "The team is waiting in the situation room."

Inside, a group of five operatives sat behind computers, not including the man who'd brought him inside. All rose as Jacob entered and gathered behind the man who was clearly in charge. He introduced himself as Kenneth Pilkington, named his colleagues and their functions, and offered to help Jacob in any way they could. "We've been given the heads-up that this comes directly from the White House." He confirmed Jacob's initial thoughts next when he said, "This kind of stuff normally gets handled with DEA and FBI involvement in liaison with the Mexicans, but for some reason, it's been handed to us." He gestured toward the team members. "Normally it's just two of us here. The others have been pulled in from other cities to see if we can get this over and done with quickly and with minimum, preferable zero, casualties."

Jacob nodded, realizing how damn tired he was despite sleeping for the majority of the bus trip. "Appreciate it. The most important thing you can do for me right now is bring me a strong, hot coffee, cream and sugar."

---

"We set to go?" said Jacob, sitting next to two men wearing headsets.

Both men nodded and gave a thumbs-up. "Make the call whenever you're ready. Trace will kick in after you've had him on the line for two minutes."

"Really?" said Jacob. "What if he–"

"Only joking," said one of the men, introduced as Spike. "That's the stuff of TV shows. We've already got a general idea of where this cell phone is. But it's a very broad area. Huge in fact. Because it's a rural location, there aren't many towers and infrastructure to make a more accurate triangulation. But getting any response from him now will help narrow that area down. The

Mexican police already obtained what we needed in order to ping his location through the provider of the 'silent number.' Which got us that massive Lacandón jungle. Now enough of my waffling. You going to call him?" The man adjusted his headset with a wriggling motion.

"I've got a text I'm going to send, demanding that he call me back," said Jacob. "The SIM inside my burner is actually Sanchez's mother's."

"Holy shit!" said the second man in headphones, Alan. "You're some kind of spy, my friend. I can't even imagine how you did that!"

"Let's get on with it, shall we?" said Jacob. He pressed the button, and the SMS was sent. "Let's wait a while. I've given him ten minutes to respond."

Ten minutes went by without a response from Sanchez.

"Not to worry." Jacob grinned. "I was anticipating this."

At the eleven minute mark, a phone call came through. Number withheld but it could only be Sanchez. Jacob pressed the green button. In his best Mexican accent, he said, "Sanchez?"

"No. A friend of his."

"Bullshit." Jacob couldn't believe the temerity. "Listen to me. You must transport Paul Brohman tomorrow into Ocosingo. Leave him on the steps of the post office at 10:00 a.m. and disappear. We will have the area covered with firepower you and your shitty cartel can only dream about. So no funny business." He waited for a reply, but none came, just heavy breathing. "Did you hear what I said, cabrón?"

"Si. And I have a message to you from Señor Sanchez. He says you can go fuck yourself!"

"Very well. I'm sorry he feels that way. We are now forced to carry out our threat. His mother Maria will unfortunately be killed, the images sent to him, and a video spread all over the Internet. He will have zero authority or credibility, and the other cartels will crush him. Perhaps that will change his mind."

Jacob glanced to his left. A nod and a thumbs-up from headphones man one.

"Ha ha! You are very confused. Drunk perhaps?" said the voice speaking on Sanchez's cell. "Because Maria is standing right here next to me. Say hello, Maria."

Jacob ended the call. "Jesus fucking Christ!" He tossed the cell at a wall, taking a chip out of the plasterboard.

"We've traced it!" rejoiced Alan, whipping off his headset. "Right to the very street address."

"Yeah, and I can tell you exactly where it is. Not in the jungle, that's for sure. Villa Serenidad in the suburbs of Tuxtla, state of Chiapas." His genius plan had come unstuck in the most dramatic, even humiliating fashion. "Somehow Sanchez figured out the AI clip of his mother was fake. How? It was next-level convincing, dammit!"

Roffey stood off to the side, scratching his long chin. "Is he right about the location?"

"Bang on target," said Spike, offering open palms and a screwed-up-lips frown.

Jacob paced the floor, then headed for the coffee percolator and poured himself a big cup. "No, it's not the clip. He's been tipped off. Maybe Alvarez, the manager of the retirement village. I know Sanchez likes to remain a phantom figure, but perhaps there are people he trusts. She could be one of them."

Roffey gave Jacob a quizzical look. "Should we advise the police in Chiapas that we suspect Sanchez has popped his head up there?"

"No. It's not him. An errand boy. His mother hasn't seen him in years. We probably spooked Sanchez with the video. My gut tells me he would've believed it at first, but curiosity made him do some checking. Now it seems obvious that a cunning prick like him won't frighten so easily."

"Then what next?" said Roffey.

"We wait on the satellite experts to find some potential

targets, then either narrow them down or target them all. Claxton won't spare the dollars to get Brohman out of trouble."

"Brohman's probably dead," said Brent, an analyst who'd remained quiet for some time. "We've got no proof he's alive."

"Nor that he's dead," Jacob pointed out. "And while we're waiting for the experts to get us what we need, I'm not going to sit idly by and do nothing." He pointed at Brent, dark haired and swarthy. Also built like a wrestler. "You. How's your Spanish?"

"Fluent. I grew up in El Paso, and my mother is Mexican."

"Combat skills?"

He laughed. "Two tours of Iraq."

"Feel like a day away from the office?"

# THIRTY-ONE

SIRENS FLASHED RED AND BLUE, STROBING AGAINST THE gunmetal gray sky. A crowd of people stood behind police tape about fifty yards away from the vehicle. She could make out a forest of arms holding phones aloft, citizens capturing the excitement for their social media accounts. Two more squad cars blocked off the road at either end. Having come via a narrow side alley the cops hadn't yet sealed off, Carmen approached the entrance to the building slowly. Small, hesitant footsteps. Her instincts yelled at her: *Turn back and go home, you've got nothing to gain by being here*. Yet she inched her way forward, looking left and right as she went. Apart from the handful of police, she was now the only person on the street.

"You have a reason to be in the area?" A well-muscled female officer in reflector sunglasses ambled across in Carmen's direction. She hoisted the glasses onto the top of her head, revealing stunning brown eyes. Inexplicably, Carmen felt an odd flutter in her stomach as the attractive cop eyeballed her. *I'm not, am I?* she wondered. "The space needs to be kept clear for when the detectives arrive, so best if you trot along."

Carmen pointed at the big black door across the street and mumbled: "I work in that building over there."

"Okay. Do you need to be at work right now?"

Carmen nodded. "Yes." She chewed her knuckle for a second and said, "What's happened here? Why are there police?"

"There's been an armed holdup at a café. A waiter got stabbed and some money was taken." The officer pointed a long index finger. It was the same cafe she'd visited with Iglesias. "We've arrested the culprit, so there's no danger to you. Still, I'd like to ask. Did you see anything suspicious on your way here?"

A quick shake of the head. "No. I've only just turned the corner up there near the alleyway. Everything looked normal." She laughed uneasily. "Then again, this is Bogotá."

The officer escorted her across the street. "You okay? You look a little shaken up."

"I've been through a lot lately. When I saw all the action going on, it made me think about that assassination the other day, the men shot in their car."

The woman shook her head. "Terrible business. We're still looking for that guy who pretended to be a cop. Can you believe it?"

"No." She *could* believe it all right. The urge to get away from the officer now was overwhelming. "Anyway, like I said, I need to get to work, if that's all right with you?" She pointed at the door again.

"Of course."

As she tapped in her PIN, Carmen thought, and not for the first time, about how wonderful it would be to get the hell out of Bogotá. Too much crime, too much poverty, too many drugs. She envied Iglesias. How lucky his parents moved from Colombia when he was a kid!

A sense of relief flowed through her body as she ascended the stairs. She'd half expected the police presence outside to be linked with her own office, to Iglesias. The sight of law enforcement uniforms was beginning to become almost a phobia for her. She didn't trust them; in fact, she barely trusted anyone now that Miguel was dead. He'd been her rock since they were children.

Iglesias had kind of filled the gap, but it was only temporary. He'd be heading back to America sooner or later.

"Great to see you back," beamed Stynes as she turned the handle and opened the glass door to the reception. Her haven in this work-prison. "You've been missed by everyone." He was fussing about in her space with a pile of papers and paperclips, everything a mess, clueless as per normal. What a hypocritical asshole.

"Great to be back," she lied, giving what she knew would be the wateriest of smiles.

"Wonderful." He stepped aside, apparently intent on getting back to his own office. The gall of the man: he acted like her being coerced into sleeping with Brohman had never happened. Perhaps he was suffering from some kind of autism? Yes, that was it. She'd read about the condition. No empathy for others. That symptom certainly applied to him. At the door, he said, "Let's get together for coffee and cookies at 10:30 with the rest of the staff, okay?"

"Lovely," she mumbled in his wake. The fake smile he wore the whole time undoubtedly reflected his sense of relief. Now he wouldn't have to find a replacement admin worker to cope with the backlog. She'd never met a more selfish person than Stynes. She took a deep breath. *Just do your job and forget about him.*

Today the plan was a basic one: immerse herself in mundane clerical tasks, but at the same time stay alert for any office talk that could point to the mole Iglesias had spoken of. She'd agreed to be his eyes and ears. How effective she'd be in that role was up for question. She didn't interact with many people in the sensitive areas of the department, where the 'real work' was done. Doing this for Iglesias was more a symbolic effort than a realistic opportunity to find out anything of value. But who knew? She remembered an English phrase she'd memorized at high school, as much for its beautiful sound as for its meaning: loose lips sink ships. Right now, her radar was switched to the 'on' position.

With the reception to herself, she settled in at her familiar desk and logged on to the system. She spent the first hour alone reading a bunch of emails, most of them irrelevant, but it was a great way to practice guilt-free procrastination. The emails were work 'related,' so it was legit to read them, but no way in hell they were real work. After that, reconciling expense dockets and typing up letters from Stynes' handwritten notes (even his blotchy handwriting was ugly, like the man himself) took her to 10:20 a.m. Stynes stuck his head in twice to ask a couple of dumb questions; she barely looked up to speak to him. Looking at his face made her want to puke.

Halfway through typing another letter, all hell broke loose.

Stynes' alarmed voice over the phone reached a volume she wasn't used to; the man was almost shouting. Not like him to lose his cool. Something extremely serious was up; she could feel it in her bones. She remembered another English expression, something about shit hitting a fan. Stynes barged into the reception, eyes ablaze.

"Men from the embassy have arrived. Most inconvenient. Please go downstairs and show them up."

"What was all the yelling about?"

"They're demanding we hand over everything for a forensic audit. They want to shut us down for a couple of days and go through our databases. All to do with this unfortunate incident of the businessman being kidnapped."

"What the hell!" He couldn't even bring himself to say the name Brohman. Perhaps the gutless wonder did have some shame after all.

"Exactly what I said." He waved his hand with a flicking motion. "Now please, let them in. The way one of the rude bastards spoke to me, I wouldn't be surprised if they busted the fucking door down."

A frisson of pleasure coursed through Carmen's body. Seeing Stynes in panic mode had made coming into the office worth it for that alone. She prayed he was in the firing line, that he was the mole, that he would suffer indignities, just like she had. "Yes, sir," she snapped, not even trying to hide the sarcasm in her voice. Yet Stynes, the self-centered moron, couldn't even detect it.

"Thanks, Carmen. You're a treasure."

The men at the bottom of the stairs were from Hollywood central casting, thriller movie department. Goons in black suits, crisp white shirts, and Ray-Bans. She didn't wait for them to introduce themselves. "Please, come this way."

She almost skipped up the stairs. Maybe they would shut the whole operation down for good. Objectively, the outpost had failed miserably to fulfil its mission. Agents being exposed all over the country and Stynes unable to figure out why. If the arrival of these heavies signaled the end of her career as an underpaid minion of the United States government, then bring it on. She couldn't wait to give her statement about what Stynes had made her do. "In here, gentlemen."

She watched closely from behind as Stynes stood, holding out his hand to the taller of the visitors. No hand extended by the CIA man. *Delicious,* thought Carmen. *He's totally fucked.*

---

SHE TRIED to focus on the translated document on balance of trade that she was supposed to be proofreading. None of it made any sense—not in English, not in Spanish. It probably did in reality, but concentrating on the complex language that she usually handled with ease was proving impossible. Then, out of the corner of her eye, she saw the two suits escorting Juan Palacio down the corridor. Palacio's head was bowed, his body barely staying upright. She jumped out of her seat, opening the door a fraction in time to see the three of them reach the bottom of the stairs. The door clicked shut, and they were gone. Butterflies swarmed in her stomach. She raced back into her office and fired off an SMS to Iglesias on the Mexican burner number he'd texted her just hours ago. *Palacio's been arrested.* Eyes and ears.

At 10:34, Stynes cradled his coffee as he addressed the staff. "I had hoped today would be a happy one, with Carmen back on deck." He gestured toward her with a wink that made her skin crawl. "But, unfortunately, we've also had some bad news. It seems Juan was feeding information to a third party and also involved in some unsavory activities. As such, he's been taken away for further questioning. If found guilty, he's off to Guantanamo."

"What the fuck did he do?" demanded Marty James. "We deserve to know."

"Apparently, we've been hacked into."

James shook his head. "Impossible! The firewalls I created can't be breached."

A deep frown from Stynes. "It seems they can. I won't go into details, but it's alleged Juan was involved in the abduction of a private citizen."

"Brohman?" said backroom intelligence analyst Fiona Giles, a pigtailed blonde with a heavy crop of freckles.

"I can't say."

"You were the one who suspected Brohman of being the mole, not one of us!" For some reason, she cast a glance at Carmen, then quickly looked away. Carmen noticed, though, and guessed why Giles might have looked at her like that. *She fucking knew.* Did they all know?

A look of horror crossed Stynes's face. "Please. I'd rather not get into specifics."

Carmen crossed her arms, staring defiantly at Giles. "Why did you just look at me like that?"

"Like what?" The woman's voice was the dictionary definition of defensive.

Tears welled in Carmen's eyes. She raised her right arm and swept it around in a circle until it finally landed on Stynes, like a prize wheel coming to rest on the winning number. "Jim here was so sure Brohman was a baddie, he made me sleep with him, plant a bug to get incriminating evidence. Turns out he couldn't have been more wrong." She scanned the staff to see if any of them looked surprised. None of them did. "I'll be talking with the same people who took Juan Palacio away, don't you worry. Spilling my guts. Telling then how I was coerced into doing something... unspeakable. Threatened with loss of employment if I refused." She watched their stunned faces again. This time, there was a spark of shock in some of their eyes. But it didn't matter. They all knew the bare bones of it. As such, they were all complicit.

She saw there was half a cup of coffee left in her cup, the dregs of a cookie she'd been dunking sitting on the bottom. She sauntered up to a stupefied Stynes and flung the remains in his face. "Fuck you!"

He recoiled but said nothing in his own defense. Because he had no grounds on which to defend himself.

She turned around and glared at the others. "Fuck all of you!"

# THIRTY-TWO

A HAZINESS HOVERED BEFORE HIS EYES. IT HAD BEEN bothering him for the last two days now. Like a permanent fog he couldn't get away from. Maybe he had a couple of floaters growing on his eyeballs. He was at the age where they can start to appear and affect your vision. He'd lost weight, too. At least ten pounds.

A bang on the door. "Brohman! Get your ass upstairs in five minutes," Javi growled. "Señor Sanchez wants a word. Dress nice and shave, 'cos you'll be on a Zoom call with a respectable lady. I've unlocked the door." A cackling laugh. "If you don't come, I'll be down with my toy taser to zap your ass."

He hadn't spoken to Sanchez for two days now. In fact, he'd been locked away in his apartment, left alone with meals brought in three times a day. The accommodation was luxurious in terms of furnishings but scant on what a modern person requires for entertainment. No TV, no phone, no Internet, but there was a radio. It only picked up Mexican stations, which gave Brohman the chance to absorb some Spanish. Not that it would do him any good if Sanchez planned on killing him. He passed the interminable hours by doing round after round of calisthenics and jerking off twice a day. He thought he might have struck it lucky on one occasion when, instead of Fernando, a bikini-clad beauty brought him lunch on a tray. But that was all she brought him. One book that had been left in the room for him. A fucking Bible. King James version in English, so at least it had some poetic value. He'd read Psalms and Revelations, got sick of it, and shoved the thing back in the drawer for the next victim.

Now Sanchez wanted to talk again?

He selected a clean shirt from the closet, chinos and a belt that he had to tighten an extra notch. The lost weight was a mystery to him; he'd been eating and drinking more than usual and exercising less. He half-heartedly chalked it up to the lack of sex, which he figured was the key calorie burner for his specific metabolism.

At the top of the spiral staircase, Fernando escorted Brohman to a large media room. On a big dropdown screen was a grim-faced woman, her hair tied back, with whom Sanchez was already engaging in an animated conversation in Spanish. The woman was familiar. He'd met her on a number of occasions in Bogotá. Laura Torres.

"Take a seat, Pablo!" said Sanchez, switching effortlessly to his perfect English with an ebullient smile. "You already told me you know the lovely Laura."

Brohman took the chair next to Sanchez. "Yes. We've met a few times before."

The obsequious waiter José appeared from nowhere and wordlessly left a platter of antipasto, a carafe of water, and two crystal cut glasses.

"We've just been discussing a very interesting development at Clandestine Operations in Bogotá, haven't we, Laura?" Sanchez dipped bread in oil and balsamic vinegar and chewed thoughtfully.

The severe woman nodded. "A very troubling development. Juan Palacio has been detained for questioning."

Brohman shook his head. "Isn't he the IT assistant? Can't say I know much about him."

"Let me illuminate," said Sanchez. "Juan Palacio was our inside man. He's the one you should be thanking for the luxury vacation you are having at my expense."

Brohman said nothing. This so-called development meant nothing to him at this point.

"He was the one who discovered you chatting with Miguel Hererra, whose innocent sister you so disgustingly defiled," said Torres, unable to hide her revulsion. "So he tipped off Adolfo about how you couldn't resist young women. Carolina reeled you in so easily, and here you are." This time she smiled.

"You've also got Miguel to thank, too, in a roundabout way," said Sanchez, turning to face Brohman. "You were the one he picked to hand over the intel which blew the cover of Palacio, as well as other agents spread all around Colombia. If you hadn't fucked his sister"—he roared with laughter—"you wouldn't even be here, do you realize that? If you need something to blame for your predicament, it's your penis." More uproarious laughter, which Torres joined in.

"But why did you kidnap me?" said Brohman. "It makes no sense. You've got the USB with the intel. You haven't asked me for money. You haven't—at least I think you haven't—asked anyone for a ransom for my release. I can only assume you plan to murder me, despite your assurances to the contrary."

"No one wants to murder anyone," said Torres.

*Tell that to Miguel and Carolina and who knows who else*, went through Brohman's mind.

"Exactamente," agreed Sanchez. "Such a drastic step and never taken lightly. At least by me."

"We want to make you an offer," said Torres enthusiastically.

Brohman shook his head. "I've got more than enough money. I don't know what you could entice me with."

"How about an endless supply of the type of young Colombian woman you desire?" said Sanchez with a wink. "All of legal age, never the same one twice. You'll be in dirty-old-man heaven."

"Hmmm." Brohman rubbed his chin. "Now that's an offer I could–"

No time to finish the sentence as Sanchez hauled back and slapped Brohman across the face with a vicious, stinging blow. "You filthy bastard!" Like a taser, the pain arced through Brohman's teeth, neck, down his spine. For his size, Sanchez was deceptively powerful. A hearty laugh came from the screen, Torres obviously relishing the violence.

"Jesus Christ!" wailed Brohman. "I was only kidding."

"Ha ha, Pablo. That's just the problem. You were not kidding. Your record and reputation go before you."

"Then, no." He sensed blood trickling from his nose, tickling his top lip. "There is nothing you can offer me."

"Hey," said Sanchez. "I just gave you a friendly slap and said you were a filthy bastard. I didn't say the offer wouldn't be a real one."

On the big screen, Torres shrugged. "Then we will simply hold you until the election is over next month. Adolfo can do whatever he wants with you then."

"The election?" Brohman scratched the back of his neck.

"If Hannah McIvor becomes president, we let you go, no hard feelings. You can chalk it up to experience, maybe start thinking more about your inappropriate behavior toward women."

Brohman shook his head in bewilderment. Surely they wouldn't just release him, would they?

"And if she loses, and it's neck and neck right now"—Sanchez snarled and made a throat-slitting gesture, eliciting a gawping stare from Brohman—"then maybe we'll have to rethink the catch-and-release policy."

Brohman drank water from a glass using both trembling hands and looked back at the screen. Sanchez noticed sweat beginning to bead on the man's brow, even though the air conditioning was set to a cool temperature.

Torres leaned forward as she peered into the camera. "I've got another proposal for you, Señor Brohman. Of course, Adolfo gets to veto it if he doesn't like the sound of it. We let you go now, a month before the election. In return, you will be our inside man in Washington. Pass on information about the Claxton campaign. Anything McIvor can use to exploit his weaknesses."

"After the election," continued Sanchez, "you will be released from your obligation to me, and I will never bother you again. You may travel to and from Mexico and Colombia with impunity, do your business, chase your women. How does that sound?"

"It sounds like a great deal," said Brohman, the smile genuine because, Sanchez was sure, he genuinely wanted to live and desperately wanted to get away from this place.

"My, my, Pablo. I expected more of a challenge." He yanked out the wedge of lemon from his bottle and guzzled half the Corona. "We'll work out the logistics after this little teleconference." He sensed a wave of relief pouring out of Brohman, like the air in the room had somehow lightened. He popped two olives in his mouth, and while chewing them on one side turned his attention back to Torres.

"Any luck with finding this mysterious American businessman?"

"No."

"Well, I think he's having a laugh at the expense of all of us."

"What do you mean?"

He explained the messages he'd received on his mother's cell number, the video of her being threatened. A look of curiosity passed over Torres, one finely plucked eyebrow hovering. "You don't seem too worried by it. I don't understand."

Two olive pips flew from between Sanchez's teeth and landed in a bowl with a ting. "It was a fake. A very good one, totally convincing. However, I smelled a rat and got Juan Palacio to investigate. He dug around and discovered my dear mother was exactly where she was supposed to be."

"A relief for you, I'm sure," said Torres.

"Indeed. Laura, what can you do to set him free? Please have a word with that Stynes fellow, offer him some incentives. A man with brains and cojones like Palacio has is the kind of person we want on our team permanently."

She shook her head. "I'm so sorry. He's totally screwed, from what I hear. Hauled away by the scruff of his neck. He'll never be heard from again."

"A shame." Sanchez nodded and tut-tutted. "I was afraid you'd say that. Thanks for your updates, Laura." He patted Brohman on the shoulder. "I'm sure your reassurances have helped convince Pablo here to do the right thing." He disconnected the call and pushed the plate of antipasto toward Brohman. "You not hungry?"

"Oh," the American replied absently. "Sure." He ate a chunk of feta cheese on a cracker.

"Now that you've agreed, in principle, to our offer, I want you to do one more thing before we organize to ship you out of here on the next donkey cart."

"What's that?"

"Place 80 percent of the money you were planning on donating to Claxton's election campaign fund into my little Panamanian trust account. He'll smell a rat if you're unable to drop at least some of your hard-earned cash into his coffers."

Brohman's face turned white. "Claxton won't be satisfied with 20 percent. He'll be expecting all of what I promised him."

"Listen. Why don't you tell him you've got unexpected medical expenses to meet after your harrowing ordeal?" Sanchez sighed. "Do I have to do the thinking for both of us?"

Brohman's hands were trembling again, droplets of sweat getting into his eyes. He blinked to get them out. "Eighty percent is a lot," he protested half-heartedly. "Maybe...a little less?"

Sanchez fired up his laptop and spun it around. He smiled. "You're absolutely right. Let's make it 75 percent. Now log into your bank account and let's get that transfer happening."

"I...can't remember the login details."

Sanchez picked up his mobile. "Javi. Our guest Pablo is having trouble recalling the details to access his online bank accounts." He ended the call, grinning at Brohman. "He's just fetching his taser. I bought it for him last Christmas."

Brohman's fingers began to dance across the keyboard. "Actually, I think I've just remembered."

# THIRTY-THREE

Slums. Jacob had been in lots of them. Shanty towns, ghettoes, favelas, down-at-heel American hellholes too. All kinds of run-down, violent neighborhoods with different labels and different demographics. And every time he'd had the misfortune to visit one, the reality was actually a lot less scary than the anticipation of what *might* happen.

"You okay, Brent?" said Jacob, making sure to speak Spanish with his new partner, even when they whispered in hushed tones. Outsiders here were not welcome; they knew that from the stares they attracted.

"Fine. You?"

"Never better. Only I'm getting frustrated at the way no one's ever heard of Adolfo Sanchez."

"Yeah," said Brent, stepping out of the way of a slack-eyed dog of indeterminate breed with protruding ribs you could scrub laundry on. "But not unexpected."

"I thought spreading around the green stuff would loosen a few tongues." He took off his baseball cap with the Los Angeles Dodgers logo on the front and wiped the dust and grime from his eyes. He squinted in the bright light of the sun. "Seems the name Adolfo Sanchez still carries a lot of weight in his old barrio. And instils a lot of fear."

Brent nodded. "Almost as much as La Unión Tepito, it seems," he said, referring to the biggest and most feared gang in the district, involved in the entire gambit of criminal activities: drugs, kidnapping, murder, extortion. "Let's try that cantina up ahead. Even if we strike out again, at least we can buy a beer. Money speaks the same language, no matter where you spend it."

They strode the litter-strewn path, keeping the brims of their hats low over their eyes. Someone had once described Tepito as a walled city with no walls, and Jacob certainly got a sense of that in this labyrinthine hood. The markets alone occupied 25 streets. Back here in the fetid shadows, where the poor suckers who lived here hung out, instead of tarps and tents, it was stucco walls, bright reds and greens mixed with pastel yellows and greens and blues. Graffiti galore. Here and there, corrugated iron constructions struggled to stay vertical while bodies full of alcohol, narcotics, or both slumped against the walls of buildings.

Jacob and Brent had decided to abandon the most densely choked areas with market stalls, known locally as tianguis in favor of the quieter back lanes of Tepito.

"You know this is a no-go zone to normal people," said Brent under his breath. "Including the police. I'm not actually sure this is a good idea."

"I'm starting to question the wisdom of coming here, too," Jacob conceded.

"Then maybe we turn back, get on the subway, and mosey on back to town. I can pick up some knock-off DVDs at the market on the way back. Maybe a second-hand AK-47."

"Maybe." Jacob liked the black humor but wouldn't be drawn into the banter, not just yet. "Let's try this street, then we go back." He scanned the dilapidated shacks running in a straight line up the narrow alley until perspective made them merge together in the near distance. "That old man back in Colombia, Zapata, said Sanchez had made plenty of enemies here before he sought out greener pastures. People he had stiffed who would love to see him carved into little pieces. You'd think at least one of them would hate Sanchez enough to squeal." He rubbed a hand over his mouth. "I could kill a beer anyways."

Brent also expressed a keen interest in slaking his thirst, even if it came at the price of wrecked nerves. They entered through a beaded flyscreen into a gloomy, cramped space. Four men sat on barstools, smoking and drinking beer from bottles, condensation running down the sides. Two of the customers were bare-chested, the other two sported grubby mesh shirts. The collective body odor from them was barely disguised by the clouds of smoke. A small fan mounted behind the bar cranked over slowly, dispersing warm air and the tobacco fog and doing absolutely nothing to cool the bar or suppress the smell. A radio played a lilting norteño tune, country music with a Mexican slant.

"What do you two want?" said the barman. He rubbed his long nose and sniffed dismissively.

"Two Dos Equis beers," Jacob replied flatly. "Ice cold."

The barman flicked a dirty dish towel over his shoulder. "Did I ask what you want to drink? No."

The men sitting at the bar laughed in a chorus. "Good one, Pancho," a skinny, bald man called out. "You let 'em know who's boss."

Jacob remained tight-lipped as he held the barman's narrowing gaze. Brent also kept silent, save for his rapid breathing.

"I asked, *What do you want?*" The man ran bejeweled fingers through long strands of jet-black greasy hair. "And by that I mean, what the fuck are you doing in this bar? I never seen you before. Any you guys seen these pendejos around here before?"

Head shakes and growls of "no."

Jacob's fingers began to flex; he presumed Brent's were doing the same. Embassy station chief Roffey had issued them the smallest pistols in the armory, a pair of .380 caliber Glock 42s. Neither men wore jackets—the heat was just bearable, but it was T-shirt weather. The little Glocks, with six plus one in the clip, were perfect to conceal in pants pockets.

"Ha ha!" cried the barman, clanking two bottles of the requested brand of beer in front of Jacob and Brent. The caps went sailing through the air as he expertly opened the bottles, a gasp of CO2 escaping. "I'm only playing with you guys. We don't mind strangers in our little corner of the world, do we, boys?"

There were general grunts of agreement that strangers were, in principle, okay.

He tapped the bar top with a long, dirt-encrusted fingernail. "As long as they're not chotas or here to cause trouble or...ask too many questions."

Jacob gulped. The suspicion they might be chotas, or cops, set his nerves alight. And the "too-many-questions" policy was going to make it hard to broach the subject of Sanchez. His cell buzzed annoyingly in his pocket—the one not containing the pistol. Whatever it was would have to wait until this little exchange was over and they were safely away from the place.

"We're just visiting," said Brent. "Doing some research for a university project."

"What kinda project?" said the closest bare-chested man, oily and wiry and covered in jail tattoos that included a network of blue ink all over his neck and face. Where there weren't tattoos, there were puckered scars and gold piercings.

"It's...ah... on the types of architecture found in highly populated urban areas around Mexico. We've always been interested in Tepito, heard so much about it."

"Not just the bad stuff," said Jacob, running his finger around the top of the bottle. "Although we're sure the stories about the violence are highly exaggerated." He gave a short laugh.

"You a couple of gays?" spat one of the men in a mesh shirt.

"Looks like it," agreed face tatts.

"You're studying together at some fancy university, that's one"—mesh shirt one pointed at Jacob—"this dude's playing with the neck of the bottle like it's the end of the other guy's cock, that's two. Add 'em up together, and we got ourselves a couple of maricas."

"I can assure you..." Jacob began, when there was another vibrating message on his cell phone. He reached into his pocket to turn it off, but the old clunker of a burner required you to actually look at it to figure out what you were doing. He pulled it out to see who the message was from, when from behind him the cell was snatched out of his hand. Jacob spun around to see the second bare-chested man waving the phone around, taunting. The man stood a head taller than face tatts but was still around three inches shorter than Jacob.

"Don't you know it's rude to look at your fucking phone when you're in company?"

"Hand it back, please. I won't do it again." He held up his hands. "We just want to drink our beers and leave."

To his left, face tatts had jumped out of his seat and wrapped a sinewy arm around Brent's neck. The left forearm interlinked with the right wrist to form a vise-like headlock. The color in Brent's face changed from red to purple in an instant, the increased blood pressure in his head forcing his eyes to bulge. He spluttered as he struggled to breathe; forcing a hand between the tight grip of the hostile had zero effect. He would soon succumb to either a sleeper hold or a spinal cord break. Neither scenario appealed to Jacob.

Coming here had been a mistake, Jacob knew now. A huge fucking mistake. Too late for regrets, though. A solution was needed and fast. The temptation was to try and talk his way out of it, but he canned that notion in a nanosecond. These men were drunk and in the mood for a confrontation. With their confidence boosted by alcohol, they thought they had the advantage in numbers and that their opponents were a couple of softies. Besides, Brent was in a world of trouble.

Jacob's hand darted into his pocket, feeling for the dwarf gun's metal handle. Before he had time to get it out, he felt the burn of a knife blade pierce the flesh of his hip. It wasn't deep, but it burned like hell.

A spinning roundhouse kick took care of the assailant at the rear, who dropped to the floor unconscious, blood spurting from a big gash above the eye. Jacob hit the deck and rolled, scooped up his cell phone and the knife, and leapt back to his feet.

"Enough!" cried the barman, who had ducked behind the bar and was waving his towel like a trainer in a losing boxer's corner. "You'll make a mess of my bar and then who'll clean it up, huh?"

"Let him go!" Jacob brandished the borrowed knife, the razor-sharp blade covered in his own blood. He screamed again at face tatts, who was laughing maniacally. "Let go NOW or I will kill all of you!" The man, whose blazing eyes darted in all directions, retightened his grip; Brent's eyes began to close, and sputum bubbled on his lips. The attacker bared a set of teeth that could probably tear through raw meat like it was soft bread.

"I'll say when it's enough," said the second mesh-shirted man. He swung off his stool like he was dismounting a horse, casually reach into his shorts pocket and produced a knife two inches longer than the one Jacob was holding. The man twisted it this way and that, holding it with a worrying familiarity, like he sliced people up with it every day. He stood underneath a softly glowing lamp about two feet away from fact tatts. The first mesh-shirted man gawked at the spectacle through a smile that was more gum than teeth. He was too old, drunk, or smart to get involved in the melee.

"Come on, pendejo!" called the man waving the knife. "Show us what you've got. You wanna save your pretty boyfriend's ass or not?"

Brent was fading fast. If Jacob didn't act now, he'd be unconscious or dead in seconds. *Why did I bring you on this fool's errand?*

Jacob reached into his cargo pants pocket and palmed the pistol, hiding it, and held up his left hand. He pointed at the ceiling with an up-and-down pumping motion. "Mira eso! Check it out!" For some reason, the men followed his gesture with their eyes.

With their attention momentarily diverted, Jacob quickly

leveled the pistol and squeezed off two rounds. One hit the lamp, sending shards of glass flying in all directions. The other bullet struck the knife-carrier in the middle of the forehead, leaving a neat, round hole. The shot had killed the man instantly.

Fact tatts instinctively let go of Brent, who fell to the floor. He held up his hands, begging Jacob not to shoot. "I was only kidding man." He caught a glimpse of the corpse on the floor and began to weep inconsolably.

"A little too late for excuses, isn't it?" Jacob leveled his gun at face tatts' nose; the man covered his face defensively. A bullet fizzed through the air, striking face tatts square in the patella. He squealed, cursing his own stupidity for falling for the simple diversion.

A quick survey of the room revealed that the barman was still hiding, yet the old man remained glued to his barstool, reveling in the spectacle.

Jacob raised Brent, heaving and panting, to his feet. "Are you all right?" he asked in Spanish, looking into his partner's bleary eyes. Even in the chaos, he had the presence of mind to stay in character. Brent opened his mouth, strings of spittle between his lips, but no words came out. Jacob draped Brent's left hand behind his neck and over his shoulder, gripped it with his left hand, right arm around the winded man's waist. He walked him to a corner booth, deposited him there, and fetched him a glass of tepid water.

"Drink this, buddy. Better for you than a beer right now. This place will be swarming with God knows who after those gunshots. Get ready to hustle out of this shithole."

Jacob leaned over the bar and demanded that the skulking barman stand the fuck up and hand him a couple of dish towels. He mopped up the smears of blood from his hip and tossed the towels back at the barman. Although painful, the knife wound was superficial, and the bleeding had completely stopped. He wiped away what he could, then donned the dead man's pants, which were a perfect fit. As they marched out the door, Jacob offered a silent prayer for the dead man and asked the good Lord to ensure a speedy recovery of the wounded one. Not that either deserved divine intervention, but—benefit of the doubt—maybe they'd had rotten childhoods.

Back out in the alley, to his pleasant surprise, there wasn't a soul around. Brent had recovered from his choking ordeal, and the two men quickly retraced their way back through the markets to Tepito subway station.

In the relative peace and quiet of the train heading back toward the embassy, Jacob checked the messages on his burner, a phone that had nearly cost them their lives.

One was from Carmen. Juan Palacio had been picked up from the office and carted off to, she presumed, the US embassy. There was more: her thoughts about what had happened, but it would have to wait.

The second message was from Mark Roffey and held a lot more interest.

*We've found Sanchez.*

# THIRTY-FOUR

With Brent in the capable hands of an embassy medical officer, Jacob took a cab back to his five-star hotel in the Cuauhtémoc neighborhood of Mexico City. His room was a huge step up in quality compared to Manuel's modest accommodation in Tuxtla. High-end furnishings, a bed fit for a king, mini gym, fridge stocked with champagne, the whole nine yards. The penthouse suite offered breathtaking, panoramic views over this pulsating megapolis of 21 million people. Fletcher's useless secretary may have finally redeemed herself with this booking.

In a privately booked conference room, across a vast glossy table that wouldn't be out of place in Elon Musk's boardroom, sat General Jaime Rodríguez. He was one of the top commanders of the Mexican Special Forces Corps, the *Fuerzas Especiales.* The soldiers in the corps had received training from the American Green Berets, so Jacob knew they must be a capable and formidable organization.

"I have it on good authority that you caused quite a stir in Colombia, Señor Montoya." The general had a thin-lipped mouth that barely moved as he spoke, yet every word was loud and clear. "Thanks to you, a little bird tells me, a traitor has been exposed. Now we are on the cusp of capturing the latest scourge on both Colombia and Mexico. So for that, I say congratulations and, more importantly, thank you."

"I cannot take credit for much of what has happened, General. Two brave agents have sacrificed their lives, and another, a civilian woman, has been to hell and back but has also made a significant contribution. Where we are now is largely thanks to them."

A second man, Colonel Luis Ramirez, sat with a pensive expression. He was in charge of the elite unit from the Joint Special Operations Command, the Fuerza Especial Conjunta or FEC. "The only reason you are tagging along, sir," said Ramirez in barely accented English, "is that I was personally contacted by our president with the order to fit you in. If it were my decision to make, you would remain here in your comfortable hotel room until we rescue Brohman and bring him back to you."

Jacob nodded. The men in their splendid uniforms commanded respect. He understood the reluctance to include him in the operation. "Believe me," he said in English, "if it were my decision to make, I would be doing exactly that." He showed a pair of open palms. "For some reason, President Claxton wants me to be present when Brohman is rescued. Assuming he's still alive, that is." He sipped water from a tall glass. "I'm doubtful that's the case, though."

"I don't know about your lack of confidence in our guest, Luis," said Rodríguez. "From what I heard, Señor Montoya managed to rescue a fellow agent from a very sticky situation today, one in which they were outnumbered and on unfamiliar territory."

"The opposition were of low quality," said Jacob. "Something tells me Sanchez and his henchmen will present a more formidable opposition."

"Indeed they will," agreed the colonel. "We must be careful. Our men have trained for scenarios in jungle environments. We are familiar with the terrain of the state of Chiapas. Sanchez will not be able to resist our overwhelming force."

Jacob drank more water. This was a tight-rope. He couldn't tell these men how to run their own show, but talk of 'overwhelming force' rang alarm bells in terms of liberating a hostage. It was as if Ramirez was reading his mind. "I can see the concern on your face. You're worried Sanchez will liquidate your man. Believe me, we have the best hostage negotiators in the business; we deal with kidnappings with the frequency America deals with mass shootings."

"Can you negotiate with someone like Sanchez?" said Jacob.

"Not all hostage negotiators are successful, and failures can be spectacular," said Rodríguez.

"We all remember the Waco siege."

"We are much better at this than the FBI was at Waco," said Ramirez. "We've had a lot more practice."

After a break for coffee, two other people arrived: a man and a woman Jacob knew, via the secret triple-squeeze handshake, were from Skia, but who the Mexicans thought were private remote sensing specialists from the US Department of Defense. The man, a John Smythe, resembled a tall, skinny geek from a popular sitcom, the woman, Mary Browne, also appeared bookish and nerdy. They were all business, however, and demonstrated how many hours of meticulous work had identified a remote location of the Lacandón jungle that was home to Sanchez's Mexican hideout.

"Our hunch that this was the area was confirmed when we sent in a drone that was shot down by Sanchez himself." Smythe, looking very pleased with himself, adjusted his black-rimmed glasses. "The camera was transmitting images back live. The machine we used resembled a hobbyist drone, except with capabilities that belie its innocuous appearance." He laughed like a small child who'd sniffed helium. "There's been an uptick in ecotourism in the national park, so we put a label on the drone. Property of Sven Ingerson and a fake Swedish cell phone number. Even a little sticker flag of Sweden."

"We couldn't have asked for a better result," said Browne, also wearing a smug grin.

Jacob coughed into his fist. "You didn't see any other people on the camera, did you?" He turned the screen around to show a picture of Paul Brohman. "This man, for example?"

"Unfortunately, no. There was another man in the company of Adolfo Sanchez, but we have been unable to identify him at this stage."

The Skia undercovers rolled a short video of the incident. Jacob shook his head in bewilderment as the sharp images showed a frantic man in a bathrobe leveling his rifle, aiming wide, then blackness as the drone was struck. "Not a bad shot," said Jacob with a note of appreciation. Finally, Browne described satellite photos of clandestine landing strips they had uncovered, perhaps belonging to Sanchez's cartel Moderno, perhaps to others.

General Rodríguez thanked the specialists for their briefing and sent them on their way. He placed a call, and three other soldiers arrived to go over the finer details of the raid. The session took four hours, with painstaking explanations of every step, alternative scenarios, and contingencies should the negotiations fail. One of the soldiers advised that three local government figures had been arrested for turning a blind eye to a number of cartels building infrastructure in the jungle in return for big bribes. Jacob smiled: If Brohman had perished and his legacy was a clean-up of the cartels, it would be a positive one for the common people.

"You know, Señor Montoya," said General Rodríguez when it was just he, Ramirez and Jacob remaining, "if it weren't for the inconvenience of your man Brohman, we could go in there and liquidate the lot of them, send a message to the other cartels in the region who are making life a living hell for the local populations. The Sinaloa and Jalisco Nueva Generación cartels have been running riot there, and it's time a signal was sent."

"If it turns out Brohman is dead," said the colonel, "we may very well do just that."

---

THE WHIRRING chopper blades overhead were like the accompaniment from the orchestra's rhythm section. Jacob listened to the lively chatter of the soldiers over the cans, the music to the rhythm; not much of the elite officers' technical jargon made a lot of sense to him, but it passed the time.

In the pre-dawn light, the Sikorsky UH-60 Blackhawk landed in a clearing, dense foliage of deep green jungle plants making for a dark environment. Even at this early hour, sweat escaped profusely from underneath his bulky gear. Jacob's body would have to cope with the weight of a full set of gear: light camo clothing, ballistic vest with ammunitions pouches, integrated comms helmet, water canteen, basic medical kit, probably a compass and a Swiss army knife buried in there somewhere. The only things that belonged to him were his underwear, his trusty boots, and his immortal soul. Weaponry comprised the same general-purpose HK21 machine gun, Glock 17 and combat knife as those carried by the other twelve members of this unit, as well as the negotiator, a steely, middle-aged woman called Imma who was built like a squat tank. Four members were assigned the task of toting Russian-made RPG-32s with a small supply of high-explosive fragmentation warheads. The load would be shared around to ease the burden.

His pulse quickened as the mission got closer and closer to the pointy end. He felt the dampness increasing under his kit. The only thing missing from his gear, he realized, was insignia denoting his name and rank. Out here he had no rank, no identity. If he died in battle, no one would come for the body, and if his corpse was miraculously found before the animals ate it, no one would be able to identify him.

The FEC response unit had been put down a couple of kilometers from the edge of the identified compound. The sound of the chopper may have been loud enough to reach the target; however, it was reasoned there was enough aviation activity, even in this remote area, for that not to raise alarm bells at the hideout.

"Remember why you are here," said the unit commander, Enrique Rojas, raising his voice as they jogged away from the helicopter. The other soldiers assembled at a polite distance behind him as the Sikorsky took off, giving Rojas and Jacob the chance to converse. "Your role is to be on hand when Brohman is liberated. I know you've been told this already, but do not engage with the enemy unless in self-defense. No matter the temptation."

Jacob nodded. "Of course. I'll be keeping my distance while you boys do your stuff."

To underscore the point, Rojas added: "This unit has a lot of experience dealing with cartels and the evil fuckers in them. Leave it all to us. I want no heroics from you."

*Fine by me*, Jacob thought.

The men listened to one last round of instructions and a pep talk from Rojas. It was almost as if they were about to take on another country in the soccer world cup final, Jacob mused. With screams of encouragement and nods all round, everybody pumped and primed, then formed a single file behind their leader, Jacob second from the end. The man behind him was nicknamed 'the goalkeeper,' there to stop unexpected shots from unexpected directions. They marched along a pre-made path, one of many identified by the hard-working remote sensing team, exchanging banter along the way. Rojas and the two men behind him at the front of the line used machetes to cut through occasional encroaching vines and fallen branches. Jacob marveled at the enthusiasm with which they wielded the blades, clearing the path with ease. The very existence of these minor obstacles gave Jacob hope: no one had been out here for a while, meaning they were unlikely to stumble upon the enemy or booby traps.

Breathing was hard with so much weight to carry, and the uneven and undulating terrain also took its toll. His own punishing exercise regime, though, ensured Jacob was fit enough to keep up with the cracking pace set by Rojas and his men. There was one short break for drinks and a piss if required at the halfway mark.

It took them a little over three and a half hours to march seven kilometers, negotiating slippery, mossy sections, rocky outcrops, and a couple of small creeks. There would be a serious leech examination when this was all over. As they ticked over the seventh kilometer, the sound of a relieved voice came over the comms. Rojas. *Compound in view.*

Now came the tricky part, the part that made the jungle trek look like a stroll around Central Park.

Confronting the cartel.

# THIRTY-FIVE

JACOB REMAINED WITH ROJAS, FACING THE WESTERN side of the compound, which was ringed by a tall razor-wire fence. With the aid of binoculars, Jacob could make out the exterior of the building. Solid brick, rendered in white stucco, not many windows. A huge swimming pool and well-tended tropical flowers and shrubs in the front garden. It reminded him of a maximum security prison with a touch of luxury. The satellite photos, which were their preliminary visual guide, showed that there was only one way for vehicles to get in and out of the property—on the western side they were currently watching. Now in addition to that valuable satellite imagery, they had a ring-side view of what confronted them.

Jacob and Rojas were accompanied by a soldier, Antonio, who'd been the last to take his turn carrying an 8 pound portable PA speaker together with a bagful of peripheral gear. Rounding off this group was the negotiator, Imma. The others had split into three groups and set up on the eastern, northern, and southern sides. They dug in far enough back from the fence to—they hoped—avoid any cameras, motion sensors, or other devices that would give away their position.

"You sure this speaker's gonna be powerful enough to reach

that building over there?" Rojas looked at Imma. "It's kinda small."

"It'll reach just fine." She nodded confidently. "We've tested the machine in a similar environment, many times. If the enemy's inside with the TV playing loudly, or even in the garage with a motorcycle engine revving, they're going to hear this device when it's cranked up to full volume."

"Hmmm. The latest high-resolution satellite images tell us there's a minimum of twelve men on site, plus a handful of women there to entertain them." Rojas made air-quotes on the word entertain. "What if they're having a party in there and they can't hear us because of sound-proofing?"

She sucked in a deep breath and wiped a smear of sweat from her brow. "Perhaps that would be a problem." She tapped her watch. "However, it's just after 9:30 a.m., so I don't think there'll be any partying going on."

Rojas mumbled something under his breath. "Very well." He tapped a button to activate the microphone boom on his helmet and gave his troops the heads-up that contact with the enemy was about to be made. He concluded with: "Buena suerte! *Good luck everyone!*"

---

IMMA PRESSED a button on her cell phone, connecting via Bluetooth to the 160W PA speaker. The device pointed due west, where the backroom techs had determined the rooms most likely to have people in them were situated. She scrolled to find the file with the sound she needed and pressed the icon. Jacob had never experienced an air-raid siren, but he imagined the racket that blared out of the speaker must have been an exact copy of that. He gritted his teeth as the deafening sound wailed for about thirty seconds. She waited ten seconds, then played the sound again. The same again, five times. Even through the headset, Jacob's ears were ringing.

She then connected Rojas's headset to the speaker via her cell phone. He activated the press-to-talk button. "Attention, Adolfo Sanchez. This is Colonel Luis Rojas of the Cuerpo de Fuerzas Especiales. My men have your compound surrounded. We ask that you release the American hostage you have taken, Mr. Paul Brohman, and the life of everyone inside the compound will be spared. Including yours. I will give you thirty minutes. Send out Brohman with his hands in the air. Wait five minutes after that, and the rest of you surrender. Failure to comply will not end well for you."

Jacob mentally applauded the commander. Cool and calm. No direct threat, but the implicated consequences of non-compliance were pretty clear.

Thirty minutes later, there was no sign of any action from the compound. The windows remained shuttered and the doors closed. No one was observed by any of the soldiers.

"Must have been something I said." Rojas grinned at Imma. "Your turn."

The negotiator was as confident in her approach as the commander had been. She introduced herself and advised that a two-way radio would be dropped over the fence via a small drone in the next couple of minutes. Negotiations would take place on a preset frequency.

Antonio sparked into action, assembling a quadcopter and attaching the two-way handset in a couple of minutes.

Jacob drew a long breath as he watched the cargo sail over the fence and land on the top sandstone step outside two big wooden doors. He feared even top-class operator Imma was going to face an uphill battle getting Sanchez to the negotiating table.

---

"WHAT THE FUCK IS THAT?" Sanchez shoved the sleeping woman square in the back. "Do you hear that noise?"

"Yes," the woman mumbled, instinctively reaching for a sheet to cover her nakedness. "It's awful. Make it stop!"

The final air-raid siren sound ended, then came a booming man's baritone voice that carried a ton of authority. It was muffled slightly due to the closed windows and doors but clear nevertheless. "Did you hear what I just heard?"

"Si!" Tears streamed down the woman's face. "Are we going to die, Adolfito?"

"Not if I can help it." Temples throbbing, he pressed an intercom button and ordered everyone in the building to gather immediately in the ground-floor gym. Paul Brohman included.

"We've got a situation here," he barked once everyone had arrived. "But one we've prepared for. We stand our ground, fight to the very last man. Right?"

"Si!" exclaimed the group.

Javi gave a fist pump. "Let's give them some heat."

Sanchez surveyed the men gathered around him. Javi's level of enthusiasm wasn't matched by the others. In fact, some had terror in their eyes. With the might of the government's most elite forces outside, they had every right to be nervous. He'd have to work hard to fire them all up. If they were going to repel the Fuerzas Especiales and make their escape before more of them turned up, unity of purpose was crucial.

The meeting was interrupted by a woman's voice announcing the impending arrival of a walkie-talkie to communicate with.

"You gonna shoot that one to pieces, too, jefe?" Javi's eyes glowed.

Sanchez pointed at Brohman. "You and I are going to take a little walk to the front door in a moment." He gestured to one of his muscle-bound henchmen. "Go stand by the window. Let me know when the package arrives. The rest of you, head to the armory and grab whatever weapons and ammunition you can carry. When we get back, Javi, take this motherfucker to his room and bolt the door. I don't want him wandering about with a gun in his hand."

Five minutes later, Brohman opened the front door and walked ten feet with his hands in the air and the barrel of a pistol pressed into the back of his neck. He picked up the walkie-talkie, did as the female voice instructed, and pressed to speak.

"Pass on the message, cabrón."

"Mr. Sanchez says you can all fuck yourselves."

"Well done, Pablo," came the whisper into his right ear and a pat on the back. "Muy bien."

"But I say...I've got nothing more to lose." He spoke fast, like a horse-race caller. "There's ten men and four women inside. Come and get 'em!"

---

JACOB LISTENED in disbelief to the brief doorstep exchange. Brohman showed plenty of balls, getting pistol whipped into unconsciousness—or worse—for his trouble. Sanchez ducked back inside before returning with another man. Together they dragged the American into the villa by the heels and closed the door again.

"What the hell?" said Rojas. He relayed to the troops stationed out of the line of sight what had just transpired. "He spoke so fast I didn't catch what he said."

"Wow! He didn't shoot Brohman," said Jacob, peeling the binoculars from his eyes. "That's a good sign. An even better one—he's alive. All this time I thought he must have been dead."

"What did he say?" barked Rojas.

Jacob repeated the details.

Rojas shook his head. "I've been dealing with these pendejos longer than I care to remember. They've got cruelty in their DNA. He could be torturing Brohman as we speak. Cutting off body parts while he's still alive. But they've got even fewer troops than us."

Imma took the initiative. "This is the police negotiator speaking, Señor Sanchez. Please listen to me. We are prepared to make concessions to you in return for the safe return of Paul Brohman."

Rojas activated his mic boom. "Group leaders, activate thermal imaging cameras. I've got a hunch he's got all his men around him for protection."

"Right away, sir!" Through his headset came the voices of the leaders on the north, south, and east sides of the building.

A crackle, and Sanchez could be heard over Imma's two-way. "What kind of concessions?"

"We take Brohman into our custody, walk away, and leave you in peace."

"But only for 24-hours," said Rojas. "Clear out, get the fuck out of Mexico, and do not come back. We know where your mother is."

"Fuck you, pendejo!" Jacob heard the heavy breathing exaggerated by anger. "You nearly had me interested until you made that threat against my mamma. Sorry, but no deal. We stand our ground."

Jacob knew Rojas's words were a bluff. Sanchez had someone visit his mother and take her out of Villa Serenidad, although where was a mystery. But old Maria was Sanchez's Achilles heel, and as such Rojas's tactic was probably worth a shot.

Word came back from the group leaders: thermal images of lots of people massed together on the ground floor, eastern side of the building. One image of a large person in a ground-floor backroom north side, not moving. No other signs of human life in other parts of the building.

"That's Brohman isolated," said Rojas. "We can't sit here all day."

Imma nodded. "I'm afraid Sanchez is one of those guys who will never cut a deal. It's do or die with him, and he doesn't care how many of his own men go down with him. He's also the first case I've dealt with where the kidnapper has no demands of any kind."

Rojas said, "South group. Any windows on your sides?"

An affirmative came from the leader. There were two small windows on the south side, both under one square meter in area, and a set of French doors leading onto a terrace.

"On my word, fire your RPG launcher at those windows and doors," said Rojas. "When the shells explode, run for the fence. One person per team hang back and watch the rooftop to cover the others. Use bolt cutters to bust your way through the wire fence. Get inside via blown-out doors and windows and subdue the enemy as best you can. Keep casualties to a minimum. Find Brohman and get him out of there. Be careful and may God be with you."

# THIRTY-SIX

THE FIRST WARHEAD BURST INSIDE THE BUILDING. THE deafening sound sent an assortment of birdlife scattering from the surrounding jungle. At fifteen-second intervals, two more HE-FRAG shells followed. The thermal imaging suggested that no one was in that wing, but mistakes happen. Anyone unfortunate to be standing near the entry points would have been vaporized.

Rojas glared at Jacob. "Wait here until you are summoned. Stay alert. There could be members of the cartel outside we haven't encountered. Protect Imma. She's the best negotiator in Mexico. We can't afford to lose her."

Jacob nodded. "You're the boss."

He sat cross-legged on the damp earth and slugged a draft of water from his canteen; Imma did likewise. They watched in silence as Rojas and Antonio scampered down an incline, breaking through foliage onto open ground. Three figures appeared on the rooftop carrying what looked like AK47s. They peered over the edge, scanned the surroundings, and marched back and forth, desperately searching for an opponent they would never see.

Jacob pressed the binoculars firmly to his eyes, spellbound by the spectacle unfolding. As if on cue, special ops shooters cut the men down, the goons' bodies juddering as bullets ripped through them.

"Bullseye!" cried Imma with a tad too much glee for a supposedly clear-headed negotiator.

"This won't take long now," said Jacob. "If Brohman had the numbers right, there aren't many left to mop up."

"Sanchez could have called for backup from friends on the outside," suggested Imma.

Jacob nodded. "Yes. But this will be over and we'll be gone before they get here. I've seen the satellite photos. Unless there are tunnels, he's well and truly screwed."

Two minutes later, a crackle came over the cans. Rojas. "Montoya. Get your ass down here. There's someone who'd be very pleased to meet you."

---

"YOU OKAY?" Jacob wasn't sure how to greet the man. A handshake, an arm around the shoulder, a hug? He opted for none of those, as he remembered his violation of Carmen Hererra. Although, to be fair and with the luxury of hindsight, it was via a dating app, and he couldn't have known it was a setup organized by Stynes.

Brohman ran a hand through his lank hair. "I'm a lot better now that the cavalry's arrived. When I heard the explosions, I thought your plan was total annihilation."

Rojas stepped up and interrupted with a curt, apologetic nod. "Just to let you know the body count, Señor Montoya. In addition to the three men dead on the roof, there are three with serious but not life-threatening wounds, and four surrendered and are uninjured."

"The women?" said Brohman, who sounded like he actually cared for their welfare.

"Safe. Our female team member is with them."

Brohman nodded. "I'm glad. This is no life for them." His

body began to tremble. "The way I'm shaking, you'd never believe this old boy was in the Marine Raiders, would you?"

"Perfectly natural after what you've been through." Jacob noted that not only was the man shaking, his teeth chattered when he spoke. "It's shock. Come on. I'll escort you out of here," he said. "We'll wait at the clearing for the helicopter, is that okay with you?"

"No." The commander shook his head. "We'll bring the dead, detainees, and wounded out. They'll be transported first, then we go. I recommend you two grab something from the fridge and wait by the pool."

"Fine by me," said Brohman.

"A mop-up crew is on its way, too. Plus a bunch of government investigators. They'll take over from there."

Jacob and Brohman headed for the door leading onto the pool deck. To get there, they had to pass seven men who sat against a wall, hands and feet bound with cable ties, gags on their mouths. "Which one of these assholes is Sanchez?" said Jacob, pretty sure he knew but wanting confirmation.

Brohman gestured toward Sanchez, eyes afire. "Not injured, I see." He bent down to within an inch of the man's face. "So you surrendered, you fucking coward." He stood and unleashed a mighty kick at Sanchez's face. Blood streamed from the shattered nose. "And this fucker—" Brohman pointed at Javi, who radiated defiance and hate through his bloodshot eyes. "He's even worse." He unleashed with a brutal flurry of punches to the man's head.

No one made a move to stop or even reprimand the American businessman. Jacob was astonished that he had snapped out of his state of shock so quickly. He stood back and watched as the thwacking hits went on for another thirty seconds, until Javi keeled over, knocked out and bleeding from a number of deep cuts.

"Oh shit," said Brohman. "Have I killed him?"

"No idea," said Jacob, grabbing him by the forearm. "Let's get out of here."

"Espera! *Wait!*" an excited voice called out, stopping them in their tracks. Jacob turned to see Antonio leading a young man. "I found this guy cowering in a cage in the basement." He looked at Brohman, then Jacob. "Either of you know who he is?"

Tears welled in Brohman's eyes as he regarded the almost lifeless figure, barely standing. His head was bowed, legs buckling like an old bridge about to collapse. Even from a distance of twenty feet, Jacob could smell the stench coming off the man's body. Antonio pressed a finger under the man's chin to force his head up so his face could be seen. Jacob gasped; he recognized him from photographs he had seen. That mop of curly hair. Miguel Hererra.

# THIRTY-SEVEN

"Can you believe that she won?" said Fletcher, gesturing toward the television. "After all we went through!"

"We?" Jacob was incredulous.

"And by we, I mean you."

Jacob burst out laughing. "That's the first time you've used that trademark cliché of yours and it's actually been appropriate."

Irina shook her head, clearly not getting the in-joke but enjoying the interaction. She placed her glass of champagne on the long table set up in the middle of the open-plan living area, moved to an armchair, and tucked her feet under her butt. They'd all been standing for the national anthem as the band played "Hail to the Chief."

"Oh shit, will you look at it!" Fletcher angled his glass of cognac at the giant TV screen. Hannah McIvor, newly elected president of the United States, waved and smiled, smiled and waved. The cheering and applause from her admirers in the massive crowd was louder than for any president at their inauguration. At least that's what the unseen television commentator said. McIvor's square-jawed athletic boyfriend stood by her side, also smiling and waving. A teenage son stood on the other side, looking almost rapturously at his mother.

"I cannot believe the American people voted for an unmarried woman," said Irina, shaking her head. "In Russia, even a married woman would never even get close to such a position."

Jacob tossed back half a glass of champagne and smacked his lips. "I suppose these days anything is possible. Before Obama, the very idea of a Black president was unthinkable."

"True," said Fletcher. "Anyway, I've had enough of this spectacle. We have a new boss, but for now I'd like to mourn the old one." He took to a fresh cigar with a guillotine cutter, lit it, and sighed.

Jacob chuckled. "What are you talking about? He's not dead."

"Again, true," Fletcher conceded. "But his spirit is broken. He was an old-school gentleman, and apparently that's a dying breed. We know he was defeated by dark forces, and despite the resources at our disposal, there was nothing we could do about it. Have you seen the crime stats for the areas the tainted drugs were released into?"

"Yes, I have," said Jacob. "And still, there's nothing to tie it to McIvor herself."

Jacob took a seat on Fletcher's soft-as-silk sofa, crossed his legs over on an ottoman footstool. "Who's to say she was even aware it was happening? Presumption of innocence, and all that."

"How could she not be?" said Irina. "What's that expression about the buck stopping somewhere?"

"Without proof..." Jacob shrugged. "Miguel Hererra's intel that the Mexicans recovered on that USB drive everyone was so desperate to get their hands on pointed only to Laura Torres and Palacio interacting with the Cartel Moderno. She received money in unaccountably large sums, unfortunately from an anonymous bank account in Panama. Palacio, too, although the amounts were much smaller. Those two will rot in jail. To their credit, they're refusing to squeal on any accomplices. It will take some serious digging to uncover the whole truth. For now, though, this is where the trail goes cold."

Fletcher pursed his lips. "They'll get her sooner or later. If this wave of dirty drugs wasn't sanctioned by McIvor herself—which I doubt—it was her campaign director. The rumor mill's running hot about that swine! The FBI are about to subpoena a lot of people, him included. That's when it'll get interesting."

"What about this Mr. Brohman you were so intent on rescuing?" said Irina. "Seems that was all for nothing, *da?*"

"Yeah," Fletcher scoffed. "The money he eventually tipped into Claxton's campaign didn't sway the vote in any way. The flood of drugs was too much to combat with fancy advertising. Worse for him, he'd already signed a large chunk of his fortune over to Sanchez."

"No way!" said Irina.

"He'll possibly get it back. There are international treaties the US government can leverage to get the Panamanian bank to cooperate. Although with McIvor in charge, who knows? Maybe they won't try too hard to help Brohman. He's no friend of hers, after all."

Jacob picked up the remote and flicked mindlessly through the channels. All about the election, no light entertainment worth watching, not even a halfway decent football game. "You gonna be able to work with McIvor?" he asked. "You've never hidden your distaste for the woman." If Skia was wound down, he'd be free; the no get-out clause would mean nothing if the organization were to be liquidated. He had enough money to last several lifetimes. Win-win.

Fletcher laughed. "I can work for anyone, as long as they pay. I'll miss old Claxton, that's true, but I'm nothing if not flexible."

"A hypocrite, more like it," said Jacob. With Fletcher still protesting his loyalty to the White House, Jacob excused himself, heading for the bathroom. He had an insatiable need to call Carmen Hererra, but not with Irina present. If she was jealous of the dead Sally-Anne Vincent, a very alive and beautiful Carmen would send her through the roof. He clicked the door shut and turned on the exhaust fan.

"Carmen? Soy yo. *It's me*. I'll be quick. Just wanted to see how you are."

"Carlos! I'm great. Can you believe they found Miguel alive?"

"What? No way!"

"It seems the cartel captured a local man who had the same kind of hair as Miguel and killed him like a human sacrifice. They made that gringo Brohman think it was actually Miguel. We all thought it was Miguel." Jacob gasped at the news. What kind of minds did those sick fucks have?

"There was an asshole there called Javi who tortured my brother." She choked up for a moment. "Miguel's going to take years to get over this ordeal. But he's strong, and I will always be there for him. The Colombian government wants to offer him a job, so that's good news, huh? I had no idea he was so smart with hacking and all that. Smarter than that cabrón Juan Palacio." She forced a laugh. "I thought it was just photography and surfing. Here's the best news. Well, not quite as good as Miguel coming home." She took a breath to recover from her rapid speech. "The entire Clandestine Operations office has been closed down."

"Stynes? Is he being investigated?" Jacob already knew the answers to his questions but wanted to hear her version of events.

She erupted into laughter. "How would I know? I hope so. I heard a rumor the cops are linking an American to the murder of Gilberto and Ricardo. I know it's Stynes."

Jacob grimaced. There was a lot a deep investigation could uncover. If Stynes was dirty, he would be shown no mercy in Colombia. He decided to change the subject. "You got a job?"

"No. Well, yes. Only part-time. A dress shop. Pretty boring, huh?"

"Listen, Carmen." He'd been in the bathroom too long. "I wish I could talk for longer, but I've gotta go. People are waiting for me."

"Hey!" She clearly didn't want the conversation to end. "A lady became your president. Isn't that fantastic!"

"Yes," Jacob said through clenched teeth. "Amazing. Look, I..."

"I told Miguel all about you. He really wants to meet you. You're coming back to Colombia, right?"

"Sure."

With a promise to call back in a few days, Jacob flushed the toilet and headed back to the party. It was no empty promise: he would call, get her bank account details, and wire her the amount of money Brohman had promised Miguel. A million dollars. It was the least she and her brother deserved.

"You were a while in there," said Irina. "I was starting to get worried."

He sat on the arm of the sofa, wrapped his arm around her shoulder, and pulled her in tight. He whispered in her ear: "Ya lyublyu tebya. *I love you.*"

There was the sound of another champagne cork popping. "Either join me for a drink, or..."

"Or what?" said Irina, too easy to take the bait.

"Or get a room," said Fletcher.

Irina held out her glass. "How about a drink first and *then* we get a room?"

"As they say in South America," said Fletcher, bowing as he poured bubbly into flutes, "salud!"

**Don't miss THE HAVANA FILE. The riveting sequel in the Jacob Hunter Thriller series.**

The mole, planted during the height of the Cuban Missile Crisis, has remained undetected for decades, feeding critical intelligence to America's enemies. Now, with a resurgence of communist influence from China in Cuba and the Caribbean region in general, the mole's activities threaten to destabilize global security.

Hunter must infiltrate the tight-knit circles of Cuban intelligence and uncover the identity of the traitor before they can execute a plan that could compromise U.S. national security. Using his unmatched skills in linguistics and espionage, Hunter navigates a deadly game of cat and mouse in the heart of Havana, where old Cold War loyalties clash with new geopolitical realities.

As he delves deeper into the mystery, Hunter uncovers a chilling conspiracy that reaches far beyond Cuba's shores. The mole's next move could ignite a conflict that would reshape the world order. From the gritty backstreets of Havana to the shadowy halls of power in Washington, Jacob Hunter must expose the traitor before it's too late. But with the clock ticking and enemies on all sides, will Hunter manage to stay one step ahead, or will he fall victim to a plot that has been decades in the making?

Scan the QR code below to purchase THE HAVANA FILE.
Or go to: righthouse.com/the-havana-file

*NOTE: Flip to the end for an exclusive sneak peek!*

# DON'T MISS ANYTHING!

If you want to stay up to date on all new releases in this series, with this author, or with any of our new deals, you can do so by joining our newsletters below.

In addition, you will immediately gain access to our entire *Right House VIP Library,* which includes many riveting Mystery and Thriller novels for your enjoyment. Including a prequel novella to this series!

righthouse.com/email

*(Easy to unsubscribe. No spam. Ever.)*

# ALSO BY DAVID ARCHER

Up to date books can be found at:
www.righthouse.com/david-archer

**ROGUE THRILLERS**

Gates of Hell (Book 1)
Hell's Fury (Book 2)
Ice Burn (Book 3)
Judgement by Fire (Book 4)

**JACOB HUNTER THRILLERS**

The Kyiv File (Book 1)
The Bogota File (Book 2)
The Havana File (Book 3)
The Amsterdam File (Book 4)
The Saint Petersburg File (Book 5)

**PETER BLACK THRILLERS**

Burden of the Assassin (Book 1)
The Man Without A Face (Book 2)
Unpunished Deeds (Book 3)
Hunter Killer (Book 4)
Silent Shadows (Book 5)
The Last Run (Book 6)
Dark Corners (Book 7)
Ghost Operative (Book 8)
A Fire Burning (Book 9)
Dawnlight (Book 10)
Dead Ice (Book 11)
No Loose Ends (Book 12)

**ALEX MASON THRILLERS**

Odin (Book 1)
Ice Cold Spy (Book 2)
Mason's Law (Book 3)
Assets and Liabilities (Book 4)
Russian Roulette (Book 5)
Executive Order (Book 6)
Dead Man Talking (Book 7)
All The King's Men (Book 8)
Flashpoint (Book 9)
Brotherhood of the Goat (Book 10)
Dead Hot (Book 11)
Blood on Megiddo (Book 12)
Son of Hell (Book 13)
Merchant of Death (Book 14)
Extinction C-14 (Book 15)
A Vengeful God (Book 16)

**NOAH WOLF THRILLERS**

Code Name Camelot (Book 1)
Lone Wolf (Book 2)
In Sheep's Clothing (Book 3)
Hit for Hire (Book 4)
The Wolf's Bite (Book 5)
Black Sheep (Book 6)
Balance of Power (Book 7)
Time to Hunt (Book 8)
Red Square (Book 9)
Highest Order (Book 10)
Edge of Anarchy (Book 11)
Unknown Evil (Book 12)
Black Harvest (Book 13)
World Order (Book 14)
Caged Animal (Book 15)
Deep Allegiance (Book 16)

Pack Leader (Book 17)
High Treason (Book 18)
A Wolf Among Men (Book 19)
Rogue Intelligence (Book 20)
Alpha (Book 21)
Rogue Wolf (Book 22)
Shadows of Allegiance (Book 23)
In the Grip of Darkness (Book 24)
Wolves in the Dark (Book 25)
Olympus Must Fall (Book 26)
Children of the Empire (Book 27)
Wolf at the Gates (Book 28)

**SAM PRICHARD MYSTERIES**

The Grave Man (Book 1)
Death Sung Softly (Book 2)
Love and War (Book 3)
Framed (Book 4)
The Kill List (Book 5)
Drifter: Part One (Book 6)
Drifter: Part Two (Book 7)
Drifter: Part Three (Book 8)
The Last Song (Book 9)
Ghost (Book 10)
Hidden Agenda (Book 11)

**SAM AND INDIE MYSTERIES**

Aces and Eights (Book 1)
Fact or Fiction (Book 2)
Close to Home (Book 3)
Brave New World (Book 4)
Innocent Conspiracy (Book 5)
Unfinished Business (Book 6)
Live Bait (Book 7)
Alter Ego (Book 8)

More Than It Seems (Book 9)
Moving On (Book 10)
Worst Nightmare (Book 11)
Chasing Ghosts (Book 12)
Serial Superstition (Book 13)

**CHANCE REDDICK THRILLERS**

Innocent Injustice (Book 1)
Angel of Justice (Book 2)
High Stakes Hunting (Book 3)
Personal Asset (Book 4)

**CASSIE MCGRAW MYSTERIES**

What Lies Beneath (Book 1)
Can't Fight Fate (Book 2)
One Last Game (Book 3)
Never Really Gone (Book 4)

# ABOUT US

Right House is an independent publisher created by authors for readers. We specialize in Action, Thriller, Mystery, and Crime novels.

If you enjoyed this novel, then there is a good chance you will like what else we have to offer! Please stay up to date by using any of the links below.

Join our mailing lists to stay up to date -->
righthouse.com/email
Visit our website --> righthouse.com
Contact us --> contact@righthouse.com

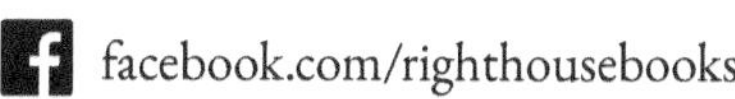


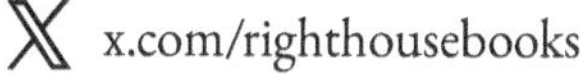


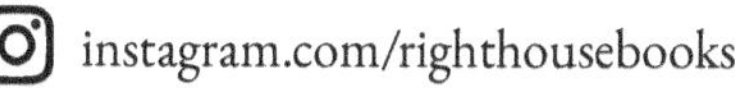

# EXCLUSIVE SNEAK PEEK OF...

THE HAVANA FILE

# PROLOGUE

## HAVANA, CUBA

THE RUMBLE OF AN APPROACHING STORM ECHOED across the expanses of the Straits of Florida, a buffeting wind creating a mass of white-caps in the waters of Havana Port. A crack of thunder boomed, reverberating through the claustrophobic streets of the historic downtown district. He pulled up the coat collar to cover his neck from the slanting rain as he wound his way through the labyrinth of streets, then felt the reassuring hard steel of the Makarov pistol tucked into his belt. This was a mission too important to be delayed by inclement weather. He quickened his step.

---

THE DILAPIDATED BAR was tucked away in a gloomy alley, a flickering neon sign swaying above the doorframe. Inside was the rhythmic clink of glasses and murmured conversations, clouds of pungent cigar smoke and softly playing rhumba music. Despite the chic ambience, an air of growing unease hung over two men sitting at a corner table, hunched over their glasses of over-proof rum. The dim light struggled to cut through the thick smoke that hovered in a haze around them.

One of the men, Cristian Passo, once a respected Cuban intelligence officer, now a man-for-hire and occasional CIA informer, wiped his brow and glanced at his timepiece, a sturdy and reliable Russian-made Vostok amphibian diver watch. His contact was ten minutes late. But that was the least of his worries. Passo knew he was sitting on information that could tear apart Cuba's delicate relationship with its foreign allies and maybe bring him a windfall —or a bullet. It all hinged on whether or not the contact coming tonight would be willing to talk to the American.

Across from Passo, a man in a brightly colored Hawaiian shirt fidgeted with his drink, his eyes darting nervously toward the door every few seconds. Frank Cain, a journalist with a nice, safe life in Washington DC, was more than just uneasy. He was terrified. And with good reason. He had come to Cuba chasing the story of a lifetime—an audacious military operation designed to make the United States look like the worst bad guy among nations. Breaking this one would make him a modern-day Carl Bernstein, the man who blew the lid on Watergate.

Cain had a long list of contacts in the intelligence world who had pointed him to Havana. They'd whispered of a dangerous man embedded within the Cuban government, passing information to America's enemies for decades. He even posed a risk to his own regime. One of those contacts connected him with Passo, who claimed this dangerous man was working with China, perhaps Russia too, to stage an operation so bold it would throw the world into chaos. If Cain could expose it, his name would be on every headline from New York to Sydney. But first, he had to survive the night.

Passo leaned forward, his voice low, his English flawless and only lightly accented. "The man you're looking for, he's not just anyone. His name is Miguel Domínguez. A big shot in the government, very close to the top, but a traitor to his own country. He's the key." Passo tapped the table with talon-like fingernails. "For years he's been feeding intel to both the Chinese and the Russians for money. And now, together they're planning something bigger than anyone realizes. A false-flag operation—Bay of Pigs all over again. And of course, they want the world to think it's America pulling the strings. You follow?"

"Yes, I follow," Cain said impatiently. He then corrected his tone, which he realized had been sharpened by his anxiety. "It was us, after all, who tried and failed the first time back in the 1960s. And with this new president about to be inaugurated...man...this is huge." Cain's heart raced, but he forced himself to stay calm. Hand wrapped tightly around his glass, knuckles white, he asked, "And you're sure it's him? Domínguez?"

"I have no doubt. His father was of a hawkish disposition too, back in the Cold War. It runs in the family." Passo shifted in his seat, his gaze flicking nervously to the entrance. "But listen to me, Cain, you need to understand. You're playing a dangerous game. These people—they don't leave loose ends."

For a second, Cain pondered the wisdom of his decision. Then all doubts vanished: the fame and glory were worth it.

"There's a man coming tonight who can confirm what I say," Passo continued. "He will provide you with incontrovertible evidence. You must talk to him." He rubbed his thumb against his index and middle fingers. "And you will pay me for this tip-off as we agreed, *correcto*?"

Cain nodded, opening his mouth to reply, but before he could speak, the door to the bar creaked open, letting in a gust of humid, rain-soaked air. A figure stepped inside, silhouetted against the storm, water dripping off his long coat.

"That is not the man we are expecting." Passo stiffened. "We need to go. Now."

But it was already too late.

The newcomer crossed the bar with deliberate, slow steps. A lean and tall figure, he approached their table; water droplets flew as he ruffled his mane of dark, curly hair. A pair of cold eyes swept the room before landing on the two men. A glint of white teeth as the man smiled with satisfaction. Passo muttered a blasphemous curse and reached for the gun tucked under his jacket. Cain's pulse hammered in his ears as he struggled to figure out what the hell was going on.

"Cristian," the man said, his voice a predatory growl. "You been talking too much, *coño*. And to the wrong people." The man nodded at a stunned Cain, only now realizing that, apart from the profanity, the man was speaking in English. Which meant he probably knew who Cain was. Or at least where he was from. Not good. Not good at all.

Passo's hand was halfway to his gun when the man moved in a flash, faster than Cain could follow. A muffled shot echoed through the bar—a suppressed pistol. Passo slumped back in his chair, a dark red stain blossoming across his chest. His eyes, wide with shock, locked on to Cain's for a split second before going glassy and closing.

Cain leapt from his chair, panic flooding his veins. His mind screamed at him to run, but his feet remained glued to the floor. The gunman, calm as a lion sizing up its next meal, stepped closer. Cain could feel the walls closing in, the air too thick to breathe.

"You should have left this alone, *gringo estúpido*," the man said, raising the gun to eye level.

Cain instinctively ducked and turned, grabbed the chair he'd been sitting on, and flung it at the man. The spine of the chair struck the stranger in the left shoulder, momentarily throwing him off balance. Cain seized the opportunity to bolt.

His feet slammed against the uneven flagstone floor as he shoved his way through the crowded bar, muted gunfire behind him, the *thwut-thwut* sound of bullets ripping holes in plaster walls. He barely registered the shouts of protest from the bar's regulars as he crashed into tables and chairs, forging his way toward the back exit. Rain lashed his face as he burst into the pitch-black alley. His heart pounded so hard, he feared it would burst out of his chest.

He ran toward a light, not knowing where he was headed—only that if he stopped, he'd certainly die.

The narrow streets of the rotting neighborhood blurred around him. He darted between dilapidated buildings, his shoes slipping on the rain-slicked pavement. Even above the noise of the growing storm, he could hear heavy footsteps pounding behind him. Too close, too damned close. He needed to shake the man, but where could he go? Havana was an alien city. He was a recently landed foreigner with no idea where he could hide, his hotel miles away.

Up ahead, the street opened into an empty square. Cain spotted a small church looming in the distance. He sprinted in a straight line with a speed he never thought possible, then, with the robotic footsteps persistent behind him, ducked down another alleyway. Maybe he could hide in an alcove or a dumpster, then try the church? For a second, the world fell silent, no more pounding footsteps. He would escape. Yes, he was certain of it now.

But just as he was about to round a tight corner, a *pfft* sound, then an agonizing pain tore through his side.

Cain gasped and fell to the ground. He crashed against hard, wet cobblestones, a grunt escaping his lips. Instinctively, his hand pawed at his side. He looked wide-eyed at his shaking hand, slick with blood. He'd taken a bullet. He clawed his way up the bricks in the wall, each breath like a punch in the guts. No good. He collapsed again, the world spinning around him. This was the end of the road. He was going to expire here, alone in the deserted streets of Havana, with the truth eluding him, his quest unfulfilled.

The footsteps became audible once more, louder by the second. He glanced up, the shadow of his relentless pursuer loomed over him.

"This was none of your business, *gringo*," the man snarled. He aimed the gleaming pistol at the middle of Cain's nose. Just before he could pull the trigger, a distant shout interrupted the moment. The gunman hesitated, glancing over his shoulder.

*A chance.*

Ignoring the excruciating pain coursing along every nerve fiber, Cain summoned the last of his strength. He unleashed a side kick, striking the man in the patella and knocking him off balance. Cain again scrambled to his feet, a new boost of adrenaline giving him a surge of energy as he stumbled back into the broader alleyway. Blood poured from his gunshot wound and his vision blurred, but he plowed on. God—or fate—had sent him a lifeline.

Ahead, approaching headlights cut through the rain, getting heavier by the minute. As it passed under a dim headlight, he made out a big, clunky Buick. Gaudy yellow.

Cain waved his arms frantically, praying for another miracle. The car screeched to a halt, and the door flew open. A figure inside yelled in urgent, staccato Spanish, "*Rápido, súbete al maldito carro!*" but Cain only understood the first word. *Quickly.* It was enough.

He yanked open the door and flopped into the back seat, barely conscious, as the car sped away into the night.

The last thing Cain saw out the window before he slipped into unconsciousness was the gunman, bent over double and furiously rubbing his knee.

# CHAPTER 1

Fletcher's Tribeca converted warehouse was enveloped in a shroud of silence. Not an uncomfortable one: Skia director Grant Fletcher and his number-one agent, Jacob Hunter, didn't need words to fill the space. They were men cut from old-fashioned cloth, comfortable in their roles.

Fletcher's raspy voice finally broke the quiet. "Have a shot of liquor and relax. Should be a CIA job, but their Deputy Director Joel McDonald doesn't want to touch it with a ten-foot pole. He's flicked it to us. And by us, I mean you."

Jacob rolled his eyes and sighed at the '*I mean you*' cliché the boss busted out ahead of every assignment.

"This is a big mission, son." Fletcher offered a look of sympathy mixed with encouragement.

"Aren't they all big missions, Grant?" Jacob grinned, pouring himself a measure of Hennessy XO into a crystal glass. He didn't drink much; only with Fletcher, and when a mission demanded it. "Not sure I'm ready for this briefing. I'm still processing Zerina's death."

"Come off it, Jacob." Fletcher clipped the end off a stogie, lighting it with a silver Zippo. Through the smoke, he added,

"You're surrounded by death every time we send you out into the wild."

Jacob leaned back, eyes drifting to the stash of cigars. Without being offered, he plucked one from the wooden box. Fletcher passed him the lighter. With both puffing away, Jacob circled back to Zerina. "Will there be a funeral?"

"Yes. Three days' time," Fletcher replied, tapping ash into a glass ashtray. "But you won't be able to make it. Unless you pull off a miracle and wrap this mission up before they lower her into the ground."

"I'll do my damndest." Jacob shook his head. Zerina Mills had meant a lot to him, and she was a good friend to Irina. The woman had been a brilliant young agent, cut down in her prime by a relentless and incurable illness. Jacob's grief was real, but years of training kept his emotions in check. Irina, though? She'd cried for days after hearing the news.

Fletcher rubbed his prominent chin. "We'll have a private memorial when you get back. How's that sound?"

"Better than nothing, I guess." That was the eternal caveat.

Fletcher nodded sympathetically. "This one's going to take every ounce of skill you've got. And then some." He blew out a perfectly formed smoke ring. "Tomorrow evening, you're heading to where these delicious tubes of tobacco come from. Cuba. There's serious trouble brewing."

"What kind of trouble?"

Fletcher rocked back and barked a laugh. "That's the problem. We don't know exactly. We suspect it involves the Russians and the Chinese. The smart money is on a plot to bring down the US government, turn the world against us. More than it already is. They believe if it is to happen, it will be soon."

"How soon?"

"On or before Hannah McIvor's inauguration as this country's new president."

Jacob grimaced. "What's this prognosis based on?"

Fletcher leaned forward. "The murder of a man called Cristian Passo. He'd been drip-feeding information about this big operation to a CIA agent in Havana. Our officers over there took his claims with a grain of salt. Too far-fetched, they thought. Now he's been assassinated in such a clinical fashion, they're suddenly inclined to believe he was telling the truth."

Jacob's nostrils flared. "I know who Passo is. I remember seeing his name high up on a list of our most valuable assets in the Caribbean. A Cuban intelligence officer, right?"

"You remember correctly."

"He's supposed to have had a lot of pull with decision-makers in the *Dirección de Inteligencia*, or DI."

Fletcher shook his head. "Must have been a while ago you saw that list. You're thinking of the old Cristian Passo. He's now an ex-intelligence officer. A traffic accident last year took him out of the game. Spinal injuries. The state was supposed to look after him generously, but instead, they tossed him on the scrap heap. He's been living on a pitiful pension in a bolt-hole outside Havana. Plus the odd bit of chump change the CIA put his way."

"You're kidding." Jacob drained his glass and wandered over to the giant aquarium, watching the fish swim lazily. "He must have pissed someone off to be treated like that. I hope I'm better looked after when I'm retired from the game."

Fletcher smirked, admiring a chain of perfect smoke rings. "You don't need a pension. You've made enough money with Skia to buy your own third-world country."

"You don't know if I've lost it gambling." Jacob cracked a wry smile. "In fact, tear up my contract now, burn it in the ashtray. I'm ready to retire."

Fletcher laughed. "I don't need to remind you of the deal, do I? No get-out clause until..."

"Until I'm 55, get fired, or disappear." Jacob resumed his seat. "There's little I forget."

"That's why we hired you. Also pattern recognition. Your knack for languages, too. You're perfect in Russian and Spanish. How's the Chinese?"

Jacob groaned. "Not great. If I'm talking to a Chinese child, maybe I can order takeout."

"Luckily, you won't need it. The language, that is; not sure about the takeout. Seriously though, the Chinese diplomats and spies embedded in Cuba will have excellent Spanish. English and Russian, too, probably."

"Still, not knowing Mandarin is a big gap in my skill set."

"Chinese is a pain in the ass to learn, I'll give you that," Fletcher said. "But let's scratch it from your list for now."

"No, I'm going to learn it properly." Last year, Jacob had quickly reached fluency in modern standard Arabic. Surely, Chinese wasn't out of reach.

Fletcher nodded. "Might not need it now, but it'd be a good addition. You're the best we have. We could fire half the China desk and replace them with you."

"Stop it, Grant. You're embarrassing me."

Fletcher clapped him on the shoulder. "I enjoy embarrassing you. One of the perks of the job." He shifted his attention to a manila folder on the glass-topped table. "Let's get to it. Yesterday, a journalist named Frank Cain witnessed Cristian Passo's murder in a dingy bar in Havana. Cain miraculously escaped after Passo was shot at close range. The killer was gunning for him too, but he got away, picked up by a man in a Buick. Cain's description of the man driving the vehicle fits Raúl Espinosa, another deep-cover CIA agent. Unfortunately, Espinosa has gone to ground. Cain's being flown out under government protection as soon as he's fit to travel, but not before you've spoken to him. We've squared that away with the State Department." Fletcher paused for a beat, then said, "Cain's psychologically scarred by what he witnessed, so you'll have to tread carefully with him."

Jacob scanned the dossier, stopping at Cain's bio. "This guy writes pieces for the *New York Times*. Syndicated to a bunch of other outlets. I've read his stuff. Sharp, knows his way around diplomacy. If he says he was targeted for assassination, I'm inclined to believe him."

"Believe him after you've grilled him."

"Fair call." Jacob nodded. "Mind if I read the file a little more thoroughly first?"

Fletcher sighed, standing. "Go ahead. Nature calls."

With Fletcher out of the room, Jacob focused on the file. Clearly, finding Espinosa was paramount. Raúl Espinosa was a former military intelligence officer turned baker, a trade he learned from his late mother. The man had also been feeding the CIA low-grade intel for fifteen years. Now, apparently, he had something big to sell. The question was: why was he bypassing the CIA and using a journalist? In Jacob's mind, the answer was simple—money.

Fletcher returned, looking relieved. Jacob said, "So we're talking about a classic false-flag operation. Bay of Pigs II?"

"That's McDonald's take. To be certain, we really need to talk to Espinosa. More precisely, *you* need to talk to him. He's been refusing to spill the details or name names to his CIA handler. It's now clear he knew as much as Passo, but we're hazy on what the connection is. Looks like he must have known Passo, who in turn lured Cain into the vortex." He poured himself a glass of fresh water. "Like I said, Passo's intel was previously dismissed as fanciful. Now it seems he was too close to something. Based on what he'd already revealed, we believe the Chinese and Russians are involved in the plot. And someone inside the Cuban government is pulling the strings."

Jacob's brain processed the web of details as he glanced over the file again. The facts blurred momentarily, subconsciously pulling him back to a different puzzle—Sally-Anne Vincent. His high-school sweetheart. A loner like him. She had been too young, too innocent to die. Twenty years had passed since her murder, and still, no answers. A wound that refused to heal, a mystery that taunted him.

"Earth to Jacob Hunter." Fletcher clicked his fingers. "You good?"

Jacob blinked. "Yeah, just old memories creeping in." He poured another half-measure of cognac.

"Irina or Sally-Anne?"

A faint smile touched Jacob's lips. Irina, the IT genius he'd saved in Moscow two years ago, was as brilliant with code as he was with languages. They were fiercely passionate and surprisingly balanced, like two pieces of a puzzle that fit perfectly. She'd even come to understand his connection to Sally-Anne, the dead girl from his past. Now she was helping him look for Sally-Anne's killer.

"Both, in a way," Jacob admitted. "What's the timeline on this thing?"

"Unknown." Fletcher folded his hands together. "But we have to move fast. If there's a loose cannon in the Cuban cabinet, the situation for us is critical. McDonald's received reports that the Ministry of the Revolutionary Armed Forces, aka MINFAR, is at the heart of this."

"That's a worry. If something's cooking, that's a good place to hide it."

"Damn straight." Fletcher nodded as his cell phone buzzed. He scanned it for a moment, then handed it to Jacob. "From Langley."

Jacob squinted at the blurry image. "This is what they call grainy."

"Yes. But read the text."

Jacob read aloud. "Deputy Minister Miguel Domínguez snorting something off a prostitute's breasts in Budapest." He looked up, smirking. "This photo could be of anyone."

"It's worth investigating. Domínguez was seen the next morning talking to a Russian businessman—Vitaly Botvinnik. The Russian has a track record of arms deals with some nasty regimes, terrorist groups. He ain't too fussy about where he gets his money from."

Jacob tapped the screen. "Okay, now we're talking. And if

Domínguez is tied up in this, why hasn't the Cuban president fired him?"

"Kompromat, maybe," Fletcher said. "Or maybe he's got dirt on the president himself." He narrowed his eyes.

"Then why not eliminate Domínguez altogether? I imagine the leader of an authoritarian country could do what he liked with impunity."

"Good question. One I'm sending you to find out the answer to."

Jacob leaned back, a smile tugging at the corners of his mouth. "Your gut is not only slightly protrusive, Grant, but sometimes right. Think Domínguez is the key?"

"I believe so. He's linked to the old guard. His father was one of Fidel's foot soldiers. If this is a major false-flag operation and it goes forward, Domínguez will play a major role. By the way, I'm filing away that 'protrusive gut' remark to be dealt with at a later date."

Jacob grinned, his mind already creating scenarios of what might await him once he landed in Havana. "Anything else?"

Fletcher chuckled. "Of course. Your legend. It's one that's been nurtured for a number of years. You'll be undercover as a freelance Argentinian journalist called Manuel Vargas. Backstops are all organized, including a shit-ton of web pages going back a decade, photos, even some lifelike AI videos, a portfolio of articles you've written on a range of subjects." He handed Jacob an Argentinian passport. Well-worn with a number of stamps and a press visa.

Jacob flicked through the pages and snorted. "Perfect. Easy to pull off. *Yeah, right.*" His command of Spanish had gotten him through tricky situations on his last mission in Colombia and Mexico, but Cuba...that was like another planet.

"The visa in there is actually a real one. Proving your legend will hold up to the highest scrutiny."

"Comforting."

"It should be. It was issued by the Cuban embassy in Buenos

Aires. We had to pay for fast-tracking since the process takes weeks, usually. The forged papers used in the application did the job perfectly. You'll find it a lot easier to get access to Domínguez and others with that visa. Hopefully."

"A lot of effort's gone into this, Grant."

"For good reason. McDonald's worried this could blow up like 1961, only much worse. He wants the CIA kept out of it as much as possible. Their track record in the region is..." Fletcher trailed off.

"Terrible?"

"Exactly. So it's up to us."

"Of course. Because we don't exist, and if we screw up, there's no one to blame."

"That's the spirit, Jacob."

Jacob's stomach churned at the thought of another Bay of Pigs happening, only this time with Russian and Chinese involvement. It wasn't just dangerous—it was catastrophic. A misstep by him, failure to nip it in the bud, could reshape global alliances in a way the US wouldn't recover from. Allies would rip up long-standing defense treaties, pointing the finger at America as the 'aggressor' state.

"You'll start by tracking down Espinosa," Fletcher said. "I'm sure he knows more than what's in that file."

"Who's looking after me when I arrive?"

Fletcher squinted. "Looking after you?"

"Yeah. There's usually someone on the ground to pick me up, or at least show me around the place. I've never been to Cuba. Be nice to have a welcoming face at the airport."

Fletcher shook his head. "You're going to have to play detective for a while."

"The file says Espinosa's a baker. Surely there's details on his employment after he left the intelligence agency. Hang on a second." He thumbed through the pages and found an address. His bottom lip jutted out in a frown. "No record of him working as a baker anywhere. It's just taken as a given that he was because that's what he told the handler." Jacob cursed quietly. "Sloppy work."

"Talk to the journalist Cain. Get him to take you to the bar where Passo was killed."

"Doesn't he know the name of it?"

Fletcher shook his head. "Passo picked him up in a taxi they hailed on the street. It was dark, stormy. Cain doesn't speak Spanish, and he can't remember what it was called. He..."

"A dark and stormy night? Spare me the clichés."

Fletcher ignored the remark. "I'm sure with a bit of driving around, he'll remember something."

"Definitely worth a shot." Jacob nodded, his mind sorting through the web of connections. Cain, Passo, Domínguez. It would make a lot more sense once he was there. "I get the feeling I'll be chasing a bunch of Cold War ghosts."

Fletcher gave a nod. "History's got a funny way of repeating itself."

"I damn well hope not." Jacob closed the file, his mind shifting into high gear. Every mission had its risks, but this one felt different. "What about Irina? Are you giving her clearance to know about this case?"

"You bet. Use her skills however you need to. She's proven herself in terms of ability, discretion, and loyalty."

"She knows the drill." Jacob stood, sliding the folder into his jacket and tucking the expandable file under his arm. "She worries when I'm away, but she understands."

Fletcher chuckled, moving back toward the aquarium. "You two are a good match. She keeps you sharp."

"She does more than that." Jacob grinned. "But I'll keep those details to myself."

The moment of levity faded as Fletcher's expression turned serious. "This one's going to be rough, Jacob. There's a lot riding on it."

"I know. I've never set foot on Cuban soil. I've got a lot of reading to do."

Concern crinkled the corners of Fletcher's eyes. "If you get even the slightest sense this thing's about to blow—back off. No one's coming to save your ass if it all goes sideways."

Jacob nodded. "I'll keep that comforting thought in mind."

As he made his way back to his apartment, the lights of Manhattan reflected off the inky-black waters of the Hudson. The mission ahead lay out like a chessboard in his mind, but his thoughts drifted, as they often did, to Sally-Anne. The one puzzle he hadn't solved. Twenty years of searching, no answers. And now, another puzzle waited in Cuba—one that, if left unsolved, could blow up in his face. And the world's.

When he reached the front door, his phone chirped in his pocket. A message from Irina: *Feel like a late-night visitor?*

He grinned as he tapped. *If it's you, always.*

Scan the QR code below to purchase THE HAVANA FILE.
Or go to: righthouse.com/the-havana-file

www.ingramcontent.com/pod-product-compliance
Lightning Source LLC
LaVergne TN
LVHW091110080826
845145LV00008B/1861

*9781636964683*